Awards and Praise for

The Promise Kitchen

First Place, Fiction, 2015, Royal Dragonfly Book Awards

Winner, Best New Fiction, 2016, National Indie Excellence Awards

Silver, Bill Fisher Award for Best First Book: Fiction, 2016, IBPA Ben Franklin Awards

"First-time author and food blogger Peggy Lampman knows the exact ingredients needed to create an appealing story . . . an eye-opening and thought-provoking must read."

—*San Francisco Book Review*, 5 stars

"A sweetly told saga, bubbling with appealing characters and food-related talk . . . A poor country girl and a fashionable city woman learn about life in a tasty novel that blends romance and recipes."

—*Kirkus Reviews*

"Peggy Lampman is an engaging writer, capturing the heart of Southern living with wit, charm, and vivid detail as she alternates chapters between Shelby, Mallory, and Miss Ann . . . For readers who enjoy a Southern flavor to their stories, spending time in the company of these fine folks . . . will go down as easily as a slice of watermelon on a hot summer's day."

—*Blue Ink Review*

"A book full of flavor and substance worth savoring. The characters, particularly Shelby and Mallory, are well drawn and three-dimensional, with roots, ambitions, motivations, and personalities . . . a story full of the evocative, powerful influence of food, cooking, love, friendship, and family on the human heart."

—Indie Reader, 4½ stars

The
Welcome
Home
Diner

OTHER TITLES BY
PEGGY LAMPMAN

The Promise Kitchen (previously published as *Simmer and Smoke*)

The Welcome Home Diner

Peggy Lampman

LAKE UNION
PUBLISHING

Published by Lake Union, Seattle

www.apub.com

Amazon, the Amazon logo, and Lake Union are trademarks of Amazon.com, Inc., or its affiliates.

ISBN-13: 9781542047821
ISBN-10: 154204782X

Cover design by Laura Klynstra

Printed in the United States of America

For Lucy

Pot Liquor: The broth leftover in a pot after simmering greens with smoked pork.

Potlikker: Viscous brew, leaked from the soil, savory and bold. Heaven's field of blackened greens, bitter and sweet.

Pronunciation Guide For Polish Words Used In

The Welcome Home Diner

Babcia: grandmother *(BAHB-cia)*

Bolesławiec: a town in southern Poland famous for its pottery *(BOL-e-swa-viets)*

Delikatnie: gently *(de-lee-COT-neh)*

Dziadek: grandfather *(JAH-deck)*

Gołąbki: stuffed cabbage *(ga-WUMP-key)*

Obrzydliwe: disgusting *(OB-ze-dlee-veh)*

Sytuacja swiatowa jest tragiczna: The situation in the world is tragic. *(sit-u-AT-sia SHVIA-tova YEST tra-DICH-na)*

Włocławek: a town in central Poland on the Vistula River *(vwo-TSWA-vek)*

Prologue

I take my seat behind the breadboard and plunge my hands into the sticky mound. The dough is a revelation, the suppleness warm between my fingers.

"The magic rests between your hands," my grandmother says, "and like your fingerprints, the bread will be your own."

I clutch the dough tighter, clenching these elements of life: flour of the earth, air, and water, which release the yeast.

"Delikatnie," she whispers, in her native Polish tongue. "Gently, my child. Let me show you." As she kneads the mass, folding and turning, it contracts and then swells. She stretches and tucks the dough into a round. Beneath her touch, everything blooms.

After returning to the stove, she stirs her spoon into a simmering soup. The kettle sings, the pans hiss. Yet the kitchen is silent.

As I wake with a start, my body's limp, loose, and my eyes are wet. I kick out of the sheets, and they twist around my feet. Adjusting the pillows smashed up against the headboard brings clarity; I'm twenty-four years older than in my dream.

I settle into the duvet, close my eyes, and drift . . . The seven-year-old is still inside me, but my grandmother fades. Don't leave, not yet! Her fingers brush away my tears and her hands smell of bread—of rye, sunlight, and dust. Shhhh, shhhh, she whispers while I am weeping but still happy beside my babcia *as we melt into the glow.*

The sudden sweep of loss tastes of wood smoke, and it bites and burns. To soothe the pain, we grieve and then accept, digging deep, tugging at the roots, and pulling them out. By sharing memories with family, and with friends whom we've chosen to become our family, all of us clouding into a misty steam rising from the brew.

Chapter One

Addie

If you're the last person to leave Detroit, don't forget to turn off the lights.

The saying amuses me, as it does my cousin Samantha, known as Sam among our friends. Several months ago, we bought a house and opened a diner together in the city. Perhaps we are, as my stepfather says, out of our minds. Time will tell.

In the meantime, here I sit, settled into the chair at my desk, gazing through the office window. Braydon, who was our first hire, is in the kitchen garden, harvesting lettuces that we'll use for tomorrow's menu. A tall, thin man with a quiet manner and perfect teeth—white, shiny, and square—he possesses an air of gravitas. At this moment, however, his motions appear broad, his gesticulations wild. What could he be saying to Sam and Sandra—nicknamed Sun Beam—that would arouse such passion?

I straighten with a jolt, my smartphone jarring me out of my reverie. Cascada's "Everytime We Touch" ringtone alerts me it's David, my live-in boyfriend. Feeling his presence in the room, I smooth my hair and moisten my lips. Dropping my voice an octave, I answer in a whisper.

"Hey, sweetie. Whatcha need?"

"Baby girl. You know what I need."

"Haven't I taught you the rewards of patience?" My inflection captures the purr of a promise.

"All work and no play makes David a very sad boy." He clears his throat. "Why was I calling? Oh yeah. Could you bring home the electric drill I lent Braydon? He was using it to install the soap canister next to the hand sink."

"No worries. It's already in my bag. Before you get going on the bathroom, you need to secure the shelf above our bed. The next time the headboard rams against the wall, the shelf might fall down. It will kill me before you do."

"God forbid we let that happen." I can see him smiling that rascal smile.

After our good-byes, I slump back into the chair and push aside a stack of cookbooks. Placing several grease-stained prep lists into the recycle bin, my gaze wanders back through the panes. Sam is my first cousin on my father's side. She and Sun Beam are harvesting the first of the late-May crops. Now that school's out for summer, Sun Beam will be coming into work with her mother, LaQuisha.

A burst of beaming light, Sun Beam wears braided cornrows pulled into ponytails that trail down her back. Her round glasses magnify her brown eyes so that they appear owlish—solemn, shiny, and believing. She is nine years old. Her molars are loose, and new front teeth are coming in crooked.

Lella, a young woman we recently hired to wait tables, walks toward the trio, a woven basket in her hands. She has the long, muscular frame, flat waistline, and chest of a thirteen-year-old gymnast. Her pale complexion and gleaming face are topped with an asymmetrical haircut, which is dyed in streaks of tangerine and strawberry, the colors of the poppy tattoo on her upper arm.

She bends down, hands the basket to Sun Beam, and throws back her head, laughing at something the girl says. At Lella's arrival, the group's tension seems to melt away. She has that effect on people. She straightens, then returns to the diner.

Braydon resumes cutting off the scalloped lettuce leaves at soil level. Afraid of bruising the tender fronds, he makes sure his motions are gentle as he hands them to Sam, who places them in the basket. In the few months he's worked for us, he's made himself invaluable. He was part of a volunteer group loosely organized to help revitalize the area. Helping us update the diner prior to its opening was his first project.

In fact, Braydon pointed out how the electrician screwed up the furnace wiring by running a 120-volt line into a 220-volt circuit. After the worker left, the motor wouldn't run. Braydon corrected the mistake, but what galls me is that the electrician claimed that he checked, and the furnace was in working order. We paid him hard cash from our closely guarded funds, while Braydon worked for free. I took solace in giving the guy a bad review on Angie's List. I hope no one else has to suffer from his inefficiencies. A place could catch fire from bad wiring.

With the savory leftovers Braydon brought the volunteers from his home kitchen—the delicate, crumbling biscuits, smoked pulled pork, and creamy chess pies—we discovered he was also an excellent cook.

Counting out the singles, I watch as Sam rests her hands on his shoulder. Their discussion appears to carry weight. Perhaps that upsetting customer returned for lunch—the guy who offended Lella with his vulgar and derisive teasing. We've been brainstorming ways of handling situations such as this, but it's not the sort of discussion they'd be having with the child.

Distracted by the scene in the garden, I lose track of my counting. I recount the singles, secure them with a rubber band, and place them into the money bag stamped WELCOME HOME. Then I tap my computer and review the employee schedule for next week. That's when Lella's moving, and she requested the time off, so I'll ask Braydon if he can, once again, work overtime.

Braydon has been whipping up soul food, which our clientele has embraced. Our most recent signature dish is what he refers to as a "mess of greens" served with potlikker. Potlikker, beloved by all citizenry below the Mason-Dixon, remains a foreign brew to most Yankees. Unless you're from Detroit, where many locals have extended roots in the South.

Potlikker is the broth left behind after simmering the greens with pork, and is best served with corn pone for dunking. Would that the world were as amicable as our menu. Who would guess Southern soul food would coexist happily with Polish cooking and farm-to-table heartland fare?

I sigh, shut down the program, and stare out the window. They've harvested a large basket of greens—plenty for the Heirloom Salad with Blue Cheese Croutons on tomorrow's menu. Braydon tucks his shears beneath his armpit. The three of them rise, and Sam pulls them into her, orchestrating a group hug. Sam can enlighten me as to their discussion when we return home after work. As the trio enters the corridor through the back door, their chatter now sounds casual.

Everyone warned us, said our going into business together would ruin our relationship. As it turns out, they were wrong. Sam and I shared the same crib, the same bottle, and the same toys. We shared our grandparents, Babcia and Dziadek. If I ever forget a piece of my history, I just ask Sam. It's only logical we'd share the same business. I could never have wished for a better partner, or a better city in which to build a career.

But, so far, we haven't attracted the customer base needed to survive. It could be the weather. These past few months, business has been conducted in a fusillade of snow, icy sleet, and rain. When it's not raining, Detroit's thinking about raining, and the walls in the kitchen sweat from the heat of simmering pans and humidity. It's difficult mustering up a smile for those few patrons who don't mind trading damp socks for a hot bowl of soup.

Aside from that one offensive man, we've been cooking for a handful of Detroit-area sympathizers—friendly folks more curious about the crazy women who had the stupidity to open a diner in one of the more dangerous parts of town than desirous of our made-from-scratch flapjacks and pastries.

And then there are the money worries. Some weeks we barely make payroll for our three-person staff, much less ourselves. Sixty percent of restaurants go under in their first year of business; eighty percent fail within five. You gotta know that stat's higher in Detroit. I worry The Welcome Home Diner might fall prey to next year's data. I try not to make this concern my mantra.

Nevertheless, Detroit is fertile ground—major corporations are beginning to pour billions into downtown revitalization, betting their money on the city's recovery. Small businesses such as ours also have a stake in this rally. If we ever get our footing, we'll hire David's father's construction company to build an addition. My eyes scan the empty, hard-packed soil bordering the garden. We have the acreage.

I shove the money bag into the safe beside the desk. Sam's dad, Uncle Andrew, configured it to be disguised as a laminate panel in the wall. If Braydon continues to earn our trust, he'll be the next employee we'll train to cash out.

After closing the office door behind me, I walk through the corridor, which divides the back kitchen from the office, and pass through the swinging doors opening to the diner. The restaurant is divided into three areas. The main floor—which would seat up to thirty-four patrons if filled to capacity—houses two six-tops, four four-tops, and three two-tops. It's framed by large windows, which suffuse the area with sunlight, and looks out to the parking lot and East La Grande Avenue.

The second area is the counter space, which is, in effect, a Formica bar, original to the restaurant. A soft shade of wintergreen, it's embossed with a pattern of tiny boomerangs the color of doves. Pearlescent stools are permanently affixed to the floor and seat an additional twelve patrons. The counter stretches the length of the diner and divides the main floor from the third space, the prep area. This is where the action takes place, and is the highlight of the performance.

The best seat in the house—if you don't mind being perched on a seat that's as hard as the head of a nail—is at the center of the counter. Sun Beam's mother, LaQuisha, works the grill. We call her Quiche, for short. Watching the blur of her arm as she flips pancakes on the flattop, your eyes wander to the stacks of mismatched china and Ball jars filled with pickled vegetables, lining shelves above the sink. When your eyes slide down the counter, you're mesmerized by the swirl of straws in iced teas and chocolate egg creams.

In the background you listen to layers of sound: flapjacks hissing on the grill; murmurs of conversation punctuated by the rattle of plates and cutlery being set at a table; hot, sultry bebop jazz tenor saxophonist Lucky Thompson, who grew up in this area—the city's East Side—killing his horn.

You inhale a tingling blast of aromatherapy when lavender-lime soda is placed between your hands. Taking a cooling sip, you feel a jolt when a child's hand knocks against your wrist as she reaches for the syrup—tapped from Northern Michigan maples. And then your fork sinks into a tender pile of buttermilk pancakes, pats of melting butter oozing down the stack, apple and walnut islands in the syrup. You slide the morsel into your mouth—*mmmmm*, this is how food is supposed to taste.

These are the sensorial pleasures we hope our customers feel when dining in our establishment. As if you're having breakfast or lunch in an anachronism, transported to an era set in the midcentury. Timeless. Floating. Blessedly minus the thorny issues of segregation that plagued the country in those swept-away years—we're proud of our diverse and talented staff.

It's a world of our creation, an oasis for our customers. This world, however, is no nirvana for the workers. We must smile when a customer complains about the wait for a sandwich, or comp a check, even if the offending item was licked clean from the plate. We take responsibility and beg pardon to other customers if someone's kid throws a tantrum, then rush for crayons and paper to placate that child.

But now it's half past two, and we're closed for the day. Free from patrons, we're transported to a place where we can let down our guard. As I cast my eyes around the scene, Braydon, Lella, and Sam are clearing tables. Sun Beam sits at the counter, in front of her a tricked-out sausage. She enjoys experimenting with leftovers after the restaurant is closed. As her mother shuts down the grill, she turns to face her child, gesturing with a knife as she speaks.

"What in heaven's name have you got on that plate, child?"

"Stop waving that blade around, Mama. You look like a flying ninja. Hot dogs are delicious with mayo and stuffed with fries." Sun Beam, throat stretched, chirps like a chickadee, twittering nonstop.

"Why, girl, I never," Quiche replies, scrunching her nose. She returns the knife to the drawer and retrieves a spatula. She scrapes it across the carbonized flattop, glistening with grease, clearing it of burned bits of bread, bacon, and other relics from today's special. With the palm of her hand, she brushes away her shiny black bangs.

"Fries have no place on a wiener. A hot dog cries out for mustard, ketchup, and relish." She pauses and looks sideways, casting her eyes over her shoulder. "And who ever heard of using mayo? It's un-American." Making *tsk-tsk* sounds, she turns to regard Sun Beam, her spatula pointing at her daughter as if she were a teacher admonishing an unruly student with a ruler.

"Pasty gobs of goo squeezing outta that bun—I'm queasy watching you eat that mess."

Her gaze holds steady on her child. They have the same heavy-lashed, wide-set eyes; round as disks, the irises are a coppery brown. I climb onto a stool and sit beside the girl.

"You tell her, Addie. She won't listen to me. You spend your life trying to get folks to eat right."

"No worries, Quiche," I say, wiping a smudge of mayo away from the rim of her plate. "Murray Hills out of Novi hand-makes the links using organic chicken. Sam made the potato buns this morning, and what could be healthier than baked sweet potato fries?" I place a hand on Sun Beam's shoulder and give a little squeeze. "She's right. I'll bet our homemade mayo tastes delicious on the dog."

"I told you so, Mama," says the child, adjusting her glasses and giving her mother a solemn know-it-all nod of her head.

Quiche raises her brow at me, seeming to weigh my words. I always get the feeling that she's not quite sure my opinions are to be trusted. Pursing her lips, she returns to the grill.

"But you need something green," I say, wiping the corner of Sun Beam's mouth with a napkin. "And so do I."

I pat her hand, slide off the stool, and circle back behind the counter. At the cold station, I make a spinach salad with hard-cooked eggs and smoky bits of bacon. I ladle on our lemony house dressing and, with prongs, pull some of the salad from the bowl and place it on Sun Beam's plate. "Here ya go, hon. A jolt of iron to keep you strong."

Babcia (a Polish endearment for *grandmother*) would have approved of my nurturing. I regard her portrait, a black-and-white photograph of her when she was in her early thirties. Sam and I consider this picture our most important piece of decor. Sacred, in fact. It was taken in the late forties, after she had arrived in Ann Arbor. The photograph is crooked, so I slide a chair under her portrait and climb on top, stretching to straighten it.

Her white-blonde hair is twisted back into a bun. She wears a floral dress and the hint of a smile. What isn't apparent is her complexion: a delicate alchemy of ivory and pearl; the color of her eyes: crystal blue; the sound of her laughter: clear and light; and her fragrance: a delicate whisper of crushed violet I always smelled on her collar.

I push the right edge of the photograph up and then wiggle the top edges of the frame so that her eyes are parallel with mine. No one could ever guess her courage by gazing into those eyes, so gentle and sweet. I can't imagine the strength of character it would take to suffer through a war, leave all that's familiar behind, and forge a new life in a strange, new land. Our eyes lock and I smile before hopping off the chair.

Braydon picks up my chair and takes it to the side of the diner. Sam, leaning into a mop handle, watches me, her eyes soft and thoughtful. We share the same memories of our grandmother. Then she bends above the bucket, returns the mop to the water, and swishes the gray ropes in the suds.

⁓

Sam

Lunch rush—if you could call it a rush—is over, and the diner just closed for the day. I glance at Addie's profile shining through the office window as she cashes out. She turns her head to watch us we collect the greens.

Braydon sits on his haunches, tearing yellowed leaves away from a bunch of arugula. He places them on a pile of compost and swivels to face Sun Beam.

"I must have told you this story half a dozen times. You're still not tired of hearing it?"

She shakes her head, a solemn expression on her cute little face.

He sighs, a smile playing about his mouth. "That dog was a sight. Poor little thing. She'd made herself a nest from rags and lived under the expressway. I'll never forget the day I found Bon Temps." He digs out a dandelion that's invaded the garden.

"A tornado struck Detroit the day before. That twister cut a four-mile path of destruction." Forehead lined, eyes stretched wide, he raises his arms, swirling them about his head. "Almost one-hundred-mile-an-hour winds, the city's never seen anything like it. I was twelve years old."

"That's the most terrible story I've ever heard. I hope a tornado doesn't hit town when I turn twelve." Through the thick frames of her glasses, Sun Beam gapes at Braydon in goggle-eyed admiration.

"Her fur was soaking wet," he continues, "clinging to her ribs, which stuck out in angles."

I wrap my jacket tighter around my shoulders. His words and the damp chill in the air are causing me to shiver. We're taking advantage of a cease-fire in the rain to harvest the first of the cold-season crops.

His dog lies next to Sun Beam, holding her muzzle high in the air. Her snout expands, as if relishing the smells emanating from the diner. Braydon brings her to work, and she often hangs out with Hero, my dog, in the garden. As our conversation loops around dogs and torna-does, Lella brings us the basket we had trouble locating.

No one can dismiss Bon Temps in a glance. In the world of unusual dogs, she stands alone. Judging from her short, stubby legs, extended body, and wavy coat of hair, Braydon guesses her to be a spaniel-dachshund mix. Her tail points to the sky in a flash of gold lightning finished off with a fluffy pom-pom. Long wisps of fur dangle from the tip, like ribbons fes-tooning a parade float. Identical tendrils dangle from the summit of her long, upright ears like an ancient Chinese headdress.

Lella returns to the diner, and Sun Beam rubs the tip of Bon Temps's cotton-ball tail between her thumb and forefinger, which she says helps the dog relax.

"How'd you find her?"

"I didn't find her. She found me. I didn't know she was following me until I stopped to tie my shoe. She trotted up and licked my fingers.

Her fur was so wet it seemed glued to her bones." Braydon puts his hand under Bon Temps's chin, lifting her head. "And look at those eyes. How could I say no to those big brown eyes?"

"Her eyes look like yours," says Sun Beam.

She's right. Braydon has large eyes, the color mirroring his skin, the golden ash brown of forest wood. He's only twenty-two years of age, but those weatherworn eyes seem to have many stories to tell.

"How old is she?"

"That I can't answer with certainty." Braydon wraps his fist around a bunch of shoots, picks up the gardening shears, and, with a swift swipe, cuts through the base of stems. While talking, he continues harvesting the bundles and handing them to me. I place the intact leaves in the basket, the more tattered ones in the compost pile.

"I'm guessing she was close to two when I found her. She wasn't wearing a collar, so I couldn't find her owner, much less find out her age. That was ten years ago. Two thousand five. Back then, she was full of energy, a young dog, but not a puppy. That would make her twelve now."

"That's old in people years, right?"

"I figure she's sixty-two, maybe sixty-four."

Sun Beam squints at Braydon. "That's really old. Same age as Granny. Is she named after a candy?"

"Nope. Bon Temps means *good times* in French. A friend of my auntie, our next-door neighbor, speaks Creole. She suggested the name."

"What happened to your mama and daddy?"

"Sun Beam," I say, interrupting her inquisition. "Enough questions, honey. You're gonna drive Braydon crazy." Poor kid. I haven't heard the whole story, but he did tell me he lost his parents when he was a child. I can't imagine the pain he must feel in the retelling.

Braydon clears his throat. "That's all right, Sam. It's a good question." He puts down his shears. His eyes are dreamy, half-mast, as if he were falling asleep. They wander from me to Sun Beam.

13

"My parents died when I was a kid. An ice storm came out of nowhere, slicking up the expressway." A reddish-pink shine journeys across his eyes. "They were a part of a ten-car collision. I was at a sleepover." He lifts his face to the sky. "I could have been in that car."

Sun Beam's chin begins to tremble, and her eyes fill with tears. Braydon looks down at her and, with his forefinger, lifts her chin to meet his eyes. "My story does have a happy ending."

Sun Beam swallows, adjusts her glasses, and nods.

"Bon Temps saved my life as much as I saved hers. We were both orphans and needed each other." Bon Temps, now sleeping in the grass, hears her name and looks up at her master. He pats the dog's head.

Picturing a young boy and half-starved dog wandering under the expressway tugs at my heart. My hands are still, and I stare at the earth, biting my lips to hold back the tears.

"So here's the happy ending," he says, taking Sun Beam's hands. "My aunt and uncle on my father's side took me in. Their kids had already left home. And as long as I kept out of trouble, they said they'd let me keep Bon Temps. You'd better believe I kept my nose clean. Bad kids skip school and smoke pot. Some start stealing cars and shooting guns at thirteen. It's not hard recognizing the kids to avoid."

He squeezes her hands. "But, just like me, you're going to be one of the good kids. We'll all see to that." He pulls at one of her ponytails, a half smile on his face. "My aunt and uncle are quiet, God-fearing Christians. But they've been good to me. Bon Temps, my aunt, and my uncle are the closest thing I have to a family."

Sun Beam stares at Braydon with a timid, solemn look. "You an' Bon Temps can be a part of our family, too. It's just me, Mama, and Granny. I'd love having a big brother." She presses her lips together and lowers her head as if she just confessed something profound.

She whispers into Bon Temps's ear, to make sure the old dog hears her words. "And for sure I'd like having a dog." The dog's tail swishes.

Braydon is quiet, and I, embarrassed by this intimate turn of conversation, am at a loss for words. I can think only to repeat Sun Beam's sentiments.

"She's right. You aren't alone, Braydon. You have your aunt and uncle, you have your dog, and now we're your family, too."

Sun Beam rubs Bon Temps beneath her collar and, with the other hand, scratches behind her white ears. She turns to me. "Would you let me build a doghouse next to the garden? So the dogs can have their own home?"

"What a wonderful idea, honey. Of course you can."

She looks up at Braydon. "Will you help me?"

Pressing his lips together, he nods. Securing his shears under his armpit, Braydon runs his knuckle under his nose. Working in the garden must be healing for him—trimming, snipping, and pinching back a harvest of grief.

I place my hand on Sun Beam's shoulder. "Why don't you make yourself one of those fancy sandwiches while your mom breaks down the grill?"

Stretching out my arms, I pull the two of them into me, patting their backs. Then, I stoop to pick up the basket of lettuces.

Traipsing through the back door and corridor, passing Addie in the office, we cross through the swinging doors and enter the prep area. Sun Beam opens the reach-in, removes a sausage, and places the link on the flattop, which Quiche is scraping down. The woman's hands are lashed with scars from years of manning grills, meat slicers, and bubbling fryers. Braydon wheels the mop bucket into the main area, and we move the chairs to one side of the room so that we can clean the floors.

As we work, Sun Beam busies herself by composing a sausage dog before taking a seat at the counter. Addie enters the prep area and makes a spinach salad for herself and the child. Then, she slides a chair beneath our grandmother's portrait and climbs up to adjust the photograph, staring at the picture, as is her habit. She then hops from the chair and retreats to the office, salad in hand.

Through the side windows of the diner, I see the familiar beat-to-hell yellow Ford pickup arrive in the open cargo area that's loaded with boxes and bags. It's Jessie, our hot sauce and garlic vendor, on her bimonthly run.

Jessie, a heavyset African American woman in her early fifties, is a Detroit urban farmer who wears waist-length dreadlocks and frayed overalls. Her only adornments, which are as much a part of her as her mud-crusted work boots, are the beads she wears looped around her neck. Strands of gold and polished amber, and teardrops of tiny gray strung-together bones, were purchased at the African Bead Gallery on Grand River. She says they tell a story by communicating information to others who know how to read them.

Born a decade after Angela Davis, Jessie reveres the activist. She participates in one of the Committees of Correspondence for Democracy and Socialism, which Ms. Davis founded after her split with the Communist Party. Jessie tells us her food enterprises may be capitalist, but they're in sync with Ms. Davis's principles and aligned toward a green-energy future that will revitalize Detroit. I could escape a trio of knife-wielding thugs more easily than I could the wrath of Jessie if I challenged her leftist ideology or got on her bad side.

A few years back, she cashed in her savings to attend Ms. Davis's Empowering Women of Color Conference in Berkeley. Jessie says the meetings changed her life, infusing her with African American pride and confidence. At the seminar, Ms. Davis told the participants she eschews anything causing harm to animals and, thus, is a vegan. The bacon Jessie had enjoyed at her morning breakfast was her last taste of meat.

Jessie also befriended a Native American at the seminar who introduced her to practices of traditional healing. She continued her education at Integrative Holistic Medicine in Detroit. Now, she concocts home remedies and practices in her tight-knit community of like-minded women.

Braydon holds the door for her as she enters the restaurant carrying a case of her hot sauce, Jessie's Hell Fire and Redemption. Thanking Braydon for his chivalry, she wedges her girth sideways through the door, caked mud from her boots making tracks on the just-mopped floor. A brown paper bag resting on top of the box slides off, toppling to the ground. I stoop to pick up the dirt-crusted heads, random cloves, and scapes, and return them to the bag. Braydon sweeps up the dirt and skins.

"Sorry, baby. Jévon's at the school and couldn't help me on my run. I'm getting too old and too fat to be doing this by myself."

Jévon is Jessie's only child and teaches art classes to youth groups in the city. Some condemn his public works as graffiti vandalism while others acclaim him as a street-art superstar. Jévon is the chink in Jessie's armor; any hurt he suffers is felt tenfold by his mother.

"How's he doing?" Braydon asks. "That mural he sprayed on Gratiot blew my mind."

"It was somethin', right?"

We nod, brows unmoving, in solemn agreement. Jessie has a titanic, head-turning voice, which would be a fine instrument if she were a performer. People tend to concur with whatever she says not only because of that voice but also because of her eyes. Her pupils, the inky shade of a fathomless night, are circled with a glow of cosmic energy—the color of ripe apricots, almost gold. When she casts her beams on me, I'm uncomfortable and feel undressed beneath her gaze. But when the light in her eyes dims, you'd better watch your back.

"A little boy skipping stones in the Detroit River makes you *know* better times are ahead," she booms, placing the case of hot sauce on the counter with a thud. "I just hope it doesn't get power-washed off like the one in Cass Corridor." She hands me the receipt, crumbled and stained with dirt.

"If the building's owner realized Jévon's work was worth twice the cost of the building, he might have thought otherwise," Braydon says, concurring with her son's worth.

"You got that right. Folks call him the Picasso of Detroit," she says, pride in her voice. "He's instructing a group of kids at the Project today." The Heidelberg Project is an internationally recognized art habitat—one man's creative antidote to the scourge of his deteriorating neighborhood.

Half-moons of moisture darken Jessie's shirt beneath her armpits. She removes a paisley bandanna from her pocket and mops her perspiring brow. "Lord have mercy, I've caught on fire. Will these hot flashes ever end? The change, the change. Going through the change."

"You poor thing," Quiche says, rinsing utensils at the prep sink. "Maybe you OD'ed on that concoction you brew. Everyone seems to love your recipe, but I can't stomach the stuff. Don't take offense by my words, Jess. I despise all hot sauces with equal contempt." She looks over her shoulder toward the woman. "Lemme pour you something cold after I finish the dishes."

"Thanks, Quiche. And loaded with ice, if you please." Jessie takes a seat at the counter.

Braydon slides a knife down the seam of the box, opening the case. "Just in time. We sold the last bottle yesterday."

As I busy myself returning chairs to the tables, he removes one of the bottles from the case. Smiling, he gazes at the label her son designed: a black background with orange-red flames lapping a caricature of Jessie holding a pitchfork. Another caricature depicts her as an angel, sporting wings and flying above.

"I was weaned on hot sauce myself—it was a seasoning as common as salt on our table." He shakes a dollop of Jessie's sauce onto his forefinger and dabs it with his tongue. "But this is different from what we used. More flavorful. Rounded."

He reads the ingredient list: "Serrano chilies, jalapeños, canola oil, water, honey, garlic, onion, and vinegar. Hmmm. Standard stuff. What is it about your recipe that makes it so much better than the rest? There's a taste I can't pinpoint. Something missing on the ingredient list."

"The ingredient, my son, is invisible," Jessie replies, rubbing the beads in her necklace between her thumb and forefinger. "The ingredient is *magic*. And I'll never disclose the full recipe. But I will tell you this." She points her forefinger toward his face, almost touching his nose. "If you season your food with my hot sauce every day, your soul will radiate sunlight forever."

Braydon shakes the liquid from the bottle into a pot of greens simmering on a two-burner, and stirs. He lowers a fork into the pot, then lifts a khaki mound to his mouth, taking a bite. He chews with deliberation, before batting his lips with a cloth.

"Turnip, mustard, and collard greens. Delectable. Your magic is all they needed." He places a colander into an empty pot in the sink and strains the greens. After ladling the potlikker into shot glasses, he passes them around. Quiche pulls a face as if Braydon were offering her poison.

I swallow the brew in a gulp. Braydon tips his glass to mine. "My potlikker seasoned with Jessie's Hell Fire and Redemption has the power to move heaven and earth."

I would be wondering if his words held a prophecy for a long time to come.

Chapter Two

Addie

The diner's closed for the Memorial Day holiday today. It's the first time we've shuttered the place since our grand opening in March. At last we've a day off, the weather pitch-perfect for the picnic we've planned. Sunlight spreads through the living room, the sky the brilliant blues of a peacock's feather, and I stretch on the sofa, summoning the energy to face the day. Done with the frigidity of winter, of snow and more snow, followed by weeks of howling, bitter hail.

I'd heard it on the roof, waking me in the morning, the downpour of frozen pellets pummeling our house like a machine gun. I'd heard it as I organized my backpack for work, click-clacking against the panes as I put on my fur-lined hat, as I tucked my hair into my down jacket. I'd heard the rat-a-tat against asphalt, plopping into pothole baths, as I waited for the bus that took me to the diner. And then came the rainy season. It was as if a spigot burst, and there was no way to stop the flow.

Considering all the miserable weather, the long hours, and innumerable stresses of opening a new business, it's a wonder I survived. A Michigan winter, though lacking soul, does have one advantage over sunnier climes. How else, come spring, would you fathom what it's like to be resuscitated after drowning?

David has a zest for the moment and doesn't appreciate my negative attitude. But there is one thing he does appreciate.

"You were something last night," he says, speaking from the bathroom, his voice raised so I can hear him.

I grab a Kleenex and blow my nose. Sniffling, I open my sewing kit and kneel beside the couch. "And look at me. Debbie Downer. Once again on my knees."

I thread a needle, knot the end of the strings together, and begin mending a hole on our sofa. Sand beige, with plushy taupe accent pillows. A small rip at the seam is the only flaw on this flea market find.

"Wouldn't you know, the first day the diner's closed, I'm hacking away? Three months of nonstop labor, as healthy as a beast, and I get sick the minute I take a break."

"You must have caught some weird virus from Berlin," David responds.

"It wouldn't surprise me. Berlin and Detroit are sharing everything these days."

The cities have inspired each other musically, as well as culturally, for decades. Every Memorial Day weekend, the downtown streets are packed with people from Germany, and the rest of the world, for the Movement Electronic Music Festival. Known as Techno Fest, it's been one of the world's premier electronic music scenes, celebrating techno in the city of its birth. For the past few days, Welcome Home's been busier than usual, with the influx of people exiting planes and coming to eat at the diner.

During the festival, the riverfront around Hart Plaza pulses with these one hundred thousand–plus visitors. The shows are performed on half a dozen stages, and the streets explode with music and streaming neon lights, participants gyrating in an electronic haze.

Techno's not my choice of music; I'm more of a Sarah Vaughan kind of a woman. The shows, however, are more inclusive than any other cultural event of which I'm aware, and they pump millions into the city. Blacks, whites, Asians—you name it—vacation in Detroit to get high and celebrate.

Today's the last day of the festival, and although the shows don't begin for an hour or so, the energy seeps through the door.

Sewing task complete, I snip the thread, return the needle to the sewing box, and pat the mended segment. I fall back onto the sofa and lie prone, even the smallest of tasks exhausting me.

"There's nothing worse than suffering through a cold the first day of summer."

"Official summer doesn't begin until mid-June," David replies.

"For me, summer begins on Memorial Day." I pinch my nostrils to stifle another sneeze and rub my itching eyes. "It's a miracle you didn't catch this. Must be those kale smoothies you inhale. But I'm past day three now, the contagious stage. At least according to Google. I may sound like a frog in a paper bag, but I'm over the hump."

He sticks his head out of the bathroom. His mild, disarming smile reminds me of a classics professor I once had—not quite sure whether I was worthy of that B plus he bestowed on my midterm.

"Forget your saltwater gargles and echinacea. Take some more Alka-Seltzer. That's what puts you back on track."

"On the passion track." I manage a shadow of a wink, which never fails to turn him on. But really, can't I ever get a break? Can't he suppress his supercharged libido even when I'm sick?

The past year's been insane. Sam and I purchased the diner two months after we bought our home. Sam's eyes, unsullied by my gloomier point of view, unlocked a world of opportunities to me.

Through the prism of her vision, I came to imagine the decrepit diner as a canvas on which to revitalize the surrounding neighborhood, our decaying home as a palace of potential delight. In Greece they bulldoze the earth to begin construction on an apartment complex and discover an ancient, lavish tomb. Who knows what riches lurk beneath our home—the ruins of a royal residence from some ancient civilization?

We divided the two-story house into separate living quarters. Sam lives on the first level, and I've set up house on the second. Each floor is about 1,500 square feet. Enough space so we each have a kitchen, living–dining room area, and a bedroom.

Thankfully, we both have our own full baths. I delight in the elegant claw-foot tubs original to the home. When emerging from a long, hot soak, I imagine myself as Venus, rising from the sea. But I take care not to step onto the center of the floor, as the tiles are sinking. If enough weight is placed on them, a person might fall through, landing on Sam's kitchen table. For the time being, we skirt the periphery of the room and caution our guests to do the same.

We purchased the house for three thousand dollars in a land-grab auction, sight unseen, and it's in dire need of repair. But everything's relative. All that remains of several other houses on our block—as well as those in the vicinity of the diner—are burned wooden beams to suggest there was once a home, a pile of rubble in front to remind us it had a porch.

Throughout the winter, we scattered buckets in some of the rooms to capture the water seeping through the ceiling. David plans to put on a new roof this summer. The shingles he's been collecting differ in color, but he assures me no one will notice.

David's privy to leftovers from home renovations in the affluent suburbs that keep a wary distance from Detroit, known to locals as The D. David's handy—this house could employ his skills full-time—but his availability is limited, as he works for his father's company. He also takes online business classes and hopes to have his MBA in a year.

I have an extra room upstairs. It's my favorite, just large enough to fit my desk and chair. But the room's containment is the point. There's only space enough for me and Chester, my worn, frayed sock monkey. Dad gave him to me when I was a child, and he sits flopped into the seat. As a kid, I had a habit of chewing his paw whenever I was upset. I still do, at least when no one's around.

The one time my mother summoned the courage to visit our East Side digs, she referred to this as my bonus room. Attempting to compose a cheerful face as I showed her around—pointing out, for instance, the massive blocks of original molding adorning the doorways—her moist, blinking eyes betrayed her brave smile as she poked about our dingy dwelling.

When we opened the diner, afraid to upset her further, I encouraged her to visit after we got our footing. My mother, my mother. I love her dearly, but her lifestyle troubles me. Trapped within a soulless marriage, her self-worth is defined by her beautiful home and possessions.

David saunters into the living room, a towel wrapped around his torso. I stand and tighten the sash around my robe. He pushes back my hair, and his eyes, eager and sparkling, express admiration. His lips brush mine, and with my fingertips, I push him away. There's no time for this. We're supposed to be going on a picnic today. Smiling into his eyes, I run my hands down his biceps and whisper, "Later."

I wouldn't champion boudoir skills as the enlightened woman's approach to securing matrimony. But they don't hurt. I'm thirty-one and am feeling every one of those years since opening the diner. I've slept with enough toads, traded enough notes with girlfriends, to understand that guys like David—handsome, smart, and sincere—are rare. If I want my happy-ever-after to be shared with a husband and children, I'd better soften my moodiness.

I remove his towel, roll it into a whip, and swat his lovely torso.

"I like it when you play games," he says, laughing, jerking away from the reach of the snapping towel. "Speaking of play," he continues, placing his hands on his hips and raising a brow, "have you got a name for that thing you do?"

He's so easy—*that thing*. But it works like a charm.

"No time for *that thing* now. Simmer down, cowboy." I kiss his cheek. "Save it for later."

The front door buzzer rings, and then a bone-chilling howl echoes up from the lower level, reverberating through every corner of our home. Sam's dog, Hero, has a nerve-jangling howl, and his whine could wake the dead.

"There goes the alarm," David says, glancing at the clock. "Ten fifteen."

"Kevin must have arrived. Let's get moving. They'll be up in a few."

Entering the bedroom, I cover my ears, muffling the noise from Hero's commotion below. My backpack rests on top of the armoire, so I climb on top of a chair, stretching to reach it. David tickles my exposed midriff.

"Stop it!" I yelp, giggling in spite of my irritation. I jump from the chair, bag in hand, landing on the floor with a thud.

"One of these days you're going to kill me." I drop the pack and bend, rubbing my foot. "I could have broken my ankle." He tries tickling me again, and I swat his hands away.

After selecting clothes befitting a picnic on Belle Isle, we slide into jeans. We'll be sitting on a blanket spread across a plastic liner, which will protect us from the damp ground. I don a red shirt and David wears blue; no one can accuse us of not being patriotic.

My straight, white-blonde hair falls past my shoulders. Born and raised in Michigan, I carry the creamy, porcelain complexion of my Polish ancestry. My glossy mane is a family trait—the exact shade as Babcia's, my grandmother's, when she was my age.

David's hair, gold and streaked with brown, is a shade darker than mine. He combs it to the side, and it grazes his left brow, lying shaggy around his ears. He claims to be void of vanity, but he trims his three-day stubble with the precision of a surgeon. I like that he cares about his looks and works out regularly, chiseling the lean, hard body I love.

I walk into the bathroom, closing the door behind me. I drop two snowy tablets into a glass filled with water, then gulp down the frothing brew. I'm bringing out the big guns to get through the day; my holistic remedies haven't helped a lick. I check my face in the bathroom mirror, steamy from his hot shower. Two red-blotched cheeks and a crimson nose. Pale-blue eyes, watery and red—rabbit eyes.

My eyelashes are white blonde, almost invisible, and I brush mascara over them so my eyes don't disappear into my face. I take time to perfect my lips, first lining them in pencil, then filling them in with Demon's Delight, an almost-black shade of plum. My skin hasn't felt the sun's warmth in months. I burn easily, so I layer SPF 50 sunblock on my face and arms. I'm annoyed with myself for being concerned with the way I look, even when under the weather. What if I skipped the makeup, the randy flirts? Would David still love me?

Under the scrutiny of his wolf whistles, his eyes traveling down my body, I strut to the kitchen and select a Cabernet from a closet serving as our pantry. Inexpensive, yet decent enough for quaffing, it will be bastardized by my syphoning it into Cherry Coke bottles. Consuming alcoholic beverages on public land in Detroit can land you with a hefty fine or, worse, a stint in Wayne County Jail.

I cleared out Welcome Home's fridge yesterday. No need to sell food less than fresh after a holiday. For the time being, Sam and I aren't getting a paycheck, but at least we don't have to buy groceries—one of the little perks food entrepreneurs can sneak under Uncle Sam's hard-boiled eyes. We don't need much money in general. It's amazing how cheap it is to live in Detroit.

We're betting our dwindling start-up capital will tide us over until we can make an income. We couldn't have opened the diner without Kickstarter, which is an online way of soliciting folks who may be interested in patronizing entrepreneurial ventures. What a godsend, that money. That plus the ten thousand dollars my mother lent us.

I remove chicken, a mix of spicy greens harvested from the diner's garden, and mayonnaise from the fridge. Goat cheese rests on the counter alongside bread Sam baked yesterday. As I slice the bread for sandwiches, I regard David. The man knows how to wear a pair of jeans. Not too tight, not too loose, and faded to perfection. Remote in hand, he flicks on the TV. He cracks open a peanut pod with his teeth, pops a nut into his mouth, and chews with exaggerated relish.

"Don't do that," I reprimand, shaking my head.

He looks at me in his innocent-babe, adorable way. "*Whaaat?* I put the empty shells in a bowl." He points to an empty half pod resting in a bowl, the other half scattered alongside bits of wheat-pocked peanut debris. "Nuts are packed with protein, plus these are unsalted."

I deflect my voice to a lower, sultry octave to ensure it's not the high-pitched whine of a shrew. "It's not the nuts, silly. It's that god-awful TV. Come on, *please?* Turn it off. Open the windows. Let's listen to birds."

"Chill, baby girl. This is a Reggie Roberts rerun. You'll get a kick out of this guy." He points the remote to an African American man built like a linebacker. Dressed in a baby-blue tuxedo, his large-toothed grin's the size of Lake Superior. "All this time we've been together and we've never watched Reggie Roberts? The city's mascot? It's *Name Your Price.* Pure Detroit kitsch. Everybody loves him."

I shake my head, a smile tugging at the corners of my mouth. When I look into his eyes, a lovely blur of teal, I have the unnerving sense that I'm staring into my own. Many confuse us for brother and sister, and I'm happy watching our elongated shadows walking together in the afternoon sun. Whenever I happen upon my solitary outline, I feel sliced in half. I wrap the finished sandwiches and put them aside.

Antique wood groans as feet trudge up the stairwell.

Laughing, I tackle David, trying to grab the remote. "I don't want them thinking we watch daytime TV." He waves it above his head, defending the remote as if I were trying to pull down the American flag. While we're wrestling, the door opens—Sam and Kevin.

"Are you guys practicing to audition for Jerry Springer?" Kevin asks, his voice as soft, deep, and familiar as my feather comforter. He places Sam's pack on the counter.

"Oh, Kev. Aren't the baby tigers cute?" Sam drawls, elongating her vowels, her voice oozing sarcasm. "They're fighting over Reggie Roberts." She looks at me, eyebrows raised. "Addie, you continue to amaze. I had no idea you were a fan."

"I'm fighting him to turn the damn thing off." I give one last lunge toward the remote, to no avail.

"Here's your mail." Sam sighs and shakes her head, placing the pile next to her backpack. "Look at all this garbage."

"Thanks, Sam. I keep forgetting to bring it up."

She places her hands on her hips, a question in the furrow of her brow. "What was all the jumping and hollering about? A chunk of ceiling fell down. Came close to landing on my head."

I wince, walk to the counter, and gesture toward David. He's describing to Kevin how Reggie Roberts earned the NFL's Offensive Rookie of the Year Award when he played for the Detroit Lions.

"Sorry, Sam. Blame David and his usual high jinks. The guy won't give me a minute of peace. I'll make sure he patches it up next week." I give her the once-over. "Wow. Love your dress."

"Thank you," she replies, thumbing through the stack of mail. Peering at a grocery flyer, she tears off a coupon for dog biscuits and slides it into the zippered pocket of her pack. She looks up, catching my eyes, a big grin on her face. "I'm wearing it to celebrate the beautiful day."

Sam in a dress: that's incongruous. But it's becoming—her long, shapely legs are too often hidden in jeans. Scanning the TV screen, her almond-shaped eyes, the irises a periwinkle blue, reflect amusement. Sam, David, and I have eyes in different shades of blue: blue grays, blue teals, blue greens. David's eyes are both—sometimes blue, sometimes green. Gazing into his eyes is like watching the meandering hues of the capricious Great Lakes.

Reggie Roberts's voice swells against the canned laughter.

"Buckle up your seat belts and hang on tight. Sexy's coming back to daytime!"

A contestant sashays across the stage, impersonating Lady Gaga, her butt swaying like a pendulum, skirt wiggling up meaty thighs, threatening to reveal her panty line.

"Are you kidding me?" My words are directed to Sam and then to the screen. Shaking my head, I'm at a loss to express my distaste for this show.

"Addie's just jealous," David says. "Don't fret, sweet thing. You've got the same swing in *your* backyard."

He wears an expression of a young boy teasing a girl because he hasn't a clue about how to act around her. He shrugs, and offers peanuts to Sam and Kevin, who each take a handful.

"Really, David," I say, ice in my voice. "One step forward and two steps back. That woman alone can turn back the dial on everything women have worked for in the past fifty years."

Another contestant parades onto the stage, a tacky parody of Lady Diana. Sam snorts with laughter, drops her peanuts on the counter, and scampers toward the screen. Bored, I lower my head and shuffle through the pile of catalogs and letters. It was worth buying that half-off throw from Pottery Barn to get on their mailing list. I study their decorating style and look through the glossy pages so I can find similar knockoffs at Detroit Resale Outlet.

A letter with a familiar scrawl makes me flinch. A distant life peeps out from beneath the stack, my name—Adelaide Jaworski—written with a jet-black pen on the envelope. The noise in the room fades beneath the thud of my beating heart. My breath quickens. I stuff the letter in between the Pottery Barn pages. David would never thumb through this.

I'm not going to open it. I'll get rid of it, along with the other recyclables. I'm the most determined woman I know. I will erase this letter from my brain. But what if I open it? What's the big deal? It's been close to—what—ten years? I'm not the woman I was back then.

I open the fridge, pour a glass of tea, then wipe the droplets off the countertop. With the side of my palm, I slide the scattered peanuts into a pile and then polish the laminate with such force, the cracked and yellowing surface glistens.

Sam's giggles subside, and she returns to the counter, regarding me with a curious look, a question in her eyes. Her lips tighten, and she tilts her head to the side, as if wondering what's up. Damn my sweating brow.

"Sorry, Addie," she ventures. She straightens her dress, her voice now restrained. "I forgot to ask if you were feeling better." She returns the peanuts, one-by-one, to the bowl.

"I'm on the mend. But the sun's so warm." I place the chilled glass against my fiery cheek. "I'm not used to it."

The letter's fate will be decided at another time. What a way to ruin a day. I glance at the clock and relax my shoulders, which have worked their way up, nudging my earlobes.

"Let's get this show on the road." I stuff my bag with the sandwiches and the wine-filled soda bottles.

Normally I'd be delighted with the way the day's unfolding, even suffering through a cold. But that letter knocked me off my game. Maybe I'll burn it.

Chapter Three

Sam

The buzzer zaps my nerves, a terrible jolt of a sound. I check the clock: ten fifteen.

With a ferocious gnashing of teeth followed by an eerie whine, Hero gallops to the door. The Hound of the Baskervilles comes to mind, as if he races baying across the moor. With his white coat of fur, Hero resembles a ghost, as well. Standing on his hind legs, he stretches long against the doorframe, his front paws scratching the weathered oak panels.

Amid his yowls, I hear a commotion, sounding like it's coming from Addie's bedroom above. She screams, "Stop it," her words followed by a loud thud. A chunk of plaster dislodges from the water-stained ceiling and hurtles down, crashing next to my foot. Thank God it didn't land on my head. Hero, oblivious, continues barking at the door, but his ruckus earns his room and board. Who needs an alarm with him around? If an unwelcome stranger pays a call, it's amusing to watch the fool stumbling down the crumbling steps, hightailing it down the street.

Hero's daily rubdowns are well deserved. The reality is he's just a lapdog with a bark far worse than his bite.

I adopted him from the Humane Society on Chrysler Drive. He's a pit bull with a smattering of hound, evident in his floppy ears and resonating wail. Although abandoned and starved down to bones, he did have a collar. The round metal tag affixed is stamped HERO, to which he responds when called. That's it. Hero. No owner's name or number. I've always wondered if he'd done something special to earn his name—like dragged a baby with his teeth from a burning building, or attacked a thug before an elderly woman was robbed.

Weighing in at fifty-five pounds, Hero has the wide-set eyes and musculature of a pit, with the goofy playfulness of a mongrel. He was estimated to be around two years old when I adopted him, soon after we purchased our home.

Hero and I've made a comfy nest in this house—all cinnamon smells, dog biscuits, and soft Pandora radio. Except for that buzzer and bark. I still jump when I hear the commotion. Gotta hand it to Kevin: prompt to the minute. He'd never sacrifice a moment in my company.

"Just a sec," I shout, giving Hero a biscuit to shush him. I dash to my bedroom, shake off my robe, and shimmy into a dress. I smooth the folds: pale peach with delicate green vines stitched at the hem. One hundred percent cotton, it accentuates my curves at the bodice and spills into an umbrella, landing just above my knees. Last week I spied it in the window of Vanguard Vintage. My size, so I couldn't resist.

I rarely wear a dress. When was the last time I've felt so feminine? For once my given name, Samantha, suits me. Addie's always one-upped me on beauty, but she works it with makeup. Perhaps today I'll be in her league.

I unlatch the three locks and unbolt the door, Hero panting by my side. I've trained him not to jump on friends.

"Great dress," Kevin comments, his skin dampening as he regards me. I back away and he clears his throat. "Happy Memorial Day," he adds as an afterthought, careful not to cross the boundaries I've set.

He hands me a folder. "April and May's hard copy for your files." Kevin, an accountant at Bradley and Collins, does our books and payroll in exchange for meals at the diner.

With his wide-set brown eyes, thick, muscular frame, and big, toothy smile, he reminds me of Hero working a party, tail wagging and drooling. And when one annoyed guest bops him on the nose, he ducks his head, gives a shy, loping grin, and pants on to the next person.

"Thanks, Kev. What a nice day for a picnic." I keep my expression neutral to ensure he doesn't get the wrong idea. He's well aware I want nothing more than friendship—says that's fine—but I see the yearning in his gaze.

I step outside to empty the mailbox. Most of it, as usual, is for Addie. For someone so concerned about waste, she sure gets a lot of catalogs.

"You and Addie must have cooked up some sorcery to bring us a day like today. I don't think I could have stood another day of freezing rain."

Here we go, at it again, conversation about the weather. *Boring.* I'm so sick of it. Doesn't anyone have anything to say besides relating the latest weather update from their smartphone? I, for one, have never minded our frozen winters and saturated springs.

Babcia, my grandmother, always said she had a winter's soul, which I must have inherited. When the freezing air shrieks over the Detroit River, the wind whipping the water into angry blades, I wrap my scarf across my face and pretend to be a samurai warrior. Using my umbrella as a shield, I ward off the stinging ice and pelting hail as it thrashes me from all sides.

Fearless, I endure our endless winters, for the reward is exhilarating. When the new season shows her gift in the tip of an asparagus helmet funneling above the soil, when baby lettuce leaves curl above the earth in a sigh, I'm walking on air.

Unlike Addie, I believe the foul weather was good for the diner. Even though we're in the midst of a cash-flow problem, the last thing we need is a rush. We've had an opportunity to get our footing, tighten the menu, and build relationships with those folks who didn't mind getting a bit damp.

Making sure Sarah Montgomery, for instance, had two pieces of cornbread with her greens, and omitting the onions from Lenny William's sweet potato hash, while always remembering to inquire about his newborn. The weather, from my vantage point, has been a blessing.

To say I'm the executive chef at Welcome Home is inaccurate, considering I left cooking school before earning my whites. I couldn't stand another minute with the arrogant instructor, who imagined himself Gordon Ramsay. Besides, I'd already completed the pastry division, which is my calling.

I spent the following year working in New York's Levain Bakery, whose cookies have been written up as *fucking insane*. You can get away with writing that in Manhattan. I learned more working at Levain than I ever did in school. Its infamous cookies inspired our Heartbreakers, a gargantuan chocolate cookie, the diner's most popular treat.

Calling myself the executive chef is, furthermore, absurd, since we're just a small eatery open only for breakfast and lunch. But I do have control of the menu and the kitchen. Down the road, we hope to expand the restaurant beyond the current forty-six-person seating, and remain open for dinner. We'll have to jump through a million hoops to get a liquor license, but booze is where the real money's made.

Kevin's in the bathroom, the top of the tank on the floor by his feet. He examines the inside basin, jiggling the toilet's handle. "Still having issues with the toilet?"

"No, Kevin," I say, sweeping up the plaster shards that fell from the ceiling. "Thanks to you, the flush is now a gush. A perfect potty."

He regards me, a question in his eyes, as if asking, *Did you wear that dress for me?* After today, this dress will be banished to my closet until I meet a man I'm into.

"That whatchamajigger—the flapper valve you replaced—did the job. Thanks again." He smiles, as if I tossed him a bone, and bends to scratch Hero beneath his ears.

Our house, even if falling apart, is ours. How lucky we are to live here, in a neighborhood so rich with history. What other major American city has homes with this amount of square footage that one can purchase for three thousand dollars, vacant acreage included? The floors are buckled, sinks are stained with rust, cabinet doors don't close all the way, and most of the outlets don't work. I love it!

Ninety years ago, this home would have been worth three hundred thousand dollars in today's money. Back then, home ownership was emblematic of Detroit's promise to Poles and Italians, who could not find basic sustenance, much less purchase land in their home country. The unskilled laborers flooded the city to work in slaughterhouses and automobile factories. During this era, Detroit made the same promise to blacks across the American South desperate to escape poverty, lynching, and lack of work.

Today, Detroit is making a new promise to Addie and me: *Stick with me. Believe in me. One day I will rise like a phoenix from the ashes.*

I grew up an hour's drive east of Detroit. The city's road map to economic desolation is old news to me: the riots in the sixties followed by the frantic white exodus to the suburbs, people who fled with incalculable wealth and future tax dollars in hand. I understand how crack decimated forgotten neighborhoods, turning them into crime-infested ghettos; how city schools and infrastructure nose-dived into third-world chaos, culminating in Detroit having the dubious distinction of being the largest municipal bankruptcy in US history.

There was blame enough to pack the city landfill. And when the car industries collapsed under a government corrupted by greed, it was as if someone poured gasoline over the city and lit a match. *And the fiddler played while Rome burned.*

I get that. I live in the fallout. Every day I trudge through the ruins of our burned-down, boarded-up, graffiti-stained neighborhood. It's as if the area's been erased, but the outline remains. A few intact homes, such as ours, serve as commas in a run-on sentence of skeletal frames lining our street. I've become desensitized. It's a feeling that might be shared with someone who lives in a war-ravaged city that was once beautiful. Like in Syria or Lebanon. But this is the United States.

It's hard to wrap my head around. It's too much. You have to shut down to survive. I try, however, to discover beauty in the ruined acreage, finding poetry in the rubble, in the promise of a daisy rising through crumbling asphalt.

Driving down Grand Boulevard you see the hard stuff, when the abandoned Packard Automotive Plant explodes between your eyes like a paintball pellet. There's no shutting down the magnitude of that thirty-five-acre industrial grid of busted-out windows and collapsed roofs. It's a decaying fortress—dystopic, apocalyptic—a testimony to the Motor City gone to hell. That place is cool.

The shock on my friends' faces when they visit from Ann Arbor, and the fear in my parents' eyes when they make the drive from bucolic Manchester, is my slap in the face—when I realize our living situation is not the norm for intelligent women who should know better. In truth, with Hero as my bodyguard, my only day-to-day fear is crossing paths with Curtis, a retired autoworker. The vinyl siding of his home is only a foot away from ours.

Having lived in his house his entire life, he considers himself the neighborhood militia. He pesters me with his opinions about our setting up shop in what he considers to be a bad section of town. And he thinks our neighborhood's safe? A security light is attached to the side of his home. It blazes into my living room like a searchlight through the night and I'm forced to wear sunglasses.

But Addie and I are opportunists. We're betting on Detroit's comeback, rooting for our city, investing our youth and energy in the place where our passion lies. When given a gift horse, don't inspect its teeth.

I took a risk going into business with Addie, and I'm not the gambling kind. She's an only child, and—I'd never be so cruel as to say this to her face—she's spoiled. She plays the victim card, rehashing what her therapist has deduced about her childhood: the damage inflicted by her absent dad, and her mother, whose only concern is that her next husband support her Neiman addiction. Granted, Aunt Teresa's flaky, but she's not a bad person. She's worried about her daughter's future, and she lent us a solid chunk of start-up cash. Addie has an undergraduate degree in classical civilizations. What else could she do after college but go into the service industry?

I've been relieved and surprised she's pulled her weight at the diner. While planting vegetables and tending sheep on summers spent at my family's farm, she must have developed a work ethic.

I've a picture of the two of us holding hands when we were girls. I'm laughing, wearing mud-caked jeans and a tattered T. Addie stares down the photographer with solemn warrior eyes. Her long, white braids are tied at the tips with pink ribbons, the same shade as the OshKosh overalls she always wore. She'd plead with Babcia to work out the stains and wash them each evening.

I remove the asparagus salad from the fridge and put the container in my backpack, which is already loaded with a plastic liner, blanket, plates, and napkins. No need for forks—asparagus is finger food. Crisp, tender, and sweet, young asparagus have a delectable hint of bitterness. Some dislike the flavor of the spears, while others say they don't like the smell of their pee after eating them. Granted, there is no smell quite like the smell of asparagus pee. Sulfuric and malty, it's another fragrance of spring.

"Ready to rock, Kev. The party's on."

Hero understands the signals; I'll be leaving him alone. He emits a shuddering whine, more of a wheeze, and rolls over onto his back. I squat down and scratch him on his stomach. Pale pink with charcoal splotches, it's the one portion of this animal that's soft and vulnerable.

"OK, boy. I'll take you on a long walk when I return. But with those ecstasy-baked kids from the Techno Fest running loose, I need my Hero to guard the fort." He jumps to his feet, panting, and gives a sharp bark as if he just punched the time clock. Kevin and I giggle. Kevin takes my pack, and I grab Addie's mail.

Heading up the stairs, I hear television voices hovering in the stairwell.

"Are you kidding me?" I say to Kevin. "TV on a day like today? They should have the windows open, let some fresh air into the place."

I open the door—they're fighting over the remote. My astonishment turns to amusement. Addie's so obnoxious when she launches into her diatribe about television being the opiate of the masses. Gotcha, girl. Placing the mail on the counter, I can't resist the wisecracks. At the same time, I'm envious that Addie and David have such a fun-loving and goofy relationship. My eyes slide to Kevin, so serious as usual.

Taken by the silliness of the show, I begin spinning about the room, enjoying the feeling of the dress billowing about my legs. I fall into David, who catches me, laughing. I glance at Addie, now frowning, her brows scrunched together as she tidies the stack of mail. Does she think I'm making eyes at her man?

Unsure how to handle the situation, I distance myself from the guys and rejoin her at the counter. She's never reacted to my roughhousing with David this way. I inquire about her cold; she's been ill the past few days.

"We're riding bikes, right?" says Kevin, breaking the tension. "Public transportation's sketchy on a holiday."

"On a holiday, Kevin?" I raise my brows. "When is Detroit public transportation ever *not* sketchy?"

As we pedal through the streets, the distant pound of Metallica reverberates through the city. The rhythm's as repetitive as a whirling dervish, shaking the marrow in my bones.

Avoiding potholes and crumbling asphalt, the four of us whiz past fenced-off parking lots, abandoned churches, and faceless industrial walls. Wheeling onto East Grand Boulevard, we see a burst of yellow and purple tulips redeem an otherwise tawdry apartment building. And then, again, more grids of disintegrating concrete, pavement, and gutters littered with debris.

When we make a sharp left turn to cross the MacArthur Bridge, the landscape, at once, changes. Belle Isle, a pastoral park resting between Detroit and Canada, is only four miles from our home. But from the abrupt change in scenery, it may as well be four thousand. Lush foliage and woodland trails meander alongside a well-tended beach. Boathouses, a conservatory, an aquarium, and a zoo dot the thousand-acre island. Last year the management was taken over by the state, part of a lease agreement with Detroit, and the park is being restored to its former glory.

After chaining our bikes to a rack, we head to our favorite spot. Addie and I organize the picnic beneath the sprawling maple, and we sit on the blanket. My back is to the Detroit River, and beyond its jade waters lies the skyline of Windsor. I'm happy but anxious, not quite sure what to do with myself on a day off. What's wrong with me? At last I've an occasion to relax, but I'm as jittery as the squirrels darting around the trees. I remove the salad, plates, and napkins from my pack. Addie hands me the chicken sandwiches, each wrapped as carefully as a gift. I arrange the food on plates, then pass them around.

Addie's lightened up. That scene in the kitchen, or whatever it was that was bothering her, seems to be forgotten. Now she's flirting with David, trying to draw us all into her rainbow cheer. I glance at her, noting the red sandals she wears are the exact shade of the color of her backpack. That's no accident.

Maybe I'm on edge because of Kevin, knowing he's crushing on me. It's exhausting screening my every movement and comment to ensure they won't be misinterpreted. Trying to stem the flow of his unspoken desire is like pitting cherries in July: The buckets keep replenishing, and it's draining trying to keep pace. A lot of sweet goodness, but you want them to go away.

I adjust my knees under the folds of my dress, arranging the fabric over my legs. I glance at Kevin, and he shifts his eyes. Watching those two, all goggle-eyed with their amorous teasing, may, however, be as uncomfortable for him as it is for me. The way David touches her and how her eyes flash when she speaks to him remind me I haven't been properly kissed, much less made love to, in over two years. Here I am, thirty-one years old, and I may as well be a virgin.

My last boyfriend, Andy, was a barista at a coffee shop near Levain. We lived together, but his degrading machismo was the main reason I left New York. Since I was a girl, I've worked to quieten the voices in my head that tell me I must live up to some sort of masculine ideal. Lessons taught by my parents—*never let someone's opinion define my reality*, and *I am the only person accountable for my happiness*—were a gift they gave me at an impressionable age.

As I bite into my sandwich, chunks of chicken drop from the bread, falling onto my plate. I glance around the group, but no one seems to notice my messiness. The sandwich is delicious with these spicy greens. I wipe my lips.

I stand over five feet ten inches and am a heavy-boned woman. Not fat, but curvaceous. Men have told me I'm sexy, and, until Andy, I'd always felt that I was alluring. In a natural, healthy way. I ride my bike, take speed walks with Hero, and I'm addicted to the adrenaline the fast-paced diner demands. I've a good appetite and, as a pastry chef, indulge in my art. Maybe it's tucked an extra few pounds around my hips, but that's a small price to pay for a scratch-made buttery scone.

I've always loved my body. Until I fell for Andy, who told me he'd never before dated a woman who wore clothing sizes in the double digits. (The average clothes size for American women is fourteen. I googled this. I wear a ten, sometimes a twelve, depending on how it's cut.) He told me in graphic detail what he could do with his former size-zero partners that he couldn't do with me.

The scary thing was that my love for him was so big I started to believe him. And along came the voices of self-loathing. I imagined myself as a bull in a china shop—obese, unfeminine, and worthless. After starving myself on rabbit food and then zipping my jeans, I'd note the soft bulge of flesh plumped over my belt line and cry.

On Addie's sole visit to New York, I introduced her to Andy over drinks. Into our second round, he said if I lost thirty pounds, I'd almost be as pretty as my cousin.

Addie was horrified. *Toxic jerk,* she exclaimed to me in private after I described to her his litany of abuses. *And you're living with him? Andy is unleashing his own insecurities on you so that he feels more like a man.* After I told her he wouldn't hold my hand in public, she asked me why would I date a man who was such a misogynist.

Maybe I put up with Andy because I was lonely and he was handsome. Or maybe there's something about me that prefers cruel dudes. Who knows? But those early lessons resurfaced after Addie's visit: My power does not rest in my ability to be physically attractive to men. My power comes from my intelligence, humor, values, and kindness.

Andy wounded me, but he taught me a valuable lesson. It was not about my weight. It was about him and his lack of self-worth. He tried to bring me down to his level by projecting his own inadequacies onto me.

As if Andy weren't enough, losing ground in the exorbitant rent we were paying dealt the final blow. It was time to leave the East Coast and surround myself with the people who loved me. I've vowed to stay away from men like Andy, but the experience has made me gun-shy.

It's not that I haven't had opportunities since I've returned home. I'm aware of the way men regard me when I enter a room. Especially Kevin. Poor guy. He has everything going for him, but I don't feel so much as a spark. Since the beginning of time, women have been making bad choices about men. But you can't force yourself to fall in love with a person just because they look good on paper. Hormones and pheromones—those two cataclysmic atomic levelers—call the shots. Not your brain. That's why the fallout's often a disaster.

I watch him finish his sandwich, fold up the wax paper, and clean his plate with a napkin. Then, with a sweep of his hand, he brushes away a trail of ants heading toward our picnic. If I settled for him, I'd end up hurting him. It would ruin a pleasant friendship.

Perhaps I should take notes from Addie. With her intellect and soft wit, among her girlfriends she talks the feminist talk of an awakened woman. But watch that size-two girl in action around an attractive dude. Even if she gives him the finger, it's as if she's giving an invitation. She's onstage, acting the part of a sexy, fun, girly-girl type. When I try mimicking her flirty ways, she seems to disapprove. I think of that scene in the kitchen when I was joking around with the guys—she was frowning, scrubbing the counter. Trying to understand what makes my cousin tick is like trying to read a sentence in a bowl of alphabet soup.

I'll stop focusing on the voids in my life, the mistakes I've made in the past. I will celebrate the life I'm building now. Frankly, aside from romance and sex, I'm not convinced I want to share my life with a man. It's too much drama. I like the freedom this singleness allows. I like being surrounded by *my* things. *My* photographs of *my* family and friends. *My* cookbooks. *My* yard-sale furniture and the decorative finds I've painstakingly collected. Perhaps that seems selfish, but the knick-knacks I've chosen to embellish my home are a distillation of me. The memories they hold make me happy.

My parents—aging hippies, refugees from the seventies—always encouraged me not to accept the status quo. I was even conceived in an

Oregon commune. But when I was a baby, we returned to Michigan. We moved to the quiet community of Manchester, a twenty-minute drive from my grandparents' Ann Arbor home. My folks purchased an old farmhouse, acreage, and sheep.

They make just enough money to pay their bills, and they paid off their mortgage last year. They're proud of the organic business they've created selling lamb to restaurants and other venues.

Growing up, every Saturday during the summer months, my brother and I drove to Ann Arbor and sold the meat at the farmers' market. When Addie was around, she'd come, too. We fantasized about owning our own business together. With elbow grease and determination, the opportunities in Detroit are granting us our wish.

It's a beautiful day and here I sit, obsessing about men and work. No wonder I'm off-kilter. With a napkin, I wipe the remaining vinaigrette away from the now-empty container of asparagus and return it to my backpack. Inhaling the awakened ripening of spring, I smell the buds on nearby plants as they unfurl their fists. I relax, sighing, and happiness begins to bloom in me, as well. Nature has this effect.

David, taking note that Kevin and I are quiet, tears his eyes away from Addie and removes his smartphone.

"Take a look at this, you gorgeous babes. Kevin and I made a spreadsheet comparing costs of produce from Sanchez Imports and what you're buying from Sarabeth's Greens."

He hands me his phone showing an Excel document lit across the screen. Calculations, charts? Damn it. I was just beginning to unwind.

"If you guys shift to Sanchez, you'd shave close to thirty-five percent from the bottom line of your produce costs."

Addie's neck muscles twitch as she glances at me to gauge my reaction. Now I'm annoyed. What right have they to tell us how to run our business?

"You guys, that's unthinkable," I say. "You know the importance of sourcing local. I can't imagine you'd believe we'd consider this."

"You're always worried about having the funds to pay your staff. Not to mention utilities and rent," ventures Kevin in a soft voice, his head ducking, as if to suggest apology. "David and I are trying to fix the problem."

The guys may think they're trying to help, but their words simply annoy and are having the opposite effect. Why do men always want to fix everything? Just be our sounding board and listen, mouths shut.

"Money's money. Are gold nuggets implanted in Michigan corn kernels? Can a Traverse Bay cherry tempt me away from the latest episode of *House of Cards*?" David dangles an asparagus spear over his plate. "Can this vegetable keep me from pirating the next bootleg Dylan?"

He drops the asparagus to his plate and levels us with his gaze. "I think not. For most people, buying organic food, which happens to be expensive, is low on their list of priorities. Don't you two want to stay in business?"

"Not if it means compromising our values," I reply. "There's a guy in upstate New York who makes every dish he serves from the acreage surrounding his home. His flours, his oils—everything. I'd love to make the trek and dine there, but there's a ten-year wait list."

"Damn it, David. Just listen to us," Addie says, her voice rising sharply. "Welcome Home is about being proud of what we serve to our customers."

I rest my hand on Addie's shoulder. "Supporting Michigan farms and the people who work in our state is our way of helping the economy." Addie nods her head in enthusiasm.

"Frankly, I'm surprised at you, David," Addie says, before grabbing a napkin and sneezing into the folds. Sniffling, she stuffs the linen into her bag. "We've been together over four years and you love my cooking. Why? It's because the ingredients are fresh, locally sourced, and, therefore, delicious."

She grabs my hand and raises it as if to suggest sisterly solidarity. She just sneezed into the hand now clenched in mine. It feels moist.

Yuck. Releasing her grip, she tips her head toward mine. "You could catch my cold if you touch your face. Sorry about that. Let me get you some sanitizer."

She grabs her bag and rummages through the contents. Relieved, I hold out the palms of my hands, and she pours one of her remedies into them.

"There you go. Lavender and tea tree oil with a dollop of witch hazel." Sitting rigid, I rub my hands together fiercely, irritated with David, who seems to be reciting grad-school text he recently memorized. Kevin, afraid of annoying me further, is silent. He spreads goat cheese on a cracker, edging out of the conversation.

"You'd better raise prices across the board. At least by twenty percent. Your margins are too slim. And sooner rather than later, so your customers don't get used to the current prices." Kevin shrugs, but nods, agreeing with David's proposal.

I give David a salute. "Aye, aye, captain. You may be right about the prices, but you're wrong about everything else."

Addie titters.

Folding his arms across his chest, he turns to Kevin and pats him on the back. "My man, we just got whipped. But it's nothing new. Business as usual on the home front. Why don't we drown our sorrows? Splash something on my machismo, would ya? Open some *cherry soda*?"

Addie, laughing, reaches into her pack and pulls out the bottles filled with wine. Enough talk about work, already. It's time to party. Turning her face into the crook of her elbow, she suppresses a sneeze. I'll dole out vitamin C when we return home.

I take a sip of wine. Vanilla, currant, and tobacco. Delicious. Something to smooth the rough edges. A mosquito buzzes around the lip of the bottle and nose-dives into the Cab. My arm jerks, and half of the wine sloshes out, spilling over the front of my dress. I look down at my bustline. It looks as if I've been stabbed in the chest.

Addie cries, "Your dress. Your beautiful dress."

45

Kevin winces. "Did anyone bring soda water? That should get it out."

"I've got something better," Addie says. "It's a stain stick that removes red wine spills." Once again, she reaches into her bag of tricks and pulls out what appears to be Chap Stick. She waves it across a horizon of blooming peonies. "Where I go, so goes my wine wand." She looks at David and winks, as if carrying around stain stick was another one of their inside jokes.

That's Addie, the magnificent magus. Forever the mother with a cure for all of life's problems, remedies arranged on her tidy shelves as well as in her backpack. Spices alphabetized, cleaning solutions systemized, holistic cures organized—all the labels facing the same way. She rubs the waxy stick over the front of my dress and then sponges the stain with water.

"There. Almost gone."

"I'm such a klutz."

"It was nothing you could control." She returns the stick to her bag. "The mosquitoes are fierce after breeding in all that rain. First they want our blood, and now they're after our wine."

David laughs, but Kevin's face slackens as he gazes at the shadow of a stain on my dress. The spill ruined his fantasy of what he thought could be the perfect day. He's such a nice guy. Totally cute and totally unaware of it. What's wrong with me? Why can't I fall for a nice one?

I should stick with jeans and T-shirts. I'm the type of girl who's better off with nothing nice. No nice dress. No nice guy.

Chapter Four

Addie

Chewing with deliberation, the woman looks up as I approach her table. She wears a billowing, sleeveless dress, patterned in a crimson-and-gold block print. A half dozen or so strands of sparkling beads drape around her neck, cascading into her significant cleavage. I'd put her in her midforties. After swallowing, she smiles.

"What type of wood did you use to smoke the chicken?" She points her fork at the thigh. "It's delicious."

This woman is Karen Bennington, famous in Detroit food circles for her cheeky up-to-the-minute restaurant blog. She's also known for her outrageous wardrobe and is proud to proclaim she's growing old disgracefully. Her persona is unapologetic: big, bold, and bright.

"We used birchwood chunks for this batch," I say, refilling her glass with cold tea. "And we harvested the first of the pattypan squash this morning in our kitchen garden."

She scribbles in a small spiral notebook and then removes purple-framed glasses that encompass half her face. She snaps a picture of the shredded chicken carcass with her phone. I hope she doesn't put that on Instagram.

"I wish I had room for two meals," she says, pointing to a plate at a table nearby. "Those lamb burgers look divine."

"They have been popular. We'll put them on special next Wednesday. Stop by if you're in the neighborhood." I glance about the room. Most tables, for a change, are occupied. "I must say, Karen, your *Detroit's Cookin'* posts featuring Welcome Home have certainly helped increase business. We appreciate your kind words."

She wipes her mouth, slick from the reddish-brown barbecue sauce, and takes a lingering sip of tea before speaking.

"It's my pleasure. I'm loving your food and the overall homespun whimsy of this place." She points her forefinger at me. "I want to ensure you ladies stay in business. I've several thousand subscribers to my blog."

"You can count me as one of them. Reading your reviews is the highlight of my week."

It's a good thing Sam's in the kitchen. If she heard me brownnosing this woman, she'd want to barf. Still. I'm appreciative of the business her blog's encouraged, and we must play the game.

"Could you bring me the bill?" Karen gestures to her plate. "This will be gobbled down by the time you return."

"No worries." I pick up the tea to replenish her glass yet again and then head to a four-top, refilling their glasses, as well. Our customers are especially thirsty in this heat. Thankfully, most of the orders have been filled, and our patrons appear content.

Returning to Karen, I hand her the bill, alongside a small brown box tied with twine.

"What's this?"

"It's our signature cookie. The Heartbreaker. A token of our appreciation."

"I've sampled these gooey clouds from heaven. And that name, *Heartbreaker*." She purses her lips, shaking her head. "Thank you. You ladies are simply too much." She fans herself with a menu.

"We're planning to install air conditioning. After such a chilly spring, these temperatures caught us off guard."

"This heat is uncommon for June, but I'm glad the windows are open. That gospel singing from across the street is magnificent."

I flash her a smile. "I agree. Our prep cook, Quiche, attends the church. I'd like to record their music. Maybe play it here on the Sundays when their windows are closed."

I turn and retreat to the prep area. In the past few weeks, business has improved over 30 percent. And that jump comes on the heels of an embarrassing Yelp review. Someone wrote they found a clump of long blonde hair in their soup. How disgusting. I worry that Sam removed her bandanna while she was stirring the pot, and some of her hair fell in the soup. At least the comment didn't hurt business—today's sales are sure to break the record.

Maybe it's the weather; more people are out and about. More likely, it's the attention local food bloggers have been giving the diner. Sam says I should be thrilled with the uptick in business, and I am. But the diner is drowning in a vanilla milkshake: our customers, flocking in from suburbia, are a sea of Caucasians. Over 80 percent of our city is African American, and that stat's closer to 100 percent around here. Where's Detroit?

Our closest neighbor's only ten feet from the diner, yet he sits on his porch, eyeing us with disdain. Why is that? What can we do to have our customer demographics represent our actual community of diversity?

At the moment, however, I've more pressing matters. When you don't turn compost, the stench gets worse. I wave at Lella and Braydon, pointing toward my office. They nod, smiling. Those two can handle the floor from here. Smiling at patrons, I weave around their tables as I head toward the office, locking the door behind me. The backs of my thighs are moist and stick to my sundress as I sit at my desk. The window is open, and an electric fan circulates the warm air, as fans do in every corner of the building. Sadly, the last thing we can afford is air conditioning.

I remove the letter from the drawer and reread the familiar scrawl. Respond to it or burn it. Make a decision.

> Bet a note from me's a shock. It's been a good ten years, but, at last, life cut me a break. I'm out of prison. Released—ha ha—on good behavior. I'll be working for my dad. I thought of you every day and have something of yours you'd want. Please call me: 313-841-3020. (BTW: You don't have to ask, but I'm clean.)
>
> Graham

The only rebellious act, which, in retrospect, could have ruined my life, was falling for Graham Palmer when I was attending the University of Michigan. We met at Rick's American Café, one of those typical heavy-drinking, heavy-pickup watering holes popular with students.

One of the things I like most about Michigan is its diversity. I was majoring in classical civilizations, and I had hoped to meet a guy from, say, Rome or Athens. Someone who'd inspire philosophical thinking. Someone with a worldly take on life. Typical I'd fall for a Grosse Pointe WASP.

The son of a father who owned a foreign-car franchise, Graham Palmer was a year older than me. I remember him from his brief stint at Cranbrook Upper—how could you not?

He was a straight-A dude with a bad attitude. In his second year at Cranbrook, the prestigious boarding school we both attended, he adopted a sinking-pants, splayed-finger, *wassup Detroit* gangsta swagger.

It was borrowed from Eminem, a rap star who glamorized the music, poetry, and vibe of the streets.

This was the turn of the century, when heroin, ecstasy, and meth became purer and cheaper and took root in predominantly white, middle-class communities. Imagine the horror of parents in their mowed-lawn, Suburban-in-the-driveway cocoons, witnessing their Dylans, Lukes, and Adams getting high and copying the language and attire of the ghetto—the very place they had fled, en masse, after the riots.

Graham had the image down to a science. But it was a look that didn't translate well in the regent's office, not the image Cranbrook wanted to set for the rest of its students. Graham Palmer was a memorable addition while he lasted.

What a hoot seeing his face after a couple of cucumber martinis at Michigan. I'd just turned twenty-one, was in the middle of my junior year, and, at last, of legal age to drink. I was partying with a pack of girlfriends when Graham and I caught each other's eyes across the bar, which was set into the arena like a fishbowl.

I can't remember much about the next six months except that I was wired, burned out, and my GPA was sinking as fast as I could snort the next round. Sunday afternoons spent with Sam and Babcia were my life raft. One of those Sundays may have saved my life.

In my junior and senior years, Sam attended cooking school in Livonia, which is a thirty-minute drive from Ann Arbor. We made it a priority to spend afternoons with our grandmother after she'd returned from Mass. Our grandfather had died the year before, and it became our tradition to cook a meal together in her kitchen. Splashed with sunlight, the walls and open shelves were decorated with Bolesławiec, a Polish pottery.

After Babcia died, Sam and I divided her collection of ceramics. I selected the cream teapot with matching cups, two candlesticks, and a serving bowl. Sam selected the soup tureen and fermenting crock, which we use at the diner to pickle vegetables. The collection is hand-painted with royal blue, yellow, and pinkish-red peonies. Sapphire-blue butter-flies, the uplifted shape and color of Babcia's eyes, fly above the garden scene into the speckled heavens.

None of Babcia's recipes were penned, but her eighty-six-year-old hands and taste buds bore the stamp of her own mother's when she learned to cook in their Włocławek kitchen. This was during the era preceding World War II, the years before the members of her family were forced to leave their home, and the city became occupied by Nazis.

Seventeen-year-old Krystyna, the delicate girl with the crystal-blue eyes, relocated with her family to an area outside Warsaw. It was there she met my grandfather, Fryderyk, whom we call Dziadek. While sand-wiched between the war machines of the Soviet Union and Germany, they survived on whatever their ration cards and the black market could provide.

After the war, Babcia and Dziadek immigrated to America, where, at last, they were married. Dziadek, holding a PhD from the University of Warsaw in archeology, found work as a university professor at the University of Michigan. The couple made their home in Ann Arbor and parented two sons. They never forgot the horrors of war and taught our fathers that they were the lucky ones.

It was Babcia who inspired our love of cooking. With her deep disdain of manufactured foodstuffs, she instilled in her granddaughters a distrust of processed fare.

But we were slow learners. As a child, I remember our humiliation grocery shopping with her. With the intensity of a brain surgeon, she would study the ingredients on the kid-friendly fun-in-a-box packag-ing lining the shelves. She pronounced each word on the ingredient list carefully, as though she were tasting dirt. Her blonde wisps of brow furrowed as she *tsk-tsked*, muttering *obrzydliwe*—disgusting—in earshot of all the shoppers on aisle nine.

How horrifying it would be to run into a friend who could scru-tinize our cart. Pizza, mac and cheese, and sugary cereals were the unrivaled preferences of our friends, the staple of birthday party and sleepover fare. No matter how much we begged, how much we cajoled, *Rugrats* mac and his partner, neon-powdered cheese, were denied. Sam and I'd retreat from the midcenter aisles, tears rolling down our cheeks, as Babcia led us to the periphery of the produce section—no man's land—where fruits and vegetables rested quietly in their bins.

Of course we came to share her point of view, our teen years in sync with the farm-to-table movement. The grassroots lobby to produce and consume locally harvested foods was no revelation to us; we'd eaten at this table our entire lives. Babcia was the original pioneer, the Alice Waters of Polish grandmothers.

When she died in her sleep, heartbreak blindsided Sam and me. Foundering under the weight of trying to bear such a loss, we broke down, we grieved, we grew up, we grew older. I compulsively checked my calendar, counting the Sundays the three of us met to cook—seventy-eight slashes in my timeline. I would give anything to fall back into one of those Sundays. All of those Sundays still weren't enough.

One Sunday in particular stands out in my mind. It was during the time I was dating Graham Palmer. I was wrecked—my head pounding, *rode hard* from the prior evening's partying. That morning I'd awakened in a room I didn't recognize surrounded by stoned-out strangers, powder-smeared mirrors, and needles. There were more drugs spread out over the carpet than ground into the floor of a Nirvana tour bus.

Graham was nowhere to be found, so I called a cab and returned to my apartment. In an attempt to mask my shame, I patched myself up with a hot shower, Visine, and lipstick. But when rolling out the pierogi dough, I burst into tears, retreating into my Babcia's arms.

I broke up with Graham just in time. Two weeks later he was busted for possession of heroin and dealing coke. Michigan has some of the most draconian drug-sentencing laws in the country, and he was sentenced to prison. No amount of his daddy's money could buy him out of sixty-two grams of powder sold to an undercover agent—a Pakistani-American Ann Arbor detective posing as a party store owner.

Staring at the letter, I pinch my lips between my teeth, trying to make up my mind. Is whatever he has of mine worth my calling him? It's a coin toss. I record his number in my smartphone, shred the letter, and bury the paper bits in the recycling bin. I've never told David about Graham. He'd wonder about my character if he'd known I'd dated such a thug.

Massaging my temples, I sigh. I slide open my desk drawer and pull out last week's employee time cards to get started on payroll.

～⑨～

Sam

Sweat trickles down the sides of my face and dribbles in between my breasts, sliding down my stomach. I loosen the back ties of my apron strings, which are chafing my waistline.

The six burners of the stove are working overtime as the blue flames lap the bottom of pans. Paul, our new hire, is beside me, placing a pot filled with water, vegetable scraps, herbs, and bones on the back burner. With his athletic build and clean-shaven, conventional demeanor, he looks like a professional soccer player. The fan's not doing much good—eighty-six degrees outside must equate to ninety-six in this kitchen. We shouldn't have spent all available funds on a walk-in cooler when what we really need is air conditioning.

I untie the bandanna around my head and mop my face. Every window is open in the diner, fans are whirring, and gospel singing filters through the screens. When the weather cooperates, the windows and doors of Detroit Tabernacle are flung open, and music fills the air. Church is a powerful force in this community, and the hymns infuse me with yearning. It's as if within the stanzas lie answers to questions I've long forgotten to ask.

But there's no time for contemplation now. Today's special is Lamb Burgers with Tzatziki and Beetroot Relish, and their popularity has not shown signs of abating. In the prep area, Quiche is flipping the burgers on the grill while Braydon stands beside her, spreading the tangy yogurt-dill sauce and relish on potato buns. They're running low on buns, but we've enough lamb patties and accoutrements to feed an army.

"Paul, I've got a bag of potato rolls in the freezer. We'll switch the special from burgers to sliders. I can't leave these eggs. Can you take the rolls to Quiche? In this humidity, they'll be thawed in no time."

"Pas de problemo," he replies. After reducing the flame under the burner of his now-bubbling brew, he strides toward the freezer. The smell of his stock perfumes the air and comes alive in the back of my throat as I imagine the sauce it will soon become.

A familiar twinge of irritation tugs on my emotions. Addie. Our division of labor isn't fair. I sweat it out in the back of the house while she works the front. All she does is clear tables when business demands, be charming to our customers, organize schedules and bills, and promote the diner on social media.

I stick my head over the swinging doors to see if the rush is dying down. Thankfully, it looks like most of the customers have been served. There's no need to make sliders after all. There's Addie, chatting it up with a blogger whose articles about the diner have created a buzz. I've got it wrong. Success begins at the front door. Gracious hostess skills and networking are *essential* to Welcome Home.

I return to the kitchen to garnish plates with pickled carrots and lightly dressed microgreens. A cacophony of bells rings out from the church's steeple. What a crazy day. Thank God Mom and Dad were forced to cancel their plans to have lunch here today. One of the sheep has bloat and needed treatment and observation. It's hard for them to leave the farm.

My dad, Andrew, is one year younger than Addie's father, my uncle Michael. As a teenager, Uncle Michael brought home the exemplary grades and was elected president of the student council. Dad enjoyed championing environmental causes and playing guitar in a local band. You'd never guess the two of them were brothers. The academic environment of a college town suited my uncle. The eccentricities of growing up in a town such as Ann Arbor, complete with alternative schooling, were the perfect fit for Dad.

He met my mother, Becca, in Lansing, where they both attended Michigan State. Their dream was to escape Michigan winters, move out West, and live off the land. Juniors in college, they married and then focused their studies at the Sheep Teaching and Research Center at State.

After graduating, they moved to an Oregon commune to practice animal husbandry, but they were miserable. They didn't agree with the way communal funds were managed, and the division of chores turned ugly. A vegan couple were in charge of the labor charts, and they demonstrated their hostility to Mom and Dad's practice of harvesting sheep with passive aggressiveness. Mom and Dad were assigned to bathroom janitorial duty their entire stay.

My parents also missed Babcia and Dziadek. Dad and Dziadek enjoyed woodworking and restoring old tools. Mom appreciated Babcia's frugality, her hand-stitched linens, her traditional ways of gardening and putting up the harvest.

Mom's pregnancy with me, six months after Addie's parents announced their pregnancy, was the final impetus. They repacked their bags and returned to Michigan. The winters, after all, weren't so bad. Mom could make sheepskin coats and gloves to keep her children warm.

Of course, Babcia and Dziadek were overjoyed and spent much of their time, particularly during the busy summers, at our Manchester farm. Mom turned the dated parlor into a cozy guest room. Addie, lost in the shuffle between her hostile parents, spent weeks at a time working at the farm when she was out of school.

Babcia, Addie, and I planted, harvested, and put up vegetables through the summer. Dziadek helped Dad and my brother with the sheep and the myriad chores involved in day-to-day farm life. I wish we had more family to help run the diner. My brother works in a micro-brewery in Denver.

Living off the land reminded my grandparents of their life in Poland before the war, and softened the blow felt by the absence of their other son and daughter-in-law. Uncle Michael and Aunt Teresa's visits were rare when they were fighting. And, after their divorce, they ceased altogether.

Braydon enters the kitchen, interrupting my thoughts. "The rush is over. All the customers are praising the food."

I wipe my hands across my apron. "Speaking of praise, we should be praising the heavens. If that music isn't proof there's a God, then nothing is. It's a pity they've stopped, now that I've the time to listen."

"They outdid themselves today. A double whammy. Aunt Suella says they brought in a sister choir from Birmingham."

"Who knew? A gospel choir in Birmingham?" I'm taken aback. The suburb's only 10 percent black. I don't, however, voice that statistic to justify my surprise.

Braydon snorts, reading my thoughts. "I'm talking Birmingham, Alabama. One of the couples is staying with us. The Birmingham choir hosts Detroit Tabernacle in March, when their weather's headed into spring."

I glance at the clock. "It's almost two. I'll lock the doors and put up the Closed sign."

Walking to the floor, I segue toward the grill and remove my apron. Quiche kneads the knots in her neck with her fingers. She gazes at me as if she's been through a storm.

"I've seen more white people today than I've seen my entire life in this neighborhood. And who'd ever guess lamb burgers would be such a hit? Hamburgers I get. But lamb burgers? Yuck."

"Broaden your horizons, Quiche. But then again, maybe not. We've enough trouble keeping the lamb in stock." The lamb we use is harvested at our family farm. Mom told me Welcome Home is their best customer. We refused their offer for a discount—profits for everyone are marginal enough.

"You told me to remind you the teacher is stopping by around three. Remember? He was Sun Beam's math teacher last year." She grabs the grill brush and begins scraping burned bits off the flattop.

"Oh, right. He wants to bring a class to the diner for a field trip." Sun Beam attends Detroit's Boggs School, a reimagined education model that focuses on academic as well as practical life skills. A charter school, it's an oasis in the midst of other schools operating in third-world conditions. "I'll give them some vegetable seeds to plant." One day we plan to expand the plot. We envision inner-city kids learning how to grow, harvest, and utilize fresh produce in cooking classes geared to children.

"Growing vegetables is not what interests him—the garden is going to be an example for a math project when his class resumes in September."

"Math? Really? I won't be much help in that department." I shrug. "But, whatever. Of course, I'm delighted to have the class pay us a visit."

Quiche puts down the brush and appraises me, head to toe. "You may want to rinse your face and pull a comb through your hair. His name is Uriah. And I'll wager there's a long line of women waiting in line to buy a ticket on *that* ride."

I stop, surprised. Unless she's praising Sun Beam's grades, Quiche rarely doles out compliments. Especially in reference to men. With her wide, full lips and svelte waist, no doubt she's had her share of suitors. But try engaging her in conversation about one of our favorite topics, the male species, and the woman shuts down. Heaven forbid we ask about Sun Beam's father. For all we know, it was an immaculate conception. Who knows the sort of man she'd find attractive?

I put up the CLOSED sign, go to the restroom, rinse my face, and remove my bandanna. I linger at the mirror a moment longer than usual. On impulse, I unknot my braid and run my fingers through my hair, flecking out bits of flour.

Returning to the prep area, I fish today's sales from the register and take the wads of cash and receipts to the office. Placing the bag into the safe, I hear a ruckus on the floor—Sun Beam's high-pitched squeal and a man's deep voice. The teacher must have arrived. Returning to the floor, I see a large man kneeling down with Sun Beam in his arms, the muscles of his broad back shifting beneath his shirt.

Quiche's forearms rest on the counter, and she chuckles. "You're gonna smother him, honey."

"But what a great way to go." His vowels are relaxed and rolling, a snatch of Southern accent in his words.

He unwraps himself from Sun Beam, stands, and removes his backpack, placing it on a chair. Hands on hips, he swivels, regarding the panorama. He removes his baseball cap, revealing dark hair cropped close to his head. When he sees me in the doorway, he stops. Smiles.

My pulse flares, and my legs soften beneath me. Just looking at this man—who is a good four inches taller than me and built like an ox—makes my teeth rattle. I'm tumbling into a lake with stones tied around my ankles. Sinking. Drowning. Inescapable and inevitable.

He saunters toward me, takes my hand, and shakes it, pulling me back onto the shore.

"I'm Uriah. And you must be Sam. I've heard so much about you from Sandra."

Who's he referring to? At a loss for words and clearly confused, I glance at Quiche, hoping she'll rescue me. "Sun Beam, Sam. He's talking about our Sun Beam."

My face grows hot. One minute with this man and my mind is mush. Hormones have me in a vise, and it's impossible to escape. I push my hair behind my ears. Braydon glances my way, a quiet smile playing about his lips. He and Lella roll the mop and bucket to the center of the room, I'm sure to get a better view of this performance.

"Of course." I turn to Sun Beam. *Sandra.* My face must be radiating heat, and my smile's so wide my cheeks ache. Swallowing hard, I try collecting myself.

"Well, I see—"

"I've just gotten used to calling her Sun Beam," I stammer, interrupting him, talking in distracted spurts. Then my eyes travel back to his face, his clean-shaven jawline with the whisper of an afternoon stubble. I feel like an animal shaking off the effects of a long hibernation.

"Of course, we're the only ones who call her Sun Beam," I continue. "I guess we've made our own little family here."

He looks around the room. "This place is unique. Like it's trapped in another era." He picks up a vintage teacup, painted with pale-pink roses. "A gentler time."

His eyes meet mine. I swallow hard. "You must be thirsty. Can I pour you a glass of iced tea?"

"That would be wonderful. It's blazing out there. I'm parched."

Walking to the fridge, I can feel his eyes sliding down my body. I try imagining how Addie would act at this moment. I stop, turn sideways, catch his eyes, and smile. I'm glad I wore my blue T-shirt, as the shade matches my eyes. Placing my hand on my hip, I cross my right foot over my left. Addie instructed me on this pose, which improves posture and is the best way of giving full attention to curves. "Instead of tea, perhaps you'd prefer our Lavender-Lime Soda."

He gives a little smile, a nod.

"Maybe I'll join you," I add, lifting my brows.

Alerted to the play in my voice, he walks to the counter, his eyes on my face. The air feels electrified. Am I emitting sparks? I walk around the counter, a sway in my hips, and fill two tall glasses with ice.

I've now become an actress behind a bar in an Old West movie. The cowboy was just cued to stride up and take a drink from the little lady. Quiche, Sun Beam, Braydon, and Lella are quiet, pretending to be occupied with their tasks, but not missing one beat of this show.

"Quiche tells me you want to use our vegetable garden to teach your students math." I pour us each a soda and slide one his way. Imagining myself as Mae West, I tilt my head to the side, batting my eyes furiously.

"I've found the only way of teaching that sticks with students is learning through practical life-skill exercises. Do you have paper and a pen? I'll show you."

Without moving my eyes from his, I grab an order pad from under the counter. As he takes it from my hand, his fingers linger on mine a second more than necessary. A thrill shoots up my spine. I pull a pen from my back pocket and give this to him, as well.

He sits at the counter, tapping the pen on the pad. "For example, in a traditional classroom, a student learns a formula—say, area equals length times width—does the practice problems, and then takes a test. After the test, the kid forgets what they've learned. But if the formula is made relevant to their life, demonstrating something useful to them, they retain the information."

At the moment, arousal for this man has trumped all knowledge. I take a sip of soda and try to summon an articulate sentence. Listening to him speak, I feel as if I know only a sliver more than nothing. Thankfully, a fragment of that sliver rises to the top.

"That's similar to the Montessori approach, right? Where students learn concepts from working with materials, rather than by rote memorization?"

"Exactly." He gifts me with a beatific smile, and I admire the shape of his full lips, the gleam of his teeth, and the cleft in his chin. "What

I'd like to do is have my students take the measurements in your garden and show them how to do the formula, which would demonstrate how much soil they'd need to fill it."

He draws a rectangle, and I rest my elbows on the counter to observe his calculations, cupping my chin in my hand. He smells of sap and perspiration, like a pine forest after a downpour. Pheromones. Delicious and intoxicating. I wish they could be bottled.

"See," he says, tapping the pencil on my wrist, and catching my eyes. "I multiplied the width and length of the garden. That gave me the square footage to calculate the amount of soil they'd need to fill the plot." He scribbles numbers on the pad and slides it under my eyes. "Since the garden is forty-five square yards, and we want to cover it in four inches of soil, we'd need five cubic yards of dirt."

"Fascinating." I lean my head toward the pad. I don't have a clue as to how he came up with his final number. I'll make sure to assist Sun Beam with her next math assignment. I tip my head to the side, looking up into his eyes. "Consider taking it a step further and having your students plant vegetable seeds." I straighten, looping my hair, which has fallen into my face, across my shoulder. Mae West blossoms into a honey-blonde Nigella Lawson. I imagine myself fresh from the garden, wearing a sultry smile while admiring my basket of eggplant, tomatoes, and spinach. "You know, I grew up on a farm. I could teach your students how to utilize their harvest. Give them a cooking class."

"Now that's a thought." He considers me, the side of his mouth ticked up, a look of admiration. "I grew up in Nashville, and my favorite memories are when we visited my grandparents on their farm. It was an hour's drive south from our home. I was named after my granddad."

"When does your class resume?" I say, smiling ear to ear. I have to admit, I love to show off my dimples.

"After Labor Day. Ten weeks or so." He finishes his soda in a gulp. "That was refreshing. Lavender. Hmmm. Who knew?"

"We harvested it from a clump out back. Their lilac blossoms are just beginning to appear. Let me show you around." I wave him toward the back door. "Follow me."

Addie and I cross paths as she exits the office. I touch her arm. "Addie, this is Sun Beam's math teacher. He's going to use our garden for a school project."

"Nice to meet you," she says, extending her hand.

"You, as well," he replies, taking her hand to shake it. He's a fox, yet she barely registers his presence. Her jaw is clenched, and thin lines crease her forehead. She's been holed up in that office awhile. I'm glad I don't have to do payroll.

I open the back door leading to the garden. Uriah places his fingertips in the small of my spine, and my tailbone feels as if it's being zapped by a cattle prod. Hormones. Pheromones. Will he be another addition to my history of making bad choices about men? Man, oh man, am I in for trouble.

Chapter Five

Addie

"I've never seen you wear that," David says, toying with the tiny cap sleeve of my dress. His fingers slide down to trace the piping at the top of the fitted bodice.

"Mom bought it for me last summer. The last time we were shopping together. Pink and green, somehow, does not seem right in this city." I eschewed my dark shade of lipstick, as well, selecting a pale-pink gloss. It complements the shiny ribbon, tacked around the seam at the waist.

"The girl wears only black in The D." Howling like a wolf, he runs his hands down my torso.

I smile, fluffing the bell-shaped skirt. A subtle pattern of roses and vines are printed on the silk and cotton blend. It feels soft and cool as it billows around my calves. It's odd how a dress can be transformative. Today I feel both modest and sexy.

"Mom will be happy to see me wearing it."

David's staying home today to work on the roof, so I'm borrowing his truck. He thinks shopping and lunch with my mom are all that's on today's agenda. I figured it best not to tell him the real reason I'm going to Grosse Pointe.

"Dad's dropping off the shingles," he says, taking a sip of coffee. "He has no problem with me taking off work today. But he'll be sorry he missed you." David appraises me head to toe. "I'd love to watch his expression seeing you in that outfit."

"I'll wear it next time we get together with your parents. Give him a kiss from me."

He pulls me into his arms and plants his lips onto mine. I pull away, giggling. "But not like that."

"Ha. Dad would die of shame if I even gave him a man hug." He laughs, but I can see the pain in his eyes.

My hand explores the side of his face, rubbing my fingers across his three-day stubble.

"I love your dad, but he is a pretty stern dude. Even when we're just spending time together."

His parents have a cottage on Higgins Lake, which is three hours north of Detroit. On past vacations, when everyone's hanging on the deck sipping beer, his dad rarely cracks a smile. So unlike his son, who can't get through a couple of sentences without making a joke.

"Dad's saving all his strength for his backhand." He rolls his eyes.

He's referring to his father's tennis game. Nationally ranked, his father's a tournament competitor. Back in his college days, he led Michigan in a series of consecutive-season wins.

I lean into him, stroking the hairs on his bare chest. "I know, I know. Daddy issues. I understand firsthand what that emotional distance feels like. But you know he loves you. He shows it in other ways. Like paying your college tuition. Like giving us supplies to help fix this house. He's a good guy, David." I try to catch his eye, but he stares off into the space above my shoulder.

"Hey," I say, snapping my fingers at his face. "When things get settled at the diner, I'll invite your mom and dad over for dinner."

He gives me a sad little half smile and shrugs. "That would be nice. But it won't be easy to cook for him. Since his bypass, he's cholesterol-free."

David's face falls, as it does every time our conversation circles around his dad. Several months ago, his father was having severe chest pains. It was discovered he had a blocked vessel leading to his heart. He had open-heart surgery, which scared the hell out of us. But his dad's a healthy man and made a speedy recovery.

I place my forefinger on his lips. "No worries. I'll let your mom dictate the menu."

"She'd do that anyway," he remarks, his features blank. I refrain from comment. His mother has to be the most controlling person I've ever met. She even makes me seem laid-back. Through the years, David and I have found it best to just go along with her dictates. David's sister left home after high school and remained in Ohio after graduating from Ohio State. She told David she needs distance from their mom. Who could blame her?

"Seems you need some cheering up. I'll make breakfast for us before I leave." I pour us each a second cup of coffee, feeling guilty about the day I've planned.

"OK, baby girl. Lemme hop in the shower." He flashes a broad grin. "And I'm not on any special diet, so don't forget the bacon." He yelps, "Bacon, bacon, bacon," as he scampers toward the bathroom.

I smile. I know my man. I know how to make him happy. I want us to be dancing this way for the rest of our lives. I open the fridge and remove eggs, bacon, and butter. The oatmeal and berries can wait until tomorrow.

As I'm slicing a loaf of bread, my eyes wander to the faded, floral wallpaper and then to the window frame peeling with curls of paint. Four shades of color—white, yellow, green, and blue—I counted them once. Eastern Europeans who immigrated to America built the house in 1910. A patchwork of ethnicities has lived here since. If walls could talk.

A couple of blocks from our home, there was once a thriving open-air market, Chene-Ferry. It was one of several such markets established in Detroit in the 1850s, which still influence our city's dynamic food culture today. The market was vacated in 1990, when the north end of Poletown was demolished for an automobile factory. Soon after, the factory itself was abandoned after the collapse of the car industry. Once a Polish oasis, and now a burned-out wasteland. Way to flatten a culture.

I take the breadboard to the sink, brushing the crumbs into the drain. Some say our neighborhood sums up Detroit: a city of blight run by a government caring more about corporate greed than it does its own people. But it's not productive to focus on former city politics. Yesterday is over, today is where I'm standing, and Detroit is on the brink of something grand, something transformative.

You can taste it in the smoke and tartness of the Grilled Quail with Pickled Cranberries when dining at Selden Standard, the latest darling in The D. You can smell it in the air at the Eastern Market, in the wafts of roasted garlic and yeast at a new upscale Italian restaurant, where there's always a wait. You can see it in the brows of young people—like David, Sam, and me—who are rehabbing old homes and turning urban prairies into organic farms. Neighborhood by neighborhood, our dreams are turning Detroit into a leaner, greener city.

More than one hundred years of families lived in this house, painting, scraping, and repainting this windowsill. It's the one part of our home I don't want David to restore.

As I place the bread in the toaster, the bathroom door opens. I turn. David looks so hunky leaning into the frame of the doorway, his naked body blanketed in a fog of steam. Desire hits me like a crashing wave. We lock eyes. I moisten my lips.

He grins. "Do married people ever look at each other this way?" The spell is broken.

Driving onto the expressway, I head east to Grosse Pointe, rationalizing today's agenda. So I called Graham. What of it? He has something of mine, and whatever it is, I want it back. I dared not meet him in The D, which is like a small town. David and I are an item. Everyone knows everyone's business, and if anyone saw me with another man, tongues and texts would fly.

On the phone, Graham's voice sounded just as I remembered: Grosse Pointe prep, which is a nasal tone, unenthusiastic with a hint of irony. It's a voice that sounds perennially bored, a voice particular to the Great Lakes elite.

I'd thought serving time would exhaust a voice, render it tired, gravelly. Maybe he'd copped some weird prison lingo—*Hey, girlfrien', I got jigs while you make that juice card.* But his speech had the same confident cadence as always, as if he'd returned from Princeton and recently passed the bar instead of exiting the gates of Michigan State Prison.

That voice annoyed me then, and it annoys me now. It's as carefully cultivated as the street look he copped when he was a kid. Graham's hardly Mayflower blue blood. He's Ukrainian. Second-generation Ellis Island. The grandson of a car salesman who capitalized on the irony that selling foreign cars in Detroit's Made in America culture might prove to be a profitable niche.

His grandfather changed the family name from Palamarchuk to Palmer before opening his dealership. An exotic name, especially in sales, can be a liability. Graham's dad took over the business after his father retired, with hopes his own son would one day carry the torch. Ten years of lockup cast a cloud over that dream.

Mom has her issues, but she knows my history with Graham, has never cast stones, and only voiced relief I had the sense to break up in time—that I didn't go down with him. Besides, it was party drugs, not armed robbery. And she and my stepdad, Max, belong to the same club as his parents.

Mom is curious as to what Graham wants to return. I also suspect she'd like sticking it to the controlling asshole to whom she's currently married. Max would be outraged to know she's allowing a convicted felon into the sacred gates of his enclave. He'll be at work across town, so the coast is clear until late afternoon.

Mom plans to keep to herself, a safe distance away in her bedroom, but the acoustics are excellent in the open floor plan of their contemporary home. *You won't even know I'm here,* she told me. *And there's plenty to keep me busy. Here it is almost July, and I haven't sorted my summer wardrobe from the spring.*

These days Mom is proud of me and has collected every article written about the diner. On a couple of occasions, she's even braved the city, stopping by with her lady friends to lunch, our restaurant now trending even in Mom's social milieu.

Neither Bio-Dad (my biological father), Band-Aid Dad (another ex, Mom's temporary fix), nor Douchebag Dad (zillionaire Max, to whom she is currently married) has shown any interest in stepping foot in Welcome Home. I couldn't care less about my stepdads, but it hurts that Bio-Dad, Michael, hasn't stopped by. I want him to see his mother's photograph in our place of honor.

My father and Sam's father are brothers. They were born and raised in Ann Arbor, which is a lively, colorful town. Small businesses and fast-growing tech companies flourish on the capital the university brings to the city. The town hosts an eclectic cast of characters and ethnicities. You can find a place, whether your thing is writing a thesis on biomedicine, getting high at the annual Hash Bash, or painting tribal stripes down your cheeks to cheer the Wolverines at Michigan Stadium.

Because of his PhD in archeology, Dziadek was granted professorship at the university, and Babcia found a welcoming niche at St. Thomas the Apostle. Polish tradition was strong in the Jaworski home, and the parents kept their Catholic and gustatory customs, reminding their sons at evening meals that they were the lucky ones.

My father, Michael, kept a watchful distance from his parents, as if they carried an exotic disease he was terrified of catching. He was embarrassed by their fierce Polish pride and ethnic eccentricities, and shaken by their stories of poverty during the war.

He believed his salvation lay in wealth. His grades at Huron High were exceptional, ensuring him a full ride through Michigan's undergrad program, followed by the university's prestigious business school. Majoring in finance, he met my mom, Teresa, at a frat party. She was a student in the School of Nursing.

The dazzling daughter of an Illinois farmer, Mom believed in beautiful things. Like my father, she also believed wealth would secure happiness. The end of her senior year found her pregnant with me. They were married just out of college and would have been splendid partners had their love not been crushed by materialism.

Dad became a stockbroker, and his career blossomed during the eighties era of Reaganomics, followed by the roaring nineties and the soaring Dow. He was the brother with a Midas touch, and when his portfolio began to reach well into seven figures, his touch began to reach well beyond my mother.

Their divorce was brutal and swift. I was the fallout, the neutral country in their world of astonishing bitterness. Growing up, I was despondent, yet anxious to please and to control. Or so says my therapist.

The drive from Detroit to Mom's new house in Grosse Pointe is less than twenty minutes, but driving along the glistening waterfront of Lake St. Clair on this bright summer morning is like tunneling from a war zone into Oz. The diesel smells of Detroit have been replaced with the intoxicating fragrance of lilac. The palatial estates with their ethereal landscaping of flowering trees, rose bushes, and rhododendrons merge into one collective bliss.

Mom told me she had to sign a prenup with Max before she married him, and if they were to divorce, her settlement would be small.

This had been Max's home before he met my mother. As I pull into the driveway, I feel Mom, like myself, is just a visitor. More apt, an accessory.

The flat-roofed, four-thousand-square-foot home looks like brown cardboard boxes randomly stacked in the back of a grocery store. Not that it's unattractive—the architect won several awards for his design—but that was my first, and lasting, impression.

She stands inside the open door, waves me in with an exaggerated swoop, and gives me a hug, brushing a kiss against my cheek.

"I was just telling Max how much I missed seeing you, and then you called. Serendipity, right?" Grinning ear to ear, she stands back to regard me appraisingly. "And look at you. You're wearing our dress. I'm so glad we bought it. The cut accentuates your silhouette to its best advantage." She places her hands on my shoulders, rotating me in a circle. I feel like the ceramic ballerina executing a pirouette in my old music box. "It's timeless. It could be vintage or a design just released."

"Oh, Mom, thanks again. The detailing is exquisite." She beams as I bend to lift the hemline; the fabric feels fine and thin beneath my fingertips. Now that it's summer, I'm going to start wearing dresses more often. Maybe I can find something less expensive at the resale shop; all of our clothes take a beating at the diner.

"Pastels are so pretty on you, honey. You should wear them more often."

I straighten, smiling at Mom but tired of this conversation. "It's good to see you. I've been working nonstop, and it's nice to take a break. Business has improved quite a bit since the latest blogger attentions."

"I'm so proud of you. Stress must become you, sweetie. You look radiant." She ushers me into the living room.

What's most appealing to me about Mom's latest abode is the floor-to-ceiling windows exposing the vast beauty of the lake in every corner. It's as if you aren't confined by walls, but floating over an infinity pool.

I never developed nostalgia for our previous homes, as my visits with her were sporadic. I boarded at the school and on weekends alternated between her, Bio-Dad, and my grandparents. I spent a good chunk of each summer helping out on my aunt and uncle's farm.

Lately she's said she was done with the clutter of traditional decor—the uncrowded style of midcentury modern suits her. She traded her Victorian mahogany armchair for Eames, the scrolled, slue-footed dining table for the clean lines of Arne Jacobsen. The teak kitchen, sleek and stainless, is three times the size of Welcome Home's, yet only the microwave's used. Where are the wastepaper baskets, the paper towels, the pepper grinder? Where are the pictures of me, of Max's children?

My opinion is she's watched too many episodes of *Mad Men*. She identifies with, and strongly resembles, the main character, Betty, Don Draper's wife. Take away Betty's cigarettes, pour another martini, and there you have my lovely blonde mother. Even at fifty-three, with a bit of surgical assistance, she's retained the same anxious, yet delicate, beauty of a Betty Draper.

Also, like Betty, Mom put up with Bio-Dad's philandering ways for only so long before divorcing him, and had trouble understanding her desolate daughter—that would be me. But we're mining the mess in therapy. I get to select the baggage I want to bring from my past into my life as an adult. I chose the suitcase filled with her love. But I worry she doesn't love herself. There's a thing as too much beauty, and her beauty crippled her feelings of self-worth.

She picks up a *Dwell* magazine, fanned open on the sofa, and places it on a side table next to a bulbous, tangerine vase. Sitting down, she arranges her skirt and then clasps her hands together, thrusting her head toward mine as if hoping I'll share some juicy gossip.

"So tell me. How's Sam? Did you tell her about today's bit of espionage? I'm sure you didn't tell David." Her lips twitch into a smile, as if reminded of an inside joke.

I've got to hand it to her. She did teach me a few tricks about handling men—what to tell them, what land mines to avoid.

"No. There was no reason to tell Sam." I glance at her. "And you're right. Certainly not David." She gives me a conspiratorial wink.

I did, however, feel guilty saying good-bye to him this morning, even after that zinger he shot about marriage. He's sacrificing a day's paycheck to work on the house. Back in college, I was young. Immature. Experimental. But so was David. Would he really think I was a bad person because I'd dated Graham? And would I, indeed, want to spend my life with a man who would judge me like that? Maybe Mom's lessons are something I need to revisit. I smile at her and shrug. I'm not up to prattling right now, nervous knowing Graham will be here soon.

I walk to the wall and study an abstract expressionist painting, Max's prized Clyfford Still. Max says Still's genius is in his ability to focus on the dark and the light, the intense and mysterious. Max's focus, however, is on ownership bragging rights. The painting was almost the price he paid for this home. I turn and look at Mom, tittering and anxious, playing with her rings. And the price she's paying?

Yet her timing with men has always been exceptional. She ditched my roving-eyed dad and her elegant home at the top of his career, eschewed child support, and settled for a hefty lump sum. Plus, Dad was responsible for paying for my education. Smart move. Fast-forward ten years and Dad would lose a bulk of his fortunes in junk bonds, dicey dot-coms, and speculative markets. He never told me as much, but I'm sure the crash was devastating to him, rekindling his parents' stories of impoverishment during the war. He struggled paying my tuition.

Mom should have been the financial adviser in their relationship. She invested her settlement in a conservative portfolio, which has been growing—untouched—as her consecutive husbands paid, and are still paying, her maintenance.

Dad showed his support of Welcome Home, our start-up, with three hundred bucks. I appreciate his vote of confidence. These days that's a lot for Dad. Despite all of Max's wealth, he donated only fifty dollars to our Kickstarter campaign. Over Easter, when he thought I was out of earshot, I overheard him saying, *I may as well have flushed that money down the toilet.*

If the diner's a success, proving him to be the asshole he is will be my greatest triumph. I glance around the room, at the painting, the table, and the chairs. The art books lined up on a shelf have never been read and serve only as ornamentation. Is it worth it, Mom?

The doorbell rings. Mom jumps and collects herself, smoothing her skirt. "Call me if you need me. I'll be nearby. Iced tea's in the fridge if you want to offer him something. But don't take too long." She shoots me a warning glance. "Just settle things with him and escort him out the door." She glides across the room and up the spiral stairwell to the second level.

I open the door and there he stands, a silver Mercedes glimmering behind him in the driveway. His ironed khakis, polo shirt—Pepto-Bismol pink—and Top-Siders complete the look. Always the master of disguise. But his clothing appears tired and hangs off him as if he were a coatrack. This dude is skin and bones. Delicate, even. I glance at the bag he holds in his hand and indicate, with a tilt of my head, he should come in.

He offers me a nervous half smile and enters the house, glancing around as if uncertain. There's no semblance of the bedraggled yet handsome stoner rich kid I dated way back when. I'd imagined his bad-boy image would have been stepped up by all those years in the pen. Where's the stamp of prison on his brow, the swagger in his gait? If David were standing next to this man, he would look like the felon.

"Have a seat, Graham. It's been a while."

He selects a black leather lounge and runs his hand along the curved rosewood arms. Except for the lush shape of his lips and his steely-gray eyes, I don't recognize him. I feel uneasy. What was I thinking, letting an ex turned ex-con back into my life, even if for only a few minutes? I'm glad Mom's upstairs.

"Can I get you a glass of iced tea?"

"No thanks. I'm good."

One thing hasn't changed: that voice. I take a seat on the sofa and look at him, my eyebrows raised in inquiry, as if asking, *You were the one who staged this meeting. What do you have that's mine?* He stands and saunters to the window.

"Your gardens are beautiful. My folks are thinking about unloading their house. Scaling down, getting something more contemporary." He chuckles. "Of course they'd never leave Grosse Pointe." He turns his head and smiles. "It's nice by the water. Let's catch up on the terrace."

"No. I've got to get back to Detroit."

"Choosing the slums over paradise?" He winks at me. "Still adorable."

My lips twitch, annoyed that he's flirting and making light of my choices. Even more annoyed at myself for wearing this dress. What was I thinking?

"I don't see things that way. I'm happy building a business, making a life in The D."

He returns to his chair, shoves the bag under the seat, and slumps forward, dropping his head into his palms. Pushing his elbows into the crook of his knees, he emits a slow, whistling sigh. After a moment he looks up, catching my eye.

"Awkward. Me showing up out of prison. Acting stupid. Implying you're the one who made a bad choice. Pretending the past ten years didn't exist."

"So how did it go for you?" I glance at the bag and return my eyes to him. "I mean, prison and all."

"Prison's a compressed version of the real world—at least society's underbelly. The other inmates knew I was in for drugs, pretty minor stuff. So, for the most part, they left me alone. For a couple of years I shared a cell with another guy also doing time for possession. He was OK. Played the guitar. He taught me a few chords, which helped me relax." Graham closes his eyes and strums an invisible guitar.

"I've heard it's not so bad in prison," I venture. "That it's just the child molesters who have it rough. Tortured and whatnot."

"Those dudes, the real sickos and pervs, were separated from us. At least I never saw them. But life was harsh for all of us."

"You don't have to talk about it, Graham."

"No. I'm good. My parents have me seeing someone. It helps having a circle of people I can trust."

So now he considers me a confidante. Agreeing to meet him was such a mistake.

He continues. "I know people say prisoners are taken better care of than kids in public schools. But that's total bullshit. I was in level one, for the lowest offenders, and it was no cakewalk. Breakout fights and stabbings were a regular occurrence." He studies his nails. "I did my best not to stand out."

He sits directly across from me, staring at my legs. I shrug and cross them, once again regretting I wore this dress. I push my hair behind my ears.

"You've got a restaurant, right? Why did you decide to get into the food business?"

"While trying to figure out my next move after graduating, I got a job at Zingerman's Roadhouse. I learned quite a bit from their business model. We understood our goals, had regular meetings, and spoke up if we had ideas for addressing a concern. We also received a share of the profits. Besides, working in the food industry seemed a good fit for me." Zingerman's was also the place I met David. As he looked up from his menu to order, his electric-blue eyes startled me. I'll never forget the jolt that traveled up my spine.

"Mom says your place has been featured in some food blogs she subscribes to."

"Business has definitely improved, thanks to the attention. But today's news is tomorrow's fish paper. We still have a long way to go. Sam and I are hoping honest food will stand the test of time. We're taking advantage of the opportunities in Detroit, the Promised Land," I add, managing a smile.

"At least you're able to eat tasty, nutritious food. God, prison food is nasty. Dogs eat better than inmates. I lost thirty pounds, and I was thin to begin with. I have stories, man. Don't get me started."

"I've never known anyone who's served time." I look about the home, noting the irony of prison talk in this environment. "I guess I've lived my life in a glass house."

"But glass walls shatter. One of the guys I was friendly with was a classical pianist in a previous life. Went to Juilliard, where drugs were thick. He claimed he was at the wrong place at the wrong time . . ." A few seconds pass and his eyes, glassy, return to meet mine. "My biggest accomplishment in prison was staying away from drugs. They were everywhere." He catches my eye as I glance toward the clock.

"And so often I was tempted. But that would mean hurting my parents. Again. The only people who believed in me. Who loved me." His voice is elevated now, and he speaks rapidly, in earnest, as if to make sure I understand exactly what he is saying. He leans forward in his chair, his hands gripping the handles.

"All I ever wanted was love, and I threw it away. Ironic, right? So now you got me started, and I can't shut up."

A shred of what attracted me to him years back rises to the surface—his lips, the color of his eyes. And despite his voice, despite the clothing attempting to disguise his skinniness, the lines around those lips and eyes tell me he's broken, vulnerable, ruined. Disgust melts into pity.

"Ten years is a long time. But it's behind you. You survived. You're lucky to have a supportive family."

"I know. I kept Dad and his money a secret, even from the guys I came to trust. To fit in, I cooked up some lame past for myself about my parents being separated and my mom living on public assistance. My folks understood. My parents dressed in thrift-shop clothing when visiting. And they never came together."

I smirk thinking of his mother, with her glossy coiffed hair and immaculate clothing, wearing resale. And what about his preppy voice? As if readying my mind, he continues.

"You may recall I'm a master of impersonation."

"You got that right." I smile at the memory of the high-school boy who so arduously studied Eminem. "As a kid, you had that street rap yodel down to a science."

"In jail, I copied the tougher guys' movements, the way they talked. I sure didn't share the fact I had a guaranteed job at Dad's dealership when I was released. All anyone in prison wants is a job when they get out. But how do you find work when your teeth are rotting and you've no computer skills?"

He shuffles, uneasily, as if the question he's always wanted to ask is finally surfacing. He catches my eye.

"I'm assuming you have a boyfriend."

I'm drained by this conversation. Whatever's in the bag is not worth this effort. A moment passes.

"Yes. I have a boyfriend. And he's home now, replacing our roof."

His eyes sweep across my body. "Of course you do. I was hoping, praying . . ." He shakes his head. "Whatever."

He pulls out the bag lying beneath his chair, places it in his lap, and clutches the handles with both hands, as if he's reluctant to give it to me.

"This is just a placeholder. Until my parents return. They're in Scandinavia until the end of August. The original piece, the one belonging to you, is in their safe. Before I was sent away, I stashed it in one of Mom's jewelry boxes. My brain was kinda scrambled."

What is he talking about? His posture is ramrod straight in the chair, and his thigh jerks up and down to the rhythm set by his wildly tapping foot. He reminds me of an idling race car before it roars down the track.

"Mom put all of the jewelry in the safe before she left for Sweden." He places his palm atop his leg to quiet his movements. "I messaged my folks and asked them for the code, explaining the situation. Of course they refused." He shifts his eyes away from my face, gazing at the lake. "I don't really have their trust back."

He pulls a box from the bag and holds it, his hand trembling, as words tumble from his mouth.

"The truth is I couldn't wait any longer. I wanted to see you and apologize to your face. I didn't think you'd agree to meet me unless I could pique your interest." Beads of sweat dot his brow, and he swipes them off with the back of his hand.

"I'm so sorry for what I put you through when we were dating. When you left me, I was furious. I wanted to get even. To take something of yours you treasured. I—the drugs. I was messed up."

He doesn't need to say more. I know what he has: a piece of my family history I thought I'd lost so many years back. He hands me the box and I open it. A cheap tin chain dotted with rose-colored glass beads linked to a plastic cross. A sour taste trails up my throat as I choke back a sob. He stole my most cherished possession: Babcia's rosary. I refrain from throwing the cheap imitation into his face. How could I have ever pitied this creep?

When Babcia left Poland, all she brought with her were her mother's antique amethyst rosary beads and a pair of cameo earrings. On my eighteenth birthday, she gifted me the necklace and, later, gave Sam the earrings. I kept it buried under my underwear in a chest of drawers. I'd thought I'd lost it.

I didn't realize it was missing until I'd graduated. I was moving and tore up my apartment looking for the rosary. I never suspected Graham would have stooped so low. He may have been a druggie, but I never imagined he was a thief. I kept the loss a dark secret, confiding only in

Mom. The thought that Babcia would ask to see it haunted me until the day she died. Tears blind my eyes.

"I'm so sorry, Addie. Coming here was a stupid idea. I didn't mean to hurt you. My folks will be back at the end of the summer. I'll return your necklace then."

The rosary pricks the palm of my hand. "You need to go. Now."

He comes to my chair and places his hand on my shoulder. I brush it away, but the imprint of his fingers burn. Rage creeps up my neck.

"Please go. Just go." I drop the fake onto the floor and put my face into my hands, choking back tears.

Pulling his keys from his pocket, he looks down at me. "This was a mistake. I'll call you when my parents return."

If Babcia were alive, she would not want me to pursue getting her rosary back. Not if it meant seeing Graham again.

The second the door closes, Mom rushes down the stairwell. "So, the mystery of the missing rosary's been solved. Please don't cry. I hate to see you cry." She stretches out her arms. "Give me a hug."

I stand and she pulls me into her, stroking my hair, as if I were a child.

"I'll take over from here. When Anne returns from Sweden, I'll call her and get the real rosary back."

"I never want to see him again. I never dreamed he'd be capable of stealing."

"There's no need for you to be involved with Graham Palmer. But wine will most definitely be involved at lunch. Freshen up your lipstick. It's smeared." She rubs her forefinger on my chin. "Now it's time to go spend your stepfather's money. There's a new fusion restaurant that just opened at Somerset. Asian-Mediterranean. And then we can work off our meal shopping for summer handbags at Gucci."

She laughs at the thought, and then her mirth segues into a fit of coughing, sudden and swift, like a dog's barks, bouncing from wall to wall.

Chapter Six

Addie

"I know, Mom, I know. I can't believe it, either. The press is back to get a comment, and the line out the door has never been longer. I've gotta get out there."

She tells me, again, how proud she is. I'm grateful for the relationship Mom and I've been forging over the past two years, but I would never consider her my best friend. As an adult I get to select my closest friends, and I can defriend them, for instance, if they inflict wounds. But my mother, no matter the wounds that she's inflicted in my past, will always be my mother.

Best friend also implies equality in a relationship. Our therapist counseled us that healthy mother-daughter relationships are built on a hierarchy rooted in a mother's unconditional love.

Mom's mother died when she was a child, and her dad, my deceased grandfather, was overwhelmed by the demands of his farm. I've never asked Mom if she had received unconditional love as a child. But from the snippets she's shared about her solitary childhood and his heavy-handed discipline, I doubt it. Mom's always been adept at not sharing information about her past.

Yet when the *New York Times* called to fact-check and said they were doing a review in their Sunday paper, I called my mother before any of my friends. Even David.

Most of Grosse Pointe, Birmingham, and Bloomfield Hills must read the *Times*. Our parking lot is filled with flashy cars, and the line outside the diner loops halfway around Welcome Home. Two photographers, I assume from the *Detroit News* and *Free Press*, wander around the building and snap pictures of the diner from across the street. I freshen my lipstick—I'm sure I'll be in some of them.

The article was highly flattering:

> Ask any patron about the Welcome Home Diner and their answer will be "charming, old-fashioned." Known for their Heartbreakers—massive cookies that are the stuff of legend—the diner is the antidote to today's hypercharged society. Don't miss the Buttermilk Pancakes with Apple-Maple Syrup and Walnuts or the pork and savory greens. Their menu items are simultaneously unique and traditional . . . their desserts, ambrosial.

We've made Braydon the floor manager, and he's at his happiest when the diner is packed. He's learned every regular's name, knows just what to say to elicit a smile, and wants everyone to like him. But aside from a couple of lawyers who've become regulars and Quiche's pal Danita, our employees are the only African Americans who've ever taken a seat in our restaurant.

It's as if our neighbors go out of their way to avoid us. In the press, the popularity of our diner is touted as a symbol of promise, our eatery a microcosm of a soon-to-be-realized Detroit. The city, however, will never live up to their pledge if our own neighbors refuse to join us for a meal.

My eyes travel across the line of patrons pattering about this or that while accepting a bit of cake that Braydon passes. Some are hipsters and live downtown. But most, judging from their appearance and the cars they're driving, are affluent professionals venturing into the city from suburbia. I have a secret fear that one day Graham may be a face in line. Thankfully, I haven't heard from him since we met last month. I told Sam about Graham and the rosary, but I'm uneasy that I've never mentioned any of this to David. He has enough trouble with my desire to get married. Our parents' marriages paint a grim portrait of the institution.

My mood lifts as a woman wearing large hoop earrings and hemp-woven wedges enters and takes the one empty seat at the bar. She swivels in her chair and regards the customers surrounding her. It's Danita, Quiche's friend from church.

I greet her with a menu, glass of water, and relieved smile. Even if Quiche is the only reason she's here, it's a good enough excuse today. I carry the water pitcher from table to table, refilling glasses, asking patrons if they'd like something else. I'm hoping someone asks for the bill, so I can clear the table and lighten the line. One of the photographers and another young man approach me.

"We're from the *Free Press*. We'd like to hear your thoughts regarding the article about you and your cousin in yesterday's *Times*. It was quite flattering. We'd also like a picture of you two."

"Wonderful. Of course, we're thrilled about the piece. And the *Times*?" I shake my head. "Incredible." I make a swooping motion with my arm across the tables. "As you see, we're really busy. I'll have our manager take Sam's place in the kitchen." I turn from them; then I stop. I've a better idea. I walk back to the men.

"Actually, it would be great if you could include our manager, Braydon, in the picture. He's our main man, essential to Welcome Home's success, and should be credited. Our prep cook will be able to handle the kitchen."

"Sure," the photographer responds. "We'll take a couple of you and Sam with the manager, and a couple with just the two of you. We know you're busy. This will only take a minute."

I trot to the kitchen. At the stainless-steel table, Paul is deboning and gutting trout packed into an ice-filled bus tub. His recipe for Crispy Corn Trout will be tomorrow's special. I ask him if he can manage the orders so I can steal Sam for a few minutes. He agrees, delighted to be relieved of one of the more odious prep tasks. Lella darts into the kitchen, places several finished plates on a serving tray, and grabs a cloth to clean smudges of oil away from the edges. She places the tray onto her palm, then stretches her arm over her head and retreats to the floor, the doors swinging behind her.

I grab Sam's hand and lead her into the dining area. The photographer is taking a light reading by the window. Cupping my hand over my mouth, I whisper into her ear. "Before they take photos, let's position ourselves to ensure the photographer's lens will capture Danita at the counter."

She tilts her head to regard me, a question in her eyes. I head outside to get Braydon.

The man with the short, grizzly beard who lives in the house next door to Welcome Home is sitting in his chair, rocking back and forth, glaring at us. He wears the same short-sleeved denim shirt he always wears. When he sees me, his pace quickens, as if he's ready to launch from his porch. Even from this distance I can read the anger in his eyes. I link my arm with Braydon's.

"We want to make sure you're in some of the photos. You've earned it."

"Really?" His eyes widen into saucers. "I've never had my picture in the paper before. My aunt and uncle will be freaked." He dips his head toward the man. "He looks more pissed off than ever."

"What's up with that dude?" I shrug.

We just closed the diner for the day. Braydon, Sam, and I are exhausted but elated, basking in our recent successes. Sitting in lawn chairs, iced teas in hand, we admire the vegetable garden. David just joined us, and I'm content watching the dogs stretched beside us in the sun.

"It's crazy how long the days are in July," I comment. "It feels as if the sun should be setting now." I check my phone. "Three fifty-five. We still have five hours until sunset—another six until it's dark. Maybe we should consider keeping longer hours in the summer."

"Oh God, no," Sam says. "Eight hours in a sweltering kitchen is all I can stand."

"Next year we'll install air conditioning and hire some more cooks." I rise and stretch, placing my arms above my head and bending forward. "I need to place orders and restock the perishables before five. Today's business wiped us out." Walking toward the kitchen, I stop and turn to Sam.

"Great that the photographer caught Danita in the photos."

"Why's that?" Braydon asks.

My eyes meet his. "I hate the thought of the diner being portrayed as just another hip, white-bread restaurant testing the waters of gentrification."

His mouth twists into a wry smile. "Is that why you also asked me to be in the photograph? To make doubly sure everyone knows the diner also serves pumpernickel?"

I freeze, at a loss for words. He's never spoken to me like this before. "No, Braydon. Of . . . course not," I stammer, feeling my face grow hot. What did he mean by that comment?

"Sorry, Addie. When you said *white-bread*, I couldn't resist." He shrugs. "But seriously. I've been thinking about our neighbor. Maybe he dislikes us because we ignore him." Wearing an unreadable expression, he pinches suckers off the tomato plants. "None of us have even bothered to introduce ourselves." He glances at me over the side of his shoulder. "I'd wager he judges me to be Welcome Home's token black. A hire made to fill a quota."

My pulse races and my response is quick. "By this time, Braydon, you must know that couldn't be further from the truth."

"I know that, Addie. I know. I'm talking about our neighbor's perceptions, not my own."

Clutching my hands together, I take a deep breath, trying to settle myself.

"Braydon has a point," Sam says, shaking the ice cubes that remain in her drained glass. "Trying to paint this so-called *community of color* seems forced. That photograph was contrived. It doesn't reflect reality and makes me uncomfortable. It's a different sort of discrimination, which is hard to articulate."

"That's too simplistic, Sam. It gets us off the hook. Dismissals are like a teacher who limits the number of questions that can be asked. We *need* to ask questions. We need articulation."

"Perhaps the diner's customer base should evolve without our meddling," she replies, looking into her glass.

Now I'm upset. I slap my fist into the palm of my hand. "Our meddling? Welcome Home's more than a diner, Sam. Remember? We had a vision. We operate in a culinary wasteland. Besides us, the only edible options are to be found in gas stations, liquor stores, and that godforsaken burger joint. We wanted our neighbors to have something better to choose from. Our dream was to shape an old-fashioned neighborhood gathering spot—authentic and welcoming to all races and creeds—where everyone has a seat at the table. Not some trendy, shabby-chic, elitist establishment."

"I haven't forgotten our mission statement, Addie. And I *am* asking the questions. For example, what have we done to integrate ourselves into the community?" She places her glass atop an overturned produce crate and stands to face me. "Just because we rehabbed a decrepit diner, should we expect our neighbors to fall at our feet in gratitude? And try this one on for size: Is it wrong to open old wounds? Maybe that will cause too much pain for everyone."

"But, Sam, most of those wounds never healed. Prayers and hopes won't make them disappear. Detroit is being shaped and changed by actions, not wishful thinking. Wishful thinking is just another way of worrying." I place my hands on her shoulders and peer into her face. "And we're spending too much time worrying about the wounds, worrying about relationships that have broken down. Pressing the bruises, prodding at the sore spots, ironically, just might be the sweet spots for healing our community." The muscles along my jawline clench. I drop my arms and turn to Braydon. "Let's go."

"Where?" he asks, looking startled, as if he thinks I'm planning to gag and stuff him in the back of David's truck.

"You're right, Braydon. Of course you're right. Let's introduce ourselves to the neighbor. We should have done this a long time ago. I'll grab some food. Make him a goody bag." I dash to the kitchen before Sam and Braydon can make further comment.

Walking to his home, I never realized how close we were to him. The edge of our garden can't be more than ten feet from his lot. We climb the rickety stoop, pass the empty rocking chair, and Braydon knocks on the door. A minute goes by, and he raps the door again, with a heavier fist.

A voice from behind the door. "Can't you read? The sign says No Solicitors. Get outta here before I call the cops."

Braydon clears his throat. "I'm sorry to bother you, sir, but we're your new neighbors. We want to introduce ourselves."

"You're the last people I want on my property. So get going."

"Sir, I'm sorry to hear that. My name is Braydon. I manage the restaurant, and one of the owners, Addie, is with me."

"I said get outta here," he shouts, his voice rising to a threat.

"You may know my aunt and uncle, Sam and Paula Stokes? They live a few blocks away. My aunt sings in the Tabernacle Choir. The choir director, Laurice, your neighbor down the street, is one of their good friends."

Two bolts unlock and the door cracks open. A yellow eye threaded with red veins peers at us over the brass chain. The man behind the eye unlatches the chain and opens the door. For a minute he examines us, mute, before pointing his forefinger in my face.

"You and your restaurant are turning my neighborhood into a three-ring circus."

He turns to Braydon. "I quit going to church a while back. But I do remember your aunt and uncle. And of course I know Laurice. He keeps pestering me to come back to service. My name's Angus. You can stay." He turns to me. "But she goes."

My throat tightens, and I hold the bag toward him. "We've brought over some food we thought you might enjoy. It's raining cherries in Northern Michigan right now. So we made cherry pie. The house-smoked chicken is also tasty—I could bring over some sauce if you like."

"I smell that chicken smoking every Saturday morning." His voice is at least triple the volume of mine. "How can I avoid it? I smell every-thing that goes on in your place. Most times it stinks." He grabs the bag from my hands. "But not that chicken."

I emit a shaky breath, feeling the moisture collect under my arm-pits. I don't know if I've ever been faced with such rudeness.

I turn to Braydon. A shadow crosses his face. "Like I told you, Braydon. I've got to place orders for tomorrow."

My head bobs at Angus, and I stumble down his porch steps, restraining myself from breaking into a run. The group remains in the garden, in the same position where I left them. I couldn't have been gone for more than five minutes, but the emotional roller coaster I just exited made it feel more like five hours. Plopping on David's lap, I feel one of the vinyl pieces beneath our weight dislodging from the aluminum frame. I jump up, afraid the seat will collapse.

"Whoa, baby. You look like you just met the devil."

"That man, David. His name is Angus." I pinch my lips between my teeth. "He hates me, David. He doesn't know a thing about me, but he really hates me." My jaw and hands are trembling, out of control.

David stands, brushes my hair away from my face, and peers into my eyes. "What did he say?"

"That we've turned his neighborhood into a circus. That our place stinks." I raise my voice, my breath catching in my throat. "He doesn't get what we're trying to do. He was yelling in my face."

Sam approaches and rests her palm on my shoulder. "Where's Braydon?" she asks.

"He was invited in, but the old man demanded I leave. What have I . . . what is it about Welcome Home that could have made him so upset?"

Anger swells in my chest, and I stomp my foot on the ground. "For God's sake. Billions of dollars are being invested in midtown and downtown, but they've left out the neighborhoods. So we're busting our butts trying to improve the area, but our neighbors want us to leave." I burst into tears, emitting long, rattling gasps as I try to compose myself.

"Black, white, rich, poor—we all have problems to deal with," David says, gathering me into his arms, wiping away my tears with a corner of his sleeve. "And face it. Change is inevitable. You can't swing a dead cat without hitting a disintegrating house around here. You and Sam have made significant improvements to the East Side, and it's catching on. I've had my eye on those two dudes down the street who just purchased a home. They replaced the windows, began scraping paint away from the siding, and last week they tore down the porch. You guys are inspiring change already." He shakes his head, stroking my hair as if trying to settle a spooked mare. "I don't know, baby girl. I don't know. Don't cry. He's just one old man, and we'll fix it with him."

He turns his head toward Angus's house. "I don't know how—there'll be some heavy sledding up ahead—but we'll fix it."

"What if we'd turned the old diner into a strip club? The action would have gone on through the night. Pimps. Prostitutes." I lift my arm, fanning it across the landscape in a shaky arc, before bringing my fist to my chest. "Would the neighborhood be safer then? Would he have preferred that sort of clientele?"

Shaking my head, I grab my phone from the table. "Yikes. I've only forty minutes to place the orders." I look at David, a surge of love bubbling to the surface. My man is here, right now, exactly when I need him to comfort me. "I love you so much, David. Sorry to get all histrionic."

His mouth brushes against my ear. "It will all be fine. You'll see."

"Let's do the orders together," Sam says, putting her arm around my shoulder. "Focus on what a terrific day it's been, not on what just happened." Regarding me, her brows furrow, and a crinkle of lines crawl around the corners of her eyes. I must look a wreck. I give her a tight hug.

"Thanks. If you do perishables, I'll deal with the rest. But let me order the trout." I look at David and summon up the old Addie with a wink. "Our fish vendor has the hots for me." A collective laugh of camaraderie. Relief.

At least we know the enemy. But that the enemy is our next-door neighbor fills me with a profound sadness.

❦

The orders placed, I hang up the phone. I check myself in the reflection of the windowpane, then grab a cup of ice in the prep area. I'll rub some cubes under my eyes, which are puffed out like marshmallows. My hair hangs in singular ropes, and my face is oily in the humidity. A vague plum line edges my lips; I've chewed off most of my lipstick.

I look like a corpse pulled from the Detroit River. Serious repair's in order. As I head for the bathroom, David enters through the back and grabs my arm.

"Braydon's back from his reconnaissance mission. Thought you'd want to hear what he has to say."

"Just give me a couple of minutes. Need to visit the loo."

I scurry to the bathroom, splash cold water across my face, brush my hair, and freshen my lipstick. No time to ice my eyes, but I rub off the mascara smeared beneath them. Mental note: replenish Visine. With these pink eyes, I look like a frightened rabbit. I scamper to the garden.

Iced tea has been replaced with cold beer. Even Braydon has a brew. Although he's of age, he's never joined our after-hours tippling. Today's put a toll on us all.

David has a small speaker attached to his smartphone. As if aware of Angus's silent presence, the volume's half of what it usually is when we meet in the garden. Aside from fifties jazz, our group prefers the songs our parents enjoyed from the sixties and seventies, the era of Woodstock we've musically enshrined. David's mom gave him her record player and original vinyl collection that she'd listened to in high school and college. Jimi Hendrix; Crosby, Stills & Nash; Creedence Clearwater Revival; and Marvin Gaye, to name a few. Although the music is fifty years old, it's about freedom, revolution, and change. We relate to the lyrics.

"Well, Braydon," I say, dragging a chair next to David's. "I hope your interaction with Angus was more fruit bearing than mine."

"I'm not sure. I mainly asked him questions about his story. His life. How he came to live in his home."

"And?"

"He's an old dude, Nam vet, Jim Crow in his eyes. What little he's worked for has been taken away. Except his home. You know his thumb and forefinger were blown off? The right hand, the one he used on the assembly line at Ford. When he returned from the war, he said it was hard to find a job. Said the line was all he knew, and the—"

"That war was such a waste," David interrupts, leaning back into his chair and crossing his arms over his chest. "Such bullshit. Did I ever tell you guys about the trick my dad pulled to keep from serving?" I nod at David, my forefinger at my lips, shushing him. I turn to Braydon, whose mouth twitches, no doubt annoyed himself.

"Did he buy his house after the war?" I ask.

"The house belonged to his folks," Braydon continues. "It was the home he was raised in and the home he returned to after he served. He was their only living child. His twin brother was killed in the war, and he inherited the home after his folks died."

"Is there a silver lining in this story? Did he ever marry? Raise kids?"

"He said he never married, but he did have a child. At least one that he was aware of." Braydon sips his beer, and his back, usually pencil straight, is humped over. His eyes travel around our group.

"He saw his daughter from time to time, but she lived with her mother and was always in trouble. At sixteen she gave birth to a boy. She couldn't take care of him, so the old man stepped up to the plate. He raised his grandson ever since he was an infant."

"So where's the kid now?"

"He asked me not to talk about it." His lips purse together, and he shakes his head. "But you can guess. A young black man raised in Detroit? He's locked up—the same ol', same ol'. Angus said the boy did well in high school and was a good athlete. Two or three Big Ten schools were even considering him for a football scholarship. But apparently the boy also learned to play defense on the streets, by keeping his head down and the focus on his body."

"Malcolm X said if you're black, you were born in jail," David muses, his voice low and gravelly, picking at a cuticle on his finger.

Braydon's nose twitches, and he pinches his nostrils. I'm sure he's annoyed that David quoted the man most famous, and most vociferous, in his condemnation of white crimes waged against blacks. David sometimes talks like some badass raised in the ghetto, but he doesn't understand the scope of what he's talking about. I don't either, but at least I admit it. We really could use a road map. And I really could use a beer. I rise and grab one from the cooler.

"During his senior year in high school, a friend coerced him into robbing a convenience store," Braydon continues, "and the rest is history. A history looping itself round and round and round. It was the only time he'd ever screwed up, but that time was for real."

Braydon puts his beer down, clasps his hands behind his neck, and leans back into his chair, his words directed to the sky. "The other kid was armed, but, thankfully, not Angus's grandson. Which meant less jail time. Angus said he should be released in a few months, and is moving back with him."

"Maybe his grandson's return will be his silver lining," Sam says, a gleam of hope in her eyes. Braydon, shrugging, bites his lower lip.

"So he's lived in the very same spot for over sixty years," she continues. "Did he share any memories about the way things used to be in this neighborhood?"

"He remembers the old diner. To him it was his second home. He and his parents ate there at least twice a week, and always on Sunday after church. The church and diner were the heart of the community. It sat vacant for thirty years before you two bought it. Maybe that's what's sad to him," he continues, his voice heavy with emotion. "The diner's rebirth reminds him of the old days. Of good times. Today, he's an outsider."

Bon Temps sleeps in a patch of shade. Hero trots to her side, lies down, and joins her, emitting a yowling yawn before laying his head on the ground.

"So what was your response?" I ask, directing my gaze to Braydon.

Braydon sighs, shaking his head. "I just listened and acknowledged his feelings. No resolutions were made. Of course not. His point of view encompasses more than the diner."

"I think I get where he's coming from," Sam says. "Welcome Home's symbolic of change. He's coming from a place of fear. And fear makes everyone lash out."

"You're right, Sam," Braydon agrees. "His car was repossessed last year because he couldn't pay the insurance premiums. Then he sees two white women sniffing a bargain and moving onto his turf, settin' up shop. He's on a limited, fixed income and worried about gentrification. He's concerned taxes on his home will rise and he will lose it. He has no place to go. Why wouldn't he consider the diner's resurrection to be just another betrayal in the city's history of economic abandonment?"

Braydon places the tip of his thumb in his mouth, closes his eyes, and shakes his head. We're all silent, fixated on this man who has experienced so much that we could never, and will never, fathom. But we can, at the very least, listen. He opens his eyes, breaking the silence.

"Angus is scared. He's lonely. And he wants someone to talk to. But I didn't leave without saying my piece." Braydon shakes his almost-empty beer, takes a last lingering sip, and places the bottle on the table at his side. Standing, he walks to the garden's edge and lifts a green tomato.

"You should see the tomatoes growing in his garden. Twice the size of ours." He gestures toward the large fence behind Angus's home. "His lot shares space with broken-down equipment he's repairing. My dad liked to fix things, too." He turns to face us.

"To me, the twenty-foot plot of land separating the diner and Angus's home is like the center line of I-94 at rush hour." His palms are upturned and his fingers outstretched, as if he were cradling the city. "Half of the expressway represents your people, and the other half represents mine. The line divides us, and we're both driving away from each other in opposite directions, as fast as we can. Meanwhile, the air shrieks with the sounds of honking cars, trucks, and deafening sound systems, and stinks with the smells of exhaust."

Bon Temps, sensing anguish in her master's voice, ambles awkwardly onto all fours and walks to his side. The pom-pom tipping her tail drags across the ground. He leans over to scratch beneath her ears.

"Since I've started working at Welcome Home, I've begun to feel like my home is in the middle of the road, dead center on the line. But no one wants me here. It's as if I must make a decision to cross over and join the traffic in the left lane or the traffic in the right."

He sighs, exhausted. "The trouble with me is"—his eyes move around our group, lingering a second on each of our faces—"I don't want to make the choice."

Sam stands, rushes to Braydon, and grabs his arm, shaking her head. "You know us better than that. All of us are with you in the center, all of us on neutral ground. There's no choice to be made."

He winces, and his eyes take on a wounded look. "I get what you're saying, Sam. But I feel as if someone, something, is going to force me to choose sides." He drops his head. "And it makes me sad."

Bon Temps looks up at her master. Her ears tip back and she whines. "I'm OK, girl," Braydon says to the dog as he bends to stroke her back.

"And there lies the holy conundrum," David says. Folding his arms across his chest, he raises his face to the sky, shaking his head. "To quote Rodney King, *'Can't we all just get along?'"*

Braydon straightens, his chest rises, and he looks askance at David. I know David's trying to be sympathetic, but the next thing you know, he'll change the music to Jay Z, pull Braydon in for a backslap hug, and call him a brother. David's overdue for a smackdown, but I refrain.

Braydon clears his throat. "As I was saying, that's what I said when I spoke my piece to Angus. I didn't talk about the diner. I wanted him to understand that I, speaking as a black man, have my own concerns about the future. And I don't want to choose sides. Maybe I laid it on thick, but I wasn't there to make small talk. I didn't expect a response from him and didn't receive one."

I regard Braydon. "Did you get a sense whether he feels friendlier to Welcome Home after your visit? Friendlier towards me?" I steel myself for his response.

He gives me a long, appraising look, as if he were summing me up, gauging whether or not I was strong enough to hear the truth. Then, he shakes his head, as if dismissing a thought, and smiles. "Well, he polished off all the food you gave him. He's loyal to your chicken."

We laugh, trading quick glances.

He walks to my chair and places a hand on my shoulder. "You can't take what Angus said personally, Addie. We must all be patient. Remain sensitive."

His eyes soften, and the sound of his voice fades under the blast of horns on La Grande.

"The conversation has just begun."

Chapter Seven

Sam

"Ya got that right, Addie," Lella says. "Just because a dude gives me a big tip, it doesn't give him license to be lewd." She chews her gum with abandon. "The know-it-all customers are also obnoxious." A bubble emerges from her mouth, swelling into a shiny pink blossom.

It's Wednesday, 3:30 p.m. The floors freshly mopped, we're seated around a six-top finishing up our weekly meeting. My eyes wander around the table: Braydon, Quiche, Lella, Paul, Addie.

Lella's bubble pops and she continues. "One woman said our goat cheese wasn't local because it had the flavor of a grass that doesn't grow in Michigan. She insisted it was crafted in Point Reyes. Wherever that is."

"Northern California," Addie replies, adjusting a strap on her sundress. It's pale blue with lemon-yellow piping around the middle, accentuating her long waist and slender frame. Her mother just bought it for her. Must be nice.

"Superior cheeses do come from that region," she continues, smoothing her skirt, "but their flavor profiles are different from the Michigan cheeses we serve."

"Point her out to me next time she's here," I say, bristling with irritation. "I'll set her straight. Our cheese is handcrafted in small batches at a creamery in Tecumseh. It's fifteen miles from my family's farm, and I'm friends with the owners. In fact, I'm pals with their goats, who will testify under oath they only nosh on Michigan grass."

"Baaaaaaaa . . . ," Paul mewls, his staccato sound mimicking a baby goat. "That dude needs to get a life."

"It was as if she expected me to hand her a DNA report," Lella continues. "It's hard to have a ready answer for these entitled gastronoids."

Mouth pursed, Quiche repeats the word as if she were sucking on a lemon. "Gastronoids?" Her brow furrows, as if confused.

Lella raises her brow, nodding at Quiche. "That's my name for this type of customer."

I smile. The staff is coming up with a language of its own. In a couple of years, we'll be the only ones who understand one another.

"A gastronoid," Lella continues, "is a human subspecies that only lives to eat and complain."

I widen my eyes into Os and mime pulling my hair out at the roots. "Gastronoids are full of gas." The group giggles.

"Seriously, guys," Addie says. "You should have a ready answer when customers have a question. When things settle down, Sam and I will host a tasting seminar for the staff and invite our vendors. You can become acquainted with these folks and discover the passion they bring to their craft."

"That's a great idea," Lella says. "I can become a gastronoid myself."

Quiche snorts. "I think I'll pass."

"Settled," I say, scribbling a notation in my notebook. "Do any of you have any further suggestions for the team? Any earth-shattering revelations before we disband?"

Braydon lifts his hand. "Addie. Sam. All of us are aware that funds are tight, but business is out the door. I know you ladies are working crazy hours trying to keep up, but we could still use another set of hands."

Addie nods at me before turning to Braydon. "It's you guys who are the champions. Welcome Home would be nothing without your hard work and dedication. Sam and I have discussed this, and we hear you loud and clear. We plan to set out some feelers and will make a hire as soon as the right candidate presents themselves. It may take a few weeks, but rest assured our burned-out bodies share your concerns."

"Full time?" Paul asks, his voice hopeful.

"Yep. Either one full-timer or two half-timers."

The group applauds.

"How about tacking on a dishwasher while you're at it," Paul says, ducking his head sheepishly.

"I'll bet you drove your parents crazy when you were a kid," Addie says, smirking. "When they gave you a basketball, you asked for a hoop."

"You knew my folks?" He leans back into his chair, a grin spread across his face. "You ladies are the ones who always say to dream big."

I rise from the table, so proud of the team we've created. "Next week, let's revisit the issues we're having in the neighborhood. I'd like each of you to come up with one solid idea to increase foot traffic. We want to encourage people who live in walking distance of the diner to feel welcome. There are unspoken boundary lines that need to be erased."

"The old man next door will be an especially tough sell," Paul says, unaware of Addie's encounter with him. Last week's episode was a wake-up call that we needed to take action. Addie and I had no idea as to the extent of his resentment.

"Maybe I'll offer to lend him a hand and replace his front steps," he continues. "They're rotting away. If he's not careful, he could take a mean tumble."

Lella turns to him, her smile so broad it appears to crack her face. "You are one awesome dude, Paul. I know a thing or two about carpentry. I'll help."

Our staff is phenomenal. "The diner will pay for whatever materials you need to get the job done." I glance at Addie; I'm sure she concurs.

She clears her throat. "To quote Plato," she says, her gaze to the ceiling, forefinger resting on her chin, "'The community which has neither poverty nor riches will always have the noblest principles.'"

The staff becomes quiet, trading glances. So now our meetings are a forum for Addie to reveal her book smarts? I thought we were trying to figure out how not to alienate the neighbors. We understand what she's saying, but when she quotes these philosophers, it sounds as if she's showing off. Aside from Paul, there's not a one of us who's ever set foot in a college classroom. Talk about alienating.

I sigh and glance at the clock: 4:00 p.m. "This meeting is officially adjourned."

I've a couple of hours to organize tomorrow's prep list, catch the bus, and change clothes. Uriah's picking me up at six. We've met for coffee a couple of times, but tonight he's taking me to dinner, on a real date—a Mediterranean restaurant he feels sure I'll enjoy. I bite my lower lip, my pulse quickening in anticipation of seeing him.

"You're right, Uriah. This food is delicious, the flavors so fresh." I place my napkin on the table, push my plate away, and take a sip of wine. "The lamb's juicy and tender. It has such a sunny, lemony tang." I tap the prongs of my fork at the bulgur wheat speckled with greens and tomatoes. "Usually parsley is the only herb used in tabbouleh. This one also had thyme and oregano." I catch Uriah's eye. "It's such a treat having someone else do the cooking for a change."

He laughs, shaking his head. "When you said that, I thought of my mom. She'd say those exact words every time we'd go out to dinner."

"I've been thinking," I say, fiddling with the napkin. "The last time we met, you said that you couldn't stop thinking about her signature dessert. A combination of a sweet potato pie and a pecan pie, right?"

He leans toward me, his eyes glowing. "She'd also add a splash of bourbon to the batter."

"How yummy. I love old-fashioned desserts."

"It sounds like something your grandmother would have made."

"Babcia and bourbon?" I giggle at the thought. "Ha. Maybe if she'd been born in Tennessee instead of Poland."

He studies me thoughtfully. "I still can't believe you've never been south of Ohio."

"What can I say?" I shrug, embarrassed that aside from my stint in Manhattan, I've spent my entire life in Michigan. "I told you I'd like to go down there one day."

"And I told you I'd love to be your travel guide. Remember?"

I inhale sharply. How could I ever forget that conversation? It was the first time he held my hand.

"The area where my folks live has some of the best whiskey distilleries in the world," he continues, a gleam in his eyes. "And the countryside surrounding Nashville is beautiful. All of those farms and rolling hills. You'd love Lynchburg. It's a quaint little town with some amazing antique stores."

"Seriously, Uriah. I'd love to visit Tennessee. But back to that pie." I wink into his deep, dark eyes. "Let me make it for you. Do you think your mom would share her recipe with me?"

"Heck yeah, Sam." He rubs his hands together. "And you sure know the way to a man's heart. I'll have Mom e-mail it to me. I can't think of anything I'd rather do."

He looks at me, blowing out a long breath. "I take that back. I can think of one other thing . . ."

Oh my. I feel the warmth of a flush creeping across my face. I can't stop my grin, or these dimples that are burning holes into my cheeks. I drop my eyes, feeling shy, and then reach for my wine. He turns his attention to his dinner, finishing his meal in a couple of quick bites.

Looking up, he wipes his mouth with a napkin before pointing to my plate. "You've only eaten half of your supper. And what about dessert? The baklava at this place is amazing."

It's unlike me not to clean my plate. But it feels as if I've swallowed a bag filled with butterflies. There's not much room for food.

I smile, beaming at him across the table. "You go ahead. I'll have a bite of yours." I gesture to my plate. "I'll ask the waiter to box up the leftovers. It's going to be insane tomorrow at work. I'll have something to look forward to after the day."

Tilting his head to the side, he narrows his eyes as if studying me. "I don't know how you do it. I can't imagine what it would be like to own a restaurant."

"I can assure you I had no idea what I was in for." I pull my hair around my neck. It falls into soft waves shining down the front of my blouse. "The responsibilities of running Welcome Home remind me of a Cirque du Soleil performance I once saw."

"That troupe's incredible," he replies, grinning widely. "I saw them perform at an arena in Nashville. They take theatrics to another plateau."

"I know. Literally, right? The performers juggling dozens of balls in the air across the stage, intercepting and passing them from one to another. Without even one of the balls hitting the floor." I straighten in my chair, speaking quickly, my fingertips darting to my lips. "I, too, feel like a professional juggler. One minute I'm texting a menu proposal for an office luncheon, the next I'm describing the daily special to Lella and Quiche. The next thing I know, I'm answering the phone, taking an order." I fan myself with the palm of my hand. "All the while making sure I don't burn the soup."

"And God forbid you drop a ball on that beautiful head." Leaning across the table, he tucks a long, wavy curl behind my ear. "I couldn't bear the thought of even one of those golden tendrils disturbed." I feel my face getting warm. My pulse quickens at the touch of his fingers as they slide down my neck.

"But, honestly, Uriah." I take a deep breath, trying to corral the stampede in my chest. "The largest problem we face is trying to get our neighborhood community to warm up to us. It's not their dollars we're after. It's their fellowship. The area's a disaster zone. We want them to know we're all in this together. There's a congregation of churchgoers right across the street. You'd think at least they'd want a cup of coffee after Sunday services."

"I'm sure it's economics. They lack the funds for discretionary dining. I've had kids in my class from your area. It's a struggle for some of these families to even pay their gas bill. Junk food's affordable."

"I get that. But they flock to that place—what's it called? Hungry Boy Burgers? Their prices aren't that much cheaper than ours—at least not when compared with their supersize options."

Uriah squeezes my hand. "From what I've read, the garbage they put in commodity food is highly addictive. More's the pity. Malnutrition's a serious threat to folks living on cheap, processed food. Why is it that in the neediest communities, only the worst food options are offered?"

"I know we're dreaming big, and there are a lot of moving pieces, but that's what we want to change. Addie and I believe that if better food options are made available in low-income communities, and the residents became familiar with their delicious flavors, it could be a game changer in their lives."

He snaps his finger and thumb. "I've got it. Why not give everyone who lives in a one-mile radius of Welcome Home a twenty percent discount card?"

I clap my hands together, smiling ear to ear.

"That's a wonderful idea, Uriah. It will wipe out a chunk of our profit margin, but at least it's a step in the right direction."

"You've got my brain churning, Sam. I'll speak to school officials and ask them to write a bit about our garden math project on their website. We'll include photographs of the diner, of course."

"And don't forget," I say. "Next spring I want to have the kids plant seeds and harvest their own vegetables through the growing season."

He speaks quickly and pats my hand across the table. "We can invite the parents to tour the plot. That way you can introduce yourselves by demonstrating, through the garden project, that you're a part of their community by your work with their kids."

"The website's a great idea. You'd do that for us?"

He weaves his fingers through my hand. His grip is strong. I've large hands for a woman—farm-girl hands. But they feel small and protected wrapped in his. A current tingles between our fingers.

"Of course I will. The next time our web designer updates the site. We'll make this happen."

I squeeze his hand as he asks for the check.

"No dessert?" I ask. "A reliable source told me the baklava's good."

He winks at me. "I'll have something to look forward to the next time we eat here."

Next time. Those words sound like a symphony in two movements. *Next time.* I remove my wallet from my bag.

"Absolutely not," he says, pushing the wallet away.

Not putting up an argument, I smile into his eyes, returning my wallet to my bag. A man like Uriah has been a long time coming.

Holding hands, we exit the restaurant and stroll across the lot toward his pickup. He opens the door for me, helps me in, and leans across me to fasten the seat belt. This feeling of being cared for, of being protected, fills me with happiness.

"So, what was the impetus for your becoming a teacher?" I ask, wanting to learn more about this man who has such power over my emotions.

He smiles, folding his fingers over the steering wheel, checking the rearview mirror as he backs his car out of the parking lot.

Stopping at a red light, he swivels to face me. "My mother was my inspiration." He pulls in a deep breath, letting it out in a soft whistle between his teeth. "She is something else. I never told you this." He bites his lower lip.

"What?" I ask, concerned about the sudden pain traveling across his face.

"She was diagnosed with breast cancer several years ago. It was hard on all of us." He hits his fist on the steering wheel. "But she beat it back."

"I'm so sorry. For her. For your dad." I touch his arm. "For you. But doctors have made great headway in fighting the disease."

"They have. And never once did she complain. She seemed to be more worried about my dad and me. I love and respect her so much." His eyes dampen. "When I was growing up, she was a sixth-grade schoolteacher. I believed there was no finer career. Knowledge is the greatest gift I could ever give a child." He places his palm just above my knee, below the bottom edge of my skirt.

The light turns green, and he guides the steering wheel with his left hand, his right remaining on my thigh. "There is no word to me more splendid than the word *teacher*," he continues. "When a student refers to me as their teacher, my entire being is filled with joy."

It takes him fifteen minutes to drive me home. Feeling the warmth of his hand on my thigh, I can't remember a thing we discussed. When we arrive at my place, we remain in the truck. Taking me into his arms, he gives me a long, lingering kiss that I will, however, be remembering for a very long time.

⌒୨

Addie

"Thanks, Addie," Kevin says, looking up at me as I pick up the empty plate that rests between his hands. "You don't need to wait on me." He stands. "Let me do the dishes."

"Oh no," I say, tipping my head to David. "When I fix dinner, David does the cleanup."

"Hey," David cries. "Not fair. All you did was reheat leftovers from work."

"You got that right, David. Work. That's what I did all day. Work, work, work. And now it's your turn."

He smacks his palms against his forehead. With an exaggerated sigh, he rises from the table. I shake my head, laughing at my adorable boy.

"I was just testing you. Seriously. You put in a day yourself. You and Kev have some catching up to do."

Carrying the dishes to the sink, I notice through the window the lights of a pickup truck creeping down the street. It can't be going more than five miles per hour. It stops in front of the house, and the lights dim.

I'm sure that's Sam with Sun Beam's math teacher, Uriah. They've been seeing each other. David and I haven't hung out with them, but I met him once in passing. She told me it's the first time she's felt this way for a man since her fling with that creepy barista in New York. Of late, there's a lightness about her. Nothing seems to get under her skin. Yesterday she mentioned she'd lost five pounds. I told her not to lose more; she doesn't realize the power she holds over men in the curve of her hips. My eyes dart to the window. It's certainly a lengthy good-bye.

I worry about Kevin. David's had the *man-to-man* talk and told him that if he thinks Sam will fall for him romantically, he's wasting his time. Last week we fixed him up with one of my most adorable girlfriends, but she reported that Kevin was distracted, uninterested.

Sam and Kev are a regular topic of discussion for David and me. If Sam and this teacher become serious, he'll be joining our group. Kevin's crush on Sam might, indeed, crush Kevin in the end. Is there something about his psyche that seeks rejection? I glance over my shoulder at Kevin deep in discussion with David. Maybe it's an affirmation of negative feelings he has about himself. Or maybe I've been in therapy too long and overthink relationships. With his attractive face, muscular frame, and promising career, the man's a catch. Just a tad too serious.

As I dry the last dish, the front door closes and Hero begins to howl. Curiosity has the better of me.

"Hey," I say. "Sam's home." Kevin straightens in his chair and begins tapping his foot. His eyes dart about the room, as if unsure of his next move.

"I'll go down and invite her up," I say, heading for the stairwell. "We've some thoughts regarding payroll that will affect your accounting."

David groans. Kevin, however, smiles, and his foot slows, as if relieved our conversation will be treading on his turf.

"David. Can you see if we've another bottle of that Zinfandel I fell in love with? If so, could you open it and let it breathe?"

"Aye, aye, Little Caesar."

I shake my head at him and make my exit, scampering down the stairs.

Sam sits slumped at the kitchen island, elbows pressed against the countertop, with her face buried in the palms of her hands. Hero stands at attention by her side, regarding his master. His ears are pricked in concern, and his tail is stiff, hanging down between his back legs. She drops her hands and looks up at me. She appears not to be seeing me, but seeing right through me.

I shake her arm. "Sam? Are you all right?"

She sighs, her eyes glazed over. "I've never been kissed that way in my life."

"My God. For a minute you scared me. You were with the teacher, right?"

She bends to pat Hero. He wags his tail, and his ears relax.

"Yep. Uriah. The man's incredible. Not only is he a hunk, he's thoughtful and generous." She straightens on her stool and shakes her head, as if not believing her good fortune in meeting him.

"And get this. He keeps talking about his mom. He really respects her. He actually told me he loved her." Mouth agape, she shakes her head in disbelief. "Can you imagine a guy saying that on a first date? I've read that men who have healthy relationships with their mothers are sensitive and attentive in romantic relationships."

Relationship-speak. It's my favorite sort of chitchat, yet it makes David crazy. "Are you sure?" I take a seat at the counter, eager to hear more. "All the times I've hashed out David issues ad nauseam with my therapist, she never asked me once about his mother."

Sam narrows her eyes. "You're kidding." She scrutinizes me, lifting an eyebrow. "Maybe you should skip the therapy and order a woman's magazine. Better yet, save a tree and subscribe to them online. Respectful, loving mothers teach their sons how to value women. I'll see if I can find that article for you."

I lean into her, placing my fingers on her forearm. "Maybe that's what's wrong with David. His mother's so domineering he's afraid of crossing her. His dad sure is. Do you think that's why David doesn't value me?"

Sam's eyes widen in incredulity. "What? You must be kidding. The way David looks at you? The way he treats you? He spends every spare second fixing up this home, and his name isn't even on the title. What does that tell you? Of course he values you. He adores you."

I spread out the fingers on my left hand, wiggling my ring finger. "He could prove it by giving me a ring. I'm almost thirty-two."

"I'm not far behind," she says, taking my hand. "Listen, Addie. You're living your life as if you're in some sort of race. Slow down. What's the hurry?"

"The hurry is that I—"

"Hey, ladies, I've uncorked that bottle of wine," David shouts, his voice bellowing down the stairs and into the kitchen.

I stand and cross the kitchen toward the stairs, cupping my hands around my mouth.

"Up in a minute," I shout.

I turn to Sam and shrug. "Hey. Let's table this discussion for later. Meanwhile, if you don't mind, why don't you keep Uriah under wraps. Just around Kevin. Let's not mention you've been seeing someone."

Sam sighs, the V between her brows deepening. That's her look when she's irritated.

"Just for another week or so," I add quickly. "He's so fragile. I think he's still got it bad for you."

I exit the kitchen and clamber up the stairs. Without a word, she follows me, Hero tagging behind.

David's poured the Zinfandel into four of my oversize glasses, the ones almost large enough to bathe in. Resting on the counter, the round bowls of my red-wine glasses allow plenty of area for the flavors to explode. For once, he chose the proper stem.

After giving Hero a dog biscuit, I distribute the wine and then press my nose over the rim, taking a deep sniff of the rich aroma. I turn to Sam, who still appears annoyed. "I know your taste, Sam. You will love this—"

"Hold your horses," David interrupts. "Kevin and I'd like to make a toast."

I stop speaking, my lips still parted.

"We haven't officially congratulated you ladies on the recent success of Welcome Home." He tips his glass to Sam and then toward me.

"I've just finished July's books," Kevin adds, "and for the first time, you ladies are officially out of the red." Our glasses clink together, and we all take a sip.

David plops into an armchair. I place my wine on the side table and fall into his lap. Flinging my arm around his neck, I burrow into the solid, familiar comfort of the man I love. The back of his neck looks so innocent and fragile. I touch his earlobe. In a glance, he catches my eye, and we giggle, in spite of trying to keep straight faces. We've been together four years, and this man still makes me blush. The two of us are so playful with each other, so much in love. So different from our parents. How can I make him understand that marriage for us would be different, as well?

Facing us, Sam and Kevin sit on opposite sides of the couch, silently. Kevin's foot starts that tap-tap-tapping again. What's with Sam? Can't she bother to make small talk?

He clears his throat and darts his eyes toward her, his forehead beaded with moisture. "Addie mentioned that you two are making changes I should be aware of."

Sam takes a long, lingering sip, her brows unknotting.

"We haven't mentioned it to the team yet," she says, crossing her legs, glancing sideways at Kevin, "but when you're reconciling next month's books, you'll notice a significant jump in payroll."

"Did you make a new hire?" Kevin asks, brushing his sleeve across his damp forehead.

"No. Not yet. But soon enough. In the meantime we're increasing everyone's hourly wage, giving Quiche, Braydon, and Paul an extra two bucks an hour. And we plan to pay Lella an income she could actually live on "

"She's currently making three bucks," Kevin says. "But tips should make up the difference."

"When the diner's slow, there are no tips," Sam replies. "Yet she's still at work, mopping floors, cleaning tables, for less money an hour than it costs to buy a latte."

"When the diner's dead, you aren't making money, either," David retorts, raising his brow to regard me, curious as to my role in this conspiracy. "And you and Sam are making less money than Lella." He shrugs. "Anyway, it's a moot issue. The law states that if income combined with tips are less than minimum wage, restaurants must pay the difference."

I lean into David, narrowing my eyes. "It's spottily enforced. She deserves a wage that she can live on. Sam and I've agreed. We're increasing her salary to ten bucks an hour."

"Ten dollars plus tips? How are you supposed to be competitive with restaurants paying three? Why are you guys paying your workers this exorbitant amount?"

"Ten dollars an hour is not exorbitant," Addie says, shaking her head with an exaggerated sigh. "Imagine, David, living off ten bucks an hour."

"That's why I'm studying my brains out in business school."

"And your dad pays the tuition," Addie says, kissing her forefinger and planting it on his lips. "Not everyone's as fortunate as us."

He hesitates, biting his lower lip. "Touché, Addie." He takes her hand and squeezes. "It would be much harder to go to school without their money."

"All my parents gave me was a suitcase and bus ticket when I graduated from high school," Sam says with a tiny frown.

I glance at my feet dangling across David's lap, hanging over the armrest. I reach over and grab my wine, taking a sip. She's right. I study the imprint of my lipstick on the rim and then return the glass to the table. But at least she grew up in a loving home with parents committed to each other. Money can't buy that.

"David," I continue, avoiding Sam's gaze, rubbing his neck. "We're not trying to wage war. Our customers know the waitstaff is paid fairly, so patrons are relaxed. They aren't pressured into thinking a large tip will garner better service."

I catch his eyes and stretch mine wide. We fall silent, trying to out-stare each other. He stares at me as if he were gauging a thunderstorm that might be worth the trouble to wait out rather than drive through. At last, he drops his head in resignation. I always win at this game.

After a pause, he looks up and shrugs his shoulders. "Well, if you two insist on paying these sorts of wages, you should knock the prices up another ten percent across the board."

I roll my eyes, but flick my hair, flirtatious, and then take his hands in mine. "We're proposing a new restaurant model. An honest and egalitarian system. We've got a hardworking, loyal staff and want to keep them. Employee turnover in restaurants is far more costly than taking care of the workers who've earned your trust."

"Someday we might give them options to buy into the business," Sam says, her fingertips making tiny circles on her thigh, just above her knee.

That devilish twitch returns to David's grin, and he shakes his head, laughing. "I propose you change the name of Welcome Home to the Radical Diner."

Even Sam giggles at that one, duly noted by Kevin, his laughter joining ours.

"Hey," she says, her mood improved with the depletion of her wine. "Here's an idea. It's cut from chapter two of Sam's manifesto." She winks at David. "What if we give everyone who lives in a one-mile radius of Welcome Home a twenty percent discount card?"

David applauds, returning the wink. "Actually, that's a great idea, Sam. Marketing 101. You didn't need college after all."

Her face colors and she smiles.

"We could have them laminated, and commission a mailer," I say, excited to be brainstorming a concrete plan that could warm our neighbors up to us.

"A mailer would be expensive," Sam replies. "Quiche told me discussions are held and opinions formed in churches, barbershops, and ladies' hair salons. You'd be surprised how many churches and salons there are in the few-blocks radius surrounding the diner." She bends to scratch her dog behind his ears. "I'll take them door-to-door with Hero."

"I'll come with you," says Kevin. "To make sure you're safe."

"Sweet of you, Kev," she says, flashing a smile, "but I'm sure Hero and I will be just fine."

Kevin's eyes drop into his hands. Sam shot that little zinger right into his chest, and it pains me to look at him. That girl can be heartless.

I untangle myself from David's arms and stand, the atmosphere now tainted. "Well, I don't know about you people, but I'm exhausted." I blow them a kiss. "Stay as long as you like, but I'm going to bed."

Not surprisingly, David jumps up, wrapping his hands around my waist. "Not alone, you aren't."

"Good night," Kevin says, his words a whisper. "I've got a busy day at the office tomorrow."

"'Night," Sam says. She stands and claps her hands, alerting Hero it's time to depart. The evening has expired.

Chapter Eight

Sam

It's said, "All good things in moderation." The last days of August must have missed that memo, because everything about this week is excessive.

The excess of vegetables and fruit cracks a whip beneath my feet every time deliveries are made. The excess of heat in this kitchen—combined with the sloth of midday humidity—blankets my body like a wet quilt. Even my eyelashes drip with moisture.

And then, there's this excess of passion. I have the hots for Uriah so bad I can't tell if the temperature is having this effect on me or not. If it were a frigid day in February, I suspect my cheeks would still be burning.

A bowl of heirloom tomatoes, the sultriest of the nightshades, rests on my table beside me. I select a Cherokee Purple, which has a rusty, orange-red belly with lime green shoulders spanning out from the stem.

Yesterday he picked me up from work. When we arrived at my place, he kissed me, pressing me against the bumper of his pickup. His breath smelled of citrus and ginger, from the lemonade I'd brought to cool us down. Then, without a word, we went into the house, into my bedroom, and I let him—for the first time—undress me. In my bed, we kissed again, harder. I bit him gently on his lower lip before releasing myself into carnality.

I hold the tomato gently in my palm. It's large, heavy, and thick with flesh. Even a twitch of my fingers could bruise the delicate skin. Like most heirlooms, the Cherokee's surface is split in several places and appears to be bursting its seams. In their quest for size, shape, and flavor, cultivators accidentally eliminated most of the heirlooms' defensive genetics, rendering them vulnerable.

He's a wonderful lover, knowing just the right words to say. And with those thick, lingering fingers, he touched me as if I were something delicate, fragile, a treasure he wished to protect. I moved like a cat beneath his hands.

I slice the tomato into five thick pieces. The seeds—which define tomatoes as a fruit and not a vegetable—are embedded in the purplish-red flesh and circle the stem like spokes on a tire. I sprinkle the slabs with kosher salt. Holding a piece between my fingers, as if it were the most delicate of petits fours, I bite into the juicy morsel. The flavor reigns triumphant, bursting between my teeth—the perfect balance of sweet to sour. Pink liquid drips onto the plate beneath my fingers.

I wipe my fingertips on a dish towel. Comparing an heirloom tomato to one of those rosy, round poseurs found in grocery stores would be like comparing the intensity of lite beer with a hand-crafted ale, or tap water with Bordeaux.

I resume my task of chopping, dicing, and mincing as an electric fan circulates warm air across my back. The kitchen staff and I are working around the clock canning and pickling eggplant, peppers, zucchini, okra, and tomatoes. The pace won't let up until the first frost, but I could work a twelve-hour day and still have the desire to replay last night again and again. If Detroit could harness my energy, they could relight every broken streetlight.

Desire ripples through me. Sparkles, even. I wish it weren't Addie's day off; I'm dying to confide. But then again, maybe not. The few times I've mentioned Uriah, she seems distant, removed. And it blows my mind that I can't bring him up when Kevin's around. Am I supposed to hide him under a rock?

Lately, it's all about Addie. Her obsession with the past and future are also driving me nuts. Quit worrying about the future, live for today. Enough wasting precious time in therapy and searching for solace in ancient Grecian scripts. It's all Greek to the rest of us. Close your books and put away your fairy tales. Breathe, Addie, breathe.

Lella pops her head into the kitchen and slides several orders up into the rack, all for the Green Zebra Tomato Curry. She reminds us of Pixy Stix, those long, thin sticks of powdered candy: her temperament—like the sugar—both sweet and tart. She's easily excitable but can shut down just as fast when she's annoyed.

"Everyone is loving your curry," she says. "The last bowl I set down created a chain reaction at a table nearby. You'd think in this heat everyone would want salad." Her jaws grind quietly, working a stick of gum.

"Actually, spicy foods cool you down. Cultures in the hottest spots on the planet eat the spiciest foods," I scrape away the seeds of a jalapeño with the blade of my knife. "Something about your internal body temperature rising to match the temperature outside."

"Well, I should have a bowl after lunch rush. That or join the kids across the street playing in the broken fire hydrant." She edges in closer and lowers her voice so Paul's out of earshot.

"I just said good-bye to that guy I've been telling you about. Brett actually requested I be his waiter today. He ordered *the usual.*" She giggles, tightening her apron strings. "Two eggs over easy, bacon, blue-corn grits, and red-eye gravy." Looking at the ceiling, she hugs herself, elated.

Man, the heat's got us all hot to trot.

"He even congratulated me on the article in the *Times*. He actually congratulated *me*, like I was the reason for all of this attention."

"Well, you are. Everyone who works here shares equal responsibility for the diner's success."

"Thanks, Sam. And we also share responsibility when we piss someone off. Did anyone ever figure out who wrote that nasty review about the chicken?"

I put down my blade, my mood darkening, pinching the skin at my throat. We've just received another potentially destructive comment on Yelp. "No one has a clue. Addie and I've spoken to every employee, and no one remembers any customer complaining about anything besides having to wait too long for a table."

"And I always rectify a complaint with a sweet treat," Lella replies.

"Serving undercooked chicken is a big deal," I add. "You'd think the customer would have sent it back."

"As long as the person is writing the truth." Lella pushes her pen behind her ear. "Quiche and Paul always temp the chicken. Whether it's roasted, fried, grilled, or smoked, it's always cooked to perfection."

"I wish they would have complained to our face. Especially since they wrote they'd become ill after eating it."

"I think the person is a coward trying to hurt us. And really—all caps followed by a million exclamation points? Just like the comment written about the soup, it hurts your eyes to read it. It was wonderful so many customers leaped to our defense."

"I know. Sticks and stones. The positive backlash was tremendous, and now both reviews are past tense. We've still maintained our average of four and a half stars. In the meantime, I'm pleased Brett congratulated you on all of the great press we've received."

I pick up my knife and begin slicing a potato into rounds. I am pleased he thought to thank her. We can't take all the credit for Welcome Home's success. We were thrilled the photo including Braydon was chosen to be in the paper. His aunt had it framed. I hope Angus saw it, too, although he probably thought it was window dressing. Braydon said he refused our offer to rebuild his steps. He never, however, refuses our chicken. It's a start.

Lella interrupts my thoughts. "Can you meet me at the pottery studio after work, say around four? I want to tell you more about him. And I owe you for a Heartbreaker. Brett asked for two to take back to his office, and I slipped him an extra." She jumps up and down, clapping her hands. "I have this feeling he's going to ask me out."

"Well, you're so dang cute, I'm sure he will."

"More good news," she says, her hazel eyes dancing to the rhythm of the chase. "He's not wearing a ring." She gathers up the finished plates and exits the kitchen. Three plates balanced on her arm, she can still work the floor with the energy and swish of a goldfish in a small tank.

Lella extricated herself from an affair with a married man, a fellow potter, a few months back. He swore he was going to divorce his wife once his children had graduated high school. After the kids graduated, he showed no signs of divorcing her. Lella broke it off, leaving him to sulk behind his wheel. I hope Brett works out. She seems reckless in her choice of men.

This morning, Uriah and I had planned to meet the minute after I left work to spend the afternoon and evening together. Alone. But now I'm reconsidering. As much as I hate sharing him, I should introduce him to my people. Addie and our group are meeting in the garden tonight, and David's bringing his guitar. We can all hang together.

My heart sinks. I'm sure Kevin will join us. He's shy, and we seem to be his only friends. But I'm done hiding Uriah because of Kev's crush on me. I've never led him on, and can't imagine why he doesn't get it. I feel bad for him—love's a battlefield—but I have to live my life. Let time do its thing. One day Uriah and Kevin may even become friends. I'll also meet Lella at the pottery studio after work. I'm not the kind of woman who blows off her friends when there's a new man on the scene.

When we first opened the diner, David suggested we draw a line between our private and professional lives with the staff. He explained it's difficult to delegate to friends; they will take advantage of our good natures, and mediocrity will flourish. What he's suggested is impossible. Working side by side in the trenches with our employees has made us as loyal as a team, as intimate as a family. Addie and I empower every employee. Our weekly meetings have created an environment where they're comfortable challenging our procedures. We encourage them to go off script from the handbook and bend the rules if the situation merits. They were thrilled with their raises; newly invigorated and enthusiastic, they seem to shimmer these days, a lightness in their feet.

I head toward Paul, standing in front of the prep table. Kosher salt streams from his fist over a gazpacho he just made. He grabs a spoon and tastes the cold soup. "Just a tiny bit more, and the flavor will explode." He grabs the box, shakes salt into his hand, and sprinkles it over the orange-red soup, which is thick with cucumber, peppers, and tomatoes.

"Can you handle the orders? They're slowing down, and I need to check the floor." He nods, mopping away a rivulet of sweat running down his cheek. After covering the soup with saran, he takes it to the cooler. Head down, I exit the kitchen and squeeze in a text to Uriah, wondering if he'd mind changing plans.

The main floor is at least ten degrees cooler than in the kitchen, but several customers are fanning themselves with menus. Installing air conditioning must be made a priority next spring. Tory and Wally Spitts are sitting at the counter, chatting it up with Sun Beam. They're a husband-and-wife law team in Detroit and supporters of every local, independent business that comes to their attention.

Sun Beam waves her arms in exaggerated swoops above her head as she carries the conversation. The summer's almost over, and all of us will miss her regular appearances during her mom's shifts. I approach and ask the pair if they'd like a coffee refill. Tory places her palm on top of her cup.

"We've had our quota, but thank you. Sun Beam is warning us we're in the middle of hurricane season." She turns to the child. "I didn't know we had hurricanes in Michigan."

"We don't." Sun Beam studies the pair in the silent, steady reproach of a teacher regarding students who aren't paying attention in the classroom. "You didn't let me finish what I was saying. The Great Lakes region's too cold to make them. I was trying to tell you that it's hurricane season down South."

"Well, Sun Beam," Wally says. "What a relief. Tory won't insist I rush home and batten down the windows and doors. At least there's one advantage to suffering through the snow."

Sun Beam nods her head vigorously. "You can say that again. But Michigan does get tornadoes. They happen when cold air collides with warm. Did you know that Braydon found Bon Temps after a tornado hit Detroit?"

Tory looks at me, amused, a question in her dark, lovely eyes.

"You remember Braydon. He's our manager. Bon Temps is his dog."

Sun Beam turns her attention to a sandwich she made from the previous day's leftovers. I lift up the bread to peek: a slice of eggplant, uncooked, and several slices of cheese. Spread on the bread is a copious amount of a metallic caper-pickle sauce, which we use as a tart counterpoint to the buttery lake trout we feature.

"Sun Beam. What a remarkable sandwich. Don't you find raw eggplant bitter?" Her brows furrow, and she pulls her plate toward her. She takes a large bite as if to defy me.

"It's delicious," she retorts, her mouth full. Squinting as if in pain, she puckers her lips as she swallows, eyeing the sandwich with suspicion. "But I'm losing my appetite eating all of these sandwiches I'm imagining." She pushes the plate away and takes a large swig of water.

I smile, casting a swift wink toward Tory and Wally. They're wearing new watches, and I lean across the counter to admire their jewelry.

"Love these. Shinola, right?"

Tory stretches out her arm to admire her watch, the orange leather band looped twice around her wrist. "This one's called the Birdy. Look at the craftsmanship, the design." The word *Detroit* is stamped on the pearly face, beneath the gold-numbered dial.

"That's the coolest watch I've ever seen." I hope one day I can afford to buy a Shinola watch.

Shinola's hired over four hundred Detroit residents, many laid-off autoworkers, to craft their watches. Last year they presented the city with four public clocks and partnered with officials for an off-leash dog park. Hero and I have a blast there, but the other dogs make Bon Temps nervous.

"Detroit is primed," Wally says, regarding his watch, pride in his eyes. "The cost of doing business here is the best in the world. Downtown has seen over a twenty percent increase in demand for residential properties."

"Oh," I say, grabbing a piece of paper from the pocket of my apron. "I almost forgot. I was hoping you'd stop by. Seems I did something stupid. I signed a contract with a linen company, thinking my costs would be reduced. Turns out, after the first discounted delivery, the price shoots through the roof. We'd end up paying far more than we do with our current vendor. The salesman lied to my face."

I sigh, knocking the toe of my kitchen clog against the counter base. "It was a bait and switch. I called the company and canceled the delivery. But they said it was too late."

Wally picks up the contract, examines it, and then regards me, a smile playing about his lips.

"No worries, Sam. The contract is one-sided to the extent that no reasonable person would agree to such terms. It's unconscionable, which would render it void. Furthermore, the clause is inconspicuous. Even with glasses it's almost impossible to read."

Wally pulls the paper up to his eyes, which are magnified behind heavy frames. Then, he slides the contract to Tory, turning to face his wife. "What do you think? This couldn't be more than an eight-point font."

She picks up the paper with her fingertips. As her eyes skim the document, she holds it at arm's length, as if it had been used to wrap fish. "This is a joke," she says, her nose crinkled in disdain. "Linen Express. Humph. If memory serves, the owner of the company has seen the inside of a courtroom before." She puts the letter in her briefcase and catches my eye.

"I'm sure he expected you to roll over and take it, but the last thing he'll want is litigation. When we return to the office, I'll draft a letter to the company and send it certified mail. If the delivery shows up before they receive it, make sure it's refused."

"I really can't thank you enough. Please bill me for your time."

"No way," Tory says, smacking her fist into her palm. "Knocking down hoodlums who threaten the spirit of the new Detroit is our favorite sport."

"We have plenty of clients who pay the big bucks," Wally adds. "We'll take our fee in your soups of the day."

My face burns, amazed by the generosity of this couple.

"Well, again," I say, at a loss for words. "Thank you." I glance at Sun Beam's plate. "And don't let Sun Beam scare you away with her lunch."

"I'm finished," the girl says, sliding off the counter stool. Only one bite was taken from the sandwich. She rolls up her sleeves and tightens her ponytails. "I'm going to the garden to work on the doghouse."

Ping. I fumble for my phone. Uriah!

Dribbles of sweat roll down my spine. I press Sun Beam's glass of ice water against my cheek and roll it against my pulse. Then, I make my exit, scurrying out the back door to read the latest text.

You must be tired because you've been running through my mind all day.

A cornball sense of humor. That's OK. It's like David's.

I'll keep busy until this evening, but it will be hard.

What will be hard? I giggle. But he does have plenty to keep him occupied. His classes resume soon, and he's been working on the curriculum.

Closing my eyes, I remember the smell of his chest after we made love. Leather and starched cotton, the aromas made more potent mixed deep into his sweat. There's no sexier smell than a man's sweat. And there's no more powerful drug than the love drug, the endorphins turning your mind into goo.

Since last night, our text play keeps me craving him. I wipe my damp fingers against my apron, and then my thumbs fly over the keyboard in response and then freeze.

Stay in the shallows, girl, don't wade deep. A sobering thought crosses my mind. Maybe last night to him was just a hookup. I'm the stopgap until he finds someone more attractive—a hotter, skinnier girl he'd shower with affection.

CTFD—calm the fuck down. Seriously. Chill. I backspace and type:

Look forward to seeing you.

I press "Send" and then check tomorrow's forecast: high, seventy-seven degrees. Thank God. Maybe the cooler temps will contain me.

෨

Addie

"Nice work at the studio today, Sam," Lella says, kicking off her sandals. She takes a beer from the cooler and sits in a lawn chair. "The way you threw that bowl made it look as if you've been at it for years."

"Thanks," Sam replies, as she turns to her new man, Uriah. "Lella showed me how to make pottery today. It was cool. I love the way clay feels in your hands when it's spinning, all slippery and soft."

The slight slur in her voice makes her sound as if she's drunk or talking in her sleep. But she's had only one beer. She stares, mesmerized, at her outspread hands. Uriah moves his chair next to her so that the handles are pressed together. He stretches his long, well-muscled arm across her shoulders.

"But look at these fingertips." She wiggles them in front of her, the cuticles of her nails edged in clay. "What a mess. I've been scrubbing and scrubbing and still can't remove the gunk." She leans into him, wearing her special smile, tentative and wan, which says it all: Sam's deep in love—or lust. In the early stages of a romantic relationship, the two are often confused.

Uriah grazes the tips of her fingers with his, as if on his way to holding her hand. He gazes into her face, with not so much as a twitch. Her relationship with that arrogant barista, in retrospect, was a healthy experience. Ironically, in the end, it strengthened her sense of self. She now refuses to be degraded and is quick to call out bullshit. Any dude who can look at Sam without shifting his gaze is as fearless as a tightrope walker.

This aura of hot, new passion electrifies me. I glance sideways at Kevin, who is pretending to be interested in Lella's description of a sushi set she's glazing. But his face is pale, and he coughs, as if the air is suffocating him. It irritates me that Sam would rub Uriah in his face. Why did she invite her new boyfriend to join us? Her behavior's insensitive.

A good friend enters the garden from the street. Hero jumps up and barks, and Sam gives him a biscuit to settle down.

It's Tim, who works in the tasting room at Two James Spirits downtown. He pulls a couple of bottles from a brown bag. Two James is Detroit's first licensed distillery since Prohibition and produces an array of spirits.

"The rye," he announces, wandering to each of us, showing us the label of the Catcher's Rye whiskey bottle. "As classic a whiskey as the novel is a read." He unscrews the cap, pours shots into glasses, and passes them around.

"Smell the rye from Michigan's heartland as it swirls into the waters of the Great Lakes." We obey, lifting the cups under our nostrils and sniffing. "Now taste. *Ummmm . . .* spicy, with the taste of sweet fig at the finish. Delicious, right?"

I take a sip of the amber liquor, swish it around my mouth, and swallow. A fire lights up in my chest. "There is a God, and *she*," I say, winking at David, "lives in Michigan." He smiles at me, strumming his guitar, as our glances flit up and down each other's bodies.

Uriah's fingers spider up Sam's shoulders, and she cuddles into his arms. We take tiny sips, but Kevin finishes his in a gulp, requesting his next be a double. David and I trade glances.

"My man," Tim says, pouring a hefty amount into Kevin's cup. "What's the occasion?"

"Does a man need an occasion to drink a fine whiskey?"

"A fine whiskey, like a fine woman, should be treated with respect," Tim says. "Be mindful. This stuff's close to one hundred proof."

"Just paying my respects to the heartland, bro," Kevin replies, taking a long, deep swallow.

"Good thing I brought an extra bottle," Tim remarks, shaking his head with a sidelong glance at Kevin.

As the evening continues, our liveliness amplifies in sync with the bottle's depletion. Except for Kevin. He answers in monosyllables when conversation is directed his way, and has moved only twice, to replenish his supply. Uriah strokes Sam's shoulder, and she turns her face into him, kissing his neck. Now I'm angry and tempted to pass her a note—*Get a room.* Poor Kevin.

David's strumming amplifies as he picks out the tune of "Baby, Won't You Be My Baby," his fingers pressing strings on the fret of his guitar. It's a song he's been working on from one of Dylan's recently released bootleg series. I point to Angus's home, placing my fingers over my lips. "Shhhh. You don't want to upset him further."

"OK, OK." He puts down his guitar and folds his arms across his chest.

Everyone's now quiet, regarding me with flickering eyes as if I were a party pooper. Between being pissed at Sam and worried about Angus being pissed at me, I'm on edge. Perhaps overreacting, as well. His music wasn't that loud.

I turn my attention to the sky. It's twilight, almost dark, and the evening sky is streaked in apricots and royal blues.

Lella stands. "Gum, anyone?" She passes an open package of gum around our group. Sam and Uriah each slide a piece from the pack.

Sam glances at her phone.

"Yikes. It's close to nine thirty. Well, as much as I hate leaving this shindig, this girl's gotta be raring to go when the rooster crows."

She bends to hook Hero's collar on the leash, her jeans sliding down to reveal creamy flesh above her butt. Uriah's gaze is fixated on the patch of skin gleaming in the moonlight. They rise and leave, and Tim follows.

David slides his chair next to Kevin's and puts his arm around his neck.

"You doin' OK there, buddy?" Kevin looks up from his drink, his eyes filling with tears. "Kevin. You can't do this to yourself," David says. "I warned you about Sam. If you let this into your heart, it will eat you alive."

Oh God. I slide my chair to the other side of Kevin. "We've all been where you're sitting, Kev, and it hurts. We feel your pain."

"What's wrong with me?" he says, his words slurred. "Am I really such a bad guy? Why does she find me so disgusting?" I am furious with Sam.

Resting my forearms on my thighs, I lean my head toward his, catching his eyes. "She doesn't find you disgusting. She loves you,

Kevin. But only as a good friend. She loves you the way I love you. There's nothing wrong with you."

"Hey, dude," David says. "You're a chick magnet. Remember when we set you up with Tina? That girl is hot, man, and she said you wouldn't give her the time of day."

Kevin pushes David's arm away and half rises, stumbling. "Addie," David says, his voice crackling with concern. "Get him a glass of water." He turns to Kevin. "You're wasted. Give me your keys. We're taking you home."

"I didn't bring a car. I'll walk home. No worries," he says, garbling his *r*'s. I trot to the kitchen and pour leftover coffee from lunch into a glass filled with ice.

"You're not walking home alone. It's dark now, and the streets aren't safe," David argues. "Especially with the lights out." The failure of the city to keep the neighborhood streetlights burning has had a crippling effect on our psyches. For good reason, we stay inside after dusk, afraid of the dark.

"Come on, man," David continues. "I'm loading you into the car. We'll take you home."

Kevin straightens and drains the glass of coffee in a gulp.

"Goddamn it, David," he says, shoving him. "I'm fine. I want to walk." After a long, drawn-out burp, he weaves his way across the yard, pantomiming great effort not to stumble into the garden. He swings his cup toward a sky now filled with a high August moon, slurring verse from Henry Lawson, a poet he sometimes quotes:

"'I'll find a drunken pauper grave, and what have you to say? Good night! Good day! My noble friends, and what have you to say?'"

I've never seen Kevin such a train wreck. We stand, follow, and watch him dodging cars as he weaves across La Grande. He selects the most dangerous street to make his journey home.

David grabs his keys from his pocket. "He's too drunk to know we'll be following him."

Chapter Nine

Sam

"Jesus, Lord, I'm sweating like a pig. But I'm not complaining. Early September heat's good for growing garlic." Jessie glances out the window as she holds the door for Jévon. "But we could sure use some rain."

Judging from the empty truck bed, we must be their last delivery. In contrast to his mother's mud-caked overalls, Jévon's tall frame is dressed in a minimalistic look—clean and fresh. Today he's wearing a white crew-neck T well fitted to his muscular build, and his pressed, dark-wash jeans are rolled up at the bottom. He walks into the diner and slides the case of sauce and bag of garlic onto the counter.

"Good to have my boy helping me again," Jessie says, linking her arm into her son's. "Saving my back from the chiropractor."

"Sam. Quiche." He nods at us. "Good to see you ladies. It's been a while." He looks around. "Where's Braydon? I wanted his opinion on the Banksy mural sale."

Banksy, whose real identity is unknown, is a graffiti artist from England who creates artistic works of social commentary around the world. Five years ago, he stenciled an eight-foot mural of a forlorn

African American boy who'd just written I REMEMBER WHEN ALL THIS WAS TREES with a can of red paint. Urban explorers discovered the work on crumbling cinderblocks in the sprawling, abandoned Packard plant.

Amid a huge amount of controversy, the 1,500-pound mural was excavated by a local nonprofit art gallery, who then fought and gained legal ownership of the piece. Now the gallery's decided to sell it at a Beverly Hills auction, with plans to use the proceeds for an art center.

"Braydon's out back working on Sun Beam's house," I say, returning a chair to its table, taking deliberate steps to avoid slipping on the freshly mopped floor.

"It's for the dogs," Quiche corrects, before laughing. "Not my child." Her back is to us as she speaks, and she's arranging the china cups and saucers we've been collecting from estate sales, putting them onto shelves. "She sure loves those dogs, and figuring out how to build that house was the highlight of summer. Braydon drew up the plans and showed her how to build it. But he claims she did most of the work."

Addie emerges from the office, her hands filled with paperwork.

"Uriah's bringing his class to the garden late afternoon to demonstrate a math formula," I announce to the group. "Uriah's not Sun Beam's teacher this year, but she's tagging along."

Addie's brows furrow, a question in her eyes. I know what she's going to say before she says it. Irritation clouds my excitement over Uriah's visit. Kevin collects the bookwork today, and the two men could cross paths. I speak before she has time to open her mouth.

"Yes, Addie, *Uriah*. He's coming to the diner with the children. Remember? Part of our vision before opening was to have a garden that also served as a learning lab for local kids. Uriah happens to be their teacher."

She shrugs, as if saying *whatever*, and takes a seat at a four-top. She spreads last week's time cards in front of her and removes her calculator from her bag.

Addie was pissed at me after that evening in the garden and told me I was insensitive with Kevin. She said I should have given him more time to adjust to my new relationship before rubbing it in his face. I said I couldn't live my life hiding my reality from Kevin, and in the next moment, we were off to the races. I thought she'd calm down by now and accept the fact Uriah is a fixture in my day-to-day. But by the look on her face, I can tell her feathers remain ruffled.

"Sun Beam liking school?" Jessie asks, sensing our annoyance with each other and trying to change the subject.

"Yep," Quiche replies, securing stray bits of hair with bobby pins. "She just started fourth grade a couple of weeks ago. She can't wait to introduce the kids to the dogs and show them the house she's building with Braydon. I told her not to brag."

"I'll pull him away from his project," Addie says, looking up from her work. "He mentioned being curious about your opinion, Jévon. Whether you thought the mural should be sold or kept in Detroit."

"That's a hot-button issue—I'd love to chat," Jévon replies.

Addie stands. "I'll get him."

"Hey. Can Mom and I trade a pound of garlic for a couple of plates of greens?"

"Of course. Help yourself." She nods toward the simmering pot on the back burner, a cloud of steam wafting above the top lip of the kettle.

"I can't eat those greens, son." Jessie wrinkles her nose. "They're cooked with pork."

"Well, I don't share your aversion to the mighty pig," Jévon says. "It's been sustaining our people for centuries."

Quiche fills a bowl with greens and hands them to Jévon. She gives Jessie a piece of cornbread wrapped in a napkin. Braydon and Addie enter from the back door.

Jévon puts the bowl down and grabs his hand, pulling him in for a backslap hug. "Been a long time."

"Hey, man, I loved your work on Cass."

"Yeah? Thanks for that. The kids were a big help."

"So, what do you think about the gallery selling the Banksy piece to private collectors?" Braydon asks. "Should it stay in the city where it was created or end up in some West Coast mansion?"

"Hmm. A tough question. So much of the sale is based on speculation. That Beverly Hills auction house estimates its worth at two to four hundred thousand dollars."

"Damn. You're kidding me."

"That amount of money could remodel the new gallery and provide a hands-on learning center for our kids."

"But it's a pity it would leave Detroit. Some people were even pissed the gallery removed it from its original site," Braydon comments. "Claimed the location was part of the artistry."

"That, my friend, is a no-brainer." Jévon picks up the bowl of greens, stabs them with a fork, and takes a massive bite before batting his lips with a napkin. "They had to remove it before vandals wrecked it or bulldozers destroyed it. Look what's happened to half of my work—vanished under a jet hose."

"I'm with you on that one," replies Braydon. "But I don't think they should sell. The mural is part of our history. Remember what almost happened at the Detroit Institute of Art? To pay off debt, the museum came within a hair of plundering their finest pieces. Can you imagine Detroit without Diego Rivera? If Detroit loses its art, it loses its soul. Why would people want to even visit our city? There'd be nothing left to see."

Jévon finishes his greens in three large bites, tips the bowl to his lips to slurp down the potlikker, and then puts the dish in the sink. "Mmmm. Just what the doctor ordered. So let me see this doghouse of yours. Maybe it could use some art—a stenciled dog denouncing the mural's sale."

"We'll have to run it by Sun Beam. She's my boss, and I don't know her politics."

Quiche guffaws, shaking her head. "Sun Beam's only political concerns are animal rights and ways of preventing global warming. She's worried if Michigan loses its cold weather, we may be threatened with hurricanes."

"Girl's got a point. I was my most noble self at nine years old," Jévon says. He chuckles and puts his arm around Braydon's shoulder, and the pair amble out the back door into the garden.

A couple of minutes later, a truck pulls in front of the diner, LINEN EXPRESS written on the side. It stops and a man exits the van. He towers well over six feet, and his massive torso and legs strain against the fabric of his copper-toned uniform. A baseball cap is perched on his head, the brim shadowing his face. He walks toward the back of the van, opens the rear doors, and places folds of aprons and dishcloths onto a cart.

I hang the CLOSED sign on the front window and scurry to the door to lock it. What would we do without Braydon? He was the one who first scrutinized the fine print and told me our linen costs would skyrocket.

Wheeling the cart to the entrance, the deliveryman sees me through the windowpanes. Finding the door locked, he bangs it with the bottom of his fist. His eyes are rheumy, red rimmed, and saucer shaped, the irises the faintest of silver, almost colorless. They appear to be disembodied from the rest of his face, which has stubble and is pocked and weathered like an old tweed jacket. The nametag clipped to his pocket reads EARL.

"Why don't you let the man in?" Jessie asks.

"Long story short, this linen delivery is a big mistake."

"He looks exhausted, all red and huffing," Jessie says, perhaps in sympathy for a fellow vendor. I unlock the door, open it an inch, and speak through the crack.

"The contract was bogus, so we canceled the service. Please take your linen and leave."

He wedges the cart into the space in the door, forcing it to open. A thick hand, covered with freckles and a down of burnt orange–colored hair, flings a piece of paper toward me. It flutters to the floor. "This contract was signed by someone who works for you." His voice is barbed, wheezing, seesawing from a high octave to low.

The heat rises in my cheeks. "Your office should have a letter from our attorneys by now."

Addie joins me by my side. Her voice is as commanding as I've ever heard it. "Leave. *Now.*"

Jessie rises and with one boot-clad foot, kicks the bottom of the cart, shoving it out the door. "You heard what the ladies said. Now git." Jessie's a big woman, yet she appears petite next to this giant of a man. But the malice in his bulging eyes begins to ebb, turning into the fear of a man confronted by a grizzly. The deliveryman takes a step back and grabs the careering cart.

"You don't know who you're messing with," Earl spits, his face tight with rage. "You're playing with fire."

"You come snooping around here again, I'll put a curse on you." Jessie's words are a deep, resonating growl finished with a snort. She removes several strands of beads draped around her chest, the ones she claims were carved from the bones of her ancestors.

He retreats as Jessie moves toward him, the gold light vanished from her eyes. She waves the beads in front of his face, growling, "I said I'm gonna curse you."

He turns and rolls the cart to the back of the van.

"Earl reminds me of someone . . . something," Addie says, folding her arms across her chest and shivering. Earl tosses the linen-laden cart into the truck without effort, as if it were a pillow.

"Got it," she says, clicking her fingers. "Polyphemus. He reminds me of the hideous Cyclops in *The Odyssey*. Polyphemus was the one-eyed giant who trapped Odysseus in his cave." She is biting her knuckle, and her forehead is beaded with sweat.

After slamming the doors shut, Earl staggers to the driver's side of the van, heaves himself up into the seat, and makes the wheels screech as he tears out of the parking lot. The vehicle, hurtling onto La Grande, hits a pothole. The back doors reopen, and the cart flies out. In his haste, Earl must have forgotten to secure the doors.

Braydon and Jévon reenter the diner. "What the hell is this commotion about?" Braydon asks.

"Don't worry, boys," I say, clasping my hands together so no one will observe their shake. "We took care of things. Business as usual."

"Why was he forcing those rags on you?" Jessie asks, as I hug her.

"It was my fault. I signed an agreement without reading the fine print." I pick up the contract and place it on a table. "Thankfully, we've customers who're attorneys. I showed it to them, and they said the contract's crap." I point my forefinger at Jessie. "That dumb dude's also scared of you."

"Dumb? If you ask me," Jessie says, her nostrils flaring, "he's more like certifiable."

"They should have received the attorney's letter by now. We won't be seeing him again."

The linens and cart are scattered across the road, causing a traffic jam outside the diner. Horns are blasting, and vehicles are at a standstill on La Grande. Angus is standing on the sidewalk, staring at the commotion. He turns to face the diner, fists on hips, legs planted wide. At this distance, it's hard to read his expression. But as he walks toward his home, he shakes his head from side to side, as if disgusted.

"Braydon. Jévon," Addie says, grabbing their hands. "Help me get that crap out of the road. We'll dump it on the sidewalk." Addie turns to me. "Sam. Maybe you should call the police and have them haul it away. With all this commotion, Angus must be livid."

The police came, we reported the incident, and they cleared away the linen and cart. After Uriah arrived, Addie retreated, closing the office door behind her.

It's late afternoon and the students from Uriah's class have just begun their after-school project. Some of their parents have joined them. The group is busy measuring the dimensions of the garden to determine how much soil would be needed to fill it. Not one to cede the floor, as they work, Sun Beam recites to them a blow-by-blow description of how she's building her beloved doghouse. Once completed, all it will need is a coat of paint. That can wait until spring.

I glance at my phone—it's time to organize the snacks and lemonade I'd made for them to enjoy after completing their assignment. Uriah and I leave Quiche and Braydon outside with the group. With one hand, he opens the back door of the diner for me. With the other, he slides his fingertips down my arm. So this is what it's like to walk on clouds. Our hips brush together as I walk past him, and a new flame travels up my spine.

I pause at the sight of the crumpled contract on the table. Uriah squeezes my shoulder, knowing my thoughts have gone back to the incident. I pinch my lips between my teeth, feeling heat surge through me again, driving the bad moment away.

I glance at the photograph of Babcia. She would be pleased I'm with a man of such fine character. I point to her image, as if to introduce her—I so wish I could.

"My grandmother taught me how to cook. I could feel her love when I ate the meals we prepared together." My eyes well with tears, understanding he will never know Babcia, never know her grace. "I suppose you could say I cook professionally to spread the love. This woman, Uriah, this woman is my world, part of who I am. Even though she's gone."

His eyes gaze above my head, distant and shining, lingering on the photograph. Then he returns his gaze to me, his forefinger tracing my face.

"Your eyes have the same shape as your grandmother's. So do your lips, your nose, even your chin. All your grandmother's. Her physical form may be a memory"—he lowers his hand to my heart, thumping his fingertip between my breasts—"but her spirituality rests here."

My heart pounds under the touch of his hand.

"She's with us," he continues. "Right now. Your eyes, you know, are windows to your soul. At least that's what they say. And if the saying holds truth, they're portals to your grandmother's, too."

Searching his face, I have the oddest sensation that I'm not only watching *him*, but I'm also watching him enter my heart. Watching him meet Babcia.

I'm watching him fall in love.

Chapter Ten

Addie

I've just finished cashing out from yesterday and check my phone for last-minute messages—perhaps some random catering opportunity we shouldn't pass up. Nope. Not a thing. I look out the window. There's nothing like the beauty of October on an Indian summer day. The air is warm and the leaves are splashed red and yellow gold against a hard, blue sky.

I've a few minutes before my interview with a potential hire, so I tumble into social digital distraction. My fingers slide down the screen, pressing hearts, leaving comments about my friends' lives on Facebook.

I resist *liking* political rants and rages. Even if our ideologies are similar, I resent armchair activists who pound me over the head with their pissed-off opinions and hate-filled tirades. Online anger is cowardly, unproductive, and draining. Quit hiding behind your screen, crafting posts with your Dorito-crusted fingers. Cowgirl up and take action.

My social media platforms gravitate to two subjects: food and children. My friends salivate over the beautiful plates from Welcome

Home's daily menu, and I, in turn, coo over their adorable children, a tug at my heart.

A woman's life is a series of stages: adolescence, puberty, adulthood, motherhood, and menopause. Motherhood's the only negotiable stage. But not for me. I want children. Precisely two.

You should hear the grief Sam gives me on the subject. If a single woman crossing the threshold of thirty wants to have children, using her own eggs, and she wants that family to include a husband, life in her thirties turns into a spreadsheet of tables, charts, and calculations. Land mines dot the landscape. One misstep and my dreams for a happy-ever-after could be detonated.

After all, I tell my cousin, no one can dispute the facts. Forty-year-old women have a significant decrease of egg supply, and that dwindling supply plummets by age forty-three. A bum rap for women with parallel goals of advancing their careers and having a family. Sam tells me I'm worrying about nothing. Forty is just a number and light-years away. Sam believes relationships, like everything else in her world, should be organic—never calculated. Case in point: Uriah. It's as if he fell from the sky and into her arms. I can't quite identify why I find the two of them annoying. She claims that if she doesn't have children, it wasn't meant to be. Childhood was wonderful for her, so she never wants to grow up.

So often David, too, acts like a boy in a grown man's body. Growing up with a mother who didn't respect a masculine point of view left him emotionally stuck in adolescence. Having a distant dad threw him a double whammy. The concept of marriage scares him. He's worried, for starters, our sex life will wane. Marriage doesn't ruin relationships, I tell him. People do. He tells me I look as if I'm in my early twenties. Tell that to my ovaries, I respond.

Never wanting to grow up, David and Sam are Peter Pans. They laugh in the eyes of logic. God forbid either one of those two discuss the future. I'm living too much in the moment, Sam says, to wonder what will happen tomorrow. I could wallpaper our home with her annoying little memes.

An only child, I grew up being shuffled between divorced parents and boarding school, my lips barely moving while other kids sang happy songs. My only constants were my grandparents, Sam, and her family's farm.

I pick up a framed photograph, a close-up of David's face, and study it. If I had a daughter, she might inherit his long, dark lashes instead of my whisper of a blonde fringe. I yearn for a future with David. I yearn for stability and a family to love.

Sam says I drank the Kool-Aid, buying into Disney's Prince Charming–Cinderella narrative. Maybe so. After all, some of the most enduring folktales have been based on mythology, my area of expertise. But I'm hoping David will buy into this story, make the noble gesture, and fight for my love. Sooner rather than later. He's two years older than me. After forty, his sperm count will nosedive. Aside from Sam, most of my other girlfriends are on the same page. Last summer, David and I went to wedding after wedding. I had hoped he'd get the hint.

I've four boxes on my hypothetical spreadsheet, all with subcategories, and I've checked off the first box: #1 Find the right guy.

Three remaining checkpoints are yet to be completed: #2 Get married by thirty-three. #3 Have baby number one by thirty-five. #4 Have baby number two by thirty-eight.

Right guy is relative. David's not perfect. He's disorganized, seems to thrive in chaos, and is oftentimes silly. So in these regards, as I've told my friends, I'd be settling if we married.

But Mom warned I'd never find perfection, and David is a smart, ambitious, and objective man. Everyone settles anyway, she says, when married. He's right-brained, and I am left, which makes for a healthy, ambidextrous relationship. Mom encourages our partnership—we've been together four years, and I know she wants grandchildren.

She continues to foot the bills for my counselor, and once a month, Mom and I meet with the therapist together. Mom confided she could never undo the wrongs she made while raising me—speaking badly of my father, shuffling me off to boarding school, marrying men I barely knew. But by being a wonderful mother to me now, and a loving grandmother to my children, she could try. Her words made me cry.

I know how hurtful divorce is for a kid—I could be the poster child for a broken home. But I'm not doomed to repeat the patterns set by my parents' messy marriage. Although they began as lovers and ended up spiteful enemies, I won't repeat those mistakes. Compared with other guys I've dated, David *is* Prince Charming.

Prime example—Graham Palmer. That dude was the most disgusting man I've ever slept with. In the end, he lied about having Babcia's rosary—just to bait me into seeing him. He wanted to rekindle our relationship. Mom spoke to his mother, who said it was never in their safe to begin with. He probably hocked it to finance a coke deal. I will never forgive him for stealing the only tangible keepsake I had from my grandmother.

David's never had addiction issues and is incapable of pulling such a vindictive stunt. My moodiness confuses him, but he loves me and is supportive of my ambitions. Those are the critical boxes that must be checked on a relationship spreadsheet.

A knock on the door interrupts my thoughts. Lella sticks her head through a crack. "Your interview's here."

"Thanks, Lella. Send her in." She opens the door and smiles at the woman, gesturing that she enter.

I stand and unfold the spare chair that leans against the wall. Smiling, I extend my hand. She hesitates before accepting my handshake. Slim and small boned, she's of average height and wears a simple brown dress belted at the waist with a thin black belt. I motion her to sit and then turn my chair to face her.

Without a word, she hands me her job application.

I glance at the page. "Sylvia Atkins. Sylvia. What a lovely name." She fidgets in her seat, the corners of her mouth trembling as she attempts a smile. The color of her skin is tawny, like creamy rolls baked to perfection, and her gold-streaked hair is pulled back into a thick ponytail.

"Thank you," she mumbles, and sits on her hands to stifle their shake. She lowers her heart-shaped face, and her next words are spoken into her lap. "My mother thought so, too."

"Have you had any experience waiting tables?"

She looks up. "No. I haven't. Brenda said she told you about me, that I don't have no real job experience." I note the cracked front tooth as she speaks.

Her social worker at the High Hope Center, Brenda, informed Sam and me of her past life. The center, three blocks down on La Grande, provides shelter and medical treatment. It also offers psychiatric evaluation, counseling, and job training for the small percentage of woman who can escape prostitution.

Sam and I don't have the details of her past life, but Sylvia's CliffsNotes are gut-wrenching enough. She's from Detroit and was sold to be used for sex when she was a teenager. I've always thought sex slavery was a third-world problem, but Brenda says it happens all around us in America, in plain sight.

Sex trafficking is a booming industry in Michigan—most of its victims are kids between the ages of twelve and seventeen. Life expectancy for girls such as Sylvia is seven years after enslavement due to STDs, drug overdose, suicide, and homicide. Sylvia is twenty years of age, and quite fortunate to have escaped after four years of abuse.

Sam and I want to help girls like Sylvia. We've been inspired by Uriah's garden project to find more ways to help younger people through our restaurant. She'd be our first hire from High Hope, so this interview will be atypical. Her application states no more than her name and the center's contact information, but that's what Brenda told us to expect. She said she had an instinct about Sylvia—that she was a quick study and eager to move forward. There was a flicker of a flame not yet snuffed out. Sylvia catches my eye and solemnly holds my gaze. I see not a flicker but a fire, burning and bright.

"Brenda did tell me about your past. She's a regular here, is passionate about the center, and works nonstop finding suitable opportunities for all of you."

"Isn't she wonderful? For the first time since I was a kid, I've been given permission to hope." Her eyes light up as a bulb turned on. "To hope high. Like the center's name." When speaking, she opens her mouth only as far as necessary.

"She also spoke highly of you." I lean into my desk, trying to catch her eyes. "I'm so sorry for what you've gone through."

She looks down, studying her nails. "I'm trying to take my life back." A few seconds pass, and she looks up and peers at me. "That's not the truth. I'm trying to become another person." She pinches her lips together between her teeth.

"You know," she continues, "when I was a little girl, my parents took me every Sunday, after church, to a place that reminds me of this one." She sighs. "Welcome Home. I always thought I'd like to run me a restaurant like this."

In her face I see the darling little girl she must have been, and when she mentioned her parents, there wasn't a trace of bitterness in her voice. Circumstances of childhood are so random, so often bitterly cruel. What lurks in her past? How could anyone sell their child?

"If I had that place, I'd serve my favorite foods," she continues. "Like pork chops, twice-stuffed potatoes, beans and rice. Mama also made sponge cake and coconut pie. So light and creamy. She said the flavors reminded her of when she was a girl in Brazil." She turns her face to the side, avoiding my gaze. "When things took a bad turn for my folks, my dream disappeared."

Working here would be an abrupt change from the brutality to which Sylvia's become accustomed. And to compound potential emotional issues, Brenda said she had the equivalent of a sixth-grade education. "Waiting tables is stressful, Sylvia," I tell her. "It requires certain skills. Like juggling orders and remembering the names of regulars. And you have to be pleasant, even when someone's slobbering, undisciplined child hurls salad in your face."

She looks at me with a half smile, as if to say, *Is that all you can dish out?* Actually, no, I think, it's not.

"Most of our customers are totally cool and have become friends, but sometimes the devil's spawn waltzes through the door." Sylvia giggles, which eggs me on. "I'm talking about those entitled finger-clicking jerks who expect you to drop everything and bow and scrape to their every demand. You know who they are the second they slither through the door, demanding a six-top for two people, informing us our soundtrack annoys." I pantomime the type, snapping my fingers.

"And take this gem from yesterday," I continue, raising my brows. "A customer couldn't bother to get off her cell phone while Lella, our waiter, was taking her order. And then the woman was pissed her cream soda was too sweet. She'd been saying *extra sweet* to the other person on the line when Lella thought she was ordering her drink. Geez, Louise. Put away your phone already so we can get your order right."

"You've got to be kidding," Sylvia says, her mouth agape.

"I'm just getting started," I say, happy she's loosening up.

"You'll have to memorize every ingredient we use in each of our recipes," I continue, "including the daily specials. Several of our customers have food allergies. On the other hand, some of their issues, we're sure, are invented. And Yelp. For God's sake, don't get me started on Yelp."

"OK, I won't, I won't," she says, her eyes crinkling in amusement. "I'll bet it's fun to work here. And I'm a fast learner."

Despite my levity in describing the job, the risk of hiring this woman is real. But I must. The diner must. Detroit demands more from all of its residents—the diner's no exception.

"The job is yours, Sylvia. I'll need Brenda to fill out these forms, but you can start training next Monday. If that's convenient for your schedule."

She smiles broadly, stretching her lips to cover her teeth; her mouth a thin, pink line on the horizon.

"Thank you so much. You'll find I'm a quick learner and hard worker."

We stand and shake hands. The health care we provide our employees doesn't include dental. But maybe there are clinics in the area that provide free services to those without resources. If not, I've had the same dentist since childhood, and she's friends with Mom. An oral surgeon is also a regular at the diner. One way or another, I'll help her with those teeth.

Closing my eyes, I unleash a prayer to the universe: *Please, let her work out.*

Chapter Eleven

Sam

The alarm on my phone rings its soft chime. Ugh. Six fifteen. Rise and shine. I untangle myself from the heat of Uriah's arms and place a pillow over my head. I'm an eight-hour girl and had only five hours of sleep last night. Maybe I can grab a nap before tonight. We're hosting a party here in the backyard after dusk. David's building a bonfire.

I sigh, toss the pillow toward the foot of the bed, and stretch. I could never get back to sleep, anyway. I'm not used to having a man in my bed. Lying on the floor, Hero is stretched out in the same direction as me. His head rests on his paws, a watchful eye, rimmed in pink, turned up to catch my gaze. Poor baby. He's not used to a man, either. Leaning my torso off the edge of the mattress, I scratch him behind his ears, which perk at my touch.

My movements and the tinkling chimes wake Uriah, who groans, pulling me back into his arms. He smells like lemon verbena, my favorite soap scent. I smile. We showered together after our lovemaking last night.

I whisper into his ear. "I'm supposed to remind you that you've got to decorate your classroom for Halloween. You're also bringing the kids to the diner after lunch. I made them cookies decorated as pumpkins."

"You have such a beautiful mouth," he replies, tracing the contour of my lips. His touch is feathery as he pulls a few strands of hair from my mouth.

I roll out of bed and stumble to the bureau to silence the alarm. I turn toward Uriah, scrolling through texts.

He rubs his eye and then shifts to regard me, placing a couple of pillows under his head. Smiling, his eyes travel up and down my body. He clears his throat. "What's the status of Welcome Home?" His Southern drawl is so pronounced first thing in the morning; sometimes I can't understand what's he's saying.

I fumble with my phone. "The last message from Braydon was written an hour ago. Let me see here. Yippee!" I exclaim, throwing my arms into the air. "We survived Devil's Night without incident. Score one for the diner."

Last night the staff each took a three-hour shift from 6:00 p.m. to 6:00 a.m., every light blazing. We made sandwiches and coffee throughout the evening for anyone who volunteered to assist the authorities. Uriah, Addie, David, and I hung out from six to nine, which was intentional. I want David and Uriah to get to know each other better.

Thanks to our vigilance, a juvenile curfew, and heavy police and fire patrol, we've made it through the night. To be fair, it's not like we're a target, although with the enemies we're collecting, we may as well be. October 30 in Detroit is Devil's Night. The moniker is linked with widespread arson. With all of the abandoned homes in the area, there's plenty of kindling. The fires have dwindled tenfold through the years, but they haven't stopped. Everyone's on guard.

"I'll make coffee."

He falls back into the comforter, stretching out his glorious body. "Aaaah. Your coffee's an aphrodisiac."

146

"That, Uriah, is the last thing you need right now." I laugh. "Save it for later."

I grab my robe and blow him a kiss before walking to the kitchen. Hero follows on my heels, his nails clicking on the hardwood floor. After replenishing his bowls with water and dog food, I make the coffee—a blend I'm always tweaking—listening to Uriah's movements in my bedroom. I should feel exhausted, but his presence in my home make me feels like I've tapped into an electric current. He enters the kitchen, half-dressed in the same clothes he wore yesterday. After buttoning his woolen plaid shirt, he tucks it into his jeans.

"Will you have time to run back to your place and change before school?"

He shakes his head. "I should have remembered to bring a change of clothes. But the kids don't notice what I wear. Maybe I'll throw a sheet over my shoulders. Pretend I'm a ghost." I move toward him, my lips parted. He slides his hands down my torso. Hero, tail tucked between his legs, trots over and whines. Uriah glances down at the dog. "Poor fella. Competing for your affection must be hard on him."

He bends to scratch him around the ears. I chuckle. "Not at all. He's trying to tell you that he's the one who always plays the ghost. Maybe I should rethink the costume he's wearing today."

"Which is . . . ?"

"You'll see. Hero and Bon Temps will both be suited up to fit the occasion."

He pulls me into him and kisses me. His hardness pushes against my thigh. I wish we had the day off. Mornings are luxurious when we don't have to work. "Stay over after the party tonight," I whisper. "And bring an extra set of clothing. I'll keep it in my closet."

I dislike Uriah's place. Aside from a few kids' drawings that he's tacked on the wall, and a framed picture of his parents on his dresser, the apartment feels as cold and temporary as a hotel room.

He stares into my eyes. "I'll be counting the minutes." I hand him his coffee, and he walks to the door. Then he unbolts the locks, turns his head, and smiles. The door closes behind him in a soft thud. Hero gazes at the closed door, his tail now wagging, relieved the interloper has vanished. I laugh, bending to rub his neck. "Oh, Hero. You're my main guy. No man could ever replace you."

The ping of a text. We just said good-bye, and now he's texting me. Nice. The guy's got it bad. I straighten and retrieve my phone. My shoulders sag. It's only Addie, who wants to come down and have a quick cup before she gets ready for work. She must have heard his truck drive off.

No problem, I text. My tummy's still fluttering, and I'd rather savor the afterglow without her company. But whatever. At times like this, it would be nice to have my own place.

She walks into the kitchen, wearing her favorite robe: a robin's egg–blue silk kimono her mother brought her back from China. Her fluffy, whipped-cream bedroom slippers always remind me of toy poodles scuttling about the floor. I pour her a cup of coffee and place it on the counter.

She hands Hero a biscuit, which he gobbles from her palm in a gulp. "Morning, Hero. Morning, Sam." She slides onto a stool, and I take a seat beside her.

I catch her eye. "What's up, buttercup?" My cousin appears so delicate and vulnerable when she's not wearing that lipstick and mascara.

She takes a sip of coffee and smiles. "Mmmm. Cinnamon and chocolate, right?"

"Yep. This time I'm combining imports from Mexico with a Kenyan bean. All fair trade, of course." I glance at her. "Do you think the proportions are right?"

"It's heavenly." She sniffs at the brew, takes another sip, and looks up, catching my eye. "It was nice getting to know Uriah a bit better. A math teacher. Interesting. He seems to be so passionate about his work." She taps my side with her elbow and winks. "What a sexy drawl, right?"

I lean into her, placing my hand on her knee. "Addie. He asked if we could be exclusive." I grin. That threw water on any doubts I might have harbored that he thought I was hookup material. He's even seen me at my worst: fresh from work, exhausted, and smelling like trout.

She stares into her coffee, tapping her fingernail against the handle. "Hmmm." Her eyes flit toward me and then back to her coffee. "Don't you think you're falling into this relationship rather quickly?"

"What? We've been seeing each other since summer."

"But he sleeps over all the time."

"No, he doesn't. Just a couple of times a week." I press my lips together. Really? Is this any of her business? God, I'd like to have my own place.

"Before you know it, he'll be moving in." Twisting her ring, her eyes dart about the kitchen as she appears to be measuring her words. She straightens, then leans into me. "Remember your relationship with the barista? When I visited you in Manhattan, you two were living together. You told me you'd let him move in too soon in the relationship." She grabs my forearm. "You said that yourself. And you remember how it all came down."

My mouth falls open. "God, Addie. Andy is nothing like Uriah. Can't you see he's a very special man? You and David were chatting it up with him last night. You saw how he acts toward me, hanging on to every word I say." My head begins to throb. "Gosh. His arm was over my shoulder the entire evening. Besides, you and David live together."

"We dated three years before taking the plunge."

"That's because you worked in Ann Arbor, and he in Detroit." I straighten, folding my arms across my chest. This is nuts. She's worried about Kevin. Good lord. Why can't I conduct my love life without all this interference?

Searching my face, she flushes and pats my arm. "OK, Sam. No worries. We've got to get moving. I'll be down in twenty minutes." She finishes her coffee in a gulp and slides from the chair. "Let's take the bus together."

"Sounds like a plan." I don't offer her a refill.

 ∽

At work, most of the staff, including the dogs, are costumed in full regalia. Bon Temps strolls the garden sporting a sequined tulle tutu. Hero wears a Batman outfit, complete with bat-ear headdress and a black cape. Sun Beam's class, as well as Uriah's, will be trick-or-treating after lunch. The dressed-up dogs will amuse the kids. We're having a bonfire in the backyard of our house this evening.

Sylvia has been working full-time for two weeks and is the only staff person, besides Braydon and me, not dressed for the occasion. She began as a waiter but had issues counting back change. This could be corrected with time and training, but her lips barely opened when she was waiting on tables. Obviously, the poor thing was trying to hide those devastating teeth, but the customers had to lean toward her to hear what she was saying.

Prep work is a better fit for Sylvia. Her stiff back and pinched face relax in the kitchen. She makes herself useful backstage, scraping food off plates, washing dishes, and assisting with culinary tasks. She seems to have a knack for baking. It's hard not to watch her as she flutters about the kitchen. The poplin chef bandanna she wears on her head is decorated in a tapestry of orange, green, and yellow flowers. I imagine her as a rare tropical bird with a bright, ruffled plume trailing along a broken wing.

I've heard just the basics of her background. That her deceased father was American, and her Brazilian mother sold her after he died. A sharp pain seared through my gut when I heard this—she was just a kid. Sylvia's petite; she must have been a fragile girl. As bait on the end of a line, how did she survive? This peculiar woman piques my interest.

Braydon, Paul, and I have been training her, but most of her smiles are reserved for Braydon. I'm sure they identify with each other, having lost their families in their early teens. I pretend not to listen as I peel a bunch of onions, then chop them into a precise dice.

Braydon is showing Sylvia how to make Heartbreakers. These supersize chocolate-chip-and-walnut cookies have turned out to be our calling card. The cookies are tender and gooey on the inside and are encased in a crispy-crunchy, sugary brown crust. A few weeks after opening, a customer, swooning, licked the crumbs and chocolate from her fingers and declared, *That was so good, it breaks my heart.* And the name was born.

Sylvia retrieves containers filled with flour, sugar, baking soda, and baking powder from the dry-goods shelf and returns to the table and their conversation, paying no attention to my presence.

"I hear you, Braydon. I grew up in Rosedale Park. You know the area?"

"They've got some nice homes in that section of the city," he says as he measures ingredients and puts them in a large glass bowl.

Sylvia smiles. "I went to a regular school, and Dad worked as a mechanic in an auto shop." She pauses, inhaling sharply. "He called me his angel."

She studies the recipe in front of her for a minute, her lips pinched together. Then she scoops cake flour into a measuring cup, taps it on the counter, and holds it up to the light. "Since we're doubling the recipe, we'll need two cups, right?" Braydon nods and she adds it to the bowl. Then she begins whisking the ingredients together as if her life depends on it. She stops and points to the smooth, sandy mound. "That about right?"

"No lumps, Sylvia. It's perfect. You've got the strength of Jehovah in your right arm." She awards his comment with one of her rare smiles. I wonder if the two of them will find more than friendship with each other.

Braydon hands her the butter. "It must be cold, but not too cold. Your finger should be able to make a slight groove in it." She presses her forefinger into the pale yellow brick and then points to the indentation.

"Like that?"

"Perfect," Braydon responds, handing her a knife. "Now cut the butter into one-inch pieces and put it, along with both sugars, into the KitchenAid." She slices and then places the chunks, one by one, into the shining silver bowl. With the edge of a rubber spatula, she scrapes the sugars into the mixer, as well.

"Next, Sylvia, we beat them together until they're well combined. To turn on the machine, you push the lever forward, like this." He demonstrates the process and, after several seconds, turns it off. "See? Now it's one sticky mass."

She cranes her neck over the bowl. "Got it."

Picking up the recipe, she speaks aloud, her words directed to the sheet in front of her face. "Family life changed when Daddy's cancer began eating him alive. We had government assistance from his working in the military, but it wasn't enough. The disease sucked away our every last dime."

Braydon nods, smiling gently. Then he touches her wrist as if she were a wounded bird and points at a step in the recipe. "Beat four eggs into the mixture and then slowly add the flour blend."

She picks up an egg and, with a swift stroke, cracks it against the stainless rim. The yolk, a dazzling sunflower orange, oozes into the bowl. Smiling, she adds the remaining eggs to the batch. "I still can't get over the difference in color between a fresh-laid egg and one you'd buy in the grocery store." She tosses the shells into the compost, rubs her fingers on a dishcloth, and turns on the mixer to incorporate the eggs into the buttery mass. After turning it off, she pours a portion of the dry ingredients into the bowl and pushes the switch. She stares mesmerized at the churning machine, and in the whir and clatter of metal on metal, I can't follow their conversation. Braydon pulls the lever toward him, silencing the machine, and once again I hear their words.

"My parents died in a car accident when I was a kid," he says. "My aunt and uncle took me in, otherwise I'd have been an orphan. Didn't your grandparents help out? What about aunts or uncles?"

"Nope. Daddy's family was God-fearing Baptists, the Bible-thumping kind. I wouldn't recognize 'em if they walked right into this kitchen. They hated my mom and wrote us off. Said he'd lowered himself to marry a Latina." She turns to Braydon. " I'm so sorry you lost your parents. That must have been horrible. But you're lucky you had some relatives. How'd you learn to cook?"

"My parents taught me the basics when I was a kid, but we never used a recipe. Cooking must be programmed into our DNA. We were born knowing how to make food taste good. Especially barbecue. Man! My dad's pork had the smoke, bite, and sweet that made you glad to be alive. He converted an oil drum into a grill and smoked ribs over the same greasy asphalt every year during the Woodward Dream Cruise." He turns to regard me, a question in his eyes. "Can I do that at the diner, Sam? During the classic car parade?"

"Braydon, every idea you've brought to the table has helped improve Welcome Home. If you want to turn an oil drum into a barbecue pit, have at it." He appraises me with a half nod, a half smile, and turns to Sylvia.

"Welcome Home brings back the happy times when I was a boy and made supper with my folks. What about you? What brings you to this kitchen?"

Good, I think to myself. I'm curious to learn more about Sylvia's past. I try making myself invisible, a grease mark on the wall. I rummage through our vast collection of recipes, intent on the pages, forearms pressed into the cool stainless table.

"Mama was depressed enough when Daddy had cancer, but his death broke her for good," the woman continues. "We lost our house and had to move to a place that was a dump. To get electricity, we ran a line to our neighbor's. Our yard was littered with bald tires and rusted motor parts. But Mama said it was a palace compared to her home in

153

Rio. I suppose it was all she could think to say to cheer me up. The only time she smiled was when she was plastered. Soon enough, school for me was just a memory." Picking up the recipe, she squints to study it. "Oh, goodie. The fun part's next. We get to work the dough with our hands." She places the recipe next to the knife rack.

"There was this one woman in a suit with eyebrows plucked thin and penciled in black. She stopped by our house from time to time, claimin' she was on her way to the office. Sometimes she gave a twenty to Mama. Said it was for food. But we all knew it would go to the bottle." She pours chocolate chips and toasted walnuts into measuring cups.

"This went on, I guess," she continues, "a couple of weeks. After a while, she told Mama she could help me. Said she knew a nice couple who could be my foster parents. She said she'd take Mama to visit me every Sunday. Said I'd be homeschooled and learn life skills, even share a computer with the other foster kids. I figured if I could get on track, I could find a job and straighten Mama out, too."

Her face pales as she stares at Braydon, running her tongue across her lips. "I was sure wrong about that." She grabs a spatula, scrapes the batter from the bowl onto the prep table and then turns to regard him.

"She gave Mama five one-hundred-dollar bills. We'd never seen so much cash. When I hugged Mama good-bye, I never dreamed it would be for the last time. I'd just turned fifteen—that was five years ago. Brenda had the police go to that house to get her some help, but she's gone. I need to find her." She swipes an eye with the back of her hand. "That is, if she's still alive."

Braydon looks at her, his face pensive as he bites his lower lip. "I've a feeling she is. I've a feeling you'll see your mother again. So what happened next?"

"Foster parents?" Sylvia smirks. "What a joke. There weren't no foster parents. There was just Bobby. And three other girls. I became a part of his ring. He gave me pills, which I pretended to swallow but hid beneath my tongue. When no one was looking, I spit them out. I saw what they were doing to the other girls." She pours the walnuts on top of the batter and then lowers the empty cup on the table so hard it hits the stainless with a jolting clang. "Every day I worked the streets. Bobby laid his fist into my mouth when I didn't earn my daily quota." Her fingers dart to her lips in a subtle, telling reflex.

I swallow, choking back a gag. Sylvia pulls sordid images from her past as casually as one would wipe a smudge off their cheek.

"I quit counting the men," she continues, straightening her bandanna, "and began counting the ways I could kill myself."

Beads of sweat pop above Braydon's brow, and his eyes dart side to side like a trapped animal. He appears derailed, even panicked for a couple of seconds. Then, he composes himself, straightening his apron. He studies Sylvia, wearing an odd expression I don't recognize as she works the chocolate and nuts into the dough.

"Next," he says, "let's divide the batter into twenty-four balls. Then we freeze and then partially thaw them before baking. That step is the secret behind their delectable gooey center and exterior crispy crunch."

Her mouth, a splinter above her chin, is like a blade slice in a nectarine. She nods at Braydon and continues. "At first I was afraid of the men, but that fear went away in time. It was the mirror that terrified me—I was scared of what I'd see." She presses her palms into her cheeks. "That my face had disappeared, or something."

Braydon glances sideways toward Sylvia, lines drawn across his forehead. His lips twitch. "So how did you escape?"

She wipes her hands on her apron.

"After I got used to the job, I began to feel a sliver of hope. I quit thinking about killing myself and began thinking of ways to escape." Hands on her hips, she scowls at the prep table strewn with ingredients and empty dishes caked with batter. "Mercy. What a mess." Dirty bowls and spoons clang together as she stacks them on a sheet pan. She carries them to the sink and places them into the first compartment of the dishwater, then returns to the table.

"A year or so passed, and luck came a-calling. Rumor had it the dude who hung out on Cass and Temple was an undercover cop. Bobby warned me not to approach him. Said if I didn't like my teeth now, I sure wouldn't like them after he was done with me." Running a wet rag across the counter, she folds her lips over her teeth, darting a glance at Braydon. "The other girls were terrified of Bobby. But not me. I made my plan. I propositioned the officer and was thrown in jail. The best place I'd been since Daddy died. Turned out they'd been trying to break up Bobby's ring for close to a year."

Braydon shakes his head. "Street slime should be hosed into the sewer."

"It scared the starch out of me when I was on the witness stand, facing him, telling the court what he made me do. His eyes were like black coals, burning into me. Branding me. As if he still owned me. I make myself sick worrying he'll get one of his goons to find me. Torture me. Or worse." Biting her lower lip, her face tightens.

"Not a chance, Sylvia. You're safe now." For a moment, his eyes lock on her profile, and then his gaze returns to the heap of cookie dough, dotted with nuts and chocolate bits.

"The judge gave him a twelve-year sentence. And I'll never forget his words. He said Bobby wasn't selling only sex, he was also selling misery. He said no prison sentence could ever do justice for the pain and suffering us girls experienced, and, hopefully, his imprisonment would be the start of our healing. So I was sent to the High Hope Center, along with the rest of the women." She shrugs, glancing around the room. "And here I am. In this kitchen."

Heads down, they begin shaping the batter with the palms of their hands. I can't understand the rest of their conversation. But I've already heard too much.

I cover the onions in plastic wrap, put them in the fridge, and head toward the pantry shelf. Studying the various ingredients, I summon inspiration for pork cutlets, trying to turn my mind off to the ugliness of this poor girl's past. My consolation is her support team. The authorities, social workers, doctors, and lawyers who've given their time and hearts to help get her to this place. We'd known we wanted to help; we just didn't know how much help people needed.

I return to the prep table, a tub of bread crumbs, mustard, and dried herbs in my hands. Sylvia and Braydon are there, two sheet pans in front of them, large balls of cookie dough lined up in tidy rows.

Sylvia looks at me, her eyes soft and welcoming, as if she'd just been talking about the weather. The air is filled with the ethereal scents of sugar, chocolate, and toasted walnuts from a recently thawed batch now baking in the oven.

"Am I jabbering too much?" she asks.

I smile, checking the time on my smartphone. "Not at all. It takes me forty minutes to prep a batch of Heartbreakers. It took you only thirty-five. After a stint in the freezer, they'll be ready to bake to Instagrammable perfection. Good job, Sylvia."

"I hope it's OK to talk about my past. Brenda encourages me to grieve. She says if I tell my story, talk about my nightmare with friends I can trust, one day the sting might get lost in the telling."

"Running from emotions is more painful than feeling and expressing them. Welcome Home's your family, Sylvia. You can talk about your story as much as you like."

Her considering me a friend suffuses me with warmth, but at the same time, I feel uncomfortable about my comparably charmed life. Will I ever feel at ease around this woman—qualified to help her at all?

She removes a whisk from the mixing bowl, and moist batter clings to the metal. A bit of dough drops onto her forearm, and she stares at it, her eyes glistening as if she's tranquilized. In a flash, she brings her arm to her mouth, licks it off, and then her eyes tumble into mine, as a pair of dice being rolled onto a table.

"Making Heartbreakers suits me fine."

◠◞

Addie

The full harvest moon rises quickly, her blood-orange color native to October Michigan skies. She beams across our group as a search-light, her glint reflected in a large piece of broken glass in our neighbor Curtis's backyard. A draft of wood smoke travels from the bonfire, burning my eyes, and it spreads across the black night air in a porous cinder shade. The air is crisp with autumn, and it's refreshing—not as chilly as it usually is this late in the season.

Jévon is walking toward our circle, his hand entwined with his lady friend's. Her full-lipped, angular face is as finely wrought as a carving of ebony art, and they glide through the moonlight with catlike grace. Jévon nods at us, and Lella retrieves two additional chairs, sliding them into our circle around the flames.

Paul and Tim, in a heated conversation about the recent city coun-cil elections, smile at the couple and pass them a bottle of bourbon. Kevin mentioned he'd be partying at a downtown bar. I suspected that would be his plan after learning that Sam and Uriah would be a part of our group. I wish Sam could have waited a bit longer before rubbing her new dude in his face. And their relationship is going way too fast. This morning I tried to warn her, even after David advised me to leave it alone; that train had left the station.

"Bad news about the Banksy piece, right?" David says, addressing Jévon.

"One hundred and ten thou's not chump change, man, but esti-mates were it could fetch four hundred thousand at auction. That's a big gap."

"Imagine," Sam says. "One day a piece of graffiti is tucked away in dystopia, water lapping its base. A few years down the road, it's eye candy in some Beverly Hills mansion. Too weird."

"The gallery's official word is the proceeds will help fund an East Side art space with a focus on kids," Jévon says.

"That's all fine and dandy, but the piece is part of the soul of Detroit. It should have stayed in our city," David says, shaking his head. "The gallery would have gained prestige hanging on to it. The mural would be a tourist attraction, pumping funds into the city."

"Water under the bridge, I guess. Maybe, one day, the new owners will bequeath it back," I say, crossing my fingers.

David—his face and lips painted the pancake white of a vampire—begins strumming his guitar. Sam and Uriah rise, and bodies entwined, they slow dance around the outside of our circle. Hero clambers to all fours, and his head follows their movements. Sam said he enjoys wearing the costume of a hero, and we giggle watching the dog, so comical with those bat ears still affixed to his snow-white head.

Sitting next to David, I feel sexy and alluring, having vamped up the costume I wore at work. After showering, I traded my tattered black shirt for a corset that laces up the front and pushes up my breasts. I tied a clove of garlic around my neck to taunt my vampire and lined my eyes heavily in thick black kohl. I hope I've hit the gothic wench target.

David stops playing the Grateful Dead and, with an impish grin, kicks an orange glowing stick, which has strayed from the ring of tinder, back into the flames.

"Let's do some Johnny Cash—a little bad-boy music."

"You mean white-boy music, my man," Jévon laughs, squeezing the hand of his lovely partner.

David laughs and begins strumming the refrain from "Ring of Fire" on his guitar.

Sam pushes away from Uriah. "Ouch, you stepped on my foot." Placing her hands on her hips, she raises her chin.

"Johnny gets all the credit for the song. But it was his wife, June, who wrote it. She penned the lyrics when she was falling in love with him."

Sam begins to sing, circling the fire, her lovely soprano filling the night air as David accompanies her on his guitar.

"Johnny Cash is a legend, no doubt. But I'm with Sam on this one. I prefer listening to June," I say. "She sang the words with such emotion and passion. Her voice touches something deep."

David stops playing, and his voice is soft, his eyes rising to the moon. "God, June was a beauty in her day. The way Johnny looked at her in pictures, like he was ready to eat her alive. The song's about their forbidden love." His eyes slide down from the heavens, and he winks at me, his voice now a growl. "And we know that's a road paved to hell, the real Ring of Fire. Right?"

"She didn't set out to write a song about hell," Sam retorts, a tiny snarl in her voice. "June was writing a song about passion."

David plucks a string on his guitar, absentmindedly. "Passion, hell—one and the same."

Turning my head, my eyes burn into his. "Passion is your idea of hell?"

He puts down his guitar and inspects me up and down, mirth in his dancing blue eyes. "I'm talking *forbidden* passion—in-fi-de-li-ty—you sexy wench. June was married to another man when she wrote that song for Johnny. Move a little closer so we can bare our fangs at each other." Fitting rubber vampire teeth into his mouth, he pushes my hair away from my neck and attempts a clumsy bite.

What does David know about infidelity? I take the bottle from Tim, pour myself a short one, and then down the bourbon in a gulp. Its amber glow lights my chest.

༄

Close to midnight, everyone has left the gathering except for David and me. He stirs the embers and throws some branches into the pit, which reignites in a flash of flames.

I am mesmerized by the pops from the crackling flames. Every spitting spark sends a flash up my groin. I turn to look into David's eyes and, without blinking, yank away the garlic clove tied around my neck and unlace my corset. My breasts tumble into the moonlight, and I reach for his head, pressing it into the soft slopes of my flesh.

"Mmmmm, garlic," he murmurs.

"Sizzle it with bacon and I'll taste like carbonara."

His laughter is muffled between my boobs.

After a pause, I stagger to my feat, noticing that his face makeup has painted streaks across the pink of my nipples. Annoyance coils around my brain like a serpent, but I catch myself before frowning and rubbing it off. Forcing my smile of seduction, I grab his hands and lean back, encouraging him to stand.

The effects of alcohol have now subsided; I am in control of this performance. After instructing him to remove his shirt and shoes, I kneel and unzip his pants with my teeth, *that thing I do* in full swing. Removing his belt, I pull down his pants, and he kicks them off to the side of the fire glowing orange and red. It doesn't take a rocket scientist to know what men want. Knowledge of the basics suffices. I give him a minute or two of this head-on, full-throttle attention. Then I rise and push him into a chair. The curtain falls on act one.

After adjusting my thong and bunching the folds of my skirt around my hips, with caution, I step into the back openings of the arms of the chair. The ragged plastic scratches my thighs as I brace my heels into the ground behind him. Act two is to hex infidelity—a woman with shorter legs could never pull off this stunt.

Straddling him, my legs hooked in place, I give him a thousand-dollar lap dance. Then I worry the chair may fall backward. I could break my legs. I slow my gyrations and get off. He's so close to coming that I want to make this good.

Pausing a moment, I throw my skirt next to the coals and position myself atop the taffeta. I imagine how sultry I must look now, lying here, nipples erect from the evening chill, face made up as a vixen.

David stands, staggers, and falls to his knees. Ripping off the string of my thong, he shreds the lipstick-pink lace. Crap. Another thirty dollars sacrificed. Entering me, he whispers my name and comes after three heaving thrusts. He touches me, and I follow suit, moments after him.

Final curtain, applause, applause.

That was hot. But *that thing* is a lot of work.

"Baby girl, you care about me, dontcha," he whispers, stroking the side of my face. Goose bumps spread across my body, and I sandwich my hands, suddenly cold, in his armpits.

"I do."

Chapter Twelve

Sam

Sylvia pulls out a chair, taking a seat at the two-top where I'm working. Of late, she's been wearing her hair in two braids, which she pins up and wraps around her head. It's a darling style on her, reminding me of Heidi. Each week I notice something different about the woman, as if she's trying on new looks, searching for the person she wants to become.

"Brenda printed out the stuffing recipe you sent her." Her willowy frame appears to flutter in her seat. "Thank you, Sam. I'm so excited. This is the first Thanksgiving I've celebrated since Daddy died." Her wide-set eyes are luminous, dancing in anticipation.

"She wants to know if you could get us some fennel," she continues. "It's a part of the recipe, and the grocery store where we shop doesn't stock it."

"Of course, Sylvia. How many people will the recipe be serving?"

"There will be twenty or so people. It's mostly us women at High Hope. I guess we should triple the recipe."

"It would please me and Addie to be able to contribute to your celebration. I'll speak to Brenda about getting more ingredients to satisfy all of your recipes. After all, we buy everything wholesale."

Sun Beam walks toward the table, carrying a plate laden with a hunk of Ginger-Molasses Bundt Cake. Sylvia glances up at the child and pushes away from the table.

"Here, honey, take my seat. I've gotta get back to work."

Sylvia looks at me, her face flushed with happiness. "I'll let Brenda know. She'll be so pleased. Thanks, Sam." She scampers toward the kitchen.

Sun Beam places the dish on the table and sits down. After pushing the ridge of the latest fashion-forward pubescent frames against the bridge of her nose, she takes a bite.

"Yum. This is tasty," she mumbles, her mouth full of cake. She looks up, crumbs covering the sides of her mouth. "Whatcha working on?"

Her inquisitive expression, and those shining owl eyes never fail to lift my spirits. "Schedules. Holiday orders." I push the mound of paperwork toward her.

"I hope you have lots of vegetarian food on that menu. Last week I turned myself into one." She thumbs through the orders.

"You're a vegetarian?" I try to suppress my amusement.

"Uh-huh. Mama's irritated, says she's got enough work without creating special menus for me. But Granny said we could make vegetarian meals together. Her doctor says she needs to lose weight." She giggles. "This cake may be vegetarian, but I don't think Granny'd lose weight if she ate it."

"Not likely," I respond, and then point to Babcia's picture. "You know, Sun Beam, that's a picture of my grandmother when she was young. The cake you're eating is her recipe. Mind if I have a taste?"

She passes me the cake, and I help myself to a generous bite.

Mmmm. I close my eyes, and Babcia and I are again standing side by side in her sunny kitchen, beating ginger, lemon zest, butter, and sugar together. *You beat the mixture until it is pale,* she is telling me. I open my eyes and slide the plate back to Sun Beam, feeling a warmth radiate through my chest.

"My favorite memories are of us cooking together. But I've never been a vegetarian. So you're telling me you're not going to eat turkey on Thanksgiving?"

"Nope. Granny said she'd make a special trip to a natural store to find me some Tofurky."

She picks up the Thanksgiving special-order menu and reads aloud: "Hmmm. Wild-Mushroom Paté." She pronounces *paté* like *pate* and then narrows her eyes. "That got any meat in it?"

"Generally, patés"—I enunciate the *e* slowly, emphasizing the correct, double-syllabic pronunciation—"are filled with a variety of meat and liver." She wrinkles her nose.

"This one, however, is vegetarian." Her face lights up. "I'll make sure to send your mama home with a container for Thanksgiving."

I pick up a blank sheet and fill out an order. We've been booked for days, but we'd never refuse Sun Beam. She presses her forefinger into the plate to gather the last few crumbs and sticks her finger into her mouth. Then she takes her empty plate back across the floor and places it in the sink.

It's Saturday and the breakfast rush has passed—we've a short respite before lunch. I'm coordinating the schedules that will take us through Wednesday, the day before Thanksgiving. Miniature pumpkins and gourds splash their oranges, mustards, and greens over tables and up and down the counter. Most of the leaves have fallen from the trees, but the cabbages, kales, and sorrel are thriving in the kitchen garden.

Thanksgiving is my favorite holiday—what could be more joyous than a day celebrating family and food? But even though Uriah will be meeting my family at our traditional feast at the farm, this year my heart's not in it.

First the bad news. Another negative review was posted on Yelp. This time the concern wasn't about hair found in the soup or under-cooked chicken. The post, again anonymous, claimed the writer was employed at Detroit Water and Sewer.

They wrote that the pipes on East La Grande were antiquated and lead based, and the water coming into the diner was contaminated with lead. Tainted water is close to home. Flint, a nearby city, recently had a series of problems, culminating in lead poisoning the drinking water. It's been an unprecedented public health disaster. Young children, in particular, have been subjected to irreversible trauma.

We know for a fact this accusation is erroneous. Our water was tested as part of our purchase agreement. There were no traces of lead or any other toxins. It's poor form to feed the trolls by posting a response to negative comments. Acting defensive is a sign of weakness. But this was an outrageous post we couldn't ignore.

I framed and hung the water-test findings at the entry of the diner and invited Yelp readers to come and review the results. Mr. or Ms. Anonymous's sole intent was to scare away our patrons with false accusations. Ironically, we drummed up new customers who were delighted with our attentions to a sanitary environment. Addie and I are confident that the reviews are coming from one person. They're using different computers so it seems to be coming from different people, but the style's the same; all anonymous, with every letter capped.

Worrisome reviews aside, our business is booming. Even with the substantial increase in payroll, we've remained in the black.

Placing my head between my hands, I regard the stack of special orders. Not even one of our neighbors is a part of this pile. Three weeks ago, Braydon distributed the discount cards and menus to every barbershop and beauty shop within a two-mile radius. Quiche distributed cards to her congregation. But they still hold back. Because of the chilly temperatures, Angus has abandoned his rocker on the porch. Although he's never placed a foot through the diner's door, Braydon said he's pleased when he pays him a visit, a bag of goodies always in hand.

Customers are beginning to fill tables, and Lella's taking orders. Addie enters from a Detroit Mobility meeting with that virtuous save-the-city glimmer in her eyes, an annoying look I know so well. As she walks to the prep area, her jet-black coat billows about her ankle boots like a sail flapping in a storm. She sheds her outerwear and then grabs an apron. I collect the orders from Lella and retreat to the kitchen. Paul and Sylvia won't be able to handle this crowd on their own.

Sage-Crusted Pork Chops paired with Baked Apples Stuffed with Orange-Scented Sweet Potatoes are today's lunch special. Paul also made a Shaved Brussels Sprouts Salad, using the last of our harvest, for the side. The next two hours pass in a fury, and then the orders slow to a trickle.

Addie has retreated to the office, and Sylvia is washing dishes. I turn to Paul. "Can you take over from here? I'll start breaking down the cold station." He nods.

A couple of four-tops idle, and the counter is half-filled with customers sipping coffee. Sun Beam is having an animated conversation with some enormous, rough-cut, balding man. The seat can't contain his massive butt, which mushrooms off the stool on either side. Uneasiness creeps into my gut. Why does he seem familiar?

I approach the counter. My pulse quickens. It's Earl, the linen delivery guy. He's not wearing his uniform and cap, but I recognize those eyes, like red-rimmed saucers. Why the hell is he talking to her?

"May I help you?" I look him dead in the eyes, which are milky and vacant, set into morbidly pale skin. There's something off about him, but this fatheaded savage with his red-haired arms doesn't frighten me.

"This pretty young thing was just telling me how she wanted to be . . ." He turns to Sun Beam. "What did you call it?"

"A meteorologist. 'Cause I'm interested in weather. Especially hurricanes. And you also have to be good at math and science."

"That's right," he says, placing a swollen forefinger into his glass, stirring the ice cubes. He regards her in a way adults don't normally observe children. "You wanna be a weather girl. Wear one of dem tight dresses and shake and jiggle around a weather map."

His voice sounds scratchy, given to highs and lows, like an instrument being tuned. My nostrils twitch at the odor of his breath, which is the smell of decaying garbage. Bile rises in my throat. I snarl, spitting, "She wants to be a *scientist*."

"That so?" He swallows his drink in a gulp and rattles the ice in his glass. Pushing his face into mine, his voice rises, close to a shout. "You pissed at me? Can't a customer enjoy a cream soda while making friendly conversation with a cute little girl?" He places his palm on top of Sun Beam's hand.

Conversation in the diner stills. Quiche turns from the flattop, her tranquil expression turning to horror as she darts, spatula in hand, from the grill toward her daughter. Quiche was witness to our last scene with this man, and although he's out of uniform, his odd voice would be difficult to forget. I place my hand on her forearm to quiet her and nod at Sun Beam.

"Go to Addie."

Sun Beam, lower jaw trembling, slides her hand out from under the beast's, scoots off the stool, and runs toward the office.

Pressing his meaty palms into the counter to brace himself, he pushes his butt off the stool, leaning farther over the counter, wheezing with the exertion. I take two steps backward, toward the two-burner. This man is a giant.

"You gonna have that black bitch come curse me? Place another hex over my head? Why dontcha just come after me with that knife?" He points to a large stainless blade next to the grill. "I ain't scared. Go ahead. I dare you."

My voice is icy. "Sir. Please leave." He cuts a swift glance to the left and right of him. The patrons who've cashed out are scraping back chairs and sliding off stools, leaving the diner in a rush. One customer at a four-top is flapping her hands like a startled bird as her friends leave, pantomiming scribbling on a bill to get Lella's attention. Another man leaves twenty bucks for a ten-dollar half-empty plate and makes a swift exit. These days you never know what sort of lunatic will pull out a gun.

Lella drops a plate, which shatters on the floor in an explosive crash. She puts down her tray and stands frozen in place. For a few seconds, time is suspended, and the diner becomes eerily quiet. Earl's anger slides into a shrugging nonchalance.

"I weren't threatening nobody. Just wanted to have a neighborly chat." He thrusts a hand into his pocket, pulls out his wallet, and lays two dollar bills on the counter. "This should cover the cream soda, with a nickel left over. Keep the change."

As he slides his rear from the stool, Sylvia, Braydon, and Paul are entering from the kitchen. Wiping their hands on towels, uneasy looks cross their faces. Earl locks eyes with Sylvia, and she quickly looks away, anxiety drawing sharp creases in her forehead. When he leaves, I place the **CLOSED** sign on the door, even though it's thirty minutes early. I grab a rag from a sanitizer bucket and clean the stool he'd been sitting on with fierce, angry swipes. The stench of decaying garbage lingers.

"I told you they'd hunt me down," Sylvia cries, putting her face in her hands and shaking her head. She looks up, directing her words to me. "That's gotta be one of Bobby's buddies. Was he asking about me?"

I hurry toward her, shaking my head. "That man has nothing to do with you, Sylvia. It was Earl, that asshole from the linen company." My eyes hold steady her gaze. "I told you about that guy. Remember? A total nutcase. If he ever comes in here again, we'll all take turns with a bat. We'll bust him open like a piñata."

She attempts to smile, but the sides of her mouth twitch down, and her voice trembles. "One day they're gonna come lookin' for me. I just know it."

Addie and Sun Beam cross through the swinging doors, fingers entwined, and stand in the prep area. Quiche rushes to her daughter and bends down, her eyes hooded with relief and miserable resignation. Addie releases the girl's hand, and she falls into the arms of her mother.

"He didn't hurt me, Mama. He only touched my hand."

Quiche's cheeks are wet, her features twisted. Sun Beam is the reason she gets out of bed in the morning. This woman's had her share of heartache; I can see it in the dimness of her gaze. Another wound to etch its name across her face.

Sun Beam touches her mother's tears, her voice soft. "He was big and red. And he asked me what I wanted to be when I grew up."

I turn and walk toward the back of the room, kicking away pieces of the shattered plate. Addie follows.

"I'm calling Tory and Wall," she says, pulling out her smartphone. "I've got their private line on speed dial."

My heart's pounding, my entire being quivering with rage.

"Tory? Addie here. That linen delivery dude, Earl, paid us a visit. We told you about him. The lunatic who got so pissed about the delivery? He just threatened Sam and scared the crap out of all of us."

As Addie speaks, I take a deep breath, my optimism taking charge.

"No," Addie says in response to Tory. "It didn't have anything to do with the linen company. We never heard from them after you sent that letter. Obviously, Earl took the episode personally. He's not playing with a full deck of cards." Addie nods, pressing the phone to her ear. "Perfect. A restraining order. Thank God. And, yes, we've a diner full of witnesses."

A sharp knock on the window. Startled, Addie and I jump. It's Kevin, files in hand.

"Tory, I'll call you back," she whispers breathlessly into the phone. "Sam and I can supply details later."

I unlock the door. Kevin enters the room, lines of worry crinkling his forehead.

"Closed already? What's going on?" Everyone, except for myself, is frozen in place, like a group of startled animals paralyzed in the headlights of an oncoming truck. Addie's words break the stillness.

"That linen guy stopped by and gave us a little scare. Frightened our customers away, too." At once everyone begins talking, telling their version of the story.

Kevin nods at me and walks to Addie, handing her the folder. It would have been more natural if he'd handed it to me since I was standing beside him. But, whatever. Sylvia slumps onto a counter stool, Braydon pours her a glass of water, and Kevin takes a seat at her side. Their eyes meet, and he cups his hands over hers, which are shaking. I'm sure he's saying something soothing to calm her down. That's the kind of guy he is.

Walking back through the corridor to the kitchen, I cross paths with Addie and remark, "Water under the bridge." Her head jerks back, as if I'd slapped her, and she follows me, close on my heels.

"Is that all this is to you? Water under the bridge? Our car is crossing the Mackinac Bridge, and it's collapsing beneath us. We're about to drown, Sam. We're about to drown." She paces around the prep table, disoriented and out of control, swatting her hands in front of her, as if she were batting back flies.

"A creep is preying on Sun Beam right beneath our nose." She leans into the counter, her nostrils flaring. "And then there are the Yelpers. Who could this person, who could these people, be?"

She looks about the room wildly and snaps her fingers. "Oh. Yes. Angus. We can't forget him. Let's never forget Angus." She slams her fists into the counter. "Why does everyone hate us?" Her face is tight, eyes pinched into slits.

I glare at her from across the table, the glinting stainless splintering my vision. Anger blooms in my chest. I close my hands into fists, digging my nails into my palms.

"You've got to settle down, Addie." My voice is close to shouting, breaking under the stress. "You're always the voice of doom. Everyone does not hate us. And if you go batshit crazy, our business will self-destruct for real. You've got to get over yourself. The world, your neighbors, David, me . . . your parents. No one owes you anything, Addie. Anything."

I lower my voice almost to a whisper, speaking between clenched teeth. "And I can't be the only one strong enough to keep the pieces glued together while you're out spinning your wheels in therapy."

She clutches the lip of the counter, leaning into the table, her voice taunting and crackling with irony. "Oh, Sam. Always the toughie. Always so cool. Performing so well under stress. Especially with your latest man, all touchy-feely, not caring who you run over. I think it's you—I think it's *you* who I'm beginning to hate."

Red splotches stain her cheeks, and she looks at me, shaking her head as if trying to take back her last word. But the word hangs low and heavy in the air, like an ominous storm cloud.

"Sorry for that," she mumbles, looking down at the floor. But the damage has been done. My first cousin, my closest friend and ally, just told me she hates me.

I regard her dropped head, hair hanging down and covering her face like a veil. My mouth is agape, for once at a loss for words.

At that moment, Jessie stalks into the kitchen. "What's all this screaming and hollering about?" She looks from me to Addie.

"Braydon got me up to speed on my ragman." She kicks the toe of her boot against the leg of the prep table. "He needs to be served a cold helping of karma," she says, her voice booming.

She looks out the window, and her next words are murmured, as if she's thinking out loud. "I never did put a curse on him. I need to be damn sure it's justified, or the hex will turn back on me. Thought a little scare would do the job." She drums her fingers on the table. "But it's time to reconsider."

Grim-lipped, she crosses her arms over the bib of her overalls, and her voice returns to its usual thunder. "But in the meantime, you two are scaring your team even worse. Quiche took little Sun Beam home after you two lit into each other."

Her words diffuse the charged atmosphere in the kitchen, and Addie and I exchange looks, ashamed we contributed to making their bad day even worse.

"There's some bad juju moving about this kitchen, swimming round and round." Jessie sniffs the air, and her eyes cloud, as if something is taking possession of her. She circles the space and lifts up a cutting board, as if seeing apparitions visible only to her. Then, her gaze returns to us, the gold spheres surrounding her pupils beaming.

"What the hell are you girls fighting about? Don't you have enough problems without killing each other?"

"We were arguing about . . ." My voice trails off, raw and pained. What were we fighting about? I can't remember what caused our argument, but our words wounded each other, and we are standing here, faced off, blood on our hands.

"It was stupid, really stupid," Addie says, breaking the silence, her eyes on mine, glistening with tears. My first impulse is to hug her, but I stop myself. She said she hated me. I wonder how long that sentiment was locked and loaded in the barrel. Something has started that neither of us can stop.

With care, Jessie removes two strings of glass beads from around her neck and holds them in our direction.

"These are healing beads, which will balance your positive and negative energy flow. But they're not yours to keep, because they're precious to me. I'm lending 'em to you ladies because they've done their job for me, and they want to keep working." Gazing at the beads, her eyes soften. It's a look I've never seen worn on Jessie.

"Their origin is the West Coast of Africa. The slave coast, where millions of my people were exported and traded for tobacco and alcohol."

She turns the beads over in her hands, as if she were in a trance. "These beads are my birthright and used in the practice of African healing."

The beads dangle, falling between her outstretched fingers. The sunlight streams through their crystal cuts, making rainbow prisms that shimmer across the kitchen, glittering like fairy dust.

"Here's your prescription. Wear them every day, under your shirts, touching the skin above your heart." Her eyes scan our bodies up and down, as if taking measurements. "I think four to five weeks should do the job. But take 'em off before you sleep. Lay them stretched out beside you on your bed stand." She shoots us a warning glance. "They reclaim their energy at night."

Addie and I nod furiously at Jessie, like obedient school children when disciplined by their headmistress.

"I'm not done yet," she says, her voice fierce, the apricot glow in her eyes casting a warning flare. "Make sure you also drink half a cup of Braydon's potlikker every day. Stir a tablespoon of my hot sauce into the brew for good measure."

Jessie says her hot sauce contains magic. A good thing. Because only sorcery can rectify the damage made by the hurricane that swept through the diner today.

Chapter Thirteen

Addie

"Come on, Addie. It's Thanksgiving. It's bad enough we're not spending it together." David pours a cup of coffee and saunters to the counter. He's spending Thanksgiving at his parents' lake house. He strokes my arm as if he were strumming his guitar. "Let's kiss and make up. We can pretend last night never happened."

"This whole relationship is about pretending, David." I shake and fold a dish towel that'd been crumpled on the counter. "Why do you refuse to discuss the future? Your silence is becoming too loud in my head." I face him, a vein throbbing in my temple. "It's too powerful and can only be diffused by conversation. If I keep shutting down, trying to keep the peace, I'm not being true to myself." I nod toward the shelf. "Thanks for the vase, but you know what I was hoping for." My mouth tightens into a stubborn line as my eyes scan the floors, looking for my shoes.

Yesterday was my thirty-second birthday. At work, Sylvia made a cake, but Sam and I—as always, since our fight—exchanged only enough words to get through the day. She did lend her beautiful voice to the birthday song, but I'm sure it wasn't meant to flatter me. Sam has a great voice, shaped by childhood chorale and a love of the dramatic, and she never misses an opportunity to perform.

No matter. The day was spent anticipating my evening with David.

In accordance with my hypothetical spreadsheet, I'm supposed to be married next year. I had a hunch last night he'd propose. But the prayed-for ring turned out to be an antique Deco vase. It was beautiful, but not a little square box.

My despondency after opening the gift triggered another argument, and in the heat of our anger with each other, I, once again, approached *the* conversation: Do we have a future together, and, if so, does that future include marriage and children? He shook his head and left the room.

My therapist, Dr. Lerner, tells me the worst time to bring up a sensitive subject is when emotions are running high. But bottled-up questions can't be healthy, either. I must know: am I wasting my time? We had reservations for dinner at a terrific new restaurant in the Eastern Market. We drank too much wine, patched things up as best we could, and avoided the topic for the remainder of the evening. Until now.

"And it's crazy we're not spending Thanksgiving together." I bend to retrieve my shoes beneath the coffee table. "Everything was set with Mom and Max. It's not fair. We spent last Thanksgiving with your folks."

"You know my mother. She plays the guilt card like a maestro. Keeps reminding me about Dad's surgery last year."

I straighten, pointing the stiletto heel toward his face. "Your mother thinks that conceding anything is a sign of weakness. Your dad's fine. He's back at work and plays tennis every day. And it's not as if your parents will be alone. Your sister will be joining them."

David's sister is single, gay, and swears she never wants a child. So David and I are our families' only hope for carrying forth the bloodline. Aware of the tension, his parents invited Mom and Max up to their home. Max refused the invitation. The Detroit Lions are playing the San Diego Chargers today, and he doesn't want to risk lousy reception. And, God forbid, their screen is less than forty-six inches.

I collapse onto the sofa, slip on my heels, and buckle the ankle straps. I look up and catch his eyes. "If we ever have kids, negotiating visiting which set of parents and when would be fraught with as much angst as the passage of the latest health-care bill."

David sits next to me, placing his hands on my shoulders. "I love us, Addie. Just the two of us. I'm not ready to make space in our relationship for anything more."

I look at him, my eyes swimming.

"At least not yet." He pulls my head into his chest. "You're upset about Sam. You're upset about the incident at the diner. You've got enough on your plate, baby girl. I want to be there for you while you're dealing with all of that. Why invite more tension into our lives?" Lowering his head, his eyes search my face. "You are the love of my life, Addie. Isn't that enough?"

I push him away. "No, David. It's not. There's always some excuse not to talk about where this relationship is going. We've been together four years. If our visions don't align . . ." I shake my head, wavering, not able to say the words.

He gapes at me in stunned silence, blinking rapidly.

I close my eyes. "I need your keys." David won't need his vehicle today. His sister's picking him up on her way from Toledo.

He stands and walks to the counter. I follow. Then he takes my clenched fist, pries it open, and places the keys in my palm. They feel cold and sharp. My insides twist.

"Be safe, Addie." He crams his hands into the pockets of his pajama pants, bites his lower lip, and heads toward the bathroom. I hear the buzz of his electric razor as I put on my coat and grab the pies from the fridge.

❦

I turn left onto Chrysler, then merge onto the Edsel Ford Freeway, heading east toward Grosse Pointe.

I'm beginning to hate the holidays. Why do they have to be so complex? The game begins late afternoon. While Max is watching, Mom and I can sip wine and play catch-up, minus discussing the issues I'm having with David. I told her about my fight with Sam. That upset her enough and is enough drama for her to handle.

My thoughts turn to Sam. After Jessie calmed us down and gave us the beads, we reached a tentative truce. But when I address her, it's like I'm talking to a doorknob. She's shut down. I've launched an emotional flare and haven't a clue to as to where it will land. For the sake of our staff and business, we're trying to get through the busy holidays without further confrontation.

Every morning before work, I wait for Hero's howl, signaling that Sam's left the house. Thirty minutes later, I walk to the stop to catch the next bus. It's easy to avoid each other at the busy diner. But I'm haunted, and I feel her absence every waking moment.

The lake appears at intervals on my right, and I roll down the window. A gust of cold air stings my eyes, and I roll it back up. My life is spiraling out of control and not proceeding down the path I had planned. I can't let Max bait me into an argument today. It would upset Mom. I touch Jessie's healing beads inside my shirt. Let them work their magic.

The only good news is that Bio-Dad Michael and I celebrated my birthday by having lunch together yesterday. This was the first time he'd ever visited Welcome Home. He said he was proud and gave me the sweetest gift of a scrapbook containing every article ever written about the place. His gift speaks volumes—he's been with me in spirit ever since we've opened.

Babcia's picture was the first thing he noticed about our decor, and his expression—lips pinched and eyes brimming with tears—touched me. He apologized for his absence of late but described how his fortunes are changing. The catch-up classes he's been taking in e-commerce paid off. Several months ago, he was hired as an analyst for a promising tech start-up in Ann Arbor. That's his hometown, his college town, and a healthy place for Dad to be.

Dad is fifty-seven, but with his lean frame and full head of hair, he could pass for forty-five. His pressed dark suit has been replaced with a worn oxford shirt and khakis. The lines etched across his forehead have eased, and his laugh comes easy. He said he's on sabbatical from women and is considering buying a puppy. As a child, I'd begged him year after year for a dog. But he said they were too chaotic and would pee on his Berber. I got a goldfish instead.

I check my phone. Not a phone call, text, or e-mail from David, but I can't waltz over to crazy land. He'll be occupied with his sister on their drive. It's not right. David and I've been a couple for four years, and we aren't celebrating Thanksgiving together. Sam and Uriah have only been dating four months and will be feasting the day away together at the farm.

I make a sharp right onto Cadieux and press the radio knob. "Jingle Bell Rock" already? I turn it off. I can stomach only one holiday at a time. The side of my vision captures the blur of gleaming cars as I pass by the lot of Palmer Deluxe Auto, Graham's father's business. My chest steams with hate.

The second I pull into the driveway, Mom comes scampering out the front door, clapping her hands, her expression that of a five-year-old opening presents on Christmas morning. I step out of the truck and onto the running board before stepping down. Wearing heels, I don't want to break my ankle.

She runs into my arms, almost knocking me over anyway. I smile, my nasty mood brightening. Mental note: make an effort to see more of her outside shared therapy.

"I said I'd bring dessert, so I brought pies. One apple and the other pumpkin."

She lowers her voice. "Thanks for not getting fancy. Although he pretends to be the gourmand, he's really just meat and potatoes."

"I know, Mom, I know." My hands drop to her slim, belted waist, and I give a little pinch. "There's not even an ounce of flesh to grab."

I push her away, admiring her slim frame. "Honestly, you look great. Those yoga classes must be doing the trick."

"Yoga, Pilates, sashimi, and salads. Believe me, there's nothing graceful about aging. It's a full-time job. But I'm off work today, so let us eat pie," she says, with a Marie Antoinette flourish of her hand.

She smiles ear to ear, yet no lines crease her forehead or web the corners of her eyes. Three times a year she visits the miracle worker of Grosse Point. Dr. Patel administers the fountain of youth to area residents via syringes and needles—as long as they can stomach the bill.

Planning to sleep over, I grab my overnight bag from the side seat. I hand Mom my thermos containing a two-day dose of potlikker and hot sauce. "This is for me. Digestion issues." I pat my stomach, refraining from further comment. Jessie's potions and charms would freak her out. Mom's eyes slide to my abdomen, hope in her eyes.

"It's not what you think." I look down at my flat torso. "My cupboard is bare."

"All in good time." She squeezes my hand.

If only.

I lift the pies from the floor of the passenger side and hold them up for her inspection. "I'm concerned about the lattice-lace topping. Max's probably a full-crust guy, right?"

She shakes her head with an exasperated sigh. "He'll get over it."

Mom's a good cook, but ever since she married Max, all of her meals have been simple, void of texture and any flavor profile except for salt, pepper, and butter. Today she ordered a roasted turkey with the basic trimmings from a nearby grocery store.

The only *vegetables* I'll see will be in the casserole made from mushy green beans, canned mushrooms, and fried onions, which Max adores. I'd rather eat gas station sushi. Sam, however, will be enjoying roasted root vegetables turned into soups and side dishes, all harvested from their garden. Their turkey will have been raised eating grass on a neighbor's Manchester farm. Those birds always have such a rich, meaty flavor.

We walk into the house. Max is sitting in his favorite Danish modern chair—a splash of overripe tangerine. Chewing at the end of a cigar, he rests his laptop on his gut. He sips a red of some sort, the price of the bottle more money than I likely make in a week. He looks up as we enter.

"Financial markets are closed today. Doesn't make sense. If Wal-Mart's open, why not Wall Street?"

Nice to see you, too, Max, I think. What an asshole. He closes his computer and rises, and we give each other a strained half hug, bumping chins.

"How are the boys?" I ask. "Will you be seeing them over the holidays?" Oops. That little zinger escaped my mouth. His two sons live in Manhattan and rarely visit. Mom warned me it's a sore spot with him. He shrugs, his face colors, and his eyes blink twice as if to say, *Couldn't care less.* With his oval, balding head, stuck-out monkey ears, and that shiny black mustache, he reminds me of a Mr. Potato Head.

"I brought some desserts I think you'll enjoy." Mom nods at me, encouraged. Max glances at the pies.

"Did you weave those from scratch?" He snorts, smoke billowing out of his nostrils.

Mom stands next to him with the same frozen smile she always wears in his presence. She reminds me of a mannequin staring out of a storefront window at Versace. Mom is afraid of being alone, and that fear is her noose. I know the feeling.

"Let's have a glass of wine," she says, glancing at me. "Max brought an exceptional case of Zinfandel from Holiday Market. We all love a good Zin on Turkey Day, right?" She nods, her head bobbing as she looks from Max to me, gauging safe territory in a war zone.

Max and I remain silent, glancing about the room to avoid catching each other's eyes. "Well . . . ummm . . . let's get dinner on the table," she says with a sigh. We retreat to the kitchen.

181

We bow our heads for Mom's perfunctory blessing. It's always lengthy before a holiday meal, as if to make up for a year of ignoring the blessed Virgin.

And so she begins. "O God, we give you honor and glory for the manifold fruits of our fields . . ." I close my eyes.

At this very moment, Sun Beam, Quiche, and Granny are experimenting with their first vegetarian feast. Braydon's preparing turducken, a three-bird roast, for his aunt and uncle. Brenda and Sylvia are making a special meal for the women at the shelter—Sylvia's been rattling on about the recipes for days. And here I sit, next to Max, while David may as well be in another galaxy far, far away.

"Grant us a heart wide open to all of this beauty . . ."

I crack my eyes. Max's head is bowed, yet he fiddles with his phone resting atop the napkin in his lap. During dinner, I'll have to listen to his logic for burning down Detroit and turning it into a wine region, all the while eating overcooked turkey, a casserole that tastes like tin, and boxed mashed potatoes. *Diem perdidi*—another day wasted.

"And with thankful hearts we praise our God, who like a loving parent denies us no good thing."

Really? Tell that to the parents who can't even provide a safe neighborhood where their kids can play, much less a turkey dinner.

At once, I think of Angus. His son's in prison. Holidays must be hard for him. I hope Braydon took him a meal. Why didn't I think to suggest that? I feel Angus's loneliness, his isolation like a wound inside my chest. In sudden kinship with this man, I cast a prayer his way before raising my head.

Opening my eyes, they link to Mom's, lined in red and hooded in resignation. At this moment, I've never loved anyone as much as I love my mother.

"Amen."

Chapter Fourteen

Sam

There's several inches of white stuff on the ground, the first of the season. Lunch rush is over, the diner's closed, and the remaining staff is acting pathetic about the snow: ebullient, as if they'd never seen it before. Quiche told me the choir at the church is practicing for Gospel Fest, but it's impossible to hear their voices behind doors tightly secured to keep the cold air at bay. A headache surrounds my eyes in a web of pain, and I massage the temples with my fingertips.

Some kids made a snowman in front of the church and asked me for a carrot and beans to give Frosty a nose, mouth, and eyes. He's leering at me from across the street. *Wipe that silly grin off your face before I knock it off.*

It's the Friday before Christmas, and I'm at my usual perch, finalizing the menu for next week. Man oh man, am I wound tight. Since Thanksgiving, this place makes me feel like a hamster on a wheel: it's a continuous loop of stress. If we're not filling special orders for holiday parties, we're working crowd control on the floor. Maybe it's good we've been so busy. Addie and I are too exhausted to discuss the tensions in our relationship. Since our fight, I've yet to see her smile. When we're forced to speak, our conversation is strained.

In contradiction to my ill humor, Lella twirls around the tables in pirouettes, as graceful as Ginger Rogers. She balances a bus tub above her head, on the palm of her outstretched hand. I swallow a couple of aspirins from a bottle that I have of late kept stashed in my apron pocket.

"'I'm dreaming of a white Christmas,'" she sings, picking at the scab of my irritation. She was always the lead in her high-school musicals and is a terrific ballroom dancer. She stops to remove the dirty cups, saucers, and glasses remaining on the table next to mine and places them in the tub. A dreamlike look crosses her face. She raises a tweezed and darkened brow at me.

"Guess what?"

"What?" I say, in no mood for jokes.

"Come on. Guess. Something good came my way."

"You've been invited to compete in *Dancing with the Stars*?"

She puts down the dishes. "No. But maybe I'll audition someday. Guess again."

My voice rises. "Lella, I've got a mountain of paperwork to do before I can leave. Just tell me."

My tone deflates her balloon, and she frowns. "I thought you'd be excited for me."

She's worked her butt off in the past few weeks and still found time to make holiday gifts for everyone who works here, even Sun Beam. Each pottery bowl she crafted was customized with our unique sign of the Chinese zodiac.

I stand and give her a hug. "Sorry, Lella. You know I want to hear your news."

She smiles, all forgiveness. "Brett, at long last, asked me out on a date."

"How great," I say, forcing enthusiasm into my voice. I can't imagine a worse match. "It's what you've been wishing for the past few months."

"Seriously, it has been months. A long time to wait, right?" She pauses a moment to stare out the window. "So I gave up the ship, told myself he was too much of a suit anyway, and started trolling the dating sites."

I clap my hands, delighted with the memory.

"Remember the one from OkCupid? You met him here after your shift. He wore that Winnie-the-Pooh T-shirt."

"How could I forget? With his fuzzy facial hair, balloon gut, and brown button eyes, he even looked like a Pooh Bear." She pretends to shiver. "But not one I'd want to cuddle.

"And let's not forget the guy who took me to Sage," she adds. "Ordered the fifty-dollar Cab and a fillet stuffed with morels, and when the bill came made a great show of forgetting his wallet."

"What an ass. It's bad enough when they ask you out and request the waiter to split the tab. What ever happened to chivalry?"

"I know, I know, it's dead, right?" She removes a stick of gum from her apron pocket, unwraps it, and pops it into her mouth. It bugs me that she plays into the cliché of a gum-chewing waitress. She offers me a piece, and I decline. "So when I was ready to give up men and hang loose at my pottery wheel, Brett asked me out. And it was in such an adorable way."

"What did he do?" I can't imagine Mr. Buzz Cut Button-Up, with that uptight demeanor and a complexion like softened goat cheese, doing anything adorable.

"He wrote a note on the bill asking if he could take me out to dinner. I read it when I was at the register cashing him out. I caught his eye and gave him a thumbs-up. When I returned with his receipt, I handed him my number." She shrugs. "He called last night."

"Did you guys get to know each other better over the phone?"

"A little. He's four years older than me and lives in Livonia. An actual suburbanite. He's an accountant."

"So where does he work?"

"I'm not sure. Some company in Detroit. He says it's a family business." She tilts her head thoughtfully. "Family." She chews her gum slowly, with deliberation. "I like that."

When Lella waits tables, she chews gum aggressively, as if her life depended on it. You can always read her mood by the movement of her jaws. She blows and then pops a bubble between her front teeth, not noticing me flinch.

"He's a Red Wings fan and really close to his brother. They're thinking about buying a boat and keeping it on Lake St. Clair."

"You told me you hate hockey and boats. Hockey gives license to violence, and boats make you seasick. You shouldn't pretend to have interests you don't have. That will only end badly."

She sticks out her lower lip, and her eyes become flat and detached. "I didn't pretend anything. You know I'm not like that."

She returns to the task of cleaning tables, her jaws working a mile a minute. I regret shutting her down. I've always been a truth machine, and sometimes I'm hurtful. In fact, I'm beginning to sound like Addie. Who crowned me yenta, anyway?

"Sorry." I place my hand on her shoulder. "I'm off-kilter today. Acting like a weird, overprotective parent, I guess."

Lella steps away from the reach of my hand, placing dishes in the tub. She stacks them into towering, haphazard piles, and I worry that our treasured estate-sale finds may chip. Her words are directed to the dirty dishes. "I'm open to anything."

"Of course you are," I say, speaking quickly. "Even if you don't share similar interests now, you can let him know you're interested in learning new things."

She turns and nods at me, all smiles. The creases between her brows have ironed out, and her eyes are dancing, delighted in her belief that I'm coming around to her point of view.

"And I can always keep busy in the kitchen when games are on, right? I love to cook, and guys love to eat, especially when they're watching sports. Also, he and his brother are getting a motorboat. I only get sick on sailboats." The words spill from her mouth as bubbles from an uncorked bottle of champagne.

"Does he like to dance?" I ask, caught up in her enthusiasm. "I've always pictured you with someone who could spirit you across a ballroom floor."

"I didn't ask, but you know as well as I that the only men who can swing dance are over sixty." She sticks her index finger down her throat. "Gag. Or my gay pals," she adds. "Every time I've tried busting a move with a lover, I end up pissed off at him."

Girl's got a point. Halloween evening Uriah tried dancing with me around the fire, and the heel of his boot crushed my big toe.

She looks at me as if begging my blessing. "I'm so sick of going out with married men, hipsters, and guys who live in their van. A suit is just what the doctor ordered."

Hugging herself, she executes a tight spin. Her tattoo and hair—a twirling splash of orangy red—are testimony to her vigorous allure, an exclamation point following her chaotic reasoning.

It's sweet she's enraptured, but Lella doesn't strike me as the type of woman who'd appeal to a guy like Brett—a guy who orders the exact same thing every time he eats here. Her charm is her offbeat originality. On the other hand, the guy's single and has a stable job. The last one she dated was married, and the one prior to that tried moving in with her after the first date. This could be the best man that's come into her life for a long time.

She mimes dancing with a partner and trips over a chair. Maybe they'll balance each other. I'll give this the benefit of the doubt.

"Trust the universe, Lella. All of your past experience with men prepared you for something better. Maybe it's Brett."

"Thanks, Sam. I wanted your blessing."

My blessing? So I'm a yenta after all. In that case, a yenta gives direction. I hold her shoulders to keep her still and look into her eyes.

"Words of advice: Stay open. Don't make him a priority if he treats you as an option."

She nods vigorously.

"And something else, Lella. You've heard it before, but it never loses its punch: never sell your soul."

She winks at me and cracks her gum. Sometime soon I'll request the staff to give their gum chewing a rest when the diner's open. If your breath's bad, pop an Altoid.

She throws her arms around me, pulling me into her chest. I feel her heart pounding fast, as the flutter of wings. Then, her eyes return to the tub. She removes half of the dishes and, with care, places them into a second bus tub.

Glancing out the window, my dark mood lifts. Tonight we're hosting a holiday party at the house—a festive environment to blow off steam. I've been so frantically busy at work, it will also be the first time since Thanksgiving I can relax with Uriah. Thinking about him, I catch my breath.

I look toward the church, and the snow glistens under Frosty's adorable pose. I've got an old corncob pipe I'll bring to work tomorrow to stick in his cheeky, black-bean grin.

<9

Addie

"I'm always embroiled in some battle. I've been pissed off for so long now the feeling's a reflex. I don't waste a moment going straight for the jugular." My therapist nods. I reach for a Kleenex on the table beside my chair and dab the corners of my eyes.

"How could I have told Sam I hated her? I love her. She's like a sister. I was using Kevin as an excuse to lash out at her and had no right to do so. She's never led him on." As Dr. Lerner studies my face, I shift in my chair, trying to ease the knot in my stomach. I toss the tissue into the wastebasket half-filled with clouds of my spent grief.

"Perhaps we should examine some dynamics you might be feeling with your cousin. When we're envious of someone, we often demonize them. From what you've told me, Sam is carefree and optimistic. People are drawn to her charisma."

"You've got that right," I say. "She's everything I'm not."

"You tell me she had a happy childhood. The sort of childhood you were denied."

"It's true," I sigh, leaning back into the sleek leather. "During those summers I spent on their farm when I was a kid, I'd observe how happy her parents were."

"How did you feel about that?"

"Sad, I guess. Really sad. It was obvious how much they loved one another. Meanwhile, my parents—as you well know—were at each other's throats."

"Jealousy wears a stinky perfume." She pauses to regard me, her eyes peering over the top rim of her tortoiseshell frames. "Perhaps your words betrayed your true feelings. Your emotions, particularly after having had such a dreadful day, got in the way. If you dig beneath those words, Addie, maybe what you were really asking Sam to do was love you. It's something for you to think about before our next meeting. How are things going with your mother?"

"Honestly, Dr. Lerner." I clasp my hands together. "Since the three of us have been meeting, Mom and I've been making great strides in our relationship. I've never felt so close to her. In fact, we're having a quick lunch before I meet David."

She raises her brow, a question in her eyes. I sigh. "Yes. David. It's a struggle. Same ol', same ol'. Actually, I'm taking your advice. We're spending the afternoon taking a break from everything. The house, the diner, and all of our relationship issues. We're trying to connect on neutral ground, in a place that's special to us. I'll tell you how it works out the next time we meet." I take a sharp breath. "I mean the next time we speak alone. I don't want to upset my mother."

"Hmmm," says the doctor. "Give some more thought to that assumption. Your mother may be stronger than you realize."

She glances at the clock on her wall. "Time's up. It's eleven o'clock. Great progress, Addie." She fiddles with her phone. "I have both you and your mother in my calendar for the week after the new year."

"I look forward to our next visit." I stand to grab my coat and bag.

She nods and smiles, then removes her glasses. She rips open a wipe and begins to polish the lenses. She holds the frames into the light and, noticing a stubborn smudge, wipes the glasses again before adjusting them over the bridge of her nose. As always, she wears a dress. And, as always, it's black, as are her stockings and heels. With her thin frame and coiffed, shoulder-length red hair, she reminds me of a Bond girl. A good look, I think, for a therapist.

◠৩

David and I have entered the Polar Passage. In the interactive glass dome at the Detroit Zoo, our pals, two goliath polar bears, paddle the blue waters around us. Talina, the female, was born here ten years ago and is easy to distinguish because of a scar on her nose. Four years back, Nuka was introduced into her lair as a potential mate.

Having checked our troubles at the entry gate, we've entered a secret world of arctic waters, glacial ice, and creatures with slicked-back fur. This has always been our favorite place in winters past, when the kids are in school and we have the tunnel to ourselves.

A trout floats in the bottom of the currents, and Talina nose-dives to capture it in her mouth. Meanwhile, Nuka patrols the surface above. He is hemmed in between the atmosphere and sea, and his head and tiny ears are distorted in the prism of sunlight shining down through the water. His head turns slowly from side to side.

Talina is finished with her snack. Her hind legs push away from the bottom surface, and her curved black nails, affixed to massive, webbed paws, paddle toward us. Then, the calloused pads of her feet press against the pane as she climbs the wall to play with a bobbing soccer ball. Nuka joins the sport until they tire of the game, jettisoning back into the water's depths.

Witnessing the graceful performance of their underwater bulk, David and I are mesmerized by the couple's antics. The bears swim to us and press their front paws and black snouts into the glass. Their dark marble eyes stare into our own, as if we were the spectacle and they, the audience. For a few seconds, our heartbeats flow into theirs, and we become one with the creatures.

We giggle as the pair turns their gazes to each other, charcoal-lipped lovers seeming to say, *Check out the two across the glass, the ones in the black parkas and silly knit hats. How bored they must be just standing there, not playing.*

David kisses me. Not a peck, but serious mouth-to-mouth reconnaissance. It's been so long since he's kissed me like this . . . *You see, we're not bored. This is how we humans play, how we dance our dance.*

Today's the first day I've had off since Thanksgiving, and David played hooky from work so we could revisit this neutral ground. Our relationship is gasping, we've had no time to regroup since the quarrels on my birthday, and this is a place where we've always connected.

Since our argument on Thanksgiving, I've avoided the *M*—as in *marriage*—word. It's a word that must be spoken, but after the holidays. I'm prepared to part ways, but that frightens me. David's the love of my life. It would be so easy not to go there.

Sam and I, as well, have an unspoken truce. Although it's awkward, we're trying to get through the holidays without revisiting our fight. Tonight, we're hosting our first get-together in our home for staff and friends. David and I are making a cocktail punch before the guests arrive, and there are platters of food to be arranged.

I check my phone. "I guess we'd better get back."

David, reluctant to leave the sanctity of the bears, pulls me back into his arms. He speaks in a throaty whisper. "This was nice. I've missed us."

"I've missed us, too, David." I put his bristly cheeks between my mittened hands. "Let's get through the holidays and take it from there."

He gives a quick nod, and we exit the tunnel, the frigid air cutting into our faces, tearing our eyes.

∽

David removes the Supremes *Merry Christmas* vinyl from the record sleeve. It's an original Motown recording from 1965, and holding it by the edges, he places it on top of the turntable. After lifting the stylus, he lowers the needle onto the outer groove of the record, and the first song, "Rudolph the Red-Nosed Reindeer," ignites the party.

Whatever your faith, or lack thereof, everyone knows the lyrics to "Rudolph," and our party sings along. Lella prances around my living room—reindeer style—hands in front of her chest, curled under as paws. Sam joins her, placing her palms on Lella's hips, and waves the others to her side, shouting, "Let's make a reindeer train."

"What the heck," Braydon says, putting down his sugar cookie, a half-eaten sprinkle star. He joins the line. Sylvia adds herself behind Braydon, and Kevin follows Sylvia. She swivels her head to look over her shoulder and winks at him. We've had our suspicions about those two; a romance would be wonderful for both of them.

Sam makes a pouty face at Uriah, who sits in a nearby chair. "You sure you want me in your train?" he asks. "I've got two left feet, and your toe just healed from the last time we were dancing."

Sam laughs. "You've got a point, but we need a caboose." He joins the end of the line, grabs Kevin's hips, and the train begins hopping around the room to the old familiar tune.

Paul, Tim, Jévon, and his girlfriend are oblivious to their antics. Heads tightly knit, they're embroiled in conversation on the sofa and in chairs. David and I are at the kitchen counter, the watering hole for our guests, replenishing the punch bowl.

We've made a much-improved Singapore Sling, which is typically composed of gin, sweet-and-sour mix, and grenadine. We christened ours the Holiday Fling and used gin from a Detroit distillery; Cherry Heering, which is a Danish liquor; ginger syrup; and Prosecco. The chemistry of a proper punch is a craft, and it serves the purpose of lubricating a party just enough to swing, but without the worry someone will be wearing a lampshade.

The song's concluded, and the next track, "Santa Claus Is Coming to Town," does not kindle the same frivolity. Hands fall from hips as the reindeer train disbands. Its participants are now clustering around the punch bowl, refilling glasses, elbows knocking, smearing chutneys, cheese, and patés over breads, and forking smoked fish atop cucumber rounds.

Sylvia and Kevin take a seat next to me at the counter. Knees touching, they lose themselves in conversation as the festivity swirls around them. In the past few weeks, Kevin seems relaxed around Sam, his previous misery replaced with smiles. He told David that Sylvia is the strongest woman he's ever met. Kev's always been attracted to the tough and bold, like Sam.

And why not Sylvia? A lush, fiery personality has been emerging of late. And Kevin's so kind. The sort of guy who'd feed, nurture, and love a beaten stray. I turn my back to the pair, but I can hear their conversation as she speaks.

"Bits and pieces of the past, like snapshots in my mind, bubble up at the strangest times," she muses, her voice softening into a murmur.

It's difficult to hear their conversation now. I'm tempted to turn, to see if their knees are still touching; perhaps they're holding hands. Their voices rise, returning to a level where I can better eavesdrop.

"Kevin. You're the first man I've ever . . . I don't know."

"I'm the first guy you've ever dated."

She laughs, a tingle of silvery notes. "That word *date*. It sounds foreign to me." She sighs. "If we're dating, you must tell me a secret."

"A secret?" he asks.

"About your past."

I smile to myself. Kevin's so reserved. I've never heard him speak about himself.

"I've told you everything about me," he says, surprise in his voice. "As I recall, it only took a couple of minutes. I told you about my parents. My crazy sister."

Again, her lovely laughter. Like miniature tolling bells, it warms my heart to hear it.

"Here's a secret," Kevin says. "But you can't tell a soul."

"What?" The word sounds breathless.

"I'm a nerd."

"If you're a nerd, Kev, then I want to be one, too. You'll have to give me nerd lessons."

"No way." He laughs. "I'm not messing with perfection. I don't want anything about you to change. You're smart, fun to be with, and, I must say, the most beautiful woman in the world."

"You need to have your head examined."

I smile. They're definitely holding hands.

"Thank you, Kevin. But seriously. I want to change my past."

"You can't change the past, Sylvia. The past is always there and is a part of who you are. You may fight to try to push it away, but fighting it is the problem."

Sylvia doesn't reply. Now it's their eyes I'd like to observe. Kevin breaks the silence, his words deliberate yet ringing with passion.

"Your challenge is not to make it go away. Your challenge is acceptance, and it won't be easy." Kevin's such a serious, sensitive dude. He's gotta be loving this conversation. This is the sort of conversation I need to have with Mom. She lost her mother at a very young age. Money was tight when she was growing up, and she funded Michigan with scholarships and loans. That's all I know. It's like she erased the first eighteen years of her life.

Uncomfortable in the role of voyeur, I stand and note that several platters need replenishing. I carry them down the stairs; we're keeping the backup party food in Sam's fridge. She's at her kitchen counter, slotted spoon in hand, removing a cabbage roll—*gołąbki*. They've finished baking, and now she arranges them in a serving dish. I thought she was upstairs with Uriah. This is the first time we've been alone since our fight. My palms dampen, and, afraid to approach her, I stand in the doorway, unsure of what to do.

The cabbage smells like summer grass after a rain, and it melts into the unctuous aromas of tomato, garlic, beef, and fat. I'm transported to our grandmother's kitchen, this classic Polish recipe being one of the first we learned to make with her. The Bolesławiec terrine Sam used to bake the rolls is cobalt blue, decorated with a pattern of ferns. It's the same dish Babcia reserved for this recipe. What has it been—four, five years since the three of us were cooking together?

Sam looks up and her face tightens. She appears alarmed, taken aback. How could I have told her I hated her? Whatever feeling I'd had at that moment was tainted and a betrayal to us both. I feel the hot flush of shame staining my cheeks, and my eyes search my cousin's, begging for forgiveness.

She places a cabbage roll on a plate and spoons tomato sauce over the plump, pale-green pillow. With a knife, she divides it into three pieces. She stabs one of the fragments with the prongs of her fork and raises it to me, offering. I put the platters on the table beside her, then lift my lips toward the fork. I open my mouth, and then she feeds me, as if I were a child. And there is something sacred in her quiet movements. After I've taken the last bite, she bats the sauce that lingers on my mouth with a napkin.

"That taste, Sam." My words, spoken in a whisper, are clotted with nostalgia. "That taste. That's the taste of our memories."

"That's the taste of our love," she replies.

I pull out the beads from beneath my shirt and raise them to my lips, the tears tumbling from my eyes. I then drop them, lay my head against her shoulder, and cry into her arms, my nails digging into the wool of her sweater as she strokes my hair.

Chapter Fifteen

Sam

My heart feels as if it's been shattered, pricking my throat and eyes, threatening to break down the dam. There's another decision to be made, which may as well be made based on a coin toss.

But I keep this conflict to myself, inside the deepest fissure of my heart, blessing the January stillness of white. The decision to make is mine alone. If heads, I could very well lose the love of my life. If tails, I will certainly lose my city, my interest in the diner, and Addie will be devastated.

We took the morning off today, sleeping in, trying to recover from the holiday madness. Taking the bus to work, I glance sideways at my cousin. "I'm so freakin' relieved we can put this behind us. To have this tension between us resolved." Our shoulders bump together as the vehicle traverses the potholes and terrain of neglected asphalt.

Head down, she's absorbed in a book she keeps in a zippered pocket of her bag, retrieving it whenever she has a bit of downtime.

"No kidding," she murmurs, looking up from the pages with a smile. She wears a wan expression, which tells me her thoughts are elsewhere. I can't think of anything more to add; we've talked ourselves blue since our reconciliation. After a pause, she returns to her book. She seems content with the quiet between us. As she's thumbing through the pages, she stops to gaze at a verse. Her hands, now still, are resting on the page.

The cherished book, Patti Smith's *Woolgathering*, is the size of a folded dinner napkin. But to Addie it's a tome. The musings and prose, inspired by the author's life, surround a young girl discovering herself. The book was written when Ms. Smith—a writer, performer, and visual artist—lived on the outskirts of Detroit in the early nineties.

Ms. Smith said that the act of writing drew her away from her torpor. Addie says they're manna for her soul—daily meditations—offering her a childlike joy, pleasures she never knew growing up. All I know is that after she spends time in the company of these pages, she seems more content than when she returns from her therapist. The bill for those visits would pay our taxes and utilities. Fortunately, her mother is footing that one.

Addie once drove me to the area where Ms. Smith lived when writing the book. Addie's dream is to purchase a house with David in one of the surrounding neighborhoods. She pointed out several homes for sale in front of a canal emptying into Lake St. Clair. She said she'd lease her space in the home we currently share. I never confided my thoughts to Addie, barely allowing myself to whisper that same dream to myself: one day Uriah and I might, too, share our own little house. With shutters on the windows, it would be surrounded with gardens filled with not only vegetables but also columbine, daisies, and peonies.

Dreaming of a someday horizon is foreign turf for me; fantasies of a future that keeps its promise could deliver a painful backfire. Best to stay grounded in my comfort zone: the present. And yet . . .

The bus drops us off in front of the diner. Last month, we'd successfully petitioned the city to designate a stop several feet away from the front door.

Welcome Home has closed for the day, and a hefty, red-enameled pickup is the only vehicle that remains in the parking lot. A gold aluminum vanity plate centered between the headlights reads JESUS SAVES. The chrome-rimmed tires are the size of doughnuts on steroids—fast food's not the only consumable of supersize in the Motor City.

I unlock the door and we enter. The truck's owner, Theo, is part of a band of scruffy regulars who look like a brotherhood of outlaw bikers. They sit around a four-top, and Lella clears their table, which is piled with plates streaked with ketchup and bacon bits embedded in maple syrup.

At 1:00 p.m. on Friday, the whistle blows early at the window factory where they work, giving the men a jump start on their weekend. Buttermilk flapjacks are their TGIF ritual. Theo is the leader in their Bible studies and the most vociferous of the trio.

"Hey, Theo," I shout, forcing play into my voice. "Is Lella treating you with the disrespect you deserve? Did Quiche burn the bacon to your satisfaction?"

"Yes and yes," he says, putting his finger on a passage to mark its place. "Catching up with these fine ladies is the highlight of my week." He smiles at me, and then his head falls back to the page. He reads a verse to his pals: "'I have not come to call the righteous, but the sinners to repentance.'"

Seeing the men sitting here as they do every Friday afternoon pleases me. Their presence is an amusing antidote to the diner's regular stream of yuppies. Their conversation and manner are serious and respectable, incongruous with their appearance.

The men are grizzled, and hard-bitten fingers with dirty nails look clownish holding the dainty china cups from which they sip. Their voices are subdued as they take turns reading passages. They forged their newfound relationship with one another and Christ while spending time in the county pen. Jesus picked them up out of the gutter, they are eager to report, saving them from the temptations of the streets.

Theo, at least six feet three inches tall, has a ruddy facial complexion, patched and pocked. His thick black hair is oiled back to reveal comb marks flecked with dandruff. His eyes, however, are a thing of beauty, and remind me of Rocky Balboa. A fringe of dark lashes dance above deep pools of cobalt, and pale half moons resembling violet petals rest beneath them. Tattoos representing each stage of a complicated life cover much of his body, with the exception of his face. He has eight on his arms alone.

My favorite is the one on the top of his wrist: La Vie Est Absurde, meaning life is *absurd*. He informs that this tat was his first. At the age of thirteen, his father left his mother for her sister. The women were French Canadian, and a permanent installation of their native tongue in the young boy would not fly by unnoticed.

Also among them are two red hearts, each encasing a name of one of the children whom he's sired with different women. I get that his kids' names were tattooed in sentiment, and that's touching. But what was he thinking when branding the snake coiled around his throat? Lella told me it's his only tattoo that's prison ink, which could explain it. Between the tongue-lashing serpent, wife-beater T-shirt, and his denim jacket designed with a skull, Theo appears to be the social media director for a gang of Latino thugs. His look proclaims, *Don't mess with me. I roll with the big dawgs.*

On one swollen bicep, words are spelled out in Old English font: Fate Fell Short. He translates this to mean that believing in fate is a cop-out. Just because you were dealt a crap hand at birth, it doesn't mean you won't end up with a full house. It's up to the individual to figure out how to play the deal.

His most recent tattoo, Jesus Saves, is not the best conversation piece, either. All three of the men are eager to spread the gospel with anyone who'll give them an inch.

Theo grins at me after bookmarking a passage, which he'd boxed into a square. I'm curious to know which portion of the scriptures is so meaningful to him that he would pen red ink into his holy book. Lella, however, has warned me to steer clear of topics related to religion with the men. Therefore, I refrain. Nevertheless, a part of me hungers to take a seat with them and inquire if they've any passages that would soothe a ruffled soul.

Theo digs into the pocket of his frayed jeans. With a crooked smile and wink, he pulls out several crumbled bills and hands them to Lella. "We can't get you ladies to take a break even when your bosses are away."

I pat Theo on the back. "Good luck with that, boys. All of our women are taken." The last thing Quiche would ever want would be some tatted-up ex-con, Sylvia avoids excessive testosterone at all costs, and Lella seems content with her latest beau, Brett. Addie and I remain skeptical about that one. His mouth is as buttoned-up as the top collar of his shirt.

The men depart in a chorus of "See ya next Friday." I lock the door behind them and flip around the sign reading **OPEN** to **CLOSED**. Walking to the counter, I slide into a seat next to Sun Beam. Addie clears out the register and takes the cash and receipts to the office. Quiche is breaking down the flattop and salad bar, and Lella places the tray of dirty dishes beside the sink. She turns to face me.

"We've leftover cabbage rolls from today's special." She slides her order pad beneath the counter. "If you're hungry, lemme bring you a dish while it's hot."

"I'm starved, Lella. Thanks." A slant of late-day sun hits the stainless, ricocheting a blade of light into the corner of my eye, making me squint. My thoughts return to Uriah and the conversation we had last night; a feeling of heaviness invades my limbs. I turn to Sun Beam, sitting at my side, happy for the distraction.

"Sun Beam, precious Sun Beam, let your sun beam down on me." I cock my head at her and grin. "Got any new vegetarian recipes to share?"

"Don't distract her from homework," Quiche says, a bite in her voice. She levels a long side-look at her daughter as she carries dirty spatulas to the sink. "Unless you're asking her how many pies we'd need to bake to serve ninety customers. You can only speak to her of numbers. Only tables and formulas until she turns that grade around."

The blunt blades make loud clanging sounds as she drops them in the sink. "Little missy had me sign her report card last night. She bought home a C minus in math. Last semester it was an A, and now it's C minus."

She opens the reach-in, pulls out a jug of milk, and pours it into a glass. She places the glass next to Sun Beam's open textbook with such force the girl flinches. Her words are directed at her daughter's bowed head.

"I dreamed you up when I was scrubbing bathrooms at the Cracker Barrel and changing sheets at the Roadside Inn. I done everything in my power to get you educated right so you could make something of your life. And now you're bringing home a C minus? What happened to your dreams? You can't be a meteorologist if you make bad grades in math." She shakes her head. "A C is bad enough. But tacking on that minus? What you talking minus to me, girl? That minus is sniffin' a D, the flip side of an F."

Muttering the word *minus* repeatedly beneath her breath, she swats a rag at the soiled counters, shaking her head. Then, she returns to face Sun Beam, her eyes steely. With the tip of her forefinger, she lifts her daughter's chin. "I did not give you permission to go messin' with our dreams."

There's more to this story than a girl not doing her homework or paying attention in the classroom. Quiche told me her daughter's not sleeping well and has recurring nightmares about Earl, the fat-headed red beast. Most nights he visits her dreams, and she awakens screaming.

Quiche closes down her station, *tsk-tsking*, refilling squirt bottles of condiments with exaggerated gestures while her daughter remains quiet, head down. Her yellow pencil is stubby, indented with chew marks, and how it dangles between her fingers breaks my heart. If you ever want to level a community, first break down the kids.

My mind strips away the past seven weeks. Seven weeks back to that day in November when Earl approached the girl. The same day Addie and I had our falling-out. I only recall fragments of images: Earl's calloused finger stirring the cream soda before placing his palm on Sun Beam's hand; the red stains on Addie's cheeks after she hurled that dreadful word into my face, wounding me as if the word *hate* were a bullet.

Lella places a plate of cabbage rolls in front of me. With a fork and knife, I cut into the tender leaves, which release a sultry perfume trapped within a puff of steam. Their aroma transports me out of that craziness to December, into my kitchen with Addie, back to the fragrance of forgiveness.

I think of Angus. Braydon brought him a holiday gift basket filled with pickled vegetables from our summer harvest. He accepted our gift, but Braydon reported he barely said thank you. And not a peep from our other neighbors either. At a staff meeting, we decided it would be more effective if the discount cards were distributed by Quiche and Braydon—folks the community trusted. To date, no one has used them. But these concerns are a vanishing cloud compared to what might have been lost: my relationship with Addie. How can I bring up Uriah's proposition without her crumbling to pieces?

I turn to Sun Beam.

"Let's set up a time next week after school. Last year Uriah was your math teacher. He'll help you make sense out of all of these numbers."

Quiche stops.

"It takes a village to raise a kid, right?" I meet her eyes, which moisten beneath my words.

With the hint of a smile, she wipes her hands on her apron and returns to her task. As I finish my lunch, Sun Beam's fingers tighten around the pencil. She lifts the textbook, pulling it up in front of her face, scrutinizing, trying to discern the correct answer to a question.

"It's fractions giving me problems," the girl says, sighing as she places the book in front of her. "I don't get how to divide and multiply them."

I lean into the page and read: "'There are twelve cookies on a platter. Five-sixths of them are chocolate chip. How many chocolate chip cookies are on the plate?'"

I should know this answer. There's an easy way of figuring this out. While I'm chewing on the corner of a thumbnail, Addie storms onto the floor, an urgency about her step. She touches my shoulder and nods toward the office. She is as pasty as I've ever seen her; I wonder what bee's in her bonnet now? My heart sinks; the hits just keep on coming. I follow her into the office, and she closes the door behind us.

She hands me her smartphone, and I'm startled to see Babcia's picture on a Twitter account. I look up, sucking air between my teeth. She points to the words beneath her photo:

> Krystyna Jaworski
> @theunwelcomehomediner

"The troll has amped his vitriol," she says. "Thrown grease into the flames. He's created a fake profile of Babcia to hurt and humiliate us. This time he's hitting us below the belt." Her lower lip trembles as she turns to face me.

"Jévon just called and told me to check it out. The profile was created last week. She's following seven hundred people and already has three hundred and twenty-four followers. While eating here, the troll must have taken a picture of our photograph of Babcia. He made it look as if she's alive and tweeting this garbage. She's sent out twenty-one tweets so far—all of them denouncing me, you, and the diner. Have you noticed any creepy dudes who've been eating here lately?"

I pick up her phone and study it. "Maybe he is a she."

"Whoever, whatever it is, they know she's our grandmother, and they know she's Polish. Read her bio."

Two-timed Polish Granny Shocked by Granddaughter's Unwelcoming Diner. #unwelcomehomediner, #ashamedpolishgranny

Detroit
Joined January 2016

I look up into Addie's face. Her cheeks are crimson. "It couldn't be an employee," I say, trying to calm her down. "And no way would any regulars pull a stunt like this. I can't even imagine our neighbors hurting us in this cruel of a fashion."

"Read the latest." She taps at the screen.

Just had lunch at #Detroit's #unwelcomehomediner. The owners, my granddaughters, ignored me. My salad was wilted. The fish oversalted. Lol.

"Insults cloaked in anonymity are cowardly," I say, touching her forearm.

Addie stares at me, her eyes blinking furiously as if she were fighting back tears. "I'm using every bit of self-restraint to avoid being a drama queen. But between our neighbors and this troll, the magnitude of hate that you and I are expected to shoulder is crushing me."

I take a long, shuddering breath. "Maybe it's Earl."

"He hasn't hurled his girth about the diner since November. Aside from obscenities, the Cyclops can barely speak English, much less create a fake Twitter profile."

"Anyone who reads this will know it's absurd. A joke that some goon crafted to get his rocks off."

I tap the screen. "OK. Here's Twitter Support." I study the phone. "Impersonation is a violation. Here's the place to file the report. I'll do it now."

I sit at the desk and spend the next few minutes recording our case, while she organizes the files. Finished, I hand her the phone.

"OK, Addie. Done. I'm sure they'll take it down. I wonder if they can figure out who did this?"

"First he Yelps he found hair in his soup. Next his chicken's undercooked. The following month he writes that our water's tainted. Those lies were bad enough. But him impersonating our beautiful Babcia and making her say those awful things was effing cruel. Cruel like torturing animals is cruel. Where does this guy get off?"

This conversation is wigging me out. My head's pounding. "Let's drop it, Addie. It's over. And you keep inferring the troll's a man. It could just as easily be a woman." I shrug and change the subject. "How are things with you and David?"

She emits a long, shaky sigh. With the toe of her shoe she shuts a file drawer, then raises her brow. "David, I'm sure, feels like he's stuck between a rock and a hard place: marry me or lose me. It's like Odysseus when he had to choose whether to steer his ship past a dangerous whirlpool or a deadly sea monster."

I look at her blankly.

"You know, the Greek myth. *The Odyssey*?" Her mouth falls open and she gapes at me, as if amazed.

Where does she get off? Does she think I'm totally clueless? I sigh. "Of course I've heard of *The Odyssey*, Addie. *The Iliad*, too, by the way. And you're always carrying on about your Odysseus; you'd think he was Dave Grohl." I smirk. "But refresh me on the sea voyage. What did he decide to do? The captain, I mean."

"He chose the sea monster, Scylla, who he determined to be the lesser of two evils. And he saved the ship by sacrificing six men."

"So, if David proposes, you'll be morphing into a sea monster while he offs a bunch of dudes?" Cracking up, it feels good to laugh out loud for a change. I gasp for air. "I'll warn the guys they'd be wise to avoid David. Six men? That's brutal, Addie." My arms clutch together at my waist, and I laugh, snorting, trying to settle myself down. Sometimes the girl's pretty funny.

She raises her chin, setting her jaw. "Seriously, Sam. I'm making him a special dinner for Valentine's Day." Biting her lower lip, she sighs. "If he doesn't present me with a ring, or at the very least tell me he wants to get married, I may very well break up. And it will be awful. Life without David will be the worst possible thing." Shaking her head, she crosses her arms above her midriff, staring out the window.

At once I'm sobered. That resonates. Uriah has decided to move back to Tennessee. Last night he told me his mom's breast cancer has returned, and this time cancerous cells have been detected in some of her lymph nodes. His parents are considering renting an apartment close to the Vanderbilt-Ingram Cancer Center in Nashville, where she will be receiving state-of-the-art treatment. His dad is overwhelmed, and Uriah wants to be closer to his parents. He's worried sick about his mother.

He's been researching other jobs appropriate for him, and discovered an opening in an educational laboratory in Appalachia. It's a couple of hours southeast of Nashville. His plans are to turn in his resignation at Boggs and leave after the school year ends in June or earlier, if necessary. Land mine alert: he wants me to join him.

Join Uriah! I know we've been together for only five months, but when you know it, you know it. I pat the top of my cousin's hand, keeping these thoughts to myself. Thinking about moving is easy; telling Addie is unthinkable. If she lost David, and then I moved away . . . I sure hope David proposes to her on V Day.

"I try not to overthink the future, Addie," I say, avoiding her eyes. "What makes a solid, balanced relationship is when the man puts the toilet seat down, and the woman puts the toilet seat up."

My attempt at humor is being the self I'm most comfortable with, but in truth I'm not feeling so cavalier. For the first time in my life, I'm thinking about tomorrow. Obsessing, in fact. This diner's a pain in the ass. One problem goes away, and two pop up to take its place. Tennessee might be a good fit for a girl like me. They've got a great culture of music, food, and whiskey.

Uriah and I could knit a new life together. Help his mother. Because my life in Detroit is like a line of stitches that could very well unravel with one strong pull.

Chapter Sixteen

Addie

Nestled into the thick of winter, Valentine's Day arrives, and Welcome Home is drunk on love. Pink and red tinsel is strewn about chair backs, bowls filled with candy hearts have been placed on every table, and lacy cutout cupids are taped to the windows. We're playing an old mix of love songs from Dean Martin, Frank Sinatra, and Louis Armstrong.

Sundays are always the busiest day of the week, and today, because of the occasion, it's crazier than ever. We work the crowd in sync. Like intimate partners dancing a complicated tango, we know the direction to turn our heads according to the beat, never stepping on one another's toes. My job, as always, is to greet and seat, fill glasses with water, and ensure each of our guests is wearing a smile. That's easy today; the restaurant's filled with my favorite customers.

Tory and Wally have just entered and are lingering inside the front door. Wally holds a *Free Press* in his gloved hands. I take their coats and escort the couple to the last available two-top, seating them next to Theo and a woman I don't recognize.

Theo's cleaned up—I'll bet to impress this woman. His hair shines not with oil but from a fresh shampoo. His signature wife-beater and denim jacket have vanished, and his tats are now hidden beneath a beige cardigan. He looks up to smile, and the serpent head appears, hissing at me over the top of the turtleneck he wears. Surely, he regrets having that snake coiled around his throat 24-7. Today, it's the only indicator that this man has traipsed well outside suburbia.

"Tory, Wally. This is my friend Theo. But I haven't met you," I say to the woman, who might be attractive if she softened her liner and combed out the spikiness in her bleached hair. I extend my hand. "I'm Addie, and we're crazy about Theo. But I'm confused. He comes in only on Friday."

We shake hands. "I'm Nell. Theo and I attend the same church. Today we decided to go out for lunch." She looks like a seventies punk star, but there's sweetness in her voice; a softness, a whimsy. She smiles, glancing at Theo, and a fretwork of lines bracket her lips. She glances at her smartphone, which rests atop an almost empty pack of Marlboros. A chain smoker, no doubt. Aside from the casinos, Detroit, thank God, has a smoking ban in all restaurants. I'll bet she grew up Downriver, one of the more rough-cut areas of Wayne County. Although that's changing—there's cheap riverfront property and decent downtowns in some areas, which are ripe for picking.

Theo smiles. "She was impressed I knew the owner."

"Your place is cute," Nell says, looking around. She turns to Wally, who just unfolded his paper. Her brows lift and irises dart, scanning the headlines.

"Hey. No end to bad news," she says, her words directed to him. "What happened to Hater and Bullet? Man. What a scam." She shakes her head, and the corners of her lips turn down, indicating disgust. "How can we afford to clean up the city when our cops are the ones causing the problems?"

Wally raises his eyebrows, shrugs, and then turns to his wife. "She's referring to the Hansberry and Watson trial—the cops who made fake arrests, stealing drugs and money from their victims. Hater and Bullet are their street names."

Tory shakes her head, speaking to Nell. "Fortunately, it's isolated. I'm an attorney and know firsthand that most of our police force are honest and hardworking. Every day they take their lives into their hands to protect us. A couple of bad apples don't destroy the whole bunch."

She turns to Wally. "It's Valentine's Day, and you're not allowed to speak of anything aside from words of adoration directed towards your wife."

Wally folds up his paper, puts it beneath his chair, and places his palm over her hand. "Sorry about that, gorgeous."

Nell smiles. "Don't blame him. I shouldn't have brought it up. Still. It rankles me that our tax dollars—which are high enough, thank you very much—go towards those thugs' salaries."

She turns to Theo. "Oh. Happy Valentine's Day, by the way." She winks at him and pats his hand.

"You, too." Theo smiles. "Those cops will get theirs. 'If a man shall steal an ox, or a sheep, and kill it, or sell it, he shall restore five oxen for an ox, and four sheep for a sheep.'" He turns his palm over to hold her hand.

Love is in the air. Lella works the tables, taking orders. She wears red leggings and a billowy pink shirt beneath her apron, and her lips are painted into a sultry Cupid's-bow mouth. Sam's shaping flapjacks and any other malleable food into hearts, and she tinted the table water pink with red-and-white peppermints. With their check, guests receive a complimentary chocolate-dipped strawberry that Sylvia made.

The only thing not in sync with the spirit of the day is the smell. Valentine's Day should carry the fragrance of chocolate and sugar. But the air carries a latent aroma of burning leaves. After Twitter extinguished Babcia's profile, Jessie insisted we have a smudging ceremony.

Smudging, a practice used in many native cultures, involves burning sacred plants to create a smoke bath. Sage, in particular, possesses special healing and cleansing powers.

Last night, Sam and I indulged our friend, meeting her when evening settled and the sky was black. The ritual involved placing bundles of the dried leaves into four fireproof containers, which we placed in each corner of the dining area. Then, we lit the clumps. After the flames died down, the sage began to smolder, and soon after, the diner was filled with smoke.

Jessie, Sam, and I faced Babcia's picture, and Jessie demonstrated how to, with the palms of our hands, waft the smoke toward our hearts. As she chanted incantations, a breeze swirled up around us, which was creepy, but the draft, Jessie told us, was Babcia giving us her love and blessing. I remember glancing at Sam, and it could have been that her eyes were burning from the smoke, but tears were rolling down her cheeks. That girl seems off these days. She's never acted so emotional.

Then we opened the windows and fanned the smoke into the frigid air. Jessie claimed to see a khaki aura, which she said was the spirit of the troll. It was followed by a bubbling crimson foam, which she said was Earl. Both of them, she said, tumbled out of the window and into the night. To complete the cleansing, my cousin and I shared a jigger of potlikker. After the ceremony, we returned to Jessie the healing beads that we'd been wearing each day since late November. They've done their job. Sam has forgiven me.

Jessie's brand of woo-woo to chase away negative juju felt foreign to me. But something's working. Today I feel strong, balanced, and powerful. The Middle English word for heart is *cuer*, from which the word *courage* was adapted. It follows that courage is an appropriate sentiment on this day for lovers. If David doesn't tell me what I need to hear, I'll summon my goddess warrior. I will tell him that we're through.

A student of the classics, I loved the lessons taught in my Roman and Greek mythology classes. Before opening the diner this morning,

I gathered the ingredients for Steak Diane—a recipe inspired by the goddess Diana to bolster my newfound courage.

Steak Diane was made in ancient times using venison and served with a truffle sauce. The goddess Diana, however, inspired more than just a recipe. She was goddess of the hunt, the moon, and nature. Shakespeare romanticized her, and her image was carved into marble, Diana of Versailles, which is displayed at the Louvre.

Today, however, it's only the recipe that interests me. There are more recipes for a Diane sauce than Beyoncé had costume changes at Ford Field. And Diana, like Beyoncé, inspires me to envision myself a woman of strength and power, compassion and courage.

To make the dish, I'm using grass-fed beef from a local farm that supplies Welcome Home. I will serve it with my favorite pasta: Wild Mushroom Fettuccine. Monique, a friend and a regular patron of the diner, makes the pasta from scratch. My Diane sauce will be spooned over the beef and pasta. The dish will swirl with the luxurious flavors of beef juices, brandy, butter, and cream, which have been reduced to heart-throbbing essence. If only.

I lower my head, close my eyes, and whisper a prayer to whatever—whoever—may be listening.

❧

David's showering while I put the finishing touches on the sauce, stirring in a bit of exotica—Hawaiian black salt and truffle oil that Mom gave me for Christmas. Nina Simone's voice, accompanied by horns and strings, is playing in the background.

I join her voice singing "I Put a Spell on You," soft enough so that David won't hear my off-key vocals torture the verse. Listening to favorite music is my way of summoning the past, articulating what I'm feeling but can't express in conversation.

What I wouldn't give to have a voice like hers, or Sarah Vaughan's—even Sam's. These women have such staggering depth and range. I sing only when I'm alone. I stir minced parsley into my sauce. Not essential to the flavor, but the green bits will brighten the dish. In music, a grace note is like a garnish to the melody. Not necessary to the composition, but always a pleasant addition.

Composing a meal must be like composing verse: the emotional state of the writer governing the realm of passion in the music; the sentiments of the cook influencing the flavor profile of the menu. Tonight, I'm a woman in love with the courage of Diana. Sauce finished, I roll chocolate truffles into finely crushed peppercorns. Chocolate represents the sweetness of love, and pepper, the bite of strength. I should have thought to make a salad with green goddess dressing.

David places his fingers against the small of my back, and I turn. He's dapper tonight, more handsome than ever. His black slacks are just tight enough around his butt to buckle my knees and lower my resilience a notch. He wears a pale-pink linen shirt I don't recognize. I've always told him he looks great wearing pink, a color confident men pull off with panache. Does the fact that he purchased a new shirt mean he has something special to tell me?

I myself have pulled out all the stops. I wear a vintage red dress with a neckline revealing my décolletage. I baited the hook with a black silk bra, the edging of lace visible when I bend forward. My lipstick, as always, is painted with precision. Tonight, I upped the ante, curling and then coating my lashes three times with mascara.

I notice that his briefcase is on the floor beside the door, next to the entry, leaning against the wall. Every evening, the first thing he does when he comes home is put it on my desk in the bonus room. Maybe tonight he wants its contents nearby for ready access. Perhaps he has something special in that briefcase of his. I remove my apron, kick off my heels, and giggle, brushing up against him.

"Baby," David murmurs, after a long intoxicating kiss. His palms slide down my back, sending shivers up my spine. I grab a cloth and wipe my lipstick away from the sides of his mouth. He winks at me and turns to the counter. I watch him uncork a bottle of Bordeaux, then pour the red-black wine into a carafe. Lifting his nose, he sniffs the air, redolent of simmering beef. He turns to face me. His eyes trail up my legs and rest on my cleavage. "That thing you do."

Here we go. *That thing*, again. I should have pounded a shot of 5-hour ENERGY—there'll be no rest for the wicked this evening. My mouth twitches. But only if he earns it.

I arrange dinner on my favorite vintage porcelain—everyone's on their best behavior when dining off fine china. Then I center the plates between the linen napkins and cutlery. I glance about the room—at the discolored wood floors, the bare bulbs in the ceiling, the peeling layers of paint. Decadence in the ruins.

He pulls away my chair and I sit, crossing my legs, showing them off to their best advantage, not missing a beat in this provocative dance. He takes a seat and then raises his glass: "To Addie, my goddess, the sexiest, the most divine creature on heaven and earth."

I tip my glass to his and then lower my head, gazing up from under my lashes, to meet his eyes. Our movements synchronized, we bring the wine to our lips. I take a small sip, and the rich flavors swim in my mouth. As I swallow, the grace note strikes a tingle of raw, sensual delight.

David presses the fork prongs into a bite of the beef, swirling it in the sauce. I follow suit. Midway to my mouth, I admire the morsel. The steak is caramelized on the outside and a reddish pink in the center. Perfection. We bite into the meat at the same time, both of us chewing with concentration. The richness of the beef is mellowed with butter and cream and cut with the spike of brandy. The goddess would approve. Like me, David savors every cadence of an exemplary meal.

"Are you still enjoying that class?" I twirl a mound of pasta around the fork. "I forgot what it's called. Some guy's name." David's in school full-time this winter. January through March is the slowest time of year at his dad's company.

He laughs. "You're talking about TEM—The Entrepreneurial Manager." Placing his fork on the plate, he catches my eye. "At this point we're working on strategies for identifying opportunities and obtaining the resources for development. That's an oversimplification, of course. But the course has my brain churning."

His eyes sparkle and he speaks quickly. "All around us, all of these homes, these abandoned buildings, are being sold for peanuts. I've been talking to Dad. We've got our eyes on an investment possibility."

My pulse quickens. I showed him the string of houses for sale by the canal a few weeks ago. I lean into him, smiling broadly.

"There's this one warehouse in the Renaissance Zone. Because of the location, it would be tax-free for any business to move into. Dad's company could move there, and then we'd get other . . ."

His words fall into a vacuum as my excitement deflates; there's a hum in my ears, and I can't hear his voice. Moistening my lips, I crank up a pleased expression, trying to return to the moment.

"Oh, David," I say when he becomes quiet, looking at me as if expecting a reaction. I take his hand. "That sounds like a great investment. And it gives you and your dad a forum for more personal interaction."

"It's been great. The two of us driving around, looking at real estate. Your sharing the work you've been doing with your mom has been valuable to me. It helps me understand Dad. Where he's coming from. Of course, we never dig deep. And he would never consider therapy."

I smile at the thought of David's father spilling his guts to Dr. Lerner.

He winks. "But for the first time ever, we've been talking about Mom and her control issues." He raises his eyebrows. "We're even joking about it. As you know, getting a laugh out of Dad's a very big deal. We've decided to let her spin in her own orbit, and we'll stay out of it."

I tilt my head, truly happy that he and his dad are making progress. "That's wonderful, David."

He reaches across the table to stroke my hand. "It's thanks to you, baby girl. But let's get back to us." His eyes burrow into mine, then dart to my cleavage before returning to catch my gaze. "Have I ever told you that you've the most beautiful eyes in the world?"

Eyes? Yeah right. Here we go. Back to clichés. Every time he tries to express his love, it sounds like a line pulled from *Sleepless in Seattle*. But it's Valentine's Day. So I let him ramble on and on about his adoration of me in platitudes, trying not to roll my eyes. I'll work on him later. Once we're married. I cross my fingers under the table.

After finishing the main course, he stands and kisses me again before taking our plates to the sink. I watch him, admiring the muscles that flex beneath his shirt as he rinses off the last traces of sauce. Then he walks to the entryway and reaches for his briefcase. My heart pounds. He brings it to the table. Opening the latch, he reaches in, pulling out—what? A deck of tickets? Wearing that rascal smile, he takes his seat and hands them to me: a set of black-and-red-checked cards in the shape of a billfold decorated with pink hearts.

"Happy Valentine's Day, you stunning wench. A dozen scratch tickets to shake up our sex life."

"Sex game scratch cards? Is this a joke?" I stare at them in horror, the wonder of the evening crashing down around my ankles.

"Funny, huh? I saw them at the liquor store and couldn't resist. All we have to do is scratch off the designs. The pose that's revealed will demonstrate the sex position we'll try." He stares at my cleavage, raises his eyebrows, and then his eyes return to my face. "They won't last long the way we go at it. Perfect, right?"

He's really stepped in it this time. I throw the cards on the floor, shaking my head, furious. "This is clearly for you."

He squirms. "What about the roses?" He points at the flowers on the counter, which I'd arranged in the Deco vase. "Those were for you. What about the wine—my buying your favorite champagne? Here. Lemme grab it." In an instant, he pushes away from the table, stands, and turns toward the fridge. I jump from my chair and grab his forearm to stop him.

His jaw tightens as he shakes away my arm. "I hate this holiday. It's packed with so much pressure. I gave you roses. I bought wine and champagne. The money I spent for those alone would feed a family for a month." His face slackens, and he looks at the floor. "I thought you'd think the cards were funny, Addie." His voice now is that of a hurt little boy.

My face contorts as I fight back the tears, summoning the strength of Diana. I won't fall off my horse. I will play this out.

I bite the bottom of my lip. My next question, and his answer, will direct the course of my life.

"Will you marry me, David? Will you marry me?" The word *marry*, to my ears, sounds like the bleat of a sheep. *Maah, maah.* My face grows hot. This is not the way this was supposed to go down.

"Addie." He slides his palms down my hair and then clenches it into his fists. "Addie. Baby girl. I love you with a fierceness I've never felt for anyone, for anything, in my life. But aren't we good the way we are? I've thought about marriage—don't get me wrong. And if I ever got married, it would be to you. But I don't know, Addie. I just don't know. I feel like you're pushing me into a corner."

My voice rises. "I've told you, David. I've been telling you for over a year. I can't stay with you unless I know you're in it for the long haul." As I stare at him, he sighs and his shoulders sag, a now-familiar reaction to my words. "All I want, David, is to get married, to have children, and to be loved by you forever."

His face shifts with an array of emotions—passion, bewilderment, distress. His body is emitting an animal scent, an unfamiliar pheromone that goads me on.

"I'm not getting what I need from this relationship. I love you, David. But our bond is broken, and I'm not sure if it can be fixed. We're not on the same page. What I need is that my partner be on the exact sentence, the exact word as myself, when it comes to our future."

"Baby. I agree. We're out of sync. You're beginning to sound more controlling than my mother, and I'm crumbling under your expectations."

His face is clouded with grief, and I don't recognize the man I love. I'm trembling from head to toe. In the storm of our relationship, I've been hauling out a lifeline to this man, playing out the spool bit by bit with each passing day. I just cut bait and smell the agony. Something in this room is dying.

"We're over, David. 'David and Addie' are through." My words hit me like a punch in the gut, and I want to burst into tears. We've always been the envy of our friends, everyone pointing to our intimate, long-lasting relationship as an anomaly—an exhibit, say, in the Detroit Institute of Art that kept the museum afloat. But now, the Diego Riveras are leaving the building. Blinking my eyes, swallowing the lump in my throat, I pinch my lips together, as utter grief rages through my soul. I pull him into me so close I can feel his heart pounding. A hardening in his groin presses against my thighs. I want him to have me right now, on the floor. I want him to pound away the pain. I press my lips into his, deepening our passion in a kiss.

He pushes me away, shaking his head. His confusion, his torment, his lust have dissolved into anger.

"I'm not something to be checked off your to-do list, Addie. I'm flesh and blood. I'll pack a suitcase. I've gotta get out of here. Leave. Right now." He looks about the room, as an animal trapped in a cage.

"I'll stay with Kevin until I figure out my next step," he continues, his words breathless, rushed. "I'll get the rest of my stuff later. I understand what you need, what you want me to say to you. But I can't say the words if I don't feel them in my heart." He pounds a clenched fist into his chest. "I love you so much. But I've been forgetting who I am, how to breathe on my own. I'm suffocating."

He pins me with his gaze for a moment before he turns to grab his cell phone. "It kills me to even look at you."

Staggering into the bedroom, he closes the door behind him. Muffled words behind the door. A suitcase being dragged out of the closet. Drawers opening and shutting. The sounds of good-bye. I collapse on the sofa and expect the tears to fall, but my eyes remain dry.

He opens the door, coat on, suitcase in hand, and approaches me as if in a trance. He touches my cheek. And then . . . he leaves.

Prone on the sofa, I stare at the closed door. David's left me. It's simple, really. He couldn't give me what I needed, so I asked him to leave. And then he left. Wait. No. I didn't ask him to leave. I wanted him to make love with me. We've had these arguments before. They've never turned into this. I remind him of his mother? Oh my God. What have I done?

Feet dragging, I weave into my bedroom. There, I peel off my dress, unhook my bra, then pull off my thong—pathetic armor of the seductress. I fall into bed and curl into a fetal position. Where are my tears? I glance at the clock—it's just after ten. It's too late to call Mom because Max would be pissed.

Several minutes pass. I'm numb from the onslaught of grief and wine. Loneliness, like tiny spiders, crawls about my sheets. I slip into my robe, retreat to the office, and open my mythology textbook. Sitting down, I turn to the page about Diana.

Diana was one of the three maiden goddesses who swore never to marry, and she was true to her word.

I push away from my desk and stand; my stomach pitches. I wrap my arms around my waist and laugh out loud. I bend over, laughing so hard my sides begin cramping. My laughter turns into tears and then to crazed, wretched grief. Hero joins in the chorus of this tawdry Greek tragedy and wails from below. Hades has risen from the underworld.

The acoustics are terrible in this house, every noise magnified three-fold. It's eleven forty-five, close to midnight. I'm ruining Valentine's Day for Sam and Uriah. Embarrassed, I stuff Chester's paw into my mouth to muffle my histrionics. I stumble to my bedroom and fall facedown onto my comforter—black mascara streaks stain the fabric. The creak of the floorboards. David? Opening my eyes, I look up from my sniveling misery. It's Sam, looking at me, sadness on her face. She sits on my bed.

"Oh, honey. You found the courage."

"Yes. It's done. There was no Prince Charming down-on-one-knee proposal, no little box opening to forever. He gave me scratch cards." I look up from my pillow. "Sexual scratch cards. Can you believe it? So I executed my plan. And you're the first to know it's official."

"Your breakup?"

"No. Well, yes. The breakup's official. But it's also official that your cousin's a disaster. A mess. I put this suffering on myself. I keep begging for it to happen."

"You're not a mess. You're upset because you spoke your truth and are processing the outcome. David didn't give you what you needed. You had the courage to break up, and now you'll find the strength to move forward. You're not stuck now, Addie. Not anymore. You must go through chaos to get to a better place."

I lurch up, clutching Chester to my chest. "Chaos is the god of creation, the origin of everything that has ever existed. Chaos made Earth out of random disorder, and you're telling me I should go through chaos?" I look at her, choking beneath tears. "I love him, Sam. I don't have the strength."

She strokes my hair. Yet again, my cousin is stroking my hair. She's never seen me such a hot mess. "Let it go, Addie. It's time to let go. Time will do its thing. You'll see. Don't come into work tomorrow. Sleep it off. Everything will be fine. Just fine."

I look into her face, and her eyes—glittering and tight—tell a different story.

༄

I can't fall asleep. At 3:00 a.m., I stumble to the wardrobe and dig through David's drawer, grabbing a T-shirt. Resting my head on a pillow, I snuggle against the shirt, and sleep falls like a heavy curtain, David's musky sweat perfuming my dreams. The morning light burns my eyelids, the T-shirt and Chester twisted between my arms. I take a moment to sift consciousness from my dream state. Memories from last night wash over me like a wave crashing down on a beach. Reality's the nightmare.

Sitting up in bed, I regard the shirt, a faded shade of cinnamon. I purchased it on eBay and gave it to David on our first anniversary, three years back. It's original to the era, the words spelled out across his chest:

Bob Dylan Live in Concert

1966 World Tour Worcester, Massachusetts

I drag my feet toward the coffeepot in a haze, then stumble through the morning rituals. How am I supposed to move forward without David? Shuffling one foot in front of the other, I find myself in front of the console. I select a Dylan album and remove the record from the sleeve. Placing it on top of the turntable, I position the needle on the second groove of the vinyl: "Simple Twist of Fate," the most soulful ballad I've ever heard.

Falling onto the sofa, sobbing into the shirt, I play it repeatedly, over and over and over again. I sniff, rubbing my nose into the animal scent of David. Looking up, I drop the shirt into my lap, hearing something new in the lyrics. Something suggesting that my efforts to control destiny were pointless; in the end, fate always has the upper hand. And even though I've met my soul mate—my twin, as referenced in the song—if the timing's not right for him, our love was in vain.

But is it really a sin, as Dylan's words question, to feel this suffering so intensely, clawing at the grief of his absence? Is the price I'm paying—in this moment—too steep?

At last, my tears subside. There's something about this song—bleeding and beautiful at the same time—that's comforting. I'm reminded that heartache's universal, and all of our plots and little schemes, in the end, are futile with love hinged to the fickle whim of fate. A fate that can strip you raw, leave you empty-handed, busted, no cards left to play.

As if it were antique lace, I fold the shirt into a perfect square and smooth it out before returning it to David's drawer. I never want to see it again. With my composure somewhat regained, I call my mother, who answers on the first ring. I tell her what happened.

"Sweetie. I hear your heartbreak, I feel your pain. David was your Prince Charming. I had no idea you two were in trouble."

"You were upset enough by my episode with Sam. I know how much you love David. I know how much you want grandchildren."

"Oh, Addie," she replies, her voice breaking. "It's your happiness I want more than anything. You can tell me everything that's upsetting you. It's my greatest joy to be here for you when you need me. You heard what Dr. Lerner told me: it's never too late."

Chapter Seventeen

Sam

Quiche has the day off. I'm taking her place at the flattop, flipping trout fillets and grilling buttered bread, my thoughts to myself. Last night, while Uriah and I were shopping at Home Depot for new light-switch plates, he called me honey. *Honey, I'm thinking aged bronze will look better than the polished brass.*

Seriously? *Honey?* We've expressed our love for each other, yada yada, so why would I be thrilled when he called me *honey?* Because the word is comfortable, domestic, a sweet endearment that takes our relationship to the next plateau. Besides, aside from my dad, no man has ever addressed me using a word that sounds so sweet.

As we shopped for fixtures, I felt as if he were taking ownership in my home. But that's not the case. Last week he gave notice to the Boggs School; he will be leaving after the school year, sometime in mid-June. Here's what I dare not speak of to anyone, especially Addie: we're fixing up my area of the home so she'll have a better chance of renting it out. I won't feel so guilty about leaving. I have no problem giving her my portion of the house. Although both our names are on the mortgage, Aunt Teresa's money enabled us to buy it.

Uriah and I are fantasizing a life together outside Cleveland, Tennessee. Unlike Addie, who always speaks in past or future tense, I've never appreciated conversations about the future. This is foreign turf for me.

Uriah and I will purchase farmland and build a home. The land he's been researching is fertile, rests in a valley, and is surrounded by mountains. He'll be working on an educational model for Appalachian youth, which he's developed at Boggs, and I'll grow all of our food. Perhaps I'll even raise sheep. I could sell the meat to upscale restaurants in Nashville. Uriah will take care of me, I'll take care of him, and we'll both be closer to his parents. He likes the idea of living off the land. I do, too. Farm life suits me. It's familiar.

But the diner. More important—*Addie*. She's been working long hours scrutinizing the books, brainstorming menus, and making to-do lists well after Welcome Home closes. It hurts watching her greet our guests, cranking up a smile, with her chin held so high. Heck, in addition to the house, I'd even give her my share of this business. Scot-free. She could make Braydon a partner. She wouldn't owe me a dime. But I can't share our plans yet, and Uriah supports me on this. Her love wounds are too fresh. Only a week has passed since Valentine's Day.

But my heart feels heavy. With a spatula, I shimmy the fish onto a plate, and then the bread. With tongs, I place a side of lightly dressed microgreens beside the trout. I turn and hand it to Braydon, who places it in front of a hungry diner drumming the counter with her open fingers. I scan the room. Addie greets a regular who always dines alone. She seats him at his favorite spot at the counter, close to a stack of cookbooks he enjoys perusing.

Nothing says I have to make up my mind this minute whether to join Uriah or not. I'll just enjoy the sun streaming through the windows. Uriah's been speaking to Realtors and says daffodils are nosing their way up under a blue Cleveland sky about now. It's still too cold to go outside in Detroit without a coat, but no matter; when the frigid air stings my cheeks, I'm in the moment, glad to be alive.

Danita enters, Quiche's friend, clutching a bag of Hungry Boy Burgers in her hand. Last week she also brought fast food into the diner, but it was after hours. She sat in her usual roost at the counter, shooting the breeze. At a loss for words, we let it slide. But Addie and I traded glances as she devoured her burger and fries, slurping down her shake.

But now the diner's open, packed with people, so she can't be bringing in fast food for the rest of our patrons to see. Give me a break—no eating establishment would allow this. We get that most people don't share our farm-to-table philosophy—cost beats organic, deals trump local—but Welcome Home is for those who do. We may understand that food made from authentic ingredients better serves our bodies, but that doesn't mean we believe we're superior to Danita. I'll bet that's exactly what she'll think if confronted.

Of all days for Quiche to be off work. She'd know what to do. What do we say to Danita so she doesn't take offense? Addie smiles at her, places her arm around her shoulders, and they venture to the far side of the floor. Addie's head is bent, her mouth close to Danita's ear, and the woman nods, exiting without fanfare. She even smiled at my cousin, squeezed her hand, as if agreeing with Addie, whatever it was she said.

Addie's such a people person, with such a mindful, gentle way. She has an innate sensitivity, even when her personal life's in shambles. She should run for mayor of The D. If it had been me at the door, it might have gone down a different road. What if I'd hurt Danita's feelings? She'd tell her church congregation what a jerk I am. Or what if she told me I was discriminating against her food, not allowing her to sit at the counter? I shudder, recalling old wounds, imagining the possibilities.

I check the order bar—only a Vegetable Plate and another for the Bean and Barley Soup.

"I'll finish this up," Braydon says to me. "Check on Sylvia—she just finished making a carrot cake and wants your approval. I couldn't believe how fast she whipped it up. When it comes to making sweets, that girl's giving you a run for your money."

His words please me. Sylvia can replace me when I—*if I*—follow Uriah to Tennessee. I retreat to the kitchen.

With a spatula, Sylvia is spreading frosting on her cake. She looks up with a smile. "I used a pound of grated carrots in the batter. Carrots make it healthy, right?"

"You betcha." I walk toward the cake, cocking my head to the side. "What a beauty. My mother always made carrot cake for me on my birthday. Customers go crazy when we make treats that remind them of their childhood. Braydon tells me it took you only ten minutes to assemble."

"Oh, sweet Braydon. That boy's got my back, lemme tell ya. But it's a cinch to throw together. I guess it took . . . fifteen? An extra five to make the frosting—it's cream cheese." With a cloth, she wipes a bit of frosting away from the pedestal.

"I'm glad you're showing such a knack for baking. Takes some of the stress off my back. I'm always so stiff after lunch rush." Massaging my shoulders with my fingertips, I rotate my head in slow circles.

"Making cakes reminds me of when I was a little girl cooking with Mama. Before Daddy was diagnosed," she continues. "That sponge cake of hers—you'd like to die biting into it. It was made with Brazil nuts and had a meringue frosting. She said the flavors reminded her of cooking with her mom when she was a girl in Rio."

"That sounds heavenly—I'll add it to tomorrow's prep list. I'm pretty sure that carrot cake will disappear as soon as it hits the floor. We don't stock Brazil nuts. Would walnuts be an OK substitute?"

"They'll work just fine." She claps her hands, jumping up and down with glee. "I haven't made that cake since I was eight years old. But I remember the recipe as if I were remembering my own name."

Sylvia's a natural. The act of baking—measuring flour, beating egg whites until they're stiff, melting chocolate with butter—must nurture her, feed her soul.

"So, how's it going for you, Sylvia? What's happening in your life—besides ensuring our customers leave with their sweet tooth satisfied?"

"Not much," she replies, patting walnut bits into the cream cheese frosting. She looks up from her task. "And *not much* is fine by me."

"Don't tell me you haven't noticed Kevin can't take his eyes off of our girl," Paul says, his metal spoon making a scraping sound as he digs deep, stirring into the corners of a cast-iron Dutch oven. He's prepping Braised Rabbit with Bacon, Prunes, and Pearl Onions for tomorrow's special. Sweet, rich smells of caramelized onions and bacon waft about the kitchen.

Sylvia ignores his remark. But her face reddens as she walks to the hand sink, removes her plastic gloves, and washes her hands under the running water. Then, she retreats to the prep board to study the list.

Since the holidays, Kevin's been lingering at the counter every Thursday after dropping off the books. He orders a bite to eat, and then, like clockwork, Sylvia joins him, taking her lunch break. Picking at their food from time to time as an afterthought, they lean into each other, their foreheads almost touching in conversation.

Kevin's long lost interest in me. His manner's now relaxed, and his smiles come easy. If this was his demeanor last year, I might have fallen for him. He was so quiet and goofy when crushing on me.

"The weather report says we're going to get dumped on," Paul comments, looking at his phone. Sylvia hurries to the window and stares outside. The blue skies have been replaced with overhanging gray clouds, and she frowns, wringing her hands together, agitated.

"You've only a ten-minute walk to your place, Sylvia. Why so anxious? I've got a pair of snow boots you can borrow."

"Paul. Come look," she says, her eyes glued to the window. "It's that same rusted-out van. And it's parked in the same exact place as it was the day before yesterday." She looks at him, her eyes narrowed with concern. "And two days before that."

Paul and I approach Sylvia and stand by her side.

"What's wrong with that?" I ask. "It's not parked illegally. I'm sure it belongs to a neighbor."

"I don't think so. I'd recognize an old, beat-up van the color of collards. This makes the third time it's shown up in the past week. It pulls up, but no one leaves the vehicle. And it parks in a place, so I can't help but see it while I'm working." She turns to me and grabs my forearms.

"I'll bet it's one of Bobby's buddies. He found out where I work. He wants me to know that his goons will catch me—torture me." She releases my arms and looks down at the floor.

"Shoot, Sylvia," I say, taking her hands in mine and giving them a soft squeeze. "You're just a wee bit paranoid. If anything, it's probably some dude waiting to lay out a dope deal."

"But he never leaves, and no one ever goes to the car." She looks up at me, shaking her head.

"Maybe he works close by. He's taking a break, napping in his van. If it's any person that would be of concern to the diner, it would be the troll."

She looks at me, bewildered. "What do you mean, all this talk about a troll?"

"You remember the person who wrote those awful things about us online? The person who pretended to be Babcia? Trolls are scaredy-cat Internet predators who intimidate people because they can get away with it."

Paul places his hand on her shoulder. "No one can find out their real identity, because online they're invisible. It's as if I threw a rock at you while hiding behind my mother's skirt. Trolls are bullies who get their jollies unleashing their unhappiness on innocent people. Or on entities, such as Welcome Home."

Sylvia's eyes are bright, her mouth soft and trembling. "Thank you, both, for trying to make me feel better. Pimp or troll, whoever or whatever is sitting in that driver's seat, right this very minute, is giving me the heebie-jeebies."

I look at her, shaking my head. "Erase the thought that someone is hunting you down. See how the car windows are tinted? Trolls like it dark. They're too ugly and cowardly to let anyone see their faces. Bobby's cohorts are not in that van. The man is locked away, and the inmates are torturing him just the way he tortured you." I look at her, raising my brows. "Doesn't that make you feel just a little bit happy?"

She regards me with a slight shake of her head. "Not really. I'm not interested in revenge on him. I'm scared of him. I want him to forget me." She raises a brow. "On the other hand, that gravy train of nasty men, all those johns." Her eyes narrow, and between clenched teeth, she grinds out her next words. "Imagining something awful happening to them . . . well, ma'am, *that* is a happy thought."

Paul slides into his jacket. "I'm going out there. I'll knock on the window."

Before I've time to protest, he's out the door. Through the panes, we watch him dart across the yard, but the van pulls away before he reaches it. As it disappears down the road, the snow begins to fall.

Chapter Eighteen

Addie

Sun Beam pushes her glasses onto the bridge of her nose, then swivels to face me. "It looks like there's dirt on my face, but they're ashes. It's supposed to be a cross. Can you tell?"

The streaked marks resemble a hieroglyph of a running child, arms outstretched into the wind.

"They do look like a cross and remind me it's Lent. You also wore them on Ash Wednesday, almost three weeks back." Four days prior to Valentine's Day. I was still with David. A different woman. "Is it your church's tradition to wear them through the season?"

"No. I'm the only one who wore them today. Our fireplace is filled with soot, so I got the idea."

"When I was a girl, every Ash Wednesday my minister rubbed the sign above my brows, too. Babcia would quote from Genesis as she admired my forehead. *'For you were made from dust, and to dust you shall return.'*" I touch the girl's forehead, smiling at the memory.

Sun Beam and her mother are helping me finish up my traditional Lenten project: Polish Easter Eggs, a savory chopped egg mixture stuffed into dyed and decorated eggshells. They will be a special throughout the season.

The bulk of lunch rush has subsided, and the counter has emptied of customers. We sit on stools while Quiche stands at the prep table, her back to us, scooping hard-cooked egg out of an eggshell. There's a teachers' workshop this afternoon at Sun Beam's school, so the students were dismissed after lunch. The girl's presence at my side satisfies a maternal craving, a completion, and I inhale her presence as if my life depended on it.

I return to my task, stuffing and flattening the egg mixture into a rose-hued shell, before passing it to Sun Beam. She sprinkles panko over the top and then, with the back of a spoon, presses the crumbs into the egg mixture. They'll be fried in butter just before serving.

I hand another egg to the girl. Recipes are much more than instruction manuals. They're stories, rich with history, connecting the dots between the past and present. This traditional recipe, as lovely as a daisy chain, has been handed down from my great-grandmother to Babcia to me, and now to Sun Beam. It conjures recollections of happy times. I remember hunting Easter eggs at Babcia and Dziadek's Ann Arbor home. Memories of white dresses, ribbons, and beautiful baskets filled with decorated eggs, chocolate rabbits, and marzipan flood my subconscious.

"What's the green stuff?" Sun Beam asks, pointing at the egg mixture, lifting me from my reverie.

"I added dill and chives to my grandmother's recipe. But she wouldn't mind. She said while she was growing up in Poland, every home was doing something different with their eggs. Sometimes we'd stir Polish ham into the mixture."

"I'm glad you kept *ours* vegetarian." She wears a solemn frown on her face.

"Did you give anything up for Lent?" I ask, skirting her favorite topic next to climate change: animal rights.

"Instead of giving up, I'm giving back. For starters, I made a Valentine's Day card for Angus. Mama said he was lonely, so we took it to his house. I drew a picture of Hero and Bon Temps holding hands—I mean paws." She giggles between her fingers. "They looked like they were in love."

Giving a start, I flash a look of surprise to Quiche. "You never told me you went to his home."

Quiche turns to face me, wiping her hands down her apron. "I don't tell you every little detail of my comings and goings. Just like you don't tell me yours." She gives me a long, appraising look. "But we've talked about him in meetings, so I took it upon myself to pay him a visit."

"Well, that was certainly gracious of you." I take a deep breath, blinking quickly. "What was his reaction?"

"What do you think his reaction would be? A woman and child at his front door wearing smiles on their faces—he smiled back and welcomed us in. It was no big deal. We all had a nice little visit."

"Did you talk about the diner? You must have talked about the diner. You work here."

She sighs in exasperation, as she does when her daughter is being particularly obtuse.

"Of course he knows I work here. And not everything revolves around the diner, either. We mostly spoke of his grandson, Gary. He's been released and is back home. He was at a job interview during our visit."

"That's wonderful," I say, thankful Angus is no longer alone.

"We also talked about fried chicken," Sun Beam remarks, arranging the finished eggs in tidy little rows. "How much he loves it."

Quiche winces. "You know this *black people loving fried chicken* thing rubs me wrong. It's like us and watermelon." She picks up a jar of Jessie's hot sauce. "Or the assumption that blacks douse every morsel of food with hot sauce. I hate racial stereotypes even more than I hate hot sauce."

I pick up a finished egg and place it into the cup of my hand carefully so as not to damage it. The shell is so fragile.

I look up, catching her eyes. "Racial stereotypes can certainly be destructive. But food? I suppose it depends on the context of conversation. If the food is referenced with the intention of embarrassing a culture or race, it's cruel and can't be tolerated." I shift in my seat. "But do you know who likes fried chicken and watermelon, Quiche? Everybody. At least in this country."

Quiche gives me her usual *not sure if I've got you figured out* look, but a smile plays about the corners of her mouth. The woman's a tough sell.

"Well," she continues, "I told him ours was the best on the planet and suggested that he stop by and taste for himself."

"And his reaction?" I hunch into the counter and tip my head.

"He shrugged. Nothing more, nothing less."

She turns to her daughter. "Tell Addie the other ways you're giving back during Lent. 'Cause I need to get back to work." Quiche hustles to the prep sink and turns on the water, as if to wave off any further interrogation.

Sun Beam fidgets with excitement. "Granny and I are saving energy. We removed a light bulb from the lamp on the side table in the den. We're running wash only when the machine is stuffed, and then we hang the clothes on the line to dry. We're giving back to the environment."

"You're also giving back to my wallet," Quiche comments, glancing over her shoulder.

"The weather's cooperating with line drying," I remark. "Last week it's freezing and now it's in the sixties. In Michigan, blink your eyes and the weather has changed."

I've welcomed tepid temperatures in winters past, but not this one. I'm feeling so alone and fragile without David in my life that any excuse to bundle up in another layer of comfort would be fine with me.

"Braydon says if the weather stays nice, he'll bring Bon Temps with him to work on Sunday," Sun Beam says, sprinkling crumbs over another egg. "He promised to dress her up with bunny ears." She puts down the panko and catches my eye. "Maybe Sam can make some rabbit ears for Hero. With that creamy coat of fur, he'll look just like a jackrabbit."

I smile at the thought. Sundays are the perfect opportunity to let the dogs visit with customers before we put them outside. The Health Department's unlikely to be making their rounds.

"Let's all wear bunny ears," I say to her, brushing her ponytail off her shoulder. "I have the rabbity eyes to match."

She scrutinizes my face, before nodding in agreement. "It looks like you just got mugged."

Ouch. That stings. From the mouth of a child, so I'm sure I look a mess. This morning, while brushing my teeth, I noticed half-moon shadows under my eyes. But I don't bother to hide them with makeup. Ever since my breakup with David, I haven't worn mascara or even lipstick. I like that my eyes and mouth bleed into the backdrop of my face. I wear blankness as a mask.

Quiche unties her apron and retrieves her purse from the shelf beneath the counter. "Time to get going, honey," she says to her daughter. "You need to get your homework done. After supper we're heading back to church." She turns to me. "Sun Beam and I are organizing an Easter pageant for the preschoolers. The little ones are so precious when they're all gussied up. We're meeting with the parents to go over each kid's role in the skit."

"You know, Quiche," I say, lighting my fingertips on her arm, "wouldn't you think folks would be hungry after church let out? I don't get it. No one from the neighborhood sets foot in this place. If we were giving the food away, I'd wager they'd still never walk through the door. Why do you think that is?"

She rummages through her purse and retrieves a tube of lipstick, then a compact, which she opens. "You need to know something about black folks, at least in this community. We're skeptical about what your people are trying to sell us. Verdict's out on gentrification. No one wants to take the long con." She cocks a brow, regarding herself in the mirror. "We've been down that road before."

She pats her nose with a powder puff. "First it's you ladies and the diner. Next thing you know comes the invasion of the pierced lips and purple hairs, buying up places like Danny's barbershop. A place where five dollars once got you a haircut would only now buy a cup of coffee." She paints a slash of pale-pink color over her lips. "And following that would be the sushi train, folks lounging round La Grande on yoga mats." With a sharp thwack, she closes her compact. "My friends think you people are like exotic pets—it's hard to guess your next habitat and what you'll want to feed on."

I chuckle as she smacks her lips together and returns her makeup to the bag.

"You're pretty funny, Quiche. Perhaps you should try your hand at stand-up."

She levels me with her eyes. "In all seriousness, there's something for everyone on our menu. With those discount cards I gave everyone at church, our prices are in line with the waffle chains. That's where my group flocks after service. Our breakfasts are tastier, and we're right across the street. The chains are a drive away." She looks at the ceiling, thumbing her fingers on the counter, and then grabs her purse.

"Danita and I've been encouraging them to stop by. I've been friendly with the Tabernacle community since I was a girl. They're interested in every other aspect of my life, but they don't seem to care about my work. They may be keeping their distance, but I know they're checking the place out. Once, after hours, I spied a couple of friends wandering around the building. But I can't drag them in by their hair." She tips her head toward Sun Beam. "And frankly, I've got more pressing concerns on my plate."

I shrug as Sun Beam slides off the stool and retrieves her sweater, which has fallen to the floor. As she slides her arms through the sleeves, I bend to give her a hug. She scampers out of the diner with her mother, crossing paths with Jessie, who's making a delivery.

I wrap the eggs in saran and place them in the reach-in. Jessie lumbers toward the counter, a case of hot sauce pressed into her hip. We'll be closing soon and most of the customers have left, except for a couple of two-tops near the front entry. After writing Jessie's check, I lean into her, resting my forearms on the Formica, and peer into her eyes.

"Honest to God, Jess. I never would have believed it, but your smudging ceremony's been effective. Before you got here, I checked Twitter for the thousandth time this week. The troll hasn't resurfaced."

"A thousand times? Girl, you need to give that phone of yours a rest. All of you people wandering around, heads down, random beeps and bleeps coming out of your persons. You look like digital zombies. Whatever happened to eye-to-eye conversation?"

I pat my pocket, my cell phone removed from her suspicious gaze. "Aren't we speaking eye to eye right now? The troll could be spinning his threads in some other corner of the web, but—at least to my knowledge—silence reigns."

Blessed silence, the pause button pressed on life. It seems as if the world has been spinning so fast, it's all I can do to hold on.

"What about my ragman?" Jessie asks, the apricot glint in her eyes dimming.

"He's vanished, as well."

I regard Jessie in admiration. Not only have those two left us alone, but that van hasn't parked across the street in over a week. Jessie's our Odysseus, and she vanquished our nemesis with her burning sage. To hell with fate. Maybe she can help me conjure up some remedy to make David return.

Jessie's voice, thick with fatigue, interrupts my thoughts. "Mind if I get some water?"

"Whatever you want, Jess."

I chew on a hangnail. It's been fifteen hours and fifteen days since David left. Mom has insisted I double up sessions with my therapist; she's footing the bill for weekly, instead of biweekly, sessions. Yesterday, however, Dr. Lerner's probing questions angered me. I don't appreciate where she was going, where she tried to take my head. We discussed David until I was blue in the face: Why would he think I'd find those scratch cards amusing? Why did I find it necessary to play the vamp? Why did I do *that thing* I do, even when ill? It was as if I were being interrogated for a crime.

Jessie returns to my side, with a glass of water for each of us.

"Jessie. I've been thinking. I studied mythology back in college, and the ancients would explain you as a conduit to the gods. A contemporary goddess."

She looks at me, a thoughtful gleam lighting her eyes. And then she nods, as if appreciating the fact that I, at last, am acknowledging her gifts.

"I have mastered special tools of the trade. I can summon certain powers with my spell work." Her eyes cloud over and her nostrils flare. "But only if there's evil in the air."

"Plato wrote that love is a serious mental disease," I venture. "Think about the expressions *sick with love*, and *dying for love.* They're universal. Love causes so much pain and makes you feel that something vile is eating out your guts."

She scrutinizes me, her mouth tight. "I don't care what those ancients said, Addie. Those philosophers and gods of yours need a reality check. Love, in all of its forms, is the most blessed power in the universe. Love isn't evil. It doesn't carry a weapon or raise its fist. Love is pure. And I refuse to go messing with purity."

"Well, maybe you can take an indirect route." I push a box knife into the case of hot sauce and slide it down the seam. "Summon the powers of Aphrodite, the goddess of love."

Removing a bottle of hot sauce from the case, my words accelerate. "Ask her to cast a spell on David. Tell her to make him realize he can't live without me."

I place the condiment on a table and rotate the fiery sauce so that the wings on the label are now parallel to the saltshaker and pepper grinder.

"No. Forget Aphrodite," I say, tightening the top of a jar of mustard. "Her deal with Paris precipitated the Trojan War. She's one tough cookie. You might catch her in a pissy mood. Summon Hera—the goddess of marriage. And while you're at it"—my voice raises another notch—"send out for Eileithyia, the goddess of childbirth."

By now I'm breathless, arranging condiments on empty tables in a full-blown rant. An elderly man at a nearby two-top glances up at me before sprinkling salt over his eggs. He peers at me again before clutching the shaker in his fist as if he's worried I might snatch it from his hand.

"Hold on, Addie, hold on." Jessie grabs my hand and leads me to an island of empty tables toward the back of the floor. "Your eyes are glassy, and you're acting manic. You're riding a black cloud on a tempest thundering inside of you. You need to get off. Stop. Breathe."

Inhaling through my nostrils, I feel the twitching of tics fretting my nerves. On the exhale, they begin to settle.

"The only one who can help you is *you*. No goddess, no therapist, no boyfriend, just you. Summon up *Addie*." Jessie's eyes rise to meet Babcia's. "Summon up your granny, too. You've always spoken of her strength. Mixed up inside of you, she's stronger than ever. That's no hocus-pocus, no goddess worship, no woo-woo talking nonsense. I'm talking science, Addie. DNA."

I stare at Jessie as if she's just read a passage from an ancient oracle, and I throw my arms around her shoulders. "Babcia. Yes, I'll think of Babcia. Thank you for that bit of wisdom."

She rolls her eyes to mask her embarrassment at my boisterous display of emotion. Pink works up her neck as I release my grasp.

"You want to control your world, Addie. You want to control your man." She touches my arm and lowers her voice to a gentler octave. "But the world's too big. And your need to control his actions and love is swallowing you."

It's impossible to meet her gaze—she's reading too much in my eyes—so I walk to the counter. After removing the remaining hot sauces from the case, I begin to polish them and line them up into three precise rows. Jessie follows.

"You can't control other people. You can control only yourself. Your own emotions. And your reactions to those emotions." She places her hand on my shoulder. "You've got more power than you realize. More power than all of those goddesses combined. No matter what life dishes out, only you can control decisions that will govern your path. Only you get to decide to be happy or sad with your choices."

She crooks her head to the side and cranes her face toward mine. One of her dreadlocks dangles about my hand, tickling it. I fold the cloth, place it on the counter, and turn to meet her gaze.

"So, what?" I ask, tears burning my eyes. "What am I supposed to do?"

"When you're alone, summon your strength and unleash your wisdom. Alone time is precious. Don't be afraid of it. Treasure the gift of silence when there's no one around to tell you who you are or what you should be." She runs her hand down my back, stroking me as one might soothe a runaway dog who'd found its way home. "Find your safe place and rest."

She folds the check and slips it into the back pocket of her overalls. "Now I've gotta get going. But you call me if you want to talk." She leaves, and for a few moments, the pain I've been feeling subsides.

Sylvia emerges from the kitchen, carrying her sponge cake on a pedestal. I reach for my cell phone and snap a picture of her now-signature confection. It's on a regular rotation, alongside the Heartbreakers. I tweet:

> Come and get it! #sylviasspongecake
> #welcomehome

God forbid I forget to tweet, Facebook, Instagram, and share.

I look out the window: gray on gray, not a glimmer of sunlight, as far as the eye can see. My misery returns as if a veil were lowered across my face. I put the empty box behind the counter, slide onto a stool, and place my face into my palms.

I glance down at my kitchen clogs. Dried egg albumen is streaked across the leather. It's been there a couple of weeks. I'm not taking care of myself; I'm just not me. So who am I? What does all this mean? Braydon walks to my side and hands me a shot of potlikker. It's the only sustenance I can keep down without wanting to barf. Yet I wish people would quit treating me as if I were an invalid.

I look up at him. "Do you remember when I first met you? When you were a part of that volunteer group who helped us ready the diner for opening day?" I down the warm brew, appreciating the palliative effect on my spirit.

"How could I forget?" He removes his hand and folds his arms across his chest, a dreamy look cast about his face. "I enjoy cleaning. It's gratifying to see what brute strength can do with filth. The rewards are immediate, visible in a swipe."

"Then you must have been in a state of ecstasy back then. The place was a disaster zone."

Chaos. This place was chaos. I look about the room. Lella's wiping down tables, most of them empty after a busy lunch. And then I nod at the remaining customers chatting among one another, smiling between bites. We did get to a better place. Chaos is the perfect weapon to instigate order. That's something to think about.

"Remember that electrician who screwed up the wiring?" Braydon says, interrupting my thoughts. "I can't believe the guy was licensed."

"I forgot about him. Man. I was so incensed. You won me over when you fixed that mess. How long ago was that?" I ask.

"A little over a year, I think. Sometime back mid-February. Seems impossible." Looking around the room, eyes dancing, he slides his phone into the back pocket of his pants. "What a transformation."

"In no small measure thanks to you. I wish I'd been up to organizing some sort of anniversary celebration."

"Maybe next year we can throw out some freebies—offer discounts," he suggests. "Something to let the customers know how much we've appreciated their patronage."

An anniversary event would have been a topic I would have hashed out, and then executed, with David. He's so clever with business promotions and strategies. A plunging sensation tumbles from the hole in my heart to the pit of my stomach. I can't stand another minute not having that man in my life. Why can't I get over him? I look down at my ragged nails, my fingers woven so tightly together the knuckles are white.

Why can't I get over myself?

Sam joins me at the table. "Is this a good time to discuss the menu change?"

I look at her. "Menu change?"

"We spoke about it last week. The transition from winter fare to spring? Remember? We'd planned to update the menu next month." She scrutinizes me, concern in her eyes. "Spring lamb will be available, and we were going to brainstorm some lightened-up soups and salads.

You said you'd order cold-crop seeds. On Friday, Uriah is bringing his class in to plant the seeds in cell packs."

Oh. Now I remember. The conversation slipped my mind. I forgot to place the order, so now we'll be behind schedule. Once again, here I sit, mouth agape.

She pats my hand. "No worries. I'll pick up some packs at a gardening center."

"They won't have what we were talking about—those off-the-grid heirlooms."

I run my fingers through my hair and then tie it in a knot at the nape of my neck. "There's an organic seed shop in Ann Arbor. I told you about their chicory—the one with the lime-green leaves streaked with burgundy? It makes a stunning plate. I was going to place an order this afternoon," I say, lying to cover up my ditzy behavior.

She touches my hand softly, but her smile's tight.

"Great. Have them overnight the seeds."

She's been solicitous to me of late. Holding back. What's up with that? I miss the old Sam, her spice and spunk. I'll bet she's afraid I'll go postal again. She has good reason to be distant. These days, I barely trust myself.

With a jolt, I grab my phone, now ringing. Always hopeful it's David, I'm embarrassed how quickly I retrieved it. I look at the screen.

"No name," I say, as Sam eyes me curiously. "But it's a Grosse Pointe number."

"Maybe it's your mom."

"No. Her ring tone's a hooting owl."

Sam giggles as I answer, pressing the phone to my ear. But when I hear the nasal voice, I'm sorry I answered.

"Addie. It's Graham. Don't hang up. You'll want to hear this."

I remain silent, using every ounce of restraint not to press the red button.

"I found it, Addie. I found it." His breathing sounds ragged, as if he's been running.

My heart quickens. "The rosary?"

Sam straightens in her chair, eyes wide, head leaning toward me.

"I thought it was in the safe. Well, your mom told you the story." He speaks quickly, his words tumbling over one another. "I thought for sure it was there. I felt like such a shit when it wasn't. Anyway, I was looking for some comics I had as a kid and found the necklace. It was hidden behind a mound of old shoes."

Is he bullshitting me again? The tone of his voice, almost celebratory in its enthusiasm, suggests otherwise.

"It's in my hand, Addie. I'm holding it in my hand. I called you the second I found it."

"Describe it to me."

"I know what you're thinking, and I don't blame you. Why trust me? But it's beautiful, Addie. So beautiful. It's a long necklace made of silver links interspersed with pale purple beads. It looks as if each is hand cut, and they're different shades of violet. A cross is affixed to a strand, depicting a crucified Christ."

That's it. Babcia's rosary. Joy washes through me, which quickly turns to anxiety. He's tainting the necklace with his stinking, thieving hands. I want it back. Now. With David gone, I have no means of transportation. I'll take an Uber.

"I take it you're at your parents' house. I'll come get it."

"Addie. The least I can do is bring it to you. I'll be there in twenty minutes. I've caused you so much suffering. I'll hop in my car this instant."

I hold the phone. Silent. Not allowing myself to breathe.

"I promise." He hangs up the phone.

Sam stares at me, a look of incredulity on her face. "He found Babcia's rosary?"

"Yes. The prick had it hidden in the back of his closet. He was so doped up at the time he must have forgotten where he stashed it."

"Look at it this way. At least he didn't sell it. Score one for the inmate. If you can hold on a couple of hours, I'll have Uriah drive you there."

"No. Graham said he'd bring it here."

"Man. I can't wait to meet this dude. I'll never forget how messed up you were when you were dating him." She studies my face, then drops her eyes to the table as if to say, *See, Addie? See what you do? You're messed up again over David.*

It dawns on me: I'm a chameleon. I take on the aura of the man I'm attracted to and then turn myself into another person. Someone I think they'd desire. Someone they'd love. But with David, when I showed my real colors, revealed what I wanted from him and this life, he bolted. At least I was speaking my truth. The *outside in*, at last, turned *inside out*. But are the consequences worth it?

"He should be here in twenty minutes or so." I push away from the table and stand. "That will give me enough time to place the seed order." I bolt toward the office. "I'll also call Mom. She'll be so happy to hear some good news from me for a change."

I order the seeds, requesting an overnight delivery. Then, I call my mother. The happy words are just out of my mouth when I hear the creak and groan of Sam unbolting the entrance door.

"Mom, he's here. Gotta go. I'll call you back the second he leaves."

I check my phone. He made it here in fifteen minutes—record time. I step out of my office, then hurry through the swinging doors and into the prep area. He's standing in the doorway, facing Sam. She's talking to him, hands on her hips, and I can see her dimples from here. I know this expression well. She finds him attractive.

Graham turns, the familiar pink rectangular box in his hand. I weave around the counter, and oddly enough, we meet beneath Babcia's photograph. He hands me the box, which I open. Gasping, my eyes fill with tears. I pick up the crucifix, which lies on the same cotton pads where I'd left it, and lift it to her picture. Graham's eyes trail my hand.

"That's her, right? Your grandmother?"

I let out a long sigh. A sigh I've been holding inside my chest for ten years, since the day I couldn't find the necklace. I nod my head and motion to a chair, offering him a seat. Sam walks to my side and lifts up the beadwork, examining it. We join Graham at the table.

"It's been so long," she says, her voice cracking, sniffing back tears. "We were eighteen when she gave us our presents. She gave me her cameo earrings." She looks at me, pinching her earlobes. "Mom keeps them safe at the farm."

Graham's head hangs low and he shakes it, biting his lower lip. Then, he looks up, catching my eye.

"When the rosary wasn't in their safe, I panicked. I knew you'd think I was scum, that I'd been lying to you all along." He licks his lips. "My first instinct was to go out and score—to get high so I could detonate the slimeball who stole his girlfriend's family heirloom."

His visage has changed—sincerity is mapped across his face. His eyes are clear, and he's put on a solid twenty pounds since I saw him last year. Graham Palmer, once again, is a handsome man. And I get where he's coming from. I, too, am an addict. I will stop at nothing to score love.

Sam touches my wrist and catches my eye, shaking her head in wonder. "It's crazy it was returned to you during Lent, the season that meant so much to Babcia."

I fiddle with the beadwork, glancing up at her portrait, and my heart swells with love for my grandmother. Since she died, it's a feeling that intensifies with the passing of every year. She's gone from this earth, but she's with me. Love can't be forced, caged, or simplified. Love is eternal. Amorphous, pliable, and fluid.

I place my head in my hands, exhausted, muffling a lone, wretched sob. I'm such a list-making, organization freak, always placing lofty expectations on myself and all the people in my world. *I'll be married and raising kids by 36! I'll transform Welcome Home into an egalitarian mecca! I'll blaze the way to revive Detroit!*

Each morning after I awaken from a fitful sleep, I see a woman looking back at me in the mirror with such sadness in her eyes. Where's Addie on the list? I've built a foundation of expectations that no one can live up to. Especially myself. I stare at the rosary in my hand. *Let it go, Addie. Let it go. Don't resist the tides of fate.*

I take a deep breath, drop my hands, and stare out the window, out into the sky, which is the color of a stone. Graham's eyes wander across my face, curious.

"Are you OK? You look"—he bites his lower lip—"well, tired. Different."

I nod, furiously, and then return my gaze to the rosary, recalling Jessie's words: *Find your safe place and rest.*

Chapter Nineteen

Sam

A man stands outside the diner, his shadow long in the afternoon sun. He reaches out to open the door; his hand is large and dark, with pinkish palms. The knob wiggles, and then his torso slumps, as if he's dejected it's locked. I recognize him—Angus's grandson. Braydon pointed him out to me when the man was entering Angus's house, carrying a bag of groceries.

My heart quickens, and I look toward the counter, pretending I don't see him, relieved the door is bolted. He was released last month from prison. This man's a felon. For heaven's sake, *what am I thinking*? My eyes dart back to the windowpanes. Theo's also a felon and one of our favorite patrons. And we've been hoping this dude's granddad would stop by since day one. I stride across the floor, unlatching the door.

He enters and extends his hand, which I take. "Good afternoon," he says, his voice deep and friendly. The tailored lines of his coat accentuate his broad shoulders, his slim waist. "I'm Gary, your next-door neighbor. I wanted to speak with someone about the dishwasher position."

A smile bursts from my face. *Progress!*

"I'm Sam. So nice to meet you. Follow me to the office. We can talk, and you can fill out a form."

As we walk across the floor, Lella bolts from the kitchen, bashing into my side, an empty tray above her head. I stumble into Gary.

"Rushes like today would bring most people to tears," she offers as an apology for almost knocking me over.

Of late, she hasn't been her upbeat self. It's as if she's lost her rhythm. She's not asking random questions and making silly comments. I miss the old Lella. I hope her latest dude—what's his name?—didn't dump her.

I glance at Gary and shrug my shoulders as if to say, *Not sure what's up with that.* We walk into the office. He makes a good first impression, but I'm uncomfortable. We're desperate for a dishwasher, but will it look like we're currying favor with his grandfather? At least transportation won't be an issue for him, as it has been with the others. Unless his jail background creates a problem, in my mind, I've hired him.

I unfold a chair and motion for him to sit. I take a seat at the desk, open the drawer, and pull out a pen and a job application form. Then, I turn the chair around so that I can face him.

"It's nice to meet a neighbor." I shift in my chair and fiddle with a paper clip, uncomfortable not speaking the words I yearn to say. What the hell. I lift my chin. "Why's your grandfather so angry with us?"

"You and your cousin were the catalyst," he replies without skipping a beat, his gaze not wavering. "It's not the diner. At least not directly. He's angry about his neighborhood. Angry about Detroit. Angry about his life in general. Welcome Home's the scapegoat, and I'm sorry for that. He's complicated, but you'd find him a good man if he ever lets you in."

There's a depth of presence about Gary. He speaks from the heart. I like that.

"Does he know you're applying for a job here?"

"He knows I've been applying for jobs. Many jobs, in fact. But, no. He doesn't know I'm applying here. Your establishment has yet to break the ice with him."

"God knows we've tried. But your granddad's no different from the rest of the neighborhood. No one who calls this community *home* comes near the place. Our name, Welcome Home, in retrospect, is a joke. We've raised the flag of resignation."

"Well, you obviously don't lack for business. Every day your lot's packed. Congratulations. Your place is a zoo."

A zoo. And I, this tethered, dancing monkey, want to escape the organ-grinder.

I don't know how I'm going to find the words to tell Addie, but I'm taking a leap of faith and moving to Tennessee. I'm aware Uriah and I have been an item for only several months, and there will be a lot of stress attached to this move. But, worst case, if we don't work out, I'm thinking I'll like it down there. But I make myself sick imagining Addie's reaction to my decision.

My thoughts return to the man sitting in front of me, a pleasant expression on his face. He takes the application from my hands and scans the pages.

"Before we get started, I must tell you something. I don't want to waste your time." He points to the application. "The box isn't here."

He must be referring to the felony check box some companies put on their job apps. Twenty-five percent of Americans have some sort of criminal record, and I'm sure that stat's higher for black men living in Detroit. It's difficult for people with records to get hired.

I look at him, feigning ignorance. He's not aware I know he was recently released from prison. "The box?"

"There's a box on applications asking if I've ever been arrested for a crime. A few years back, I never dreamed I'd have to check it."

"I'm familiar with the box. My partner and I revised our job application to exclude it. Detroit's a *ban the box* city, but not so much outside city limits."

The lines across his forehead ease. "I was wondering about that. But when I don't see it, I blurt out the truth anyway."

"The truth will set you free." I try keeping my features void of expression.

"Funny you'd choose those particular words. I was just released from prison."

I raise my eyebrows.

"The stunt I pulled my senior year in high school was the most idiotic thing I've ever done in my life." He pauses a few seconds, before handing me the application, as if assuming I won't ask him to fill it out.

"When I was a senior in high school, my granddad and I, as usual, were strapped for cash. We were two months behind on our car insurance, and I needed a vehicle to get to my part-time job."

"Car insurance in The D is more than twice what it is anywhere else in the country," I remark. "My friends who have a car and live here pay over ten grand a year. That's why I bum rides and use public transportation."

He nods, and his features relax. Maybe he was worried I'd ask him to leave after his admission.

"My buddy coerced me into robbing a convenience store. But the gun he claimed was a toy turned out to be for real. The fact that he was carrying, and I was his accomplice, was bad enough. But my conviction exploded any prospects for college. Michigan was in the process of recruiting me for an outside linebacker position."

"Not good," I say, shaking my head. "And I'm sorry. But I appreciate your candor, Gary."

"Admitting the truth hasn't helped my job prospects," he continues. "No one wants to hire a man with a record. At this point, I'd be grateful for any job. You can bet I'm a hard worker." He leans forward in his chair and speaks to me in earnest. "Despite my past, you can trust me. I'd never put my grandfather through any sort of pain again. When I was convicted, he turned into an old man overnight."

He was only a step away from a scholarship. One lapse of toxic stupidity, and he threw it all away. He could have been so much more than a dishwasher. Who knows? He might yet be.

"I believe you, Gary. And yes, you have the job. I'm afraid the pay's not great and——"

"I'll take whatever," he interrupts, his eyes widening in surprise at my offer.

"But what about your grandfather? You don't want to cause him further pain. How will he handle your crossing enemy lines?"

His mouth twitches. "For the past several weeks, I must have filled out a hundred applications online. I've been called in to interview at a dozen or so of them, but when they find out about my record, I'm denied the job. They figure out some other reason I'm not qualified. But I know the truth."

I nod my head.

"When I return from the interviews, and he sees my face, the look on *his* breaks my heart. He knows that for me to be happy, I must work. Not just because we need the money, but for my self-esteem. At this point, even if it's just washing gravy off of plates, it's something. Besides"—Gary smiles—"my granddad's used to crossing enemy lines. You know he received a Purple Heart for his bravery? I'm not sure it was worth his finger and thumb, but he's a good man."

"Let your grandfather know that you were hired because of your honesty—you'll make your granddad proud." I fasten the application forms together with a paper clip and hand them to Gary. "So, let's meet some of the crew. You can also meet the sink. You two will become quite intimate in the coming weeks."

He chuckles. "Thanks so much for taking a risk on me, giving me a second chance. I can start tomorrow, if that works."

"Wonderful. Complete the forms and bring them with you."

I lead him into the kitchen. Pies are baking in the oven, and the air is filled with their sweet and buttery fragrance.

"Paul, Sylvia. You'll be thrilled with our latest addition to the staff. Meet Gary, our next-door neighbor. He'll be the new dishwasher."

"Gary. My man," Paul says, catching his eyes and grinning ear to ear. "Ever been a dishwasher before?"

"Can't say that I have," Gary replies, shrugging.

"You're gonna love it," Paul says with a wink. He stretches his hand toward the man. "Seriously. We've been missing you. A good dishwasher is key to efficient kitchen flow. The constant pileup's been a handicap around here. I'm delighted to make your acquaintance." The men shake hands.

"Are you the one who offered to fix my granddad's steps?" Gary asks. "The stairs leading up to the porch?"

Paul's face colors. "We were worried they'd rot. That he might trip walking down. One of the waiters was also going to help. We didn't mean to interfere."

"No, man, no." Gary shakes his head and wrings his hands. "He appreciated the offer. He's just not used to strangers reaching out, seeming to care. But I'm not opposed to your help. Thanks, man. Maybe we can fix them together when the weather breaks."

Sylvia stands at the window, paying no attention to the men. Distracted, she wrings her hands. Her lips are pale and her face, ashen.

"He's back," she utters, her words cracking.

Gary and I approach the woman.

"You're talking about that van, right?" Gary asks, gazing out the window. "Gramps and I've been wondering why it always parks in the same place and nobody comes out."

"It is a bit strange," I acknowledge, placing my hand on Sylvia's shoulder. I hope the heat in my palm will melt her fears, but I also hope that she doesn't launch into a diatribe about pimps and trolls. I've just hired the guy. I don't want him to think he's stepped into a nuthouse within the first five minutes.

Paul, thankfully, walks to his side. "Let me introduce you to the three-compartment. Each sink has its own sanitation procedure."

"Hold on, Paul," I say as they turn away. "You're a bit overeager. He's not on the payroll until tomorrow."

Gary removes his jacket, tosses it on the prep table, and rolls up his sleeves. "I'll do a load on the house."

"Actually, I'd rather you didn't." I point to the paperwork. "According to law, you can't work until all of the forms are filled out."

Gary raises his brow at Paul and shrugs. "Sorry about that, man."

"I appreciate the sentiment," Paul says, as the men bump fists.

Gary grabs his coat and shakes my hand. "What time do you want me here?"

"If you can clock in at eight a.m., that would be perfect. We'll discuss a permanent schedule tomorrow."

He nods. "Tomorrow." He grabs the paperwork and practically skips out of the kitchen. I approach Sylvia.

"Look," she says, chewing on a thumbnail. "It just circled the block." Her eyes follow the van, which creeps forward in front of the window. "See, it slows down when it passes us. It's done that twice."

Her eyes are crinkled, and the edges of her lips quiver as she tries to suppress tears. She turns to face me.

"That van's latched on to other images, images that are the stuff of my nightmares." Her hand hovers over her mouth as she speaks, which, when open, always reminds me of a gaping wound.

"I see Bobby laying out the clothes I had to wear on the streets. I see all those men." She grabs my hands, wild-eyed. "I see that everything my dad told me about God was a lie. No God who ever loved me would ever let such a thing happen to a loyal follower in his flock. And it's about to happen again."

Her voice has lost its soft, sweet drawl. It sounds angry and unforgiving, like the swoosh of cracking whips, or the thwack of arrows being launched by avenging angels. She lifts her head to the ceiling, and her mouth moves silently as if she were pleading with God. She tries to give a brave smile but bursts into tears.

"Enough of this bullshit," Paul says, darting out of the kitchen. As he sprints across the yard, the van speeds up and drives away. I place my palm on Sylvia's back and feel her unsteady breaths, the quiver of her shoulder blades.

Sniffling, Sylvia swipes an apron string under her nostrils and then pulls her phone from her pocket. "I'm callin' Kevin."

Head down, whispering into the phone, she begins to pace, circling the station. She trips on the rubber floor mat and grabs the rounded edge of the stainless table to keep from falling. After several moments, her movements slow down, his words, I'm sure, dividing her fear in half.

Paul returns, panting, pen and pad in hand.

"I got the first few numbers of his license plate. Whoever it is, at least now they know we're on to him." He looks up. "Or her."

He shakes his head at Sylvia. "Sorry, Syl." He turns to me. "Isn't there something we can do?"

"I doubt it. But it can't hurt to call the police."

"I'll clock out now," Sylvia says, her composure regained. "I know it's early, but I've been good for nothing for thirty minutes. Kevin's on his way—he wants to take me out for an early supper."

As she inserts her card into the time clock, she turns her head to me. Now her eyes are dry and steely, like sharpened blades.

"Nothing is fair in this world. Nothing. And no one knows this better than me. Girls like me are pitied and despised, considered something less than human. But I won't be counted in their numbers. Not anymore. I won't let my past sabotage my future."

I rack my brains trying to come up with a response that wouldn't sound feeble. Something commensurate with the grit of her words. She wants me to understand the misery she's suffered. That it matters. All I can do is gaze at her, hoping my wet eyes communicate that she does matter. She matters, indeed. I pinch my nostrils, which are stinging, and hastily turn away. If I approach her, if I hug this woman, I'll lose it.

Busying myself by stacking dirty dishes onto a tray, I wonder where it all began? Since man first pulled a woman into a cave by her hair? Underreported, stigmatized, and normalized, rape is woven into social fabric and custom. No civilization is immune. Babcia expressed her weariness with the evil of the world in a phrase: *Sytuacja swiatowa jest tragiczna*, meaning: The situation in the world is tragic. I usually take a positive spin on circumstances, but those words enter my mind more and more often these days.

Kevin enters the kitchen, breathless, the doors swinging wildly behind him. His eyes zero in on Sylvia. She takes a couple of steps toward him and stops, tilts her head. He moves forward, pulling her into his arms.

Chapter Twenty

Addie

It's late in the day, and the afternoon sky is dove gray and early-March bleary. Sooty streaks paint the horizon. I just stepped off the bus at Woodward and Washington, and out of nowhere black clouds are rolling in. At once it's raining—cold, heavy—pricking my cheeks, pelting me from all angles. It's as if winter were being ushered in instead of out. I didn't bring an umbrella and begin to sprint. My panting breath manifests in billowing clouds as I try outrunning the rain, now freezing into hail.

I'm alone now, shivering and wet in the Polar Passage, watching the bears in their silent ballet. One of the slick, white beasts paddles over to greet me. Bubbles churn from a scarred nose on an immense, furry face—Talina. Does she recognize me? I haven't been here since December. Our eyes lock as I fiddle with the rosary around my neck. Jessie's healing beads were saving the space for the real deal.

"So, Talina," I say, mouthing the words through the pane. "David called. Yesterday. Says he misses me." I clap my hands at her in glee and then glance around the passage, hoping no one is observing my communion with the beast.

She tips her head and pulls back her lips, showing her teeth. I could swear she's smiling at me. She pushes away from the wall and jettisons up, clamping her jaws around a floating fish. The last nick in my heart is healing. I'm so glad I suggested meeting David here, in our special place.

My sweater clings damp against my torso. Thankfully, it's warm in the passage, and my body begins to relax.

I suppose one could have predicted he'd call. Stories can't all be doom and gloom. Sandwiched between *once upon a time* and *they lived happily ever after*, battles are fought and corpses carried away from the field. But the knight always returns to the princess, rescuing the damsel from the mouth of the beast.

And *yet*. Don't we all hunger for stories with a moral code and happy ending? Don't we yearn for the tales our parents read to us, the promises they made when we were young—that if we were virtuous and played by the rules, we'd have a happy life? Those tales drew, at least in part, from the mythology of my later studies. My parents broke the rules, and look at the fallout. Mom, the beautiful queen of Botox, held captive in a crumbling glass tower while Dad sweeps up the shards beneath.

I shake my head and run fingers through my hair, tangled with rainwater. Talina startles me by pressing her immense stomach into the glass wall, parallel with my body. The water slaps and ripples against the pane, distracting me from my reverie. When she pushes away, I submerge, once again, returning to my reflections.

While researching the Trojan War for my final research paper, I read several translations regarding the Judgment of Paris. All the gods and goddesses are invited to attend the marriage of Peleus and Thetis. Except for Eris, who has a reputation of being a killjoy. Bitter about the snub, she crashes the party by tossing the wedding guests a golden apple with the inscription THE APPLE FOR THE FAIR.

Three goddesses—Hera, Athena, and Aphrodite—are hungry for the apple, so a beauty pageant is staged. Paris, a Trojan mortal, is chosen to judge the winner, who will then reign as the most beautiful goddess and receive the golden apple. Conniving Aphrodite has a trick up her sleeve (as I recall, picking apart a stubborn knot in my hair with my fingertips). She makes a promise to Paris: if he picks her to be the fairest, she will use her powers to make Helen, the most beautiful mortal in the world, fall in love with him.

As in all good myths, the story's complex. But, in the end, Paris—flesh-and-blood male that he is—couldn't be impartial and succumbs to the bribe. He selects Aphrodite as winner, the fairest of them all.

Aphrodite keeps her word, and her powers force Helen to fall madly in love with Paris. But Helen is already married, ergo the tragedy. The situation culminates in the slaughter of the Trojans and the desecration of their temples. Enter the Greek chorus, wailing in the rubble, blood streaked across their cheeks. Paris, using Aphrodite's spell as conduit, forces a relationship through deception and trickery. This Grecian tale does not have a happy ending.

And the moral of this story? Make sure that Eris is invited to the wedding? Don't steal another man's wife?

The moral of the story, and the moral to *my* story, as it's been unfolding, is to be brutal with the truth. Don't accept the bribe, especially those laid out in fairy tales. I've concluded—and on some level, I've known this all along—that reality is my story. I own it. I can't force David to change. I only have the potential to make changes in how I emotionally address and confront what he's capable of giving. The truth is all I've got.

And as I'm thinking this—watching Talina, and now Nuka, paddle around me—a hand rests on my shoulder. I see his reflection in the glass, his tall, thin frame, the slight tip of his head. My shadow twin.

I turn. And he doesn't say a word. Raindrops perch on his brows, dark shadows paint half-moons beneath his eyes. But happiness is written in code throughout his face: in the softness of his gaze, the gentle tilt at the corners of his mouth. We take each other's hands, and my entire being is suffused in happiness. In love. And in gratitude. He lifts my hands to his lips and kisses them, and the feeling of those soft lips on my flesh touches me in places that words can't reach. We lose ourselves for a minute or two in each other's gaze before David breaks the silence.

"What can I say, Addie? Kismet? Fate? Destiny? I've figured out a lot of things, and one of those things is—I love you. I was born to love you. Love conquers all."

I scrunch my nose. Enough of this prattle. I'm going to say what I think. "Love conquers all? I don't like it when you frame your feelings in a cliché."

A woman with two young children walks into the corridor. I place my forefinger to my lips. They walk toward us, and the woman and I exchange smiles. The boy giggles, pointing at the bear's antics, while the woman strokes her fingers through his curls.

David stares at me, his mouth agape, surprised, as if I'd poured a bucket of water over his head. I place my fingertips into the small of his back, pushing him away from the kids. Edging away, we stop at the entrance of the corridor.

He leans his mouth toward my ear, his voice lowered to a whisper. "What am I supposed to say?" His expression bewildered, his fists open and clench shut, as if he were literally grasping at straws.

The woman glances our way and then takes the children's hands into her own. As they exit the corridor, we catch each other's eyes and, with a slight raise of our brow, nod; a woman-to-woman silent acknowledgment that I need space with this man.

I wrap my fingers around David's fists to quiet their flexing. "Lines you hear in songs or read on Hallmark cards—they're someone else's words. They mean nothing to me. When we discuss our feelings with one another, we should be sincere. Furthermore, your wisecracks, those

cards you gave me for Valentine's Day, make me feel as if our sex life—
that thing I do—is the only reason you love me."

Man oh man. This honesty serum is potent, and it's liberating to
tell it, at last, as it is.

He emits a long, low whistle. "Addie. You've got it all wrong. Of
course I go nuts making love with you." His eyes trail up and down my
body. "What man wouldn't? But you've oversimplified my feelings. Our
relationship means so much more to me than sex. You're my center." He
shakes his head, inhaling sharply.

"When you tell me you love me, I parrot the words back, not even
sure what they're supposed to mean. And inside," he beats his fist at his
chest, "inside, I feel helpless. Filled with dread. So I resort to banality.
I don't know what else to say."

His face twists in anguish. "I guess I never knew how much I loved
you, or what the words even meant, until you were gone."

He's like a vulnerable little boy in front of me, and I'm sorry for
him. Sorry that being honest and sharing feelings makes him so miserable. My eyes begin to burn, and his image blurs behind my tears. I
blink several times, to stop their flow.

He looks at me, folds his arms across his chest, and angles his head
to the side, as if he were meeting me for the first time. "I thought you
liked it when I'm funny, playful, when I slap your butt."

"I do, David. I like to joke around. But not at the sacrifice of honest
dialogue. The conversation that we're having now is what I relish. When
we're speaking from our hearts." I move closer to him. "Thank you for
opening the door, telling me what's going on in there."

With shaky hands, he fumbles with the zipper on his parka, zipping
it up an inch, then down. Up and down, over and over. This conversation is so difficult for him.

"Growing up, when guys were talking about sex, it was as if they
were discussing a baseball game. *Hey man, I hit a home run with Teresa
last night,*" he says, his voice thick with irony.

I laugh. "Girls use baseball language, too. Our version of the Teresa story was that she only let him get to second base. And only with her bra on. And only after he invited her to prom."

"It's a heap of crap, right? The man and woman on opposite teams, the man trying to make it to the next base, the woman thwarting his efforts."

"But in baseball, even if you're on a team, you're standing on that field alone. Vulnerable. And someone, David, someone always loses." I brush away his hair, which has, again, fallen into his eyes. "Running from your emotions is more painful than feeling them. You should have gone to the source." I point to my heart. "Me. Asked me what I liked and what I wanted to hear. And it was my fault for not telling you. I was lying to myself and lying to you. I reinvented who I was and played the vixen. It's what I thought you wanted, when all I wanted was to be loved."

I take his hand away from the zipper and twine it with my own. We walk back to the bears, now lolling in the water, their bellies full of fish. Is reinvention what the human species does to attract a mate and ensure our survival? Do Talina and Nuka feel these sorts of emotions, these fragile complexities? Talina dives smoothly under Nuka. Who knows? Maybe.

I turn to David, looking him dead in the eye. "I'm sick of games. It's on my shoulders, too. Even if I didn't understand my actions at the time, I tried to manipulate you so that I could control you. So I could forward my happy-ever-after agenda."

His shoulders drop, as if relieved I'm the one tapping the beehive. His chin trembles as he grasps my hands. "Thank you for that, baby girl."

Taking a sharp breath, he straightens, like a soldier in line awaiting his inspection. "So here I am. Standing in front of you. Trying not to lose you. I don't know what the answer is." His voice softens, breaking.

"And right now I'm still not ready to say the words I know you want to hear."

Tears are rolling down his cheeks. "But I'm ready to try my damnedest." His shoulders heave, his words sandwiched between sobs.

I reach into my pack and remove Kleenex. I take one, brush away my tears, and then hand him the package. He mops his face with a tissue, then removes another and blows his nose.

"Some evenings, after putting down a few," he continues, shaking his head, trying to regain his composure, "I go to sleep thinking, *I'm OK.*" He gazes at me, pain drawing lines across his face. "But when I wake up in an empty bed, I realize I'm not."

"Same, David. Same with me." My gaze searches his face. "I don't want to coerce you into marrying me. Not anymore. And our personal issues are not for each other to solve. I'm learning hard lessons. I can't control your feelings, and I can't control what you do."

Relief floods through me. Is it because David and I, at last, are having a heartfelt discussion? Yes. But no. It goes deeper than a man. I remove the wad of Kleenex dangling from his fingertips, place it in my bag, and take his hands.

"This time away from our relationship has been good for me, David. At first I thought I couldn't live without you. And then, after some time, I realized that I could. I'm learning to take control of my life. Rewriting my narrative is the most honest thing that I can do for myself right now."

"But don't snuff out the Addie I love. That everyone loves. Your whimsy, your thoughtfulness, your kindness, how you care so much about the underdog. What you may consider to be your flaws, most everyone else, me in particular, see as your strengths." He drops my hand to touch my cheek. The familiar gesture's almost painful.

We're quiet for a moment, facing each other. A young man with an infant strapped to his chest walks into the passage. He smiles at us, at our leaky eyes, red noses. He smiles at us wretched, ragged mortals, who are trying to figure it out, trying to muck through the wreckage.

263

"The zoo's my favorite place in The D," he says, bouncing the baby a little.

"We hear you, man," David says, shaking his head as if switching channels. "How old's your child?"

"Eight months yesterday. The animals seem to calm him down. But maybe it's just me who needs calming down," he adds, with a chuckle. "I haven't had a decent night's sleep since the little dude was born. Colic." He bends his head to kiss the top of the infant's head.

"Maybe the pheromones in the animal smells calm you both down," I say, and adjust a tiny knit bootie, half dangling from the baby's foot.

"Could be. Could be." The baby begins to whimper.

"Gotta keep moving," he says over his shoulder, leaving the passage. "See you around."

David lifts the rosary away from my neck.

"A rosary? What's up with this?"

I sigh, massaging my temples with my fingertips. The core of a healthy relationship is transparency.

"The story of this rosary is attached to a past I've been reluctant to share with you. But now's as good a time as any. Wanna grab a cup of coffee?"

"Baby girl, I can match anything you have to dish, line by line, story by story. Let's see whose backstories scare who the most."

"Deal." I say, swatting him on the arm. "Knock, knock."

"Who's there?"

"It's still me."

"I wouldn't want it any other way." He pulls me into him, stroking my hair. "By the way, you're pretty when your hair's damp, and when you're not wearing makeup."

I look up into his face. "You like my rabbit eyes?"

"I love your rabbit eyes."

And then, under the gaze of the great furry beasts, he leans forward, kissing me, whispering, "I love *you*," against my lips.

Chapter Twenty-One

Sam

My gut churns thinking of how my decision to leave Detroit will affect Addie. A pit sits in my stomach, and procrastination is making it grow larger by the day.

We've just closed the diner, and I'm at the counter placing daffodils in vintage teal bottles filled with water. The bottles' globular bases are in the shape of teardrops, and Addie is arranging them on each table and across the counter. Trumpets of yellow-gold cheer brighten my mood, announcing the coming of spring.

Uriah's mom is on her second round of chemo. Our plans are to move to Tennessee by the end of June, but he wants to leave sooner. It will be easier on him knowing he's only a short distance away from his parents. Besides, he's a Southern man at heart; his roots in the culture run deep.

Thank God David's returned to Addie's life. I feel as if a ton of bricks has been removed from my chest. My news will now be an easier pill for her to swallow; she won't feel so alone. She doesn't, however, want him to move back in quite yet, and she tells me her alone time has been fruitful. She seems relaxed, and her face glows.

She asks if things are OK between Uriah and me. I often catch her gazing at me, as if she's wondering what's up. We've always been able to finish each other's sentences; she must know I'm harboring something. My actions in her presence—darting eyes and fluttering hands—surely betray my words. I'm a terrible bluffer, and my dimples, which puncture my cheeks even when frowning, defy my attempts at a poker face. Addie will need to make plans for my portion of the house. And she must replace me at work. I have to tell her soon.

Lella walks across the floor, her countenance somber, unblinking. Standing in front of me, she clasps and unclasps her hands, as if unsure what to do with them. Now they dangle at her side, her fingers clenched into fists.

"Sam. I need to talk to you." She doesn't meet my eye, and her chin falls to her chest. She glances toward my cousin. "Addie, if you don't mind. I need to speak with you, too." Her breath hitches, making a hiccup sound. "But someplace private."

Addie is doing what Addie does best: ensuring each condiment is wiped clean of fingerprints, the pepper mills are full, and the flowers are placed dead center on the tabletop, each stem aligned to perfection. Forefinger on chin, she pinches her lips together, frustrated. When she moves the vase a millimeter to the right, her expression relaxes. After hearing Lella's words, she strides over to join us.

"You OK, Lella?" she asks, catching the woman's expression, which is dull, lifeless.

In the past few weeks, something has changed about Lella. She's quit her impromptu little dances, and her smile doesn't come easy. She's even stopped chewing gum. Her life has always been an open book, but these days she's quiet. Nevertheless, she's punctual, is organized at work, and is pleasant with the customers. She's just not Lella, so we assume it's another man problem. I, for one, am sick of hearing about them.

"Let's just get this over with," she says with a sigh, looking for all the world like she's lost her last friend. Problem after problem, issue after issue. I'll be glad when Welcome Home is past history.

"Give me a minute to check on things," I say. "Paul's been itching to call it a day. I'll join you two in the office."

I walk into the kitchen as Sylvia removes strawberry pies from the oven. Their perfectly fluted crust is packed with the berries that we froze last spring. When thawed, they taste as sweet as jam. Juices ooze through slits in the pastry, and their fragrance casts a lingering perfume about the kitchen.

"I've finished my prep list for tomorrow," Paul says. "Mind if I clock out? I've got friends coming over this evening to watch the Michigan-Minnesota game. I gotta clean my place. It's trashed."

"No worries," I say. "You were so productive in such a short time— maybe you should invite your friends over more often." I wink at him as he removes his apron, balls it up, and tosses it into the hamper as if it were a basketball hoop.

"Thanks, Sam." He pulls out his card and places it under the time clock. Then, he walks over to the sink and bumps Gary on the shoulder with his fist. "You're a Wolverines fan. Why don't you join us?"

"I'd like that, man, I'd like that." Gary lifts his gloved hands out of the soapy water, the sleeves of his faded khaki shirt turned up above his elbows. "I almost wept when LeVert suffered those leg injuries."

Paul cracks his knuckles. "I hear ya, man, I hear ya. But Coach Beilein says he's making progress."

"I'll bring over some sustenance. Spicy grilled wings are my specialty."

Paul smiles, rubbing his hands together.

"That sounds good, man. Real good. Bring your granddad with you."

"I'll let him know you made the offer, but his buddy owns a barbershop. They're meeting there to watch the game. It's good to see him getting out, socializing with old friends. He's been a hermit a long time, man."

If these guys had to remove the word *man* from their dialogue, and sports were also taboo, would they have anything to say to each other? But I smile; it's good to see Gary's making a friend. And an ambitious friend, like Paul, who'll be graduating from Wayne State in a couple of months.

"There'll only be a few dishes to clean after you finish that batch," Sylvia says. She covers the pies in foil and puts them into the reach-in. "I have some prep work to finish. I can handle my own mess."

"Settled," I say. "You guys can clock out now. Go have fun. Sylvia, stay as long as you've the energy to work."

"I'll do that." She casts a smile over her shoulder. When Sylvia is alone—cooking and cleaning in the kitchen—she appears to leave her sordid past behind, content with culinary tasks. I sometimes watch her through the kitchen window when I'm pulling weeds and harvesting vegetables in the garden.

Standing before her flour-dusted prep table, a pile of dough in front of her, she plunges her hands into the snowy mound, forms it into a ball, and then presses, reshapes, and kneads the pastry into submission. She said her father called her *angel*. She reminds me of one, floating about the sky, fluffing up the clouds, looking down upon us mortals and praying we're behaving.

Paul scribbles a note onto a pad and hands it to Gary, who is draining the sink. "Here's my address. Around five thirty or six. Gotta bounce." He grabs his jacket before dashing through the swinging doors.

I exit the kitchen and walk into the office. Lella is leaning her head against the window, staring outside, her palms flattened on top of the desk. Addie stands nearby, head bent, fiddling with her phone.

"Stunning day, right?" Lella asks. "I can't recall the last time it's been this warm so early in the year. It's hard to believe things are popping in the garden." She juts her chin forward, squinting her eyes. "What's Sun Beam up to?"

"She's painting the doghouse," I say, closing the door behind me.

"Sweetness and innocence. God. I could use a helping of that right now."

"Quiche is at the church, organizing the hymnals for tomorrow's service," Addie says, placing her phone on the desk.

"I've missed hearing them sing. I can't wait until they open up their windows. I could use a dose of sweet gospel soul." Lella leans more into the pane, craning her neck to the right. "You can barely make out the side street from here. Lucky you. You never had to watch that van. In the kitchen, it would park right in front of Sylvia's pastry table. Poor thing. She was always so spooked by those dark tinted windows. But it hasn't been around in a couple of weeks, right?"

"Not for a while," I reply, tapping my foot. "That episode's past tense." Come on, girl. Cut to the chase. Quit hemming and hawing.

She turns to face us. "I've been dreading this talk. You may have found me a ditz before, but I'm worried you'll hate me now."

"Lella. You'd have to do something evil—like torturing-animals evil—to make us hate you." Addie touches her shoulder. "We all make mistakes. What's up?"

"What if I slept with something evil? Would you hate me then?" Her face crumbles.

"Just tell us what's wrong." I stand tall, crossing my arms in front of me. I'm sick of hearing about other people's problems when I have enough of my own. And I've errands to run shortly.

"You can put away your fears that the troll was driving the van," says Lella. "Brett's ego's attached to his wheels. He'd never drive such a heap."

"Are you saying what I think you're saying?" I drop my arms, and my shoulders slump.

"I am. Brett's your troll. He's the author of those snarky Yelp reviews, and he cooked up your grandmother's profile on Twitter. He hates you ladies and wants to bring you and Welcome Home down."

"Why? What could we possibly have done to make him so angry?" I pull out the chair from the desk and collapse into the wooden frame.

"As he put it, you asked for it." Lella touches Addie's arm. "Specifically, you, Addie. The electrician who screwed up the wiring before opening day was his brother. Apparently, your review on Angie's List embarrassed him, and he claims their family business suffered. His brother was just as pissed. Blood runs thick."

"You're kidding me," Addie says, her voice a snarl. "That guy was arrogant, his services were overpriced, and he screwed up the wiring. The place could have burned to the ground if Braydon didn't catch his mistake."

"Brett claims it was no big deal," Lella replies.

"How did you find out?" I ask.

Her chest heaves, and she takes a deep breath. "I'll start at the beginning." She twists the ends of her apron ties. "I tried to make it work with him. He's the first guy I've ever dated I felt comfortable introducing to my folks. He looks good on paper: steady job, suburban bi-level, snazzy car paid off. But he bored me to tears. And he was so uptight. Constant road rage, angry with this, pissed off about that. A meat-and-potatoes man—we had nothing in common."

"And this went on—how many months? How could you stand it?"

She shakes her head. "You ladies are with nice, smart, good-looking men. And look at you. Both beautiful. You also own a really cool business. Maybe it's my flat chest, my nutty personality. Maybe it's because I'm just a waiter. Whatever the reason, I haven't been as lucky in love as you."

"I've walked in your shoes, girlfriend. Paid my dues." I turn to Addie, touching her shoulder. "You remember that creep—what's his name—the one I dated in Manhattan? The barista who made me feel like a twice-stuffed potato? I wrote off men for two years after him." I return my gaze to Lella. "You're a living doll who's loaded with talent. Don't settle. The price is too high."

"And pardon me, Lella?" Addie says, swatting her arm with a laugh. "Just a waiter? Allow me to tick off the attributes of being a good waiter."

She lifts a finger, one at a time, as she enumerates each of Lella's strengths. "Good with numbers. Can multitask. Energetic. Can think on her feet and memorize a litany of ingredients." She catches her breath and levels her eyes at the woman. "But most important of all, a good waiter is a gracious people person, who wants to ensure their guests have a lovely meal. It's not a job for the pretentious."

Lella nods, then drops her head, her words directed at her coffee-splattered Crocs. "You're right. My head knows you're right. But I was tired, lonely, so—once again—I lowered the bar another notch. I ignored the obvious and lost myself in the process."

She raises her head. "Long story short, a few weeks back I broke up with him. He didn't take it well. Things got nasty, and he was furious. Made comments like *how dare the likes of me break up with a guy like him?* He even pulled his fist back like he was winding up to hit me. But what he told me was so much worse than a nosebleed."

"I'm gobsmacked. You were dating the troll. I played out dozens of theories of who it could be, and all of this time you were going out with him."

"Yep. Sleeping with the enemy. I had no idea he was such a creep. A wound-tight dweeb, yes. But a creep? Honestly. Not a clue. In retrospect, I figure that in the beginning, he used me to get more information about you guys. Then, I guess, he got used to having me around. I'd cook for him, we'd watch TV, have sex—I had no idea what was up his sleeve."

I emit a long, soft whistle. I'm going into hibernation, off the grid forever, when we move to Tennessee.

"He'd ask questions about the picture of your grandmother," she continues. "Who was she, where was she born, stuff like that. He took a picture of her photograph with his smartphone. He said it took him all of fifteen minutes to write and upload the profile."

She puts her face into her hands and begins to whimper. After a moment, she looks up to regard us, purple mascara streams running down her cheeks.

"As I was walking out the door, he said creating the account and pumping out her tweets were the highlights of his workweek."

Addie's eyes cloud over, and she folds her arms across her abdomen. "But it's odd, right? He decided to quit hounding us after we conducted the smudging ceremony. Jessie and her charms continue to amaze me."

She plucks a pen from her desk and waves it over her head as if she were about to rope a horse. "He may be done, but we're just getting started. Brett needs a visit from Nemesis." She lowers her arm and slips the pen into her pocket, a smile working the sides of her mouth. "Nemesis is the goddess of revenge and exacts a fate on people who have thwarted her. In the end, she'll level a curse on the troll."

"Nemesis or no Nemesis, cyberstalking's a crime," I say, shoving my hands into the pockets of my apron. "I spoke with Tory and Wally about the incidents on Yelp and the fake Twitter account. When a person spreads lies, which they assert to be factual—like our water contains lead, and we serve undercooked chicken—it's a crime. Now we know the criminal."

"I told him I'd tell you guys," Lella continues. "And he said to go for it. Brett's done his homework. He said filing a case would be time-consuming for you. And it would cost a fortune in legal fees. Besides, you could never prove it was him. He's pretty savvy about all things tech. It would be my word against Brett's, which wouldn't stand up in a courtroom."

"He doesn't know the extent of our arsenal," I say to Addie, winking. "Two weapons going by the names of Tory and Wally."

"I don't know, you guys," Lella says, shaking her head. "After all you've been through this past year, it would open old wounds—be emotionally draining."

"Actually, it would heal old wounds." My gut still clenches when I envision Babcia's picture above those detestable words. That dude must suffer.

Lella's shoulders drop, relieved. "I'm so sorry for the role I played. If you want me to help nail him in any way, it would be my pleasure."

She unties the back strings of her apron. "I'm off to the pottery studio. It's time to spin my wheels with mother earth. I'm sick of dealing with men."

We take turns hugging her. She executes a tight pirouette—a feat, wearing clogs in such a small space—and then flounces out the door, wearing her pixie grin. The girl's back in business.

I regard my cousin and emit a long-drawn-out sigh. "At last we can cross this nightmare off the list. Brett underestimated us. I'll call Tory. As they say, revenge is a dish best served cold."

Addie laughs and lifts the palm of her hand. I slap it, giving her a high five, relieved. One less worry as I pack my bags. I'll tell her my plans on Monday.

I check my phone. "Oops. Gotta dash. Theo's picking me up, and I'm running late."

"Tell him thank you. Kev said insulated windows will save us thousands in energy costs over the long haul."

My lips twitch. There's no long haul here for me. I try ignoring the sadness tugging at my heart and turn my head so my trembling chin won't give me away.

"His company's giving us the employee discount. They'll knock thirty percent from the top," I say, looking out the window, blinking back tears. "All these windows also cost us valuable shelving space." I catch Sun Beam in the corner of my vision. "But they're worth it." I grab my handbag and retreat, closing the door behind me.

The diner's empty; everyone is gone for the day. Theo's at the door, hands shoved in his pockets. I unbolt the locks.

"Afternoon, Theo. Sorry to keep a good man waiting. Another episode of Welcome Home—this one more bizarre than the last."

"It's a soap opera around here. What's it this time?"

"Dude. What a story. I'll tell you on the way to the factory."

"Did you take the measurements per my instructions?"

"I'd screw it up for sure. Uriah measured them—he's a math whiz." I remove a sheet of paper from my pocket and hand it to Theo.

He studies it, glancing at the windows. "Looks good. All you need to do is to select the frame. That shouldn't take long."

"Nothing I can't handle. Let's go the back way, via the garden. You have to see the doghouse Sun Beam and Braydon built. She's painting it now."

To say it's a beautiful day could not begin to describe it. It's an impossibly beautiful day. A day that might have inspired Shakespeare to pen a love sonnet, Monet to paint his *Water Lilies*. The first of the sorrel and chives are pushing their way through the soil. The sky, an intense shade of blue, captures my attention.

A gentle breeze blows through the garden, stirring the ribbons in Sun Beam's ponytails. Wherever she goes, she sprinkles a trail of fairy dust behind her. She holds the paintbrush above the can, and it drips with red paint. She brushes the excess away against the rim, and then her hand glides across the wooden frame in one unbroken stroke.

"That's quite a palace," Theo says, bending to admire the house.

"Thank you," she says, looking up into Theo's face, her eyes squinting in the sunlight. "The dogs like it, too. It's big enough for both of 'em." She resumes her work with the quiet deliberation of Picasso.

As we leave the garden, a smell passes beneath my nostrils. A whiff of something rancid in the air. I glance at the garbage cans lining the gutter across the street, their lids balanced atop bulging black bags. The rubbish must be decaying in the sun—the city didn't pick up yesterday's trash. I glance over my shoulder at Sun Beam. I shrug.

Theo's truck is in the lot, waxed and glistening crimson in the brilliant light. As he opens the door for me, I glimpse the top of his wrist: La Vie Est Absurde.

"OK, Theo," I say, climbing into the truck. "Ready to roll."

∾

Addie

Through the window, I watch as Theo bends down to admire Sun Beam's project. Sam's eyes are cast to the sky, a gentle smile on her face. Theo stands, and they walk away, retreating from my vision. This is what I've been working so hard on, an appreciation of the moment. It's not so arduous a task today. I feel good. Grateful. I'm in the best place I've been since those Sundays spent cooking with Babcia. I reach for the phone to call my mother. I wish she could come to know this feeling, too.

Mom and I shoot the breeze for close to an hour. With earbuds in place, my hands are free to organize the office. This week's receipts in the first folder, special orders organized by dates in the metal bin, cookbooks returned to their proper places on the shelves. Mom tells me she's thrilled about my reunion with David, and I explain the changes I've been making with myself. She believes my happiness hinges on the work with my therapist, but I know it's something else. Something not so easily explained.

I prod her gently, ask her how she's doing. It saddens me that Mom tries to erase her past. That she's never learned to love herself. Aside from our relationship, it seems she'd like to erase the present, too. She unloads a fragment of her misery with Max on me. Last week he insisted she cancel a dinner date with a girlfriend, an old roommate from nursing school. Max had caught a cold, and if he's feeling bad, so should she. He's such a controlling, arrogant prick. But Mom's frozen in place, afraid to leave him. She knows the beast and is willing to live with it. Fear trumps change. Mom's always believed in beautiful things.

We say our good-byes, our *can't wait to see yous*, and I pick up the picture of David. My thoughts drift. We're working on our stuff now. Separately. But we see each other several times a week. There's been a shift in our relationship. An honesty invading our dialogue, which is healing. With my forefinger, I trace the contours of his cheekbones . . . those beautiful lips . . .

A bloodcurdling scream. Sylvia! I drop the picture to the floor, shattering the glass, ready to rush to the kitchen. Out of the corner of my vision I catch a thick reddish hand grabbing Sun Beam's shoulder like a thief. She drops her paintbrush and looks up at the man. A second death-defying shriek. And now a third, choked back, frozen in my throat.

A hulk of a redheaded giant. Sun Beam looks about wildly as he bends to grab her. He tosses her onto his hip, as if she were a bag of feathers. A wave of terror wells up from my belly. Her face is contorted, and her arms and legs thrash in his grasp. He stumbles away, his lionesque head shifting left to right, his prey in his arms. I grab my phone. I press 9-1-1. A surge of adrenaline courses through my veins as I bolt for the back door.

My pulse roars in my ear as I scream into the phone. "Welcome Home Diner, 15953 East La Grande. A child's being kidnapped. Get here. Now!"

Sylvia is on him, clawing at his back. With his free hand, he flicks her away as if she were a pesky fly, knocking her to the ground. He staggers into the garden, moving forward, booted feet trampling through the chives. I must stop him! And then I see it. The rusty van. Dark tinted windows. The side door open.

Sun Beam's screaming our names. "Addie! Sylvia!" The terror in her voice shatters my heart.

A rustling behind me, and now a roar. From out of the shadowy bushes, Hero springs forward like a crazed white phantom. Head down, his lips are pulled back, and he snarls. Fierce teeth tear into Earl's leg as the man screams, staggers backward, and then sways. He tosses Sun Beam as one would a bag of trash onto the ground, to fend off the attacking dog. His arms swing by his sides; his eyes bulge out from their sockets, red rimmed and vacant. He tries shaking his leg free from the pointed daggers, which are digging, digging, digging into his leg.

Sylvia hurls herself at Sun Beam, who is crawling toward her with a wild look on her face. Sylvia wraps her in her arms, bending over her, using her body as a shield to protect her.

I race toward them. "Out of here. Now!" I pull them to their feet. My mind is racing, my head scanning the scene. We can't return to the diner. He could trap us there, like the Cyclops trapped the Greeks in his cave. "Forward," I shout. "To the street." Holding hands, we run, staggering, across the yard. I raise my head to the sky and wail, screaming, "Help us, someone, oh God, please help us."

Earl's pants are ripped away, shredding around his calf and ankle, exposing flesh dripping with blood. He falls to the ground, pulls his knees into his chest, clasps his hands behind his neck so his elbows protect his face. The defensive instincts of a rodent. Hero rams his muzzle into the man's armpit, and Earl has his moment.

He rolls over on top of the dog and places his forearm against Hero's throat. With his enormous heft, he leans into the dog's neck, putting pressure on Hero's windpipe. Their roles reversed, Earl has the advantage and is choking the dog. Hero's bloodied mouth emits a high-pitched keening whine. A fist clenches my heart. Horrified, I push the women forward, away from this spectacle of gore.

I take a last glance at the scene. Earl's and Hero's bodies are locked together. Amid our screams, our pleas for help, Gary dashes into the garden, racing toward the scene. We run toward La Grande just as Theo and Sam pull into the lot and screech to a halt. They bolt from the car.

"Earl tried to take Sun Beam," I shout, pulling at Theo's shirt. "Now he's killing Hero." I point to the scene. "Gary just got there."

Theo and Sam race toward the dog and Earl. Gary has Earl's arms pinned to the ground. Theo bends over and crashes a heaving fist against Earl's face. Theo keeps smashing his fist into Earl, again and again and again, until Earl's face slackens.

And the Greeks who remained alive in the cave heaved the stake of burning coals into the Cyclops eye, buried it deep into the socket, twirling it around as a carpenter does his auger, saying, "It is the stroke of the Gods, and thou must bear it."

Hero rolls away, onto his side. Sam falls to the ground, cradling his head.

A siren's wail drones louder and louder as it approaches. Relief floods my body as a police wagon roars into the lot. Two officers jump out of the vehicle. I point to Theo, now sitting on Earl's chest, while Gary struggles to hold down his thrashing arms. The police run toward the scene.

Theo stands, gasping, pointing to Sun Beam. "This bastard tried to take the girl." Releasing Earl's arms, Gary staggers to his feet and backs away. Earl jumps up and dashes toward his van.

The cops grab Tasers. Barbed electric bolts flash from the gun with a rapid stream of clicking sounds: *tick, tick, tick, tick, tick.* Earl falls to the ground, his body convulsing. One of the officers drops to his haunches and cuffs him, and the other rushes toward me, Sylvia, and Sun Beam, issuing commands into his phone.

Theo limps backward and leans against a tree, his shoulders heaving up and down. The tattoo on his bicep, Fate Fell Short, is streaked with blood.

"'And the abominable shall have their part in the lake, which burneth with fire and brimstone,'" pants Theo, his hand cradling the other bloodied fist. Gary staggers toward him, shaking out his arms, and stands by his side. Angus, his fingers spread over his heart, walks toward the scene. His steps are uneven, as if he's aged fifty years.

The wind is still. Nothing is stirring.

Sun Beam, Sylvia, and I are clutched together. My blood is pounding in places where I've never felt its rhythm before—the backs of my knees, my elbows, the lobes of my ears. Sylvia and I try to catch our breaths, and Sun Beam is sobbing wretched, heaving sounds. Red paint is splattered across her face and arms, but the girl appears to be unharmed. She breaks away, sniffling, trying to compose herself.

"I've got to see Hero." We follow her to the dog.

Hero staggers to his feet, disoriented, and Sam holds him to her chest with such fierceness the dog whines and shivers beneath her clutch. And I start to shake, as well, uncontrollably, as I gaze at the wreckage surrounding me.

Our garden is ruined, defiled, purged of all of its beauty. The splintered sunlight is garish and the air smells rancid, stained with sweat. Trampled sorrel and chives are smashed into gaping holes of soil. Sun Beam's glasses lie in the dirt, bent, but miraculously unbroken. I pick them up, try to straighten the frames, and hand them to the child.

Quiche rushes into the yard and stops dead in her tracks. The officer is leading Earl to his patrol wagon. One look at the man—his bloodied leg, purple face, his gaping mouth with spittle running down the sides—tells the story. His face is pulverized beyond recognition. He's handcuffed, and his swollen fingers dangle like the paws of a prehistoric simian; man can be the cruelest of beasts.

The policeman locks Earl inside the back of the wagon. Quiche slaps her palms across her mouth.

"Baby," she screams, running toward Sun Beam. She falls onto her knees and pulls the child into her arms.

A wail of sirens circles our tangled knots of quivering bodies. An ambulance pulls into the parking lot. Two attendants leave the vehicle, and they rush to the police officers. As the police give instructions, their eyes dart around, surveying the scene. One attendant breaks off and heads to Sun Beam, while the other approaches Theo and lifts his fist, examining his injury.

Quiche lifts Sun Beam into her arms. "I'm takin' you home. Gettin' you away from this mess." She cradles the girl as if she were an infant and stumbles away from the attendant, toward the back door of the diner.

Sam is giving the policeman a brief rundown on our history with Earl. The officer, taking notes, says, "Strong emotions combined with a mental defect can trigger violent, impulsive behavior." Then, noticing Quiche's retreat, he leaves the conversation and follows her. He taps her on the shoulder.

"An attendant's here to examine the child," he says, his Taser reflecting a piercing sliver of light. "An ambulance will take her to the hospital."

"She's not injured." Quiche releases a strangled cry. "She needs to go home."

"It's protocol. A social worker will also be there." He places his hand on her shoulder. "We must be absolutely sure this child has not been injured in any way."

Sun Beam clutches her mother around her neck, her glasses lopsided across her face.

"I'm her mother. I need to go with her." She bursts into tears.

"Of course." The officer nods.

Quiche turns and staggers to the ambulance, Sun Beam cradled in her arms. The officer turns to Sam.

"The dog needs to be cleaned and examined. We'll make a report and call a vet."

"My dog saved this girl."

"Again, routine stuff. We must check the dog to make sure he doesn't have rabies. Please put him on a leash until the vet arrives." He glances at Hero, who is twitching, his eyes at half mast.

The officer turns and approaches a paramedic, and they hurry toward the police wagon. Sam reaches into her handbag and pulls out a leash. She bends down to hook it onto Hero's collar, and the dog's creased forehead relaxes, as if relieved that at last he will be tethered to his master. Sam fingers the silver disk—the imprint of HERO glimmering beneath our gaze.

"So now we know how Hero got his name," I say, trying to calm the shake in my voice. "He must have been a guard dog or something."

"Something magnificent, no doubt." Sam crouches on the ground, running her finger under his collar. She looks up, squinting into the sunlight. Shielding her eyes with her palm, she catches my eye. "Good doesn't always trump evil. But this time it triumphed." Hero's eyes brighten as he looks at Sam. He pulls his lips back, shows his teeth, and appears to smile at his master. She kisses his forehead and then stands, his leash in her hand. The dog rises and presses his rib cage into the side of her leg. "You know how sweet he is around children. Hero's the protector of purity and innocence."

"You should breed him. I'd like one of his offspring. I can't bear thinking about what would have happened if it weren't for this dog." I bend down and trail my fingers down his spine. His tail wiggles, not quite a wag, and then he falls back into the earth, closing his eyes. The dog's exhausted.

"Time's a thief," Sam says, tucking her shirttail into her jeans, before running her fingers through her hair. "With any luck, maybe it will steal Sun Beam's memory of today."

Sylvia's nostrils flare, and color rises to her cheeks. Veins stand out in ridges on her temple and throat. "She will never forget this day," she says, ferocity attached to each word. "She will carry forever the memory of the wretched man who tried to capture her." She rubs her eyes with her apron string.

"But we'll be here to remind her he failed," I say to her, brushing away bits of grass stuck to her forearm. "That he's forever gone. And we'll remind her that most of her childhood was not like today. Most of it was filled with love."

I take Sylvia's hands. "And when she's an old woman, she'll remember that once upon a time, she loved a dog named Hero. She also loved a young man named Braydon, who loved a dog named Bon Temps."

She squeezes my hands, looking into my eyes. "And there were two brave women, Addie and Sam, who made a family from scratch, using what others left behind."

My jaw begins to tremble, and the tears roll down my cheeks. "And she'll remember a beautiful princess named Sylvia, who possessed the soul of goodness."

Sylvia drops my hands and wraps her arms across her stomach, her hands cradling her elbows. Her eyes moisten as she whispers the words—

"Troubles came, troubles passed." She lifts her face to the sky. "And they all lived happily ever after."

Her cracked and broken teeth glimmer as pearls in the sunlight, and then she unleashes a smile of such magnificence I shiver.

Chapter Twenty-Two

Addie

Sam and I slide into David's truck. My thigh is planted next to his, sittin' country, as Quiche would say. He wears a navy sweatshirt that has a gold *M*, the insignia for the University of Michigan, stitched on the front.

"Thanks for the lift, babe." I turn my head to kiss him, and my nose twitches. He smells like me.

Reading my mind, he laughs. "I know, I know. I ran out of shampoo. I'm sure yours costs a king's ransom, so I'll replenish my generic at the drugstore while you guys are in your meeting."

We fasten our seat belts as he heads north toward Woodward and Grand Boulevard. An early-morning rain washed the patina of decay away from the streets, and the sidewalks are wet, shining like silver. Scattered, low-hanging clouds resemble dandelions trembling in a breeze. They hover in the sky, the palest of blues, pooling into and reflecting away from the Renaissance Center's mirrored facade.

The RenCen, a group of interconnected skyscrapers, is world headquarters to General Motors. Last summer the GM logo was modernized, and "Reflecting a New Detroit" was introduced as the tagline. The buildings tower in the horizon, sparkling like crystals, commanding our attention in the distant sky.

We drive past one of the century-old churches lining the street. Grief-stricken angels, with their elegiac contours, and fierce, winged gargoyles, with their ragged stares and outstretched tongues, stand as sentinels at the entrance. A stained-glass window catches a ray of light, scattering a rainbow of hues across the damp street. The three of us are quiet, in awe before our city, which seems to stagger beneath this surfeit of beauty.

David stops in front of Tory and Wally's office, located in an area known as the New Center. Sam hops from the truck, but I linger next to David as it idles.

"It's hard letting you out of my sight, baby girl. Every time I think of that afternoon . . ." His face flushes, and his lips curl in disgust. "Damn it all. I should have been there to protect you." He slams his fist against the steering wheel, and I take his hand.

"Silly. You were working. Are you offering to be my bodyguard?"

He nuzzles his nose into my neck. "If something ever happened to you, I couldn't go on." His words are muffled. It tickles and I giggle, pushing him away.

"Nothing's going to happen to me." Squeezing his hand, I smile into his eyes. "I promise."

"Give me a call when you're done. Man." He swipes his bangs away from his eyes. "I can't wait to hear how everything's shaking out."

I slide out of the truck to join Sam.

We take the elevator to the twentieth floor, and the doors open into one massive room. The entire floor is their office. Decorated in the style of chic, vintage Motown, the decor reflects the couple's love of Detroit. Office chairs and sofa upholstery, as well as luxurious draperies, are designed in custom fabrics of royal purple, burgundy, gold, and black, and reflect the glamour of an era gone by. Framed albums of the Rolling

Stones and magazine covers from *Life* adorn the walls, celebrating the spirit of the city.

"Your office is fabulous." Dazzled by the opulence, I turn in a slow circle, trying to absorb every detail. "Motown's my favorite era of Detroit history."

A Detroit-based record company in the late fifties coined the name Motown, a combination of *motor* and *town*. The significance of the label was that it was African American owned, and it integrated popular music with soul.

"Our hope is that while doing business in our office, our clients don't forget they're in Detroit, and how fabulous our city was"—Tory sweeps her hand across the skyline, set in enormous windows—"how fabulous our city *is*."

"No doubt," replies Sam, walking to the wall to the left of the window, which is lined with vintage 45 records encased in acrylic. "Temptations, Four Tops, Spinners, Jackson Five . . . oh, you've got a couple of Marvin Gaye and Tammi Terrell. They're my favorite."

Humming the tune to "Ain't No Mountain High Enough," she walks to the next record and studies it, wearing such a mouth-splitting grin her dimples appear to be bullet holes in her cheeks. Placing one hand on her hip, she swirls around to Tory, Wally, and me and thrusts her outstretched palm toward us. She sings the title phrase from the song, "Stop! In the Name of Love."

"Sorry," she says, tossing back her hair, her eyes sparkling. "I couldn't resist."

"You can't imagine how many of our clients have that exact reaction when they see the forty-five." Wally turns to his wife. "But no one to date has belted it out like Sam. Perhaps you missed your calling." Sam's cheeks become pink at his compliment. Uh-oh, don't give the girl an inch.

"The song was number one on the *Billboard* chart once upon a time," Tory muses.

I smile. "I've always loved the Supremes. Diana Ross reigns forever as queen of Motown. She's still smokin' hot today. Too bad she left The D for LA."

Wally joins Sam, stands by her side, and directs her to the next series of records on the other side of the window.

"Ah yes, the sixties. Tory and I cut our teeth on Stevie Wonder and Marvin Gaye. An era of crossing bridges and making history. The music broke all of the nonsense down. Racial tension melted away every time Eddie Hendricks's voice filled the stage. That man could sing like an angel."

Tory turns to me. "Wally must have been his biggest fan. Still is," she explains, love captured in the glow of her eyes. "When I first laid eyes on my husband, we were in our second year of law school at Wayne State. It was the early nineties. Our first date he took me to Fonte d'Amore for dinner. I remember the dish we shared, Spiedini alla Romano, made with fresh mozzarella." She catches my eye, raises her brows. "Like you and Sam, they made everything from scratch. I was sad to see it go."

She walks over to her husband, takes his hand, and squeezes it. "And you were so handsome. You looked just like Eddie, minus the beard. And, oh, that smile. A smile just like his." Her eyes mist as she gazes at her husband. "You may have gained a belly—must be those gooey Italian cheeses you devour—but you still have that smile."

"Flattery will get you everywhere. But I did resemble him, didn't I?" He studies his wife thoughtfully, rubbing his chin, as if remembering their early years. They must have been good to them. Tory and Wally pull up chairs and place our file on the coffee table.

"Less intimidating than a desk, right?" She opens the folder.

Sam and I take a seat, joining them.

"Encouraging news regarding your linen man," Tory says, settling into her seat. "The court denied him bail. Turns out he said he was going to use the girl as ransom to extort money from Welcome Home."

"Money? Good luck with that." Remembering that monstrous hand grabbing Sun Beam's small shoulder, I feel a wave of acid well up from my gut. "I think he had more than extortion on his mind."

"He said you ladies put a hex on him. And he was owed." Wally's eyes crinkle in incredulity. "In all our years of practicing law, we've never had a client accused of witchery."

"Have you ever been around when our hot sauce was delivered?" I ask.

"You mean Jessie's Hellfire and Redemption?"

"That's the one," I reply.

"We love the product," Tory says. "It's delicious. I stir it into the Root Vegetable Soup I always order." Her eyes glaze over and then wander to the ceiling. "There's this one flavor Wally and I try to pinpoint. It's a flavor we've never before tasted. Tangy, spicy, and ethereal. Just like the name suggests." Her eyes refocus and return to meet mine. "But, no, we haven't met the woman who makes it."

"Well, you'd remember Jessie. She can be a bit intimidating." I exchange glances with Sam. "When Earl said we'd better watch our backs, Jessie was there and came to our defense. She may have said something about a curse, but believe me, she wouldn't hurt a flea." I'm doubtful my last statement is accurate, but it seems to be the thing to say at the moment.

"These days the courtroom doesn't place credence on curses and hexes. This isn't a Salem witch trial." A smug tug pulls at the corners of Tory's crimson mouth. "First, we'll try settling out of court. If not, fingers crossed, let's hope David Swartz will be our judge. He'll laugh Earl out of the building."

"Settling out of court? For what he did?"

"Settling a potential civil suit out of court would have no bearing on a criminal case. It wouldn't even be admissible in one. No worries, ladies. When it's all said and done, attempted kidnapping will translate to a significant amount of jail time. But we'll see. The man's likely deranged." Tory taps her pen on a legal pad. "If he's found to be legally insane, he'll likely be found not guilty by reason of insanity, and hospitalized."

"Given hospital time? He can't get away with this." I turn to Sam, grinding my jaws together. I swivel to face the lawyers. "Maybe he's not crazy, after all." My neck dampens as heat flushes through my body. "He's simply evil to the core."

"After the preliminary examination," Wally continues, "the judge determines if there's enough evidence for the case to go to trial."

"When will that be?"

"Not for several months. Sentencing follows three weeks later."

Sam stiffens, and the blue in her eyes seem to darken, taking on a hunted look. "Earl belongs under the jail, not in it." Memories from that day haunt her just as much as they do me.

Wally clears his throat. "I'm reasonably confident he'll receive the maximum sentencing. We'll keep you posted." He turns to his wife. "Shall I continue?"

"May as well. Gives them another reason to celebrate."

"Turns out the whole of Detroit is not out to get Addie and Sam Jaworski." He gives a thumbs-up. "Just one company. And only three people within said company—all folks with whom you're familiar."

I pull on Sam's sleeve, and we lean in to hear more.

"When investigating the Twitter case," he says, straightening his glasses, "we knew Brett and the electrician were brothers. But get this. Earl's their first cousin."

I glance at Sam, my mouth falling open. She cranes her neck toward Wally. "Come again?"

"Turns out they're members of a notorious Detroit family. Their company operates out of a warehouse on 8 Mile. The operation serves as an umbrella corporation for a group of small businesses catering to the needs of restaurants. You may have heard of it. Restaurant Equipment Leases and Services."

"I have," Sam says, speaking quickly. "Before we opened, I looked up the business online. That's where we found the electrician." She nods at me. "You know, Brett's brother. He works for the company. I also considered leasing a cooler from them, but their prices were absurd. I can't imagine anyone renting equipment from that place."

"Apparently, people anxious to expedite getting a liquor license for their establishment," Tory says. She clears her throat and continues. "They've ties with the Alcoholic Beverage Control agency. They also have connections for obtaining code compliance certificates and are pros at fabricating bogus permits. That's the part of their business—the most lucrative part of their business—not advertised. The operation is quite familiar with the inside of a courtroom, I can assure you. And surprise, surprise." She wiggles her eyebrows. "Their enterprises also include a linen company."

With a start, my hand flies to my mouth. "Oh God. Linen Express."

Tory nods. "Normally the linen company wouldn't have approached the diner to solicit business. You're small potatoes compared to their other clients."

"The company boss couldn't have cared less about you," Wally adds. "He had no idea what his nephews were up to. In fact, the last thing he wants is additional scrutiny via litigation. But the three men took your review on Angie's List personally. It pissed them off so much they decided to mess with you. In as many ways as they could think of. I imagine they had a grand time." He puffs out his cheeks. "Until ol' Earl got out of hand."

"So how can you prove that Brett was our troll?"

"We secured a crucial bit of evidence that links him to the defamation of Welcome Home," Tory says.

"It's the most important piece in the puzzle," Wally adds. "I had a hunch some of those tweets could have been made from the man's office at work. As part of discovery, we were allowed to subpoena the hard drives from the computers he used at the warehouse." Tory nods at her husband in admiration.

"You can subpoena a hard drive?" I ask.

"In certain matters of civil disputes, yes," Tory says. "We believed it would have been tricky subpoenaing his personal PC—invasion of privacy, and so on and so forth. But not computers from his office. Fortunately, he doesn't own the equipment. It's all owned by the corporation. Usage is not the same thing as ownership."

"As a rule," Wally continues, "we can seek material regarding any nonprivileged matter pertaining to our claims. The court allows this as long as it's reasonable and will lead to the discovery of admissible evidence." His fingertips drum the tabletop. "The hard drive was imaged. A computer forensic expert inspected the files and shared what was relevant to our case. And certain juicy morsels of those files, my fine young women, are our smoking gun." Leaning back in his chair, he takes a deep breath, as if to savor the moment.

"Bravo," Sam says, clapping her hands in glee. She grins at me. "Of all the diners, in all the towns, in all the world, the two most brilliant lawyers walk into ours."

"Oh, please," Tory says, wagging her finger at us. "Payback is a wonderful thing. We're having the time of our lives. Attempted kidnapping is one thing," she continues, her voice growing serious. "But with online defamation, we're treading terrain in a brave new world. And we've only just begun."

Her eyes harden. "The bad news is that in the end it's unlikely your troll will get the justice he deserves. Maybe a fine, at best." She shrugs. "Who knows? But the good news is their family name will, once again, be dragged through the mud. Especially in the kidnapping case." She leans back in her chair, stroking her neck while looking at the ceiling. "Maybe one day we'll be able to bring the company down. I shudder to think of what that family has gotten away with through the years."

"What about Gary?" I nod at Sam. "We're worried he may have violated parole getting involved in the fight."

"Please let Gary know that while he's on parole his involvement may be subject to parole board review," Wally says. "But since he helped stop a crime, it would be extremely unlikely that his behavior would result in a violation." He knits his hands behind his neck and puffs out his chest, stretching his upper back.

Sam smiles. "Gary said he'd take a life sentence if it meant saving Sun Beam and Hero."

"You should warn your staff they'll likely be called in as witnesses," Wally says. "Most certainly you two. This could be going on for months."

"No worries," I say, dreading the thought of having to see the Cyclops again. I now understand how Sylvia must have felt when she testified against her pimp. I nod at Sam. "We're not going anywhere." Her eyes flicker at me nervously as she clasps and unclasps her hands. I shake my head incredulously. "All of this stemmed from my giving that dude a bad review on Angie's List? Everything I wrote about his work was the truth. I wasn't being nasty or vindictive, just relating my experience. People need to be warned. But everything he wrote about us was a lie."

She looks at me, smiling sadly. "It's OK, Addie. It all makes sense. It was their form of payback."

This is too much to wrap my brain around. I'll have to assimilate it later. I'm ready to put this conversation to bed. I sigh, my shoulders sinking as I turn back to the attorneys.

"When you dealt with the contract, you said your time would be pro bono. That was so generous of you. But since you've taken on the troll and Earl, we aren't comfortable with that arrangement anymore."

"Addie," Wally says, removing his glasses and leaning toward me to peer into my eyes. "You must understand. As we've told you many times, you two have sparked an energy that's revitalizing the East Side.

Tory and I want to be on that train when it pulls into the station." He places his palm over Tory's hand. "This is sport for us. Why deny us the many pleasures life has to offer?"

Tory smiles, nodding in agreement with her husband. I shrug, holding my hands helplessly in the air.

"We'll be seeing you often in the coming months," Tory says. "You should be proud of yourselves. We'll all have a fine time sweeping up the mess in this city."

Relief runs through my body at the thought of these nightmares at last being resolved. I smile at Sam, in an attempt to catch her eye. She doesn't seem to notice. Her face is flushed, and she appears uneasy, her fingers raking through her hair. Then she reaches for her bag, making a great effort to look for something.

This behavior's not characteristic of my cousin. She's the one who's carefree, the one who'd normally be jumping up and down in glee, practically airborne at this point. What's up with her?

Chapter Twenty-Three

Sam

Heartbreak, misery, and tears are the baggage of hard decisions. At least when you're following your heart. Knowing my choice doesn't have to be forever consoled us both. *Decisions don't have to be permanent. They're made to be broken,* I had said to Uriah, before dissolving into tears. *Tennessee's only a nine-hour drive from Detroit.* But we both knew the truth. Nine hours may as well be nine months in our worlds of complexities and schedules.

I direct my attention to preparing the soil for our first spring crop. I spade the soil again and again, and with each thrust, replay the dialog. And then, with the back of my trowel, I smooth the dirt, working out my feelings.

Today's my birthday, which this year falls on Palm Sunday. It would be an anomaly for the occasion to slip by without a fuss, but with all the tumult in our lives of late, I'd be relieved if my thirty-second came and went unnoticed.

The weather, as it's been all month, is unseasonably warm. The windows and doors of the Tabernacle are open. The swell of gospel singing accompanied by organ is interspersed with clapping, punctuated with shouts of *Hallelujah—Amen!* They've sung this hymn, "Shine on Me," many times, and it's one of my favorites.

From the garden, I regard the scene in the kitchen. Sylvia arranges Heartbreakers onto a pedestal. Paul shakes excess flour from a cut-up chicken, and places the pieces in a wire-mesh basket before lowering it into the deep fryer. My eyes shift to the office window. Addie's head is bent in concentration, and her white-blonde hair falls over the keyboard. I take a sharp breath, and tears spring to my eyes. I feel the sisterly tugs on my emotions familiar to me since I was a child.

I rummage through a cigar box filled with waterproof markers, twine, and gardening bric-a-brac and locate the Popsicle stick labeled RADISHES. I stick it into the soil, and then wrap my arms around my knees, hugging them to my chest.

The garden has been repaired from the attempted kidnapping, cleansed of all ferocity and evil. We replanted the sorrel and chives, and Jessie burned sage at each corner of the vegetable plot, conducting her charms in the folds of the night.

My gaze rests on the doghouse, and I smile. Something that could have symbolized a horrific event has now been transformed into a bit of humor. With Sun Beam and Braydon's assistance, Jévon made the finishing touches to the house with a customized graffito. He painted a caricature of Hero and Bon Temps greeting each other, bumping paws, the bubble from Hero's mouth penned with the words "Wassup, dawg?"

I look down at my knees, my jeans grimy with dirt. I'm glad I thought to bring a change of clothes to work. I, at least, can honor my birthday by wearing something special: the vintage pale-peach dress with the green vines stitched at the hem. It carries a pale-pink discoloration at the bodice, the red wine souvenir from last year's picnic. Despite Addie's efforts, it never came clean.

I stand and grab the handles of the wheelbarrow, admiring my work, the tidiness of the rows. Glancing at the garden, I notice the bag of seeds on the ground, unopened. So preoccupied with my thoughts, I forgot to plant them. With a heavy sigh, I grab my trowel, kneel back on the ground, and dig into the earth.

The seeds, at last, are blanketed by rich black soil. Through the office window, I see that Addie's place at the desk is now vacated. I check my phone: 11:05 a.m. The staff is transitioning from breakfast to lunch. She must be on the floor, easing the changeover.

I won't tell her I'd even considered leaving Detroit in the first place. What would be the point? Surely everyone has the urge to run away from time to time. Listening to my heart, I decided to stay.

I grab the hose, twist the nozzle, and water the garden. Then, I rinse my hands and face in the icy flow. Task complete, I roll the wheelbarrow, filled with my gardening supplies, back into the shed. Humming under my breath, I stride into the office, where my dress hangs on a hook. I finger the hem, admiring the tight stitches. I haven't worn this since last year, but the dress holds a day full of memories. I'd promised myself I'd never wear it again until I'd met a guy I was into. It's strange I never thought to wear it with Uriah.

Uriah. I thought I'd follow that man to the ends of the earth. Why aren't I feeling more pain? After telling him I'd changed my mind, choosing not to interrupt my life, we shed the expected tears, along with the words we would manage a long-distance relationship. Was it my imagination, or did I see relief creep into his eyes?

Maybe it was all too sudden, our relationship so accelerated it burned itself out, a wildfire smoldering before leveling a forest to ruins. Perhaps just knowing I'm capable of loving someone, of being loved in return—maybe *that's* enough. I'll take it for now. I pull down the window shade and slide the dress over my head. I like the way I feel when I wear it: feminine, strong, and victorious. I'm wearing it to please me. No one else.

I walk into the kitchen, grab a bowl, and fill it with potatoes. Vegetable peeler in hand, I take my position at the stainless-steel table.

The fact I'm wearing a dress while skinning potatoes goes unnoticed by the kitchen crew. And I'm content, at the counter, peeling the skin off the tubers.

I consider other odds and ends that would blend well with the skins to make a delectable stock. Perhaps the celery stalks and carrots gasping their last breath, forgotten in a bin in the walk-in. Bay leaves, an onion, and peppercorns, for sure. I'm startled out of my reverie by a tap on my shoulder. I turn my head. Braydon.

"You'll want to see this," he says, pointing to the doors leading into the diner. Curious, I remove my plastic gloves and follow him to the floor.

Addie is sitting next to Angus at the counter. Between his out-stretched palms rests a plate loaded with fried chicken, which is cozied up to a mess of khaki greens, the sunny tip of a corn pone peeking out from beneath. As he takes a long sip from a glass of iced tea, a tingling starts at the back of my neck, working its way down my spine and into my calves. Addie smiles at me, waving me over in a gesture to join them.

"The gospel music was gorgeous today," I say, taking the stool on the other side of his perch, trying to make conversation, not wanting to make a big deal that his eating lunch at Welcome Home is a momentous occasion for us. "Don't you love it when the weather cooperates, and the neighborhood can enjoy the performance?"

He swivels on the stool to face me. "Actually, I attended the service. It being Palm Sunday and all, Gary talked me into joining him. He's still there, at the church. They made him an usher. Can you believe it?" He shakes his head in wonder. "Boy gets outta prison for robbery, and the parish trusts him to add up the collection-plate offerings. He's also in charge of depositing the funds in the bank."

Angus puts down his fork and gazes out the window toward the church. "And it was strange, sitting in the pew with friends I've known most my life. Same feeling I had after coming home from Nam." He shrugs. "You leave the church, I guess, but it never leaves you. The music's my favorite part."

"You should hear my cousin sing," Addie says, leaning in, her eyes twinkling at mine. "Sam has a voice that could coax an apple out of a cherry blossom." Of late, her face gleams as if a spotlight has been lit in her soul. She's never appeared so happy, or radiated such beauty.

"You'd be a welcome guest at the church," Angus says, regarding me with red-laced, milky eyes. "You could even join. They're always looking for another strong voice in the choir."

Gospel singing satisfies a hunger for connection and community— a community I'm not welcome to join. The congregation seems to have placed a quarantine around the diner. And though I'd love to sing in their choir, Angus is wrong. They would never welcome me.

I force a smile. "Your choir doesn't need my help. And I can assure you, they aren't interested in breaking bread with us here at the diner." I lift a brow at Addie before returning my focus to Angus. "But one day"—I shrug—"who knows?"

Frowning, seeming troubled by my words, his eyes travel to the ceiling as he shakes his head. And then the aromas of savory fried goodness ambush his concerns, and his eyes slide down to the plate resting in front of him. He selects a chicken thigh and sinks his teeth into the flesh. The skin makes a crackling sound, and juices seep out from around the bone.

"Delicious," he says, batting his mouth with a napkin. He speaks between bites and sips of tea, devouring the food as if he hasn't eaten a decent meal in years. "The thighs are my favorite. I also enjoy the livers. Do you ever serve those?"

"Oh my, yes. We cook nearly all the parts others leave behind. People think I'm weird, but I love the chew of the gizzards, myself. After we've collected enough to make them feasible for a special, they're marinated in buttermilk, seasoned with an herbal flour blend, and fried. I'll let Gary know the next time we plan to serve them."

"Reminds me of growing up in Alabama," he says. "I guess you could say fried chicken's my birthright."

"I love it, too," Addie adds. "And look at me. A Michigan Polack." She stretches her eyes as wide as she can, as if to emphasize their paleness. Then she pulls her blonde hair to the side, lifts a long piece, and twirls it around her finger. "A plate of fried chicken is a country of pacifists where everyone gets along," she muses.

"You got that right. Brings back memories from when I was a boy. I'd be sittin' in the den in my grandma's house, smelling the best fried chicken you could ever imagine." He taps the prongs of his fork against his plate, dreaminess cast about his face.

"But it was more than the smells putting my mind at peace. It was the sounds. I'd hear her moving around, the creaking of the fridge door and cabinets being opened, the hiss and snap of the oil when the bird hit the grease. And as long as I could smell that smell and hear those sounds, I knew everything was right with the world."

The plop of bones, swish of stock, and the metallic clang of stainless against ceramic as Babcia strained broth into her tureen. The aroma of onions, bay leaves, and juniper, worming its way into my subconscious. Soothing. Loving me. All was well when Babcia made her Cream of Sorrel Soup.

"Do you miss living in the South?" I ask, my thoughts bubbling into the present as Braydon pours me a glass of water, his smile indicating that he, too, is delighted to be serving this new guest at our counter.

"Sometimes. The mild winters are nice. But I don't miss the cockroaches. They're so big you could saddle 'em up. They'd crawl around everywhere. Cupboards, closets, you name it. At nighttime, when the lights were out, they'd come out from nowhere. If you turned on the lights, caught 'em red-handed, they scurry into cracks you never even knew existed. It was like watchin' *Jurassic Park* after the dinosaurs escaped."

We chuckle as he shudders at the memory. After shaking pepper vinegar onto his greens, he lifts the bottle and gazes at the pickled jalapeños, tilting his head in wonder. "You never see this in restaurants up here."

"Braydon added it to our condiment selection—he won't eat greens without it. He packs chili peppers into Ball jars and covers them with salt and vinegar. The mixture rests at room temperature a couple of months, and then we syphon it into flasks." I pick up a bottle of Jessie's Hellfire and Redemption. "If you like your greens real spicy, also add some of this. Jessie, our hot sauce vendor, tells us the secret ingredient is magic."

He takes the bottle and stares at the label—the picture of Jessie holding a pitchfork and another of her sporting wings. "Magic. Really? You don't say?" He shakes a few drops onto the greens.

I've another inkling why it tastes so much better than her competition, but I keep it to myself. Her ingredient list doesn't specify, but I've the nose of a bloodhound. She doesn't use white wine vinegar like her competitors but apple cider vinegar. Yet sorcery remains. People like Jessie, who believe in magic, can imagine possibilities where others are afraid to travel.

Holding his fork in his left hand, he jabs at the mound and takes a huge bite. Poor dude. He must have to do everything with that hand since losing the thumb and finger on his right. Closing his eyes, he chews the greens with concentration, his nod indicating they're seasoned to his liking.

Braydon brings us each a shot glass filled with potlikker. "Here's dessert. Sweeter than icebox pie."

Angus scrutinizes the pale-brown liquid with flecks of green. He sniffs it, dips a finger into the brew, and dots it onto his tongue. "Have I died and gone to heaven? This here's potlikker. The stuff of dreams. Growing up, meat was scarce. We needed the nourishment, so we drank it all the time."

We tip our glasses together and take a sip. As curative as the most miraculous of potions, potlikker's been good to us. Addie and I drank it every day during the course of our fight. Potlikker was drunk the evening Jessie burned the sage, chasing out the demons. It was the only nourishment my cousin could get down in the weeks following her breakup. I catch Addie's eye. We may very well need the charms of this elixir to get us through the coming months. As the flavor settles on my tongue, I savor its earthiness, the essence of soil and sun, of bitter and sweet. So much more than the sum of its parts.

"Listen," Angus says, a solemnity molded around the word. He puts down his glass. "As delicious as this meal's been, your cooking's not the reason I stopped by." He clears his throat and sighs, pushing his plate away.

"What I really wanted to say to y'all, the real reason I'm here"—he pauses a second, glancing at each of us—"is to thank you." He reaches across the counter and places his hand on Braydon's. "Thank you, Braydon, for your patience. And for listening to a bitter, lonely man rant on and on."

Braydon turns his palm over and squeezes the man's hand. "Sir. I've enjoyed every minute in your company. Any ax you have to grind, I'm here to listen." His head turns toward the grill. "But right now, I've gotta get back to work. I'm manning the grill, usually Quiche's jurisdiction. And your grandson is spoiling us. Things get chaotic back there on Gary's days off." He smiles and returns to the flattop.

Angus nods at me. "Thank you for hiring my grandson. He tells me you've been good to him, and he loves working with the crew."

"Neighbors helping neighbors," Addie says. "Gary's a delight to have in the kitchen."

After finishing the potlikker, he mops his glistening forehead with a napkin.

"When he was a baby, I'd rock him in my lap. In the same rocking chair that's on my porch today. We've watched a lot of changes from that stoop, my grandson and me. After the riots, the neighborhood went to hell in a handbasket. Drugs led to gangs, led to crime, led to arson. Of course, the old diner went under. No one had any money to eat out. It was looted and then abandoned. I'm surprised they didn't burn it to the ground." He sighs, shaking his head.

"The church was the only good thing left. But when Gary went to prison, I quit attending services. I quit believing in God. I quit believing in everything. And then you ladies came around and brought the diner back to life. At first it got me mad. Everyone seems to have an opinion on how to fix Detroit. Yip, yip, yipping, chasing their tails in circles, collapsing into one big dogfight." He tips his empty jigger glass at me, and then at Addie. "'Course, you gals were crazy enough to see hope where I'd been seeing despair. And you gave this place the right name—Welcome Home. You made my boy feel at home. And when I entered the diner, it felt like I was coming home, too."

He turns to Addie, his eyes searching her face. "I want you to know I'm sorry. I regret the things I said to you. I was angry at the world, spinning like a tornado, and you were in my path. I hope we can leave it in the past."

Her eyes moisten. "I get it. I get where you were coming from. And the past is just that." She brushes her palms together as if sweeping away the memory. "The past."

They smile into each other's eyes until Braydon removes Angus's plate from the counter, breaking the spell. Angus presses his feet against the base bar of the chair, then pushes himself off the stool, grabs the thighbone, and waves it in Braydon's face.

"And thank you, sir, for making the best fried chicken north of the Mason–Dixon." He resumes his seat, places the bone on the plate, and wipes his hands with a napkin.

"Today, I'm only in charge of the grill," Braydon says. "I had nothing to do with the chicken you're eating."

"Paul may have fried the chicken," I say, "but it's Quiche's mother's recipe."

"She was right about this chicken," Angus says. "It tastes as good as the memories of my grandma's."

Addie reaches into the pocket of her apron and pulls out what appears to be a tiny gray slingshot. "I found a perfect wishbone in a chicken breast I was eating last week. I dried it so we could make a wish on your birthday."

She twirls the end of my hair with her fingertips. "You know I could never forget your birthday." Leaning across Angus, she holds between her forefinger and thumb one of the two bones shaping the top V of the Y. "Did you know ancient Romans were the first to regard the wishbone as a good luck sign?"

"I did not know, Addie. But if you say it's so, I'm a believer." At once I'm relieved she didn't forget the occasion.

"So make a wish," she says, locking eyes with me.

I place my finger on the other side of the Y and close my eyes. I make the same wish I imagine most of humanity hums without even knowing:

As antidote to contagion, may the spirit of this conversation attach itself to another, leach onto the next, spider through the networks of the city, the state, and then migrate into the world.

We tug at the bone, and the smaller piece snaps off in her hand.

Addie claps her hands in glee. "You won. But don't tell us your wish or you'll jinx it." Behind the blue of her eyes, I note her wish was the same as mine.

Angus turns to me, his eyes widening. "It's your birthday? Did you just turn twenty?"

"Oh, you rogue," I say, feeling warmth color my face. "God love you for being a good liar. Today I'm thirty-two years old."

"Well, happy birthday to you," he says, pulling out his wallet from a back pocket. "Lemme pay my check now. I wanna stop by the church. See if Gary's finished his business."

"First meal's on the house," Addie says, sliding his wallet away.

"That's not right. I don't want any special treatment when I eat here. Besides, my bill helps pay Gary's wages."

"Just this once." I place my hand over his, over the nubs where his thumb and finger once were.

He shakes his head. "Well, all right. Just today."

"By the way," I say, as he slides off the stool. "Braydon tells us your tomatoes were twice the size of ours last summer. How do you get them to grow so large?"

"Eight hours of direct sun, tomato food, and a special blend of compost a friend of mine makes. I'll share some with you this summer." He ambles across the floor. "And don't forget to prune, prune, prune." Turning at the door, he wags his forefinger at us, as if in warning. "Tomatoes don't like to be crowded."

"Maybe this is it," Addie says after he leaves, sliding over to sit on the stool he vacated. "Braydon said positive change could happen one conversation at a time. We own this one, Sam. It belongs to me, you"—she picks up her empty glass—"and a shot of potlikker." My chin begins to tremble, and I press my lips together, wondering how I could ever have considered leaving my cousin, the diner, and my city.

At that moment, Jessie walks into the diner carrying a case of hot sauce. Sun Beam and Quiche walk in by her side. The girl will be apprenticing at Jessie's garlic farm this summer. The three of them head toward the counter.

Sun Beam seems to have matured in the weeks since the nightmare in the garden. Her eyes have lost their innocence, their shine. Maybe it's the contacts she just had fitted—it's odd seeing her without glasses. But she still has enough sweet to rush into my arms.

"Thank you for that little bit of loving," I say, pulling on one of her ponytails.

"I don't share my sunbeams with just anyone," she replies. "I love working with Jessie." She looks up at the woman. "We have such a good time."

Jessie pats the top of her head. "Ain't that the truth. This girl's a dream."

"From what she tells me," Quiche says, removing her hat, "the feeling's mutual."

"Jessie was telling me about the moon and how it influences her crops," Sun Beam says.

Jessie leans into the bar, pressing her elbows on the counter. "It's best to plant garlic when the moon's in the constellations of Taurus, Capricorn, or Virgo. The root system grows stronger." We nod, as if this tidbit of wisdom was common knowledge.

With her fingertips, she rubs the sides of her neck, rolling her head in a circle. "And Sun Beam here's been telling me how important it is to pay attention to long-term forecasts."

We look at the girl now fiddling with her smartphone. Quiche sprang for the device so she can keep a close tether on her daughter's whereabouts. Sun Beam holds up the screen, which is lit with neon graphs, maps, and numbers.

"I can tell you when a storm's coming within the minute," she says, pride in her voice.

As Braydon places the emptied shot glasses on a bar tray, Jessie picks one up and examines it in the light as if she were a soothsayer.

"I'm reading the dregs," she says, leveling her eyes at me. "It's amazing how much passion can fit into such a tiny glass.

"Look at this. See where the two stains collide?" She points to two translucent streaks merging at the top of the glass. "That's two women stirring up a neighborhood."

"What else do you see?" I ask, now a firm believer in the wisdom of collards.

At that moment, before she has time to reply, Angus and Gary walk through the front door, a group of people behind them. They're singing. What are they singing? Their voices swell with the refrain. They're singing the "Happy Birthday" song; they're singing "Happy Birthday" to me. And they're letting it rip through the diner in harmony. One large woman, her face a sheen of joy, hits a tambourine against her fist. I recognize the voices—it's the gospel singers from the Tabernacle choir.

Sun Beam is jumping up and down, and a woman with a staggering soprano hands the girl her maracas. Patrons who don't even know me rise from their chairs and join in the chorus. Paul and Sylvia come out of the kitchen, carrying a towering cake, which is lit with candles, singing, "Happy birthday, dear Sam, happy birthday to you."

I turn to Jessie, who puts down the jigger. She wears a smile stretching from the East Side of Detroit to a village on the western coast of Africa.

Everyone is singing and clapping, tambourines and maracas are rattling, and people are shouting, "Praise Jesus! Hallelujah! Amen!"

What is happening? God. I'm having a Norma Rae moment. Should I stand on a chair and shout out to every person in Welcome Home that this day is capturing all Addie and I've dreamed and worked for? That the past, present, and future are colliding within this very moment? The diner is packed shoulder to shoulder, all faces turned to me. My vision blurs behind tears. Black, white, olive, beige, all of their skins merge into one color—the most splendid hue ever imagined.

"Thank you," I cry, my tears stinging my eyes, and now sliding down my cheeks. I throw out my hands. "Thank you for your beautiful voices! Thank you for celebrating my birthday with me! Thank you for coming to Welcome Home!"

My heartbeat gallops inside my chest. I'm feeling so much energy, so much ecstasy and emotion that the four walls can't contain me. Sylvia places her sponge cake in front of me. Addie rests her palm on my back, and I bend and blow out the candles, making the same wish I'd made while breaking the wishbone.

Straightening, I cup my hands around the sides of my mouth, shouting out to the singing crowd, "Back in a flash. Addie will cut the cake." I turn to my cousin. "I'm bursting at the seams."

Their singing fades behind me as I bolt from the room and into the parking lot. I scurry to the sidewalk, then stop, dead in my tracks, in front of La Grande. As I catch my breath, dust swirls, and the cars and trucks whisk by, the umbrella of my dress billowing in the swoosh of passing vehicles. A cacophony of noise—revving engines, music blasting from rolled-down windows—fills the air, which smells of exhaust, of grit and burned coffee.

I turn and face the diner. The windows reflect the brilliant yellows and oranges of the afternoon sun. It looks as if the building were ablaze. Flashes of wisdom don't come to me often, but at this moment I'm filled with awareness, a profundity rich and rare.

Can a woman choose a cousin, a business, and a city over her lover? I am here to say she can. And all I want to do to celebrate this day—my birthday—is to hang out with my people. My family. Here. At the diner. Cheering. Weeping. And laughing. Out loud. So much. On the very best day of Samantha Jaworski's life.

I am Detroit. My city is me. Shaped by the grit of our ancestry, we roll onward, rubber burning asphalt, always driving forward. Yesterday we spun out of control. We crashed and burned, blind to the faces in our rearview mirrors, broken glass in the street. But that was then. This is now. And we're back at the wheel. Time to hustle our jam, here's my ode, dear D. It's time for us to shine.

Addie

"Are you praying?" David asks, as we settle into our seats at our favorite Italian restaurant.

"No. Why do you ask?"

"Because your lips are moving, and you're fiddling with your rosary."

"You know me better than that. All of the Catholic was beat out of me in elementary-school catechism."

The waiter approaches our table and describes the evening's specials before handing us our menus.

"If you're not praying, what are you thinking?" he asks, a question in his eye.

I moisten my lips. "I'm remembering Babcia. In ancient Greece, they believed that in order for the dead to have an afterlife, they must be held alive in the memories of those who're living. Shall I show you my ritual?"

He nods, the shadow of a smile playing about his face.

"So, I start by holding the cross." I look down at the necklace and place the crucifix in my hand. "I think of her whispered prayer when she'd tuck me into bed. Then, I put my forefinger here"—I tap the bead above the cross—"and remember how I'd wake up, sobbing from a nightmare." I touch another violet sphere and catch his eyes. "I remember her song, lulling me back to sleep. Her hair, when it was uncoiled from her bun, hung down her back. White, silky, glistening—it always reminded me of an angel's wing."

His eyes circle my face, with softness, slowness. And there is something else in them, something eager and humble when he begins to speak.

"I've got it, Addie. At last. It's like a complicated riddle, and I've finally cracked the code." He shakes his head in wonder, brushing his hair from his eyes. "You've been trying to show me all along, and it's the simplest thing in the world." He bumps his fist on the table. "The purest distillation of life is love. The only reason worth living is for the people we love, and for those who love us back. In the end, it's the only thing that matters."

He touches my wrist as I finger the beads. "Even death doesn't stop love from being alive." He leans toward me, pressing his torso into the table. "Love's not tangible—it's not something you can touch. At the same time, it's so big I was afraid of it. Stumbling around in the dark, I was drifting, searching, not knowing who I was or what I wanted. But when you offered me your hand, I took my own, as well. Love just *is*. That's the miracle. And loving you has told me who I am. Why I'm here."

I pause, tracing the outline of the crucifix. "It's ironic, but it's been the opposite with me. Being away from you taught me that the best lessons are often learned alone, at ground zero." I release the rosary and take his hands. "This newfound wisdom can't be contained on a spread-sheet or noted on a to-do list, but it does include you."

He smiles his rascal smile. Please, God, don't let him upset the moment with a cliché.

"Check the inside pocket of your jacket."

"What?"

He hands me my coat, which is lying next to me on a chair.

Wiggling my fingers into the pocket, I feel a small box, velvety and round.

I'm reminded of a Latin saying, *Dum spiro, spero. While I breathe, I hope.* I pull out the box, regard it a few seconds, and then open the lid. A diamond sparkles on a cushion of black velvet.

"Adelaide Jaworski. Will you marry me?"

The restaurant sounds dim as my heart jumps hurdles. I take a deep breath to compose myself—not so fast. I hesitate a fraction of a second, before meeting his gaze.

"Let's make this a promise ring. Not an engagement. I want you to be sure."

"I am sure. I've never been so sure of anything in my life."

"But, David. I wanted it too much. I was so hungry to hear you say those words that the constant craving was consuming me."

"Why not? Why not hunger for love and its beautiful symbols— marriage, children? There's too much ugliness in the world, Addie. But to be truly loved and to return that love are life's greatest gifts. The one aspect that's pure." The muscles in his jaw tighten, his eyes resting on the rosary. "The one aspect that's holy."

His fingers wrap around my wrist, and he pulls my hand forward. "Feel my heart." I stretch my palm over his chest, feeling his flesh and the imprint of the top button on his shirt. "Until you came into my life, no one had ever touched me here."

My hand trembles, feeling the strength of his hand pressing into mine and the beat of his heart. But I don't need to be rescued by that rhythm, or to feel his power when I have the same capacity of strength in myself. At the same time, my shadow twin completes me. The power of love lies is in its fluidity, its ebb and flow. I remove my hand from his chest.

"I've given so much thought as to what I would say to you at this moment," he continues. "And here's what I've come up with."

There is a new look in his eyes, something I don't recognize. "You are like a shooting star—glittering, thrilling—breaking through a pitch-black night. A star I pray is not too high for me to reach. My feeble attempt at poetry," he mumbles, removing the ring from the velvet. "I'm no Dylan," he continues, "but these are my words, *my* words, Addie, spoken from my heart. And what could be a more fitting metaphor for a star than this?" He holds the ring at an angle so the diamond catches the light.

He catches my eyes. "I'll ask you again. Adelaide Jaworski. Will you marry me?"

I stare at the platinum band, which rests between his thumb and forefinger. I know he's waiting for my answer. My gaze returns to his face, and concern flashes in his eyes. I can't find my voice. I take a sip of water and clear my throat. So this is it.

"Yes, David." The two words crack beneath my breath. "I will be your wife."

His jaw drops, and he emits a sharp breath, as if massively relieved I didn't turn him down. He lifts my wrist and slides the ring onto my finger. I stretch my hand in front of me, admiring the beauty of the stone, which is cut into the shape of a teardrop.

"Whenever I look at this ring, I'll remember how you compared me to a shooting star. It was a beautiful thing to say." With my fingertips, I stroke his hand.

My gaze returns to his face, and I feel dizzy tumbling into his eyes. "In the ancient world, stars were thought to be the souls of people we love who've died." I cock my head. "Can this also be a wishing star?"

"It's anything you want it to be."

I think of Mom, trapped inside her fears. "I wish all of the people I love can also find their path." My nostrils sting as I think how happy our news will make her. "Their courage." Biting my lips, I try to contain my tears but feel their warmth sliding down my cheeks.

He cups my chin into the palm of his hand. "I've always admired this trait of yours. How you encourage people to be their highest selves."

In the midst of our lovefest, a couple seated at a nearby table tip their glasses toward us, smiling. With my dinner napkin, I wipe away my tears. Heat rises to my cheeks, and I admonish myself for my embarrassment at being caught in this sacred moment. David and I raise our glasses to the strangers, and then we all take a sip, a silent toast in our testimony to love. *Spread it on thick, spread it on sweet, so it looks, smells, and tastes like fresh cherry jam.*

"When you taste food and wine," I say, bringing the glass to my nose and inhaling, "what makes it delicious is the roundness of flavors. And how the flavors complement one another—the bitter and sour balanced with the sweet." I place the glass to the side of my plate, and my eyes travel across his face. "I want our marriage to have the same balance, as we live our lives in that sweet spot in the middle."

He takes a sip, his expression thoughtful, and his jaw moves, as if he's chewing the wine. Swallowing, he nods his head in agreement, placing his glass on the table.

"You've taught me so many things," he says, brushing the sides of his mouth with his napkin. "About love, life." He winks at me. "Also, the proper way of buttering bread." He pinches off a bit of bread, butters it, and pops it into his mouth.

"Oh yes. The lessons taught me by my mother." I lace my voice with irony. "How could you ever live your life without my finesse, my tutelage? Seriously, David—chaos is the world in which we operate." I lean forward and brush away his hair, which has fallen into his eyes. "Chaos is like a frigid wave crashing over your head. But you keep walking forward, into the icy water. And then your body gets used to the cold, the pieces fit together, and you begin to swim deep into the lake." I raise my glass to the sky. "Here's to chaos. Bring it on."

The waiter, as if hearing my words, appears with our food.

David laughs. "So you'll grow to appreciate my balled-up laundry on the floor, dirty dishes in the sink? My stacks of papers on the dining room table?"

I frown.

"I'm kidding you. My point is that Adelaide Jaworski, the woman I love, the woman who will be my wife, finds order in chaos. You're one of those rare breeds not afraid of facing it down. That strength is another one of the bazillion reasons why I'm so madly in love with you."

A pinkish sheen creeps into his eyes, and at this moment, he is the one who cries. I hand him my napkin, which I've just used as a handkerchief. After a minute, he takes a shaky breath, wipes his eyes, and his words ring with earnestness.

"Addie. Baby girl. I am so lucky to have found you." He blinks several times, as if not quite believing this moment. "And after losing you, you let me find you again. You're not afraid of anything, are you?"

I inhale sharply. "I'm afraid of everything, David. But I can't let my fears stop me. Even when it breaks my heart."

I grab his hands, and his damp palms press into mine. "We're so lucky to be living in a time and place where we—me and you—can make change happen."

Flying on the wings of a phoenix, born again from its ashes.

Walking home in the dew-dusted night, our words drop as petals, drifting down, leaving a trail behind us. Lights from above make prisms through the moisture and are mirrored in the damp pavement, twinkling beneath our feet.

I look up into the deep, incalculable beauty. I say it in a whisper: "Streetlights. New streetlights."

He releases my hand and steps off the curb, onto the boulevard. A golden glow beams down on him as a spotlight in the blackened sky. His arms stretch out toward the heavens, and his face is radiant in a halo of light.

"Addie. Look. Detroit is shining!"

His voice echoes through the night. Ringing like a bell. Ringing like a hymn. Ringing like a benediction.

The Recipes

Quiche's Buttermilk Pancakes with Apple-Maple Syrup and Walnuts

Yield: 12 pancakes, with enough Apple-Maple Syrup* to accommodate
Time: 45 minutes
*Make the syrup before making the pancakes.

Ingredients for Pancakes

- ¾ cup all-purpose flour
- ¾ cup whole-grain pastry flour or whole-wheat flour
- 2 tablespoons light-brown sugar
- 1½ teaspoons baking powder
- 1 teaspoon baking soda
- ½ teaspoon kosher salt
- 2 large eggs
- 1¾ cups buttermilk
- 1½ tablespoons melted unsalted butter
- Canola oil, as needed
- Apple-Maple Syrup with Walnuts (recipe follows)

Directions for Pancakes

1. Preheat the oven to 200 degrees.
2. In a large bowl, whisk together both flours, brown sugar, baking powder, baking soda, and kosher salt. In a medium-size bowl, beat together the eggs and buttermilk.
3. Stir the wet ingredients into the dry ingredients, then stir in the melted butter.
4. Lightly coat a large nonstick griddle or skillet with oil and heat over medium-low heat (325 degrees). Using a ⅓-cup measure, ladle the batter onto the hot skillet. Cook the pancakes 3 to 5 minutes, or until bubbles form on top and the bottom is golden brown. Flip the pancakes and continue cooking until the pancakes are golden brown on both sides.
5. Keep the pancakes warm in the oven as you finish cooking the remaining ones. Reheat the Apple-Maple Syrup and serve over the hot pancakes.

Ingredients for Apple-Maple Syrup with Walnuts

- ½ cup shelled walnuts or pecans
- 2 tablespoons unsalted butter
- 3 to 4 large apples (1½ pounds), cored and cut into ½-inch-thick slices*
- ¾ cup pure maple syrup
- ½ teaspoon ground cinnamon (freshly ground preferred)

*Honeycrisp, Winesap, or Braeburn apples are best in this recipe. For uniformity, use an apple corer, then cut the apples lengthwise into thin slices.

Directions for Apple-Maple Syrup

1. In a large, dry sauté pan over medium-low heat, toast the nuts until fragrant and lightly toasted, about 3 to 5 minutes. Remove from the pan and reserve.
2. Melt the butter in the same pan. Sauté the apple slices until just tender, about 8 minutes. Stir in the maple syrup, cinnamon, and toasted nuts. Reserve to serve with pancakes.

Braydon's Mess of Greens with Turnips and Potlikker

Yield: Enough for a family reunion (16 cups)
Active Time: 30 minutes
Cook Time: 2 to 2½ hours

Ingredients

- 1½ pounds smoked pork hock or shank
- Kosher salt
- 2½ to 3 pounds turnip greens, bottom tough stem ends removed*
- 2½ to 3 pounds turnips (3 large), peeled and cut into 1-inch chunks
- 3 slices raw bacon, cut into 1-inch pieces
- 3 to 4 cups diced sweet onions
- 1 tablespoon light-brown sugar
- Pepper vinegar, if available, or cider vinegar combined with hot sauce, if desired

*Mustard or collard greens may be substituted for part or all of the turnip greens.

Directions

1. Place the hock or shank in a large pot. Cover with 14 cups (3½ quarts) water. Lightly season the water with the kosher salt, then bring to a boil. Reduce the heat to a simmer and cover the pot, then cook 1 hour. (If the pork is not completely submerged in the liquid, you will need to turn it over after 30 minutes of cooking time.)

1. Chop the greens into 1-inch pieces and wash thoroughly. Stir the greens into the pot and bring to a boil. Reduce the heat to a simmer and cook, uncovered, until the greens are just tender, 30 to 45 minutes, depending on the type and age of greens used. Add the turnips to the pot and stir them into the greens and pork. Simmer until the turnips are tender, an additional 20 to 30 minutes. (When the greens and turnips are tender, do not discard the cooking liquid; this is the potlikker.)

2. While the greens are simmering, fry the bacon until crisp. Remove the bacon from the pan and reserve, draining on paper towels. Sauté the onions over medium-high heat in the bacon fat. Stir in the brown sugar and cook the onions, stirring occasionally, until golden, soft, and fragrant, about 20 minutes. Finely chop the reserved bacon and combine with the cooked onions.

3. With tongs and a slotted spoon, remove the greens, turnips, and pork from the potlikker. With a sharp knife, remove the pork from the hock or shank. Discard the fat or return it to the potlikker, if reducing (see step 6). Chop the pork.

4. Combine the chopped pork, cooked greens, turnips, and bacon-and-onion mixture. Season to taste with kosher salt, if needed, and pepper vinegar (or cider vinegar combined with hot sauce), to taste, if desired.

5. If desired, reduce the potlikker over a low boil to as strong a potion as desired. Greens and potlikker are delicious served with hoecake or corn bread.

Sam's Lamb Burger Sliders with Tzatziki and Beetroot Relish

Yield: 16 sliders
Time: 35 minutes, if Tzatziki and relish have been made in advance

Special Nonfood Items Needed

A grill

Note: The Beetroot Relish and Tzatziki may be made up to 2 days in advance.

Ingredients for Lamb Burger Sliders

- 2 pounds ground lamb
- 1 pound ground beef (80/20 grind)
- 2 teaspoons finely chopped garlic
- ½ to 1 cup chopped fresh mint
- 1 heaping teaspoon ground cardamom (optional)
- 1 teaspoon kosher salt
- 2 teaspoons freshly ground black pepper
- 16 2-inch slider rolls
- Beetroot Relish (recipe follows)
- Tzatziki (recipe follows)

Directions for Lamb Burger Sliders

1. Gently knead the lamb, beef, garlic, mint, cardamom (if using), kosher salt, and freshly ground pepper together. Cook a small bit of the batch, taste, and adjust the seasonings to your palate.
2. Divide the mixture and form into 16 patties. Oil the grill grates, and heat the gas or charcoal grill to medium-high heat. Grill the burgers 2 to 3 minutes per side for medium rare. Cook 1 to 2 minutes per side longer for medium to well-done, or until the desired level of doneness is reached. Grill the buns until lightly toasted, if desired.
3. Spread one side of the buns with the Beetroot Relish and the other side with Tzatziki. Place the burgers in between the top and bottom buns and serve.

Ingredients for Beetroot Relish

- 3 to 4 medium-size red beets
- ½ medium-size red onion
- ¼ cup extra-virgin olive oil
- 2 to 3 tablespoons red wine vinegar
- 2 tablespoons light brown sugar
- Kosher salt
- Freshly ground black pepper

Directions for Beetroot Relish

Note: Sauté the leftover washed beet greens in olive oil with a bit of garlic for a savory side dish. Or use them as a topping for crostini or bruschetta and sprinkle with crumbled goat cheese.

1. Wearing plastic gloves, trim the greens and both ends from

the beets, peel, and grate, using a box grater. You should have more than 2 packed cups of grated beets. Remove the outer skin from the onion and grate.

2. In a medium bowl, whisk together the oil, vinegar, and brown sugar. Season with the kosher salt and freshly ground pepper. Stir the grated beets and onion into the vinaigrette.

Ingredients for Tzatziki

Note: Leftover Tzatziki makes a wonderful vegetable dip as well as an accompaniment to lamb, swordfish, poultry, and grilled vegetables such as eggplant and zucchini.

- 1 large cucumber, peeled, cut lengthwise, and seeded, then cut into small (1/4-inch) dice (1½ cups)
- 2 tablespoons fresh chopped herbs (dill or mint, or a combination of both)
- 1 scant teaspoon minced garlic
- 1 cup plain (2% or full fat) Greek-style yogurt
- Kosher salt
- Freshly ground black pepper

Directions for Tzatziki

1. Place the diced cucumber on paper towels or in a fine-mesh sieve. Lightly sprinkle with the kosher salt. Let drain 15 to 30 minutes, pressing into the towels or sieve with a spoon to release excess moisture.
2. In a medium bowl, combine the cucumber with the herbs, garlic, and yogurt. Season to taste with the kosher salt, if needed, and freshly ground pepper. Refrigerate until ready to use.

Paul's Great Lakes Crispy Corn Trout

Yield: 4 servings
Time: 20 minutes

Special Nonfood Items Needed

Toothpicks or wooden skewers

Ingredients

- 4 whole trout, 10 to 12 ounces each, boned
- Kosher salt
- Freshly ground black pepper
- 8 sprigs fresh sage
- ¼ cup ground cornmeal
- ¼ cup all-purpose flour
- ½ cup grape seed oil
- 1 lemon, cut into 8 wedges

Directions

1. Rinse the trout and pat dry. Season the cavity of each fish with kosher salt and freshly ground pepper.
2. Place 2 sage leaves in the cavity of each fish. Close the cavity by threading a wooden skewer or toothpick through the flaps.
3. In a small bowl, combine the cornmeal and flour. Dredge both sides of the trout in the mixture.
4. Heat two large skillets over medium-high heat and divide the oil between them. When the fat shimmers, add 2 fish to each skillet and fry until crisp and golden brown, about 5 minutes. Carefully

flip the fish with a large, flat spatula. Continue to cook the fish on the other side until just cooked through and golden, about 4 minutes.

5. Transfer the fish to a platter and serve immediately with the lemon wedges.

Sylvia's Heartbreakers

Yield: 1 dozen jumbo chocolate chip–walnut cookies
Active Time: 40 minutes
Freeze Time: At least 3 hours and up to 6 weeks*
Thaw Time: 1 hour*
Bake Time: 22 minutes
Cool Time: 10 minutes

*Freeze time and a precise thaw time are critical to ensure a creamy chocolate center and crusty cookie exterior.

Ingredients

- 2 cups all-purpose flour
- 1 cup cake flour
- 1 teaspoon kosher salt
- 1 teaspoon baking powder
- ½ teaspoon baking soda
- 1 tablespoon cornstarch
- 1 cup (2 sticks) unsalted butter, cool but not room temperature (your finger should make a slight indention in the butter, but not much more)
- ½ cup sugar
- 1 cup dark-brown sugar
- 2 large eggs

- 2 cups semisweet chocolate chips
- 1¼ cups toasted walnuts,* chopped
- *To toast walnuts: Spread the walnuts in an ungreased pan. Bake in a preheated 350-degree oven 5 to 7 minutes, stirring occasionally, until brown.

Directions

1. In a medium-size mixing bowl, combine both flours, kosher salt, baking powder, baking soda, and cornstarch. Whisk until well incorporated and free of lumps.
2. Cut the butter into 1-inch pieces. In a standing mixer, cream the butter and both sugars together on medium speed until well combined. Add the eggs and beat 2 to 3 minutes, or until the batter is combined. In ½-cup increments, add the flour mixture to the butter mixture, beating between each addition until the mixture forms a batter.
3. With a spatula, scrape the batter out of the bowl onto a clean, dry pastry table or a cutting board. With your hands, work the chocolate chips and walnuts into the batter.
4. Using a large spoon or ice-cream scoop, form twelve cookie-dough balls. They should weigh about 4½ ounces each and be of uniform size so that they will bake evenly.
5. Wrap each ball individually in wax paper and place the balls in an extra-large ziplock bag or airtight container. Freeze until frozen, about 3 hours or up to 6 weeks. (Frozen cookies may be baked as desired.)
6. When ready to bake, thaw the cookie balls 1 hour (precisely) at room temperature. (If the dough is frozen solid when baked, the inside of the cookies will be too gooey. If the dough is overly thawed, the cookie will be too crumbly after baking.)
7. Position the rack in the center of the oven and preheat to 375

degrees (convection oven; fan on) or 350 degrees (standard oven; fan off).

8. Line a large cookie sheet with parchment paper or a nonstick silicone baking mat. Unwrap the semifrozen dough balls and place them on the sheet. Bake until golden brown, about 22 minutes. (Baking times may vary, depending on oven temperature variances.) Remove the cookies from the oven and let cool on the baking sheet 10 minutes. Now is the best time to indulge, reveling in all of their heavenly goodness.

Babcia's Ginger-Molasses Bundt Cake with Lemon Curd

Yield: 1 cake (12 generous slices)
Active Time: 45 minutes
Bake Time: 45 to 55 minutes
Cool Time: 40 minutes

Ingredients

- 3 cups all-purpose flour
- 2 teaspoons ground cinnamon (Vietnamese preferred)
- 2 packed tablespoons grated fresh ginger
- 2 packed tablespoons grated lemon zest
- 1 cup (2 sticks) unsalted butter, softened
- 1 cup light-brown sugar
- 1 cup boiling water
- 1 cup blackstrap molasses
- 2 teaspoons baking soda
- 2 large eggs, lightly beaten
- Unsalted butter for buttering Bundt pan
- 4 to 6 ounces lemon curd (made from scratch or purchased)

- 1 teaspoon powdered sugar
- Devon clotted cream or whipped cream as desired (optional)

Directions

1. Position the rack in the center of the oven and preheat to 350 degrees.
2. In a medium-size bowl, whisk the flour and cinnamon together until completely combined.
3. In a large bowl, with an electric mixer, beat the ginger, lemon zest, butter, and brown sugar together at high speed until the mixture is pale, about 5 minutes.
4. In another large bowl, whisk together the boiling water, molasses, and baking soda. The mixture will foam and expand.
5. Alternate adding the flour mixture and molasses mixture to the butter mixture in three batches, mixing at medium speed until incorporated. Beat in the eggs.
6. Pour into a well-buttered 9- to 10-inch Bundt pan, and bake 45 to 55 minutes, or until a wooden pick inserted into the cake comes out clean.
7. Cool the cake in the pan 10 minutes, then turn the cake out onto a baking rack and cool an additional 30 minutes.
8. Spread the cake with lemon curd. Place powdered sugar in a fine mesh strainer and shake over cake, lightly dusting the top. Serve with clotted cream, if using.

Babcia's Gołąbki (Stuffed Cabbage or Cabbage Rolls)

Yield: 12–16 cabbage rolls

Active Time: 60 to 70 minutes (Polish grandmother recipes can be time-consuming.)
Bake Time: 60 to 90 minutes

Note: The Stuffing may be made up to 24 hours in advance. The Tomato Sauce may be made up to four days in advance. Traditional recipes for cabbage rolls often substitute a gravy, such as a thin mushroom gravy, for the tomato sauce.

Ingredients

- 1 green cabbage, the largest you can find*
- Kosher salt
- Stuffing (recipe follows)
- Tomato Sauce (recipe follows)
- Freshly ground black pepper
- Chopped fresh dill for garnish (optional)

*You will need 12 to 16 medium-large intact cabbage leaves for the recipe, depending on the size of the leaf. If only small cabbages are available, purchase 2 heads. Some find it easier to blanch the cabbage, remove the leaves, and reblanch the leaves until just tender. Or, instead of boiling, you can freeze your cabbage to soften the leaves. You will need three days to do this: 24 hours to freeze the head and 2 days to thaw it at room temperature.

Directions

1. Position oven rack in the center of the oven and preheat to 350 degrees.
2. Fill a pot that is large enough to accommodate the cabbage head three-quarters full of heavily salted water. Bring to a boil over high heat. Place the head in the boiling water and cook 10

to 15 minutes, or until the outermost cabbage leaves are tender enough to remove. Remove the head from the water and drain in a colander. (Do not pour out the water from the pot, as the inner part of the cabbage may need more cooking time.)

3. When the head is cool enough to handle, carefully peel away 12 to 14 of the outermost leaves. (You may have to peel the outer layers first and then return the cabbage to cook if the inner leaves can't be removed with ease.) With paper towels or a clean cloth, pat the leaves dry.

4. To facilitate rolling the leaf, with a sharp knife, cut out the tough vein from the stem end of the leaf. Depending on the size of the leaf, place 1 to 2 tablespoons of Stuffing in the center of each leaf. Beginning at the stem end, tuck in the sides of the leaf and roll up to completely encase the stuffing. Continue in this manner until you've filled 12 to 14 leaves. Any extra filling may be rolled into meatballs and cooked alongside the leaves in the sauce. Coarsely chop the remaining cabbage.

5. Select one or two casserole dishes large enough to accommodate the cabbage rolls and sauce. Place the remaining chopped cabbage in the bottom of the dishes. (This will keep the bottom of the rolls from burning.) Place the cabbage rolls, seam side down, atop the chopped cabbage in the casserole(s). Ladle the prepared Tomato Sauce over all the cabbage rolls, reserving additional sauce to spoon over the rolls after they've baked. Cover with nonstick foil or foil coated with cooking oil spray. This will keep the foil from sticking to the sauce.

6. Bake the rolls 60 to 90 minutes, or until the cabbage rolls can be pierced with a fork.

7. When the rolls have finished cooking, remove the stuffed cabbage leaves from the pan carefully with a spatula. Top the rolls with remaining warmed Tomato Sauce, freshly ground pepper,

and chopped dill (if using). Serve hot. The rolls may be refrigerated 4 days or frozen up to 3 months and reheated before serving. Delicious served with mashed potatoes.

Ingredients for Stuffing

- 1 large egg
- ¾ pound ground beef (80/20 grind)
- ½ pound ground pork
- 1 cup cooked long-grain brown rice*
- ¼ cup minced shallot or onion
- 2 teaspoons minced fresh garlic
- 3 heaping tablespoons chopped fresh dill
- 1 teaspoon fennel seeds (optional but recommended)
- ¾ cup sauerkraut, rinsed, drained, and patted dry**
- 2 tablespoons tomato paste
- ½ tablespoon Hungarian paprika
- 1 teaspoon kosher salt
- 1½ teaspoons freshly ground black pepper

*Don't use quick-cooking ("instant") rice. The long-grain brown rice gives the Stuffing texture without becoming mushy; ⅓ cup dry rice yields about 1 cup cooked rice. Cook the rice in chicken stock and butter for added flavor.

**Sauerkraut varies widely in flavor and texture. I select the best available refrigerated kraut.

Directions for Stuffing

1. In a large bowl, beat the egg.

2. With a large spoon or fork, mix in both ground meats, cooked rice, minced shallot or onion, garlic, chopped dill, fennel seeds (if using), sauerkraut, tomato paste, paprika, kosher salt, and freshly ground pepper.* Refrigerate until ready to use. The mixture may be made up to 24 hours in advance.

*To test the seasoning of the meat, fry up a small portion in a skillet or pop it in the microwave till it's thoroughly cooked. Taste, then add additional salt and pepper, as desired.

Ingredients for Tomato Sauce

- 28 ounces canned tomato sauce
- 14 ounces canned diced tomatoes
- 2 tablespoons tomato paste
- 2 to 3 tablespoons red wine vinegar
- 2 to 3 tablespoons light-brown sugar
- 2 teaspoons minced fresh garlic
- ½ teaspoon ground allspice or cinnamon (freshly grated preferred)

Directions for Tomato Sauce

1. In a medium-size saucepan, combine the tomato sauce, diced tomatoes, tomato paste, 2 tablespoons of the vinegar, 2 tablespoons of the brown sugar, the garlic, and allspice. Bring to a low boil, then reduce to a simmer.

2. Simmer 20 to 30 minutes, stirring occasionally. Season to taste with additional vinegar or brown sugar, if desired. The Tomato Sauce may be made up to 4 days in advance.

Sylvia's White and Dark Chocolate–Covered Strawberries

Yield: 16 to 22 chocolate-dipped strawberries
Active Time: 35 minutes
Time for Chocolate to Harden: 30 to 45 minutes

Ingredients

- 4 ounces semisweet chocolate, chopped
- 4 ounces bittersweet chocolate, chopped
- 3 ounces white chocolate, chopped
- 1 pound (16 to 20) ripe strawberries with stems, washed and dried

Directions

1. Combine the semisweet and bittersweet chocolate in a microwave-safe dish. Microwave at 50 percent power (low to medium setting) 30 seconds, then remove and stir. Return to the microwave and cook an additional 15-30 seconds, then remove and stir again. Keep doing this in 15-30-second increments until the chocolate is smooth and melted but not burned. (Alternately, the chocolate may be melted in a double boiler over simmering water.)
2. Line a sheet pan with parchment or wax paper. Holding a strawberry by the stem, swirl the berry in the chocolate, leaving a bit of red exposed at the top beneath the stem, and allow the excess chocolate to drip back into the bowl. Lay the strawberry on the parchment or wax paper. Repeat with the remaining strawberries.
3. Melt the white chocolate, per step 1. Dip the prongs of a fork into the white chocolate, then drizzle it over the dark chocolate–covered strawberries, swirling and making a pattern. (For more control, use a squirt bottle. Or place melted chocolate in a plastic

bag, then cut a small piece from a bottom corner.)

4. Allow the chocolate to harden at room temperature, then refrigerate the strawberries until ready to enjoy.

Note: Keep the strawberries refrigerated or in a cool place, loosely covered. Sylvia has kept them refrigerated for several days with good results, but the texture of the berry suffers a bit. She recommends serving them within 12 hours after the chocolate hardens.

Granny's Skillet-Fried Chicken

Yield: 7 to 8 pieces
Active Time: 30 minutes
Dry Rub Time: 12 to 24 hours
Fry Time: 22 to 25 minutes

Notes: Tastes in sodium vary. The longer the meat sits in the rub, the saltier it will taste. You may want to reduce the salt in the recipe, especially if the chicken sits in the rub more than 10 hours. Make sure the pieces are of similar size and not too large; otherwise the chicken will burn before the meat is cooked through. Select chicken (particularly the breast), ensuring the skin covers the flesh. I use air-chilled chicken: 4 medium-size split breasts and 4 medium-size thighs, selected from a full-service counter. Full-fat buttermilk makes the skin darken too soon. If you can't find low fat, mix ½ cup 2 percent milk with ½ cup buttermilk.

Ingredients

- 1 tablespoon plus 1 teaspoon garlic powder
- 2 tablespoons crushed dried basil, divided
- 2½ teaspoons plus 1 teaspoon kosher salt

- 2 tablespoons lemon pepper, divided
- 2 teaspoons cayenne, divided
- 4 to 5 pounds chicken pieces, bone in, skin attached
- 1 large egg
- 1 cup low-fat buttermilk (see Notes above)
- 1 cup all-purpose flour
- 1 scant tablespoon cornstarch
- About 4 cups peanut oil or vegetable shortening, plus more as needed

Directions

1. To make a rub, combine the garlic powder with 1 tablespoon of the basil, 2½ teaspoons of the kosher salt, 1 tablespoon of the lemon pepper, and 1 teaspoon of the cayenne. Rub the mixture over the chicken and cover. Refrigerate at least 10 hours and up to 24.

2. Remove the chicken from the refrigerator and allow it to come to room temperature, about 1 to 1½ hours.

3. In a large bowl, whisk the egg into the buttermilk. In a wide-mouth gallon-size ziplock bag or baking dish, combine the flour, cornstarch, and the remaining basil, kosher salt, lemon pepper, and cayenne.

4. Add enough oil or shortening to a 12-inch cast-iron or non-stick skillet to ¾-inch depth. (Granny much prefers using her well-seasoned cast iron skillet.) Heat the fat until a drop of flour sizzles in the skillet, or a thermometer reads 300 to 325 degrees.

5. While the fat is heating, dip the chicken pieces in the buttermilk mixture, allowing the excess to drip back into the bowl. Dredge the pieces in the flour mixture, completely coating the skin.

6. Cooking in batches, place the pieces, meaty side down, in the hot fat and fry 11 to 15 minutes, or until deep golden brown; adjust the heat, if necessary, so the chicken doesn't brown too quickly, occasionally moving the pieces with tongs, so they fry evenly. Flip the pieces and cook an additional 10 minutes, or until the meat is white at the bone (165 degrees for breasts, 175 degrees for legs and thighs). Lift the pieces from the skillet, letting the excess oil drip back into the skillet, then drain the pieces on a rack or triple layer of paper towels.

Book Club Discussion Questions

1. Who is your favorite character and why?

2. If you were in Angus's shoes, what would have been your reaction to the women and their diner? Do you believe that Angus was justified in his initial anger?

3. Do you think the women were overreacting to the fact that their community was avoiding them? Were they overstepping boundaries? If not, what other things could the women have done to encourage a welcome reception from their neighbors?

4. How much of a person's character is shaped by their parents? Are your parents easy to recognize in yourself? Do you have certain inherited traits you wish you could change? If so, do you think therapy is a route that could be productive?

5. How is your community addressing the issues of human trafficking?

6. Are there vestiges of racism in your community? If so, how are they expressed? How are they or how could they be dealt with?

7. Is there an area in your town or city that has gone through gentrification in the last five years? Were businesses and/or homeowners forced to leave? If so, do you think tax laws should be modified to address this?

8. What is your favorite comfort food? Is there a person or place that triggers this emotional reaction to the food? Does this food tell a story?

9. Theo feels believing in fate is a cop-out. Addie comes to think fate will always have the upper hand. The notion of fate is brought up several times. What does fate mean to you?

Author Note

Every day in the United States, victims of human trafficking—predominantly sex trafficking—are being exploited. In rural, suburban, and urban areas across the country, hundreds of thousands of people are trapped with the belief that no help is available.

Help exists. Polaris, a nonprofit nongovernmental organization, is a leader in the global fight to eradicate modern slavery and restore freedom to survivors of human trafficking. To make a donation go to www.PolarisProject.org.

If you suspect human trafficking, call the National Human Trafficking Resource Center hotline at 1-888-373-8888.

Acknowledgments

If not for my deep friendship with Lucy Carnaghi, I wouldn't have been able to portray my characters, the diner, and the city of Detroit with such intimacy and compassion. Sincere thanks, as well, to Molly Mitchell and my neighbor Krystyna Bobowski. As I wrote this book, your stories were on my mind.

Enormous gratitude to my family, especially to my deceased grandmother Mary Ellen. Those hours we spent cooking in your kitchen branded my spirit, shaping my life. To my husband, Richard, who understands I've the soul of a chameleon, assuming the identities of my characters. You're a gem to endure my multiple personalities. To my son-in-law, Tom Rickmeyer, mathematical whiz, who inspired Uriah. To my children, Greta and Zan. Because of you I understand the passions of a mother—of any person—who loves a child. You gave me insight into LaQuisha, who would lay down her life if it meant her daughter could soar.

Judge David Swartz, your expertise was invaluable. My prayer is that Earl and Brett will find themselves in your courtroom. And Khurum Sheik—*ahem*, the former Detective Khurum Sheik—thank you for letting me steal your cover.

I'm indebted to my agent, Wendy Sherman of Wendy Sherman Associates, for guiding this book to its home. Buckets of gratitude, as well, to Lake Union Publishing, which is an amazing team to work with. Especially Kelli Martin—thank you for taking the wheel and steering me into Detroit. To Krista Stroever, for your keen eye and razor-sharp mind; would that every writer had such a comprehensive editing experience. And Paul Zablocki—how lucky am I to have such a kindred spirit copyedit this book. Your enthusiasm for my characters, not to mention your culinary expertise, was so very much appreciated. Claire Caterer, I imagine the environment you inhabit is impeccable; you do such a precise and thoughtful job with wordsmithing and order. Thank you!

A shout-out, as well, to the original Bon Temps, a Katrina dog rescued by Shannon and Ben Jelin. When I first met this inimitable pooch, I knew one day I'd write her into a story.

Finally, heartfelt gratitude to the men and woman who work fearlessly to eradicate human trafficking. To all the Brendas in the world, thank you for your tireless efforts. May the road rise up to meet you.

About the Author

Photo © 2016 John Shultz

Peggy Lampman was born and raised in Birmingham, Alabama. After earning a bachelor's degree in communications—summa cum laude—from the University of Michigan, she moved to New York City, where she worked as a copywriter and photographer for a public-relations firm. When she returned to Ann Arbor, her college town, she opened a specialty foods store, the Back Alley Gourmet. Years later, she sold the store and started writing a weekly food column for the *Ann Arbor News* and *MLive*. Lampman's first novel, *The Promise Kitchen*, published in 2016, garnered several awards and accolades. She is married and has two children. She also writes the popular blog www.dinnerfeed.com.